D0667074

LESSONS IN LOVE

London's Perfect Scoundrel

Other Avon Romances by
Suzanne Enoch

BY LOVE UNDONE
A MATTER OF SCANDAL
MEET ME AT MIDNIGHT
THE RAKE
REFORMING A RAKE
STOLEN KISSES
TAMING RAFE

SUZANNE ENOCH

LESSONS IN LOVE

London's Perfect Scoundrel

An Avon Romantic Treasure

AVON BOOKS
An Imprint of HarperCollinsPublishers

This is a work of fiction. Names, characters, places, and incidents are products of the author's imagination or are used fictitiously and are not to be construed as real. Any resemblance to actual events, locales, organizations, or persons, living or dead, is entirely coincidental.

AVON BOOKS
An Imprint of HarperCollins*Publishers*
10 East 53rd Street
New York, New York 10022-5299

Copyright © 2003 by Suzanne Enoch
ISBN: 0-7394-3321-0

All rights reserved. No part of this book may be used or reproduced in any manner whatsoever without written permission, except in the case of brief quotations embodied in critical articles and reviews. For information address Avon Books, an Imprint of HarperCollins Publishers.

Avon Trademark Reg. U.S. Pat. Off. and in Other Countries, Marca Registrada, Hecho en U.S.A.
HarperCollins® is a registered trademark of HarperCollins Publishers Inc.

Printed in the U.S.A.

For Jackson Lee Byrne—
welcome to the clan!
But you still aren't allowed to read this book
until your Mommy and Daddy say it's okay—
in another sixteen or seventeen years.

I love you.

Prologue

"And a gentleman should realize that a lady has a mind of her own, for goodness' sake." Evelyn Ruddick set down her teacup with a clatter, surprised that the conversation she and her friends had begun on the manners of men had become so . . . earnest. She thought she'd accepted that all males were impossible, but from the ruckus in her heart, obviously she wasn't happy about that fact.

Lucinda Barrett and Lady Georgiana Halley were right in their witty criticisms, as they usually were, and damn it all, she, too, was tired of being walked all over by every cravat-wearing member of humanity. Proper behavior for men. It almost seemed an oxymoron, but clearly someone needed to do something about their arrogant, self-involved ways.

Lucinda stood, going to the desk at the other end of the room. "We should write these down," she said, pulling several sheets of paper from a drawer and returning to hand them out. "The three of us wield a great deal of influence, particularly with the so-called gentlemen to whom these rules would apply."

"And we would be doing other ladies a service," Georgiana said, her expression growing more thoughtful as her own frustration eased.

"But a list won't do anything for anyone but ourselves." Still skeptical at the usefulness of such a task, Evelyn took the pencil Lucinda handed her, anyway. "If that."

"Oh, yes, it will—when we put our rules into practice," Georgiana argued. "I propose that we each choose some man and teach him what he needs to know to properly impress a lady."

"Yes, by God." Lucinda thumped her hand on the table.

Evelyn looked from one of her friends to the other. Her brother would likely scold her for wasting her time in frivolity, but then he didn't have to know. Perhaps he would stay in India forever, and leave them with one less scoundrel to reform. She smiled at the thought and pulled her blank paper closer. Truth be told, it was nice to feel as though she were doing something productive, whatever small use anyone might make of a list.

Georgiana chuckled as she began writing. "We could get our rules published. *Lessons in Love,* by Three Ladies of Distinction."

Evelyn's List

1. *Never interrupt a lady when she's speaking to you, as if what you have to say is more important*

2. *If you ask for an opinion, expect to receive one, and don't make fun of it*

3. *Gentlemanly behavior isn't just opening doors; to make an impression, you have to be concerned over a lady's needs at least as much as your own*

4. *Don't assume, when a lady wants to take up a task or a cause, that it's just a "hobby"*

Evelyn sat back and looked at what she'd written, blowing on it to remove the excess pencil lead. There. That should do it. Now all she needed was a victim—or rather, a student. She grinned. "This is fun."

Chapter 1

In law an infant, and in years a boy,
In mind a slave to every vicious joy,
From every sense of shame and virtue wean'd,
In lies an adept, in deceit a fiend;
Vers'd in hypocrisy, while yet a child,
Fickle as wind, of inclinations wild;
Woman his dupe, his heedless friend a tool,
Old in the world, though scarcely broke from school.

—Lord Byron, "Damaetas"

One year later

"I really wish you wouldn't make such a fuss about it," Evelyn Ruddick said, taking a step away from her brother. "Lucinda Barrett and I have been friends since we came out together."

Victor closed the distance between them again, his tone clipped and annoyed. "Be friends at some other soiree," he returned. "Her father doesn't even have a vote in the House, and tonight I need you to chat with Lady Gladstone."

"I don't like Lady Gladstone," Evie murmured back, stifling a curse when Victor clasped her arm, preventing her from sidling away again. "She drinks whiskey."

"And her husband is an influential West Sussex property owner. Putting up with a little inebriation is a small price to pay for a seat in the House of Commons."

"You only say that because she won't be breathing on you. Victor, I came here tonight to dance, and to chat with my fr—"

Her brother lowered his dark eyebrows. "You came here tonight because I escorted you. And I only did that so you would be able to assist me with my campaign."

They both knew she'd lost the argument before it began; she frequently had the suspicion that Victor allowed her to debate him only so he could put her in her place more often. "Oh, faddle. I liked it better when you were in India."

"Hm. So did I. Now go, before one of Plimpton's cronies gets to her first."

Pasting a polite, friendly smile on her face, Evelyn strolled the fringes of the crowded dance floor in search of her brother's latest source of possible votes. In all truth, Lady Gladstone's choice of liquor wasn't all that troublesome. Thirty years younger than her husband, the viscountess had worse habits than whiskey. And Evelyn had already heard a rumor that one of the worst was in attendance this evening.

She found Lady Gladstone seated amidst the scattering of chairs arranged in a shallow alcove to one side of the orchestra. Emerald-green silk clung closer than paint to the viscountess' much-lauded curves as she lounged, her head tilted to one side. Indecent as the sight seemed in Lady Dalmere's conservative ballroom, the man who leaned over her shoulder, his face so close to her ear that dark brown hair brushed her burnished gold curls, was even more unsettling.

For a moment Evelyn contemplated pretending that

she hadn't seen anything and walking away, but that would only give Victor another chance to call her foolish and empty-headed. So instead she stood there until she began to feel like a voyeur, clearing her throat when she couldn't stand it any longer. "Lady Gladstone?"

The viscountess lifted dark eyes to her. "Saint, it seems we have company," she tittered, her voice a breathless giggle.

The form leaning over Lady Gladstone's shoulder straightened to his full height, and startling green eyes set in a face of dark, lean, masculine perfection took their leisure sweeping the length of Evelyn from her slippered feet to her face. She couldn't have stopped her blush if her life depended on it.

All young ladies mindful of their reputations made a point of staying well away from the tall, jaded, and devilishly handsome Marquis of St. Aubyn. If not for her brother's political ambitions, Victor wouldn't have allowed her anywhere near Lady Gladstone for exactly that reason.

"My lord," she said belatedly, gathering her wits enough to dip in a shallow curtsy, "good evening."

He gazed at her for another moment, his wicked, sensual mouth turning upward in the faintest of cynical smiles. "It's still too early to tell." Then, without another word, he turned on his heel and strolled away toward the gaming rooms.

Evelyn let out the breath she'd been holding. "That was rude," she muttered, once he was out of earshot.

Lady Gladstone chuckled again, her own cheeks flushed—and decidedly not from the warm room. "My dear Miss Whoever-You-Are," she murmured, "Saint doesn't have to be good, because he's so very . . . very, bad."

Well, that made no sense. She hadn't barged in, though, to debate the merits of poor behavior. "My name is Evelyn Ruddick, my lady," she said, curtsying again. "We attended the Bramhurst Christmas soiree together, and you said I might call on you in London."

"Oh, dear me, I am too generous sometimes. What was it you wanted from me, then, Miss . . . Ruddick?"

Evelyn hated this part, mostly because it always entailed lying. And she detested lying. "Well, first of all, I wanted to tell you that your gown is absolutely the most splendid creation ever."

The viscountess' lounging curves became even more pronounced at the compliment. "How very sweet of you, dear." Full lips smiled. "I would be happy to recommend my dressmaker to you. I'm certain you and I are of nearly the same age, though your . . . bosom is less . . ."

Obvious, Evelyn finished silently, hiding her scowl. "That would be most kind of you," she said instead. Then, though she would have rather swallowed a bug, Evie went closer to take a seat beside the viscountess. "I had heard," she continued in a more conspiratorial tone, "that you are greatly responsible for your husband's political success. I . . . am somewhat at a loss as to how I might assist my brother, Victor, in the same arena."

Lady Gladstone's distant expression warmed into one of calm superiority. "Ah. Well, first, of course, you must know the right people. That's—"

"Where is he?" Round soft face red as a beet and his prominent fish eyes protruding even more than usual, Lord Gladstone huffed toward them, planting his feet squarely in front of his wife. "Where is that scoundrel?"

The viscountess straightened, though it seemed a bit late for her to attempt innocence. "Whom are you looking for, my love? I've been having a coze with Miss Ruddick, here, but I'll happily help you search."

Wonderful, Evie thought, as the viscount's blustering gaze turned in her direction. All she needed was to become involved in one of St. Aubyn's infamous scandals. Victor would never allow her out of the house again—even if this incident was of course actually his fault.

"You know damned well who I'm looking for, Fatima. You, girl, have you seen that scoun—"

"Evie! There you are!" With her usual splendid timing, Georgiana, Lady Dare, swooped up to them and grasped Evelyn's hands. "You must come settle an argument. Dare insists he's right, when we both know that he never is."

Evie settled for nodding at Lord and Lady Gladstone as Georgie towed her to the safer, less scandal-ridden part of the ballroom. "Thank goodness," she exclaimed. "I thought I was doomed."

"What in the world were you doing with Lady Gladstone?" Georgiana asked, releasing her.

She sighed. "Ask Victor."

"Ah. Your brother's trying to take Plimpton's seat in the House, isn't he? I'd heard a rumor."

"Yes, he is. It's so . . . aggravating. He's spent most of the last five years out of the country, and he still never even asks my opinion about anything or anyone in London. He just sends me to chat with whomever he deems most useful."

Georgiana's expression became more thoughtful. "Hm. Well, siblings weren't precisely what we had in mind, but you might make Victor the object of your lesson."

"Absolutely not," Evie answered, shuddering. "I'm waiting for Lucinda to take her turn first. And besides, as close as you came to maiming Dare, I'd probably end up murdering Victor."

"If you say so. In my experience, though, the object of your lesson may just choose you."

"Ha. Not as long as I'm being charming and empty-headed for Victor's silly political friends. They wouldn't dare be anything but polite. Heavens, someone might scowl at them."

Lady Dare laughed and took Evie's arm again. "That's quite enough of that. Come on and dance with Tristan. You may even kick him, if you'd like."

"But I like your Tristan," Evelyn protested, grinning and thankful for good, apolitical friends. "He scowls from time to time."

Georgiana's smile softened. "Yes, he does, doesn't he?"

Chapter 2

Ah, me! in sooth he was a shameless wight,
Sore given to revel and ungodly glee;
Few earthly things found favor in his sight
Save concubines and carnal company.

—Lord Byron, *Childe Harold's
Pilgrimage, Canto I*

"**L**angley, have you seen my brother?" Evelyn whispered as she accepted her shawl from the butler.

"He's in the morning room, miss, finishing the newspaper," the elderly servant answered in an equally hushed voice. "I'd judge you have another five minutes."

"Splendid. I'll be at Aunt Houton's."

The butler pulled opened the door, escorting her outside to help her into the Ruddick family coach. "Very good, Miss Ruddick."

The butler softly closed the front door behind her, but Evie didn't let out her breath until the coach had safely trundled down the short front drive. Thank goodness. It was bad enough listening to Victor complain about how she'd missed a chance to charm Lord and Lady Gladstone; if he sent her out to make another attempt, or tried to instruct her about whom she should or shouldn't

10

chat with at their aunt's, Evelyn was going to flee London and join the circus.

The coach rumbled down Chesterfield Hill and turned northeast, away from the center of Mayfair. The house her aunt and uncle occupied had been part of the Marquis of Houton's property for so long that the fashionable part of London had moved on without it. Even so, it was magnificent, and if the neighbors tended to be merchants and solicitors now, then Aunt Houton just kept the curtains drawn.

Fifteen minutes later the coachman turned up Great Titchfield Road for his usual shortcut, and Evie sat forward. The Heart of Hope Orphanage, once an old troop barracks for the army of George II, loomed tall and long and gray along the left side of the street.

Most of her peers closed their coach curtains to it, as well, preferring to pretend that it simply didn't exist. For Evie, though, it had lately become much more than an eyesore. A building that gloomy would, under most circumstances, have made her shudder and look away. Somewhere between the shivering and the eye-closing, however, she'd glimpsed the children in the windows, looking out at the street. Looking out at her.

And so a week ago, toting a satchel of candy and a hefty helping of good intentions, she had finally asked Phillip to stop the coach and had walked up to the heavy wooden doors to knock. The children had been excessively glad to see her—or rather, to see the sweets she handed out—and the whole experience had been . . . enlightening.

She had immediately volunteered to make another visit, but the head housekeeper had only shooed her out, eyeing her skeptically and informing her that all volunteers had to be approved by the orphanage board of trustees.

Evelyn leaned out the coach window. "Phillip, stop here, if you please."

The coach veered to one side of the street and rattled to a halt. It just so happened that the board of trustees was meeting today—at this hour, in fact. Evie stood as Phillip pulled open the carriage door.

"Please wait for me here," she said over her shoulder, her attention on crossing the busy street to the tall, ominous building beyond. Here, at last, seemed a place, a cause, where she could contribute something meaningful.

The dour-faced housekeeper donned a surprised look as she opened the heavy door. "Yes, miss?"

"You said the board would be meeting this morning, did you not?"

"Yes, but—"

"I should like to discuss a matter with them."

When the housekeeper continued to stare at her in disbelief, Evie borrowed one of her brother's more haughty and effective gestures and lifted her eyebrow. With a nearly audible hesitation the woman turned to lead the way toward the winding staircase.

Behind her, Evelyn stifled as best she could a growing mix of anxiety and anticipation. She hated public speaking—it always left her stammering like a goose. On the other hand, the idea of sitting on her bottom or attending Victor's endless parade of oh-so-proper soirees until he married someone more suited for the task left her shuddering with distaste. This, she could do for herself—and for the children abandoned inside the large gray barracks rooms.

"Wait here," the housekeeper said.

With a last backward glance, as though to make certain Evelyn hadn't changed her mind and fled, she knocked on another of the heavy oak doors. At an answering murmur of male voices, the woman pushed open the door and vanished into the room beyond.

Evie glanced at the clock ticking against the far wall. Her aunt did expect her this morning, and if she didn't arrive soon, someone would send word to Victor that she was missing a West Sussex Wives' Political Tea—an absurdly self-important name for a group of females who did nothing but embroider handkerchiefs in political colors and gossip about absent members.

The door opened again. "This way, miss."

Clasping her hands in front of her to minimize their trembling, Evie stepped past the housekeeper into a large, plush drawing room—no doubt part of the former barracks commander's personal quarters. She'd seen greater splendor in the homes of Mayfair, and the most striking aspect of the room was how greatly it differed from the plain halls and gloomy rooms beyond.

As soon as she stepped through the doorway a half dozen men rose, waving at the smoky air as though motion would dispose of the odor of expensive cigars. Evie's initial nervousness ebbed almost immediately—she knew all of them, thank goodness.

"Good morning, Miss Ruddick," Sir Edward Willsley said, his thick brows arched in surprise. "Whatever brings you here on this fine day?"

Evie curtsied, though technically she outranked half the men present. Politeness and flattery always garnered more results than strict formality. "The Heart of Hope Orphanage brings me here this morning, Sir Edward. I was informed earlier this week that if I wished to contribute my time and . . . other assets to the establishment, I needed the approval of the board of trustees." She smiled. "And that would be you, would it not?"

"Why, yes, it would, my young miss."

Lord Talirand smiled back at her with the patronizing gaze one gave a half-witted invalid. Evie knew she appeared somewhat angelic, for lack of a better word, and that for some reason gentlemen, especially those who were marriage-minded, concluded that since she appeared pretty and innocent, she must also be an idiot. It had used to be amusing; lately, though, she had to fight the impulse to make drooling faces at the perpetrators.

"Then I ask your approval," she said, favoring Timothy Rutledge, the only unmarried member of the group, with a flutter of eyelashes. Being thought stupid occasionally had its benefits. Men were so easy sometimes.

"Are you certain you wouldn't rather spend your time in a more pleasant environment, Miss Ruddick? Some of these orphans are, I believe, quite uncivilized."

"All the more reason for me to volunteer my time," Evelyn replied. "And as I mentioned, I do have some funds at my discretion. With your kind permission, I would like to organize—"

"A tea party?" a low male voice interrupted from behind her.

Evie whipped around. Leaning against the doorjamb, a flask in one hand and his gloves in the other, the Marquis of St. Aubyn gazed at her. The expression in his green eyes stopped the retort she'd been about to make. Evelyn had seen cynicism before; in her circle its practice was so common it was nearly an affectation. In those light eyes, though, in that lean handsome face with its high cheekbones, angled jaw, and the mouth that again curved upward in the remains of a bemused smile, the jaded cynicism was so real she could almost taste it.

She saw something else there, as well. Evie swallowed. "My lord," she said belatedly, her mind dashing in a hundred directions. What in the world was *he* doing here? She hadn't thought he went anywhere in the daylight hours.

"Or an orphan musical recital?" he continued, as though she hadn't spoken.

The other men snickered. Evelyn felt her cheeks warm. "That is not—"

"Or a dress-up masquerade ball?" St. Aubyn pushed upright and strolled toward her. "If you're bored, I can suggest a host of other activities to keep you occupied."

His tone implied exactly what he was talking about. Lord Talirand cleared his throat. "There's no need to be insulting, St. Aubyn. If anything, we should be grateful that Miss Ruddick is willing to donate her time and money to our c—"

"Money, you say?" the marquis repeated, his gaze still on Evelyn. "No wonder the lot of you are panting."

"Look here, St. Aub—"

"What's your plan, then, Miss Ruddick?" he asked, circling her like a stalking panther.

"I . . . haven't quite—"

"Made up your mind?" he finished. "Do you have any idea what you're doing here, or did you ride by and decide it would be an adventure to set foot in an orphanage?"

"I set foot here last week," Evie returned, dismayed that her voice had begun shaking. It always did that when she was angry, blast it all, though in truth he was closer to having her quaking in trepidation. "I was told that I needed permission from the board of trustees to volunteer. So, if you don't mind, I will continue this discussion with them."

His smile quickened for a heartbeat, then faded again. "But I am the chairman of this happy little board," he told her. "And since you don't seem to have an organized proposal of your intentions or any idea how to contribute, I think it would be best if you pranced your pretty bottom out of here and went on with whatever nonsense makes up your day."

"St. Aubyn, really," Mr. Rutledge sputtered.

No one had ever spoken to Evie that way; even Victor generally couched his patronizing diatribes in more polite terms. Deciding that if she said another word it would compromise her reputation as a lady, she turned on her heel and stalked out the door. At the first-floor landing, though, she stopped.

Everyone knew St. Aubyn was a scoundrel. There were rumors, which she believed, that he'd fought in several duels, and that suspicious husbands didn't challenge him any longer because he never lost. As for his reputation with women . . .

Evie shook herself. She had come here for a reason. Whatever St. Aubyn might say, that reason remained—and to her, at least, it seemed important. It *felt* important, when nothing else she'd done lately felt the least bit significant.

"Miss?"

She started, looking down the hallway beyond the landing. Three young girls, not one of them older than twelve, stood by the nearest of the tall, narrow windows. They had been playing with dolls, she realized, seeing two of the ragged things seated in the windowsill.

"Yes?" she answered, giving a warm smile.

"Are you the lady who came with the sweets last week?" the tallest of them, a thin girl with short red hair, asked.

"I am."

"Do you have any more?"

Evie hid a frown. She had thought to be talking with the board today and then joining her aunt's party. Bringing more candy hadn't occurred to her. "I'm sorry, but I don't. Not today."

"Oh. Never mind, then." The girls returned to their dolls as though she'd simply ceased to exist.

If all she had to offer was sugar, perhaps she did belong elsewhere. Evelyn walked toward them, careful to keep the friendly smile on her face. For goodness's sake, she didn't want to frighten the little ones. "If you could have any kind of food or treat, would it be candy?" she asked.

The redhead faced her again. "I would want bread pudding with apples and cinnamon."

"Pudding. That's wonderful. How about you?"

The youngest of the three girls frowned. "I don't want to think about it. Are you a cook?"

"Heavens, no. I'm Evie. I wanted to come visit with you."

The girls continued gazing at her, obviously unimpressed.

"What're your names?" she ventured into the silence.

"Molly," the redhead answered, then elbowed the middle girl. "This is Penny, and that's Rose. Are you going to bring us pudding?"

"I think I could arrange that."

"When?"

"I'm free for luncheon tomorrow," Evie answered. "How do your schedules look?"

Rose giggled. "You're coming back tomorrow?"

"If you'd like."

Molly tugged on the youngest girl's hand, pulling her

back down the hall. "If you bring bread pudding, you can come whenever you want."

"I *may* come, you mean."

"No, you may not."

For a tall man, the Marquis of St. Aubyn moved very quietly. Taking a breath, Evie faced the staircase. Behind her, the girls continued their noisy flight down the hall. A moment later, a door slammed.

"Does anyone like you?" she asked, looking up to meet his eyes.

"Not to my knowledge. You were supposed to leave."

"I wasn't ready to go."

He tilted his head, brief surprise touching his gaze. Undoubtedly few people stood up to him. If he hadn't been so rude earlier, Evie wasn't certain she would have had the courage to do so, herself. As Lady Gladstone had said last evening, his reputation was very, very bad.

"I assume you're ready to go now?" He gestured toward the stairs, his expression informing her that she would be leaving whether she wanted to or not. Best to keep a little dignity if possible, she decided, giving him a wide berth as she returned to the stairs.

"Why don't you want me to volunteer here?" she asked over her shoulder, hearing his boot steps close behind her. "It won't cost you anything."

"Until you grow tired of providing puddings and sweets—or until the orphanage has to begin paying for the removal of children's rotten teeth."

"The offer of sweets was only so they would talk to me. I imagine they have little reason to trust adults."

"My heart weeps at your compassion."

She faced him, stopping so suddenly on the stairs that he nearly ran into her. St. Aubyn towered over her, but she refused to look away from the scoundrel's arrogant, cynical expression. "I didn't think you had a heart, my lord."

He nodded. "I don't. It was a figure of speech. Go home, Miss Ruddick."

"No. I want to help."

"First of all, I doubt you know the first thing about what the brats and this building might need."

"How could—"

"And in the second place," he continued in a quieter voice, moving one step down so that her face was level with his crotch, "I can think of a place where you'd be much more useful."

Heat rose in Evie's face, but she refused to back away. "And where might that be?"

"In my bed, Miss Ruddick."

For a moment all she could do was look at him. She'd been proposed to and propositioned, but never by someone like . . . him. He meant to shock her, to drive her away. That had to be the explanation. All she needed to do was keep breathing. She cleared her throat. "I doubt you even know my first name, my lord."

"Of course I do, not that it means anything, Evelyn Marie."

The deep sound of his voice curled around her name with a soft intimacy that made her shiver. No wonder he had such a devastating reputation with women.

"Well. I am surprised, I admit," she returned, trying to keep hold of her nerve, "but I believe you asked for a proposal detailing my plans for volunteering. I will provide you with that—and nothing else."

He smiled again, the expression delightfully handsome, except that his eyes retained every ounce of cynical derision he'd had from the beginning of their conversation. "We'll see. Don't you have an embroidery circle to join or something?"

She wanted to stick her tongue out at him, but he would probably consider that some sort of seduction. And what in the world was she doing anyway, standing in an abandoned hallway talking with the notorious Marquis of St. Aubyn? "Good day, my lord."

"Good-bye, Miss Ruddick."

Saint watched her out the front door, then returned upstairs to collect his coat and hat. Of all the meddling females who tried to relieve their boredom with candy-coated visits to the Heart of Hope Orphanage, Evelyn Marie Ruddick was probably the most and least surprising. Her political-aspirant brother doubtless had no idea she had gone visiting—no self-respecting female out to aid her male relation's political career would venture outside of Mayfair to go wading with the poor. On the other hand, on the few occasions he'd ventured into his peers' soirees, she and her clever friends had looked so terribly bored and self-important that undoubtedly she couldn't resist a chance to spread the joy of her presence to the orphans.

"My lord," the housekeeper peeped, lurking in a downstairs doorway, "will there be anything more?"

"No, not that you actually did anything," he replied, shrugging into his greatcoat.

"I . . . I beg your pardon?"

"Weren't those infants in the hallway supposed to be doing something useful?" he asked, shaking his flask before he stuffed it back into his pocket. Empty again. They needed to make the damned things larger.

"I cannot be everywhere at once, my lord."

"Then you might focus on keeping track of the uninvited guests," he finished, watching her step aside as he exited.

"That's why I'm seeing to you, my lord," she muttered.

Saint pretended not to hear that, preferring to escape the premises rather than stay and argue with the unpleasant woman. He could hardly blame her for her commentary anyway. The staff undoubtedly liked having him there as little as did the rest of the board of trustees. The only person who liked it less was himself.

His carriage pulled into the street and circled to meet him outside the door. As he waited, he glanced down the roadway. The Ruddick family coach turned the corner and passed out of sight. She'd hesitated to leave, then, even after he'd sent her on her way. Hm.

Attractive as she was, suggesting that she join him in bed had only been to frighten her away. God knew she was far too angelic and virginal for his tastes. Still, she did have pretty gray eyes, and they'd widened so amusingly when he'd insulted her.

Saint allowed himself a faint smile as he climbed into his coach and they trundled off toward Gentleman Jackson's. No doubt those pretty gray eyes would never look in his direction again. And thank Lucifer for that. He had enough to deal with without an empty-headed angel stumbling across his path.

Chapter 3

Conqueror and captive of the earth art thou!
She trembles at thee still, and thy wild name.

—Lord Byron, *Childe Harold's*
Pilgrimage, Canto III

Fatima Hynes, Lady Gladstone, knew how to give a proper greeting. "Please remove your hand from my trousers," Saint murmured, glancing over her head at the half-open door.

"You didn't say that the other night," the viscountess purred, continuing her caress.

"That was before I discovered you'd told your husband about our little amusements. I warned you once, I won't be involved in your domestic squabbles."

Her hand left his nether regions. "That's why you wanted to see me in private?" she asked, her eyes narrowing. "To be rid of me?"

"You're not surprised, Fatima, so don't pretend otherwise." Saint took a slow step backward. "And neither of us knows how to cry, so good evening."

Lady Gladstone sighed. "You have nothing resembling a heart, do you?"

He chuckled. "No."

22

With a quick glance to be certain the hallway was clear, Saint slipped out of Lord Hanson's library and back toward the ballroom. He'd known Fatima wouldn't object, and all he needed to do now was stay out of Lord Gladstone's way for the next few days, until the viscountess found another lover. The old goat Gladstone was volatile enough that he would likely demand a duel, and Fatima Hynes simply wasn't worth the bloodshed.

The majority of guests had arrived at the ball, and Lady Hanson's dinners were reputed to be exceptional, but he had no intention of staying. Despite the crowd here, he would find a plentitude of fat purses and more interesting conversation at Jezebel's or one of the other, less-distinguished clubs.

He headed for the foyer and the exit beyond, then stopped as a lithe figure in blue silk blocked his path.

"Lord St. Aubyn," Miss Ruddick said, dipping one of her pert, perfect curtsies.

The muscles across his abdomen tightened. "Evelyn," he said, deliberately using her Christian name, and somewhat surprised at his body's reaction to the chit.

"I would like to set up another meeting, my lord," she said, her gray eyes meeting his. Interesting, that. He didn't know too many people, male or female, who looked him in the eye.

"No."

A delicate flush crept up her cheeks. "You said you wouldn't allow me to volunteer because I had no plan. I am assembling one, and I wish to be allowed the courtesy of presenting it."

Saint gazed at her for a long moment. It would be easy to dismiss her out of hand. To be honest, however, she seemed less dull than he'd expected, and he'd spent far too much time lately being bored. A little amusement would be worth a small effort on his part.

He nodded. "Very well. We meet again a week from Friday."

Her soft lips opened and then closed soundlessly. "Thank you."

"Shall I write it down for you, to be certain you remember?"

Her blush deepened. "That won't be necessary."

"Good."

"I . . . do have another request, my lord."

Saint folded his arms. "I'm waiting."

"I insist on visiting the orphanage again first, so that I may see what the children most need. That's the only way I may be certain that my presence there would actually have some benefit for them."

He didn't laugh in her face, but the cynical humor in his eyes deepened. Evie kept her own expression stern and serious. Perhaps he found her silly and amusing, but she could accept that if he would allow her to proceed.

"And have you asked the other board members about this?" he asked.

"No. You said you were the chairman, and so I have come to you."

His look became more speculative. "So you have."

Evie kept forgetting to breathe in his presence, probably because her heart began pounding in her throat the moment she considered approaching him to speak. "Do you agree?"

"I have a condition of my own."

Oh, dear. Now he would undoubtedly make another insulting remark about wanting to bed her or something. "Yes?" she asked anyway.

"You will be escorted for the entire duration of your visit."

She blinked. "I agree."

"And . . ." he continued, that slight, sensuous smile touching his lips again, "you will waltz with me."

"A . . . a waltz, my lord?" she squeaked.

"A waltz."

If she could put him off until after he agreed to her plan, perhaps she could avoid it entirely. "I'm spoken for this evening, of course, but I'm sure I could save a waltz for you this Season."

He shook his head, a dark strand of hair falling across one eye. "Tonight. Now."

"But I told you, I'm spoken f—"

"The next waltz is mine, or you and your pretty bottom will stay out of the Heart of Hope Orphanage."

So the Marquis of St. Aubyn was making declarations again, hoping she would run liked a scared rabbit and he wouldn't have to deal with her any longer. Well, this wasn't about him; it was about her, and about how she hadn't been able to get the children or the orphanage out of her mind. No one had ever valued her assistance before; at the orphanage, what she did would be important.

"Very well," she said, squaring her shoulders. "May I inform Lord Mayfew that I must decline his invitation?"

Something unreadable touched his gaze for a fleeting moment. "No, you may not." As if waiting for his cue, the waltz began out on the ballroom floor. He gestured toward the main room. "Now or never, Miss Ruddick."

"Now."

Prior to this evening, the most daring, scandalous thing she'd ever done was put on her brother's clothes for a masquerade soiree, and that had been at Adamley Hall in West Sussex when she'd been fifteen. Her mother had fainted. This would probably kill Genevieve Ruddick.

The marquis led the way to the crowded dance floor, declining to take her hand and no doubt hoping she would take the opportunity of his turned back to flee. Evie was tempted.

At the edge of the floor he faced her, and with a last strangled breath she joined him there. His hand slid slowly about her waist, drawing her still closer while she waited for lightning to strike her dead.

Lord Mayhew appeared, but whatever protest he'd been about to utter vanished in a convulsive swallow as he saw her companion. St. Aubyn merely looked at the baron and abruptly Mayhew turned away, scurrying off as though he'd remembered the immediate need to relieve himself.

"Oh, dear," she muttered. Perhaps Georgie and Luce were right, after all. Chivalry was dead.

And St. Aubyn was kicking stones into the grave. "Changed your mind?" he asked, taking her fingers in his other hand.

This close he smelled of shaving soap and brandy. Her eyes were level with his crisp white cravat, and she didn't want to look up at him. This close, he . . . overwhelmed her, every scandalous tale she'd ever heard about him swirling about in her mind. What was she doing, standing in the embrace of the Marquis of St. Aubyn?

With a slight shift of his hand, he guided them into the waltz. She'd never seen him dance before that she could recall, but Evie wasn't surprised that he moved with elegance and grace. And light as his grip was, she felt the steel beneath. Evie had no doubt that she wouldn't be able to escape unless he let her.

"Look at me," he murmured, his soft breath in her hair reminding Evie of his intimate conversation with Lady Gladstone.

Swallowing, she lifted her chin. "You're very mean, you know."

An eyebrow lifted. "I'm giving you what you asked for."

"In exchange for humiliating me."

"I only requested a waltz. I might have asked for something much more intimate, you know."

Evie decided she might as well blush. He probably thought beet-red was her natural coloring, anyway. "You already did, and I refused you."

St. Aubyn chuckled, the sound unexpected and warm. Even his eyes lit just a little, and she wondered for a fleeting moment why he seemed so determined to be jaded and cynical all the time.

"Sharing my bed was a suggestion, not a request. A very good suggestion, by the way."

"No, it wasn't. I don't even like you. Why would I want to . . . become intimate with you?"

For a moment he looked genuinely surprised. "What does liking someone have to do with anything? It's the act that's pleasurable."

Oh, God, now she was going to faint. Discussing sexual intercourse in the middle of a ballroom with the Marquis of St. Aubyn was akin to a demand to be ruined. He'd kept his voice low, though, and she hoped no one had overheard their discussion. As for what else anyone might think she could possibly be chatting about with him, she would worry about that later. "I admit to ignorance about the details you discuss," she returned, "but I would think any interaction between two people would be . . . nicer if genuine affection were involved."

"Your naïveté is truly remarkable," he said, then lowered his head to whisper, "and I would be happy to relieve your ignorance."

His lips brushed her ear, feather-light, and she shivered. *He's just playing with me,* she told herself desperately. *He's bored, and he's trying to keep himself entertained.* "Stop that," she commanded, annoyed that her voice shook.

The waltz ended, and he released her before she could pull away. She expected another intimate, insulting comment, but instead he sketched an elegant bow. "You've fulfilled your part of our agreement," he said, lips curving in a soft smile. "Be there at ten tomorrow morning to meet your escort. If you're late, you lose the opportunity."

Again before she could react, he strolled into the crowd of guests. They parted in a wave before him. Evie abruptly felt the need for some fresh air.

The noisy, tittering crowd parted for her as well, as she made her way to the balcony. She couldn't hear what they were saying, but she didn't need to; their conversation would feature the Ruddick name and the St. Aubyn title, and that couldn't be good.

"Evie," a female voice said behind her, and a hand clasped hers.

"Lucinda," she returned, light-headed with relief. "I had no idea you were h—"

"Are you mad?" Lucinda Barrett continued in the same hushed voice, though from her smile anyone in the audience would think they were discussing primroses. "St. Aubyn? Do you know what your brother would say if he knew?"

"I'm sure he does know," Evie answered, as they stepped out onto the cool balcony. "The only time he notices I have a mind of my own is when I'm doing something he doesn't approve of."

Lucinda gazed at her with serious hazel eyes. "This time I would be inclined to agree with him. Rebellion is one thing, but St. Aubyn?"

"Did you know he's on the board of trustees at the Heart of Hope Orphanage?"

Her friend's mouth opened and closed again. "No, I didn't. The poor dears. But Evie, what does that have to do with the price of pudding?"

"I want to begin some programs there," Evelyn answered, wondering how she could convince Lucinda about the importance of her plans when she didn't quite understand yet herself why it was becoming so significant.

"That's . . . admirable."

"You don't think I can do it, do you?" she retorted, the evening's frustrations making her voice harder than she intended.

"It's not that," Lucinda said quickly. "It's . . . If you've decided how you want to focus your energies, there are other places and in better areas that aren't associated with the Marquis of St. Aubyn."

"Yes, I know. But I chose this place before I knew about him, and I think it would be cowardly of me to turn away from those in need simply because one board member has a poor reputation." He was the chairman of the board, and "poor" didn't begin to describe his reputation, actually, but that didn't change the argument.

"Even so," her friend said, more slowly, "that doesn't explain why you were waltzing with him."

"Oh. That was a trade: He agreed to have someone show me about the orphanage tomorrow if I would waltz with him."

From her expression, Lucinda remained unconvinced that Evie hadn't lost her mind. Good friend that she was, though, Miss Barrett only nodded. "Please just remember, St. Aubyn never does anything without exacting a price, and what he does is never in anyone else's best interest."

The memory of his lips brushing her ear made Evie shiver. "I do know that, Luce. Contrary to popular male opinion, I'm not a complete idiot."

"Even so, you may want to discuss St. Aubyn with Dare. They know one another."

"Oh, very well, if it'll make you feel any better."

"How *I* feel doesn't signify, Evie. Just be cautious."

"I will." She sighed at Lucinda's worried expression. "I promise."

Victor stood waiting for her just inside. "Evie."

Motioning for Lucinda to go, Evelyn wondered whether one had to be of a certain age before suffering an apoplexy, or if anyone could succumb. "Victor."

He grabbed her arm, the gesture seemingly affectionate, except that it would likely leave a bruise. "We are leaving," he rumbled. "Of all the stupid, naive, empty-headed—"

"One more word," she said in a low voice, "and I will fall to the floor in a dead faint. That will make you look very, *very* mean."

With a baleful look, he released her. "We will continue this at home," he growled.

Wonderful. "Undoubtedly." She glanced over his shoulder, seeing a dark-haired savior approaching. "Now, if you don't mind, my partner for the quadrille is waiting."

Victor swung his head around. "Dare."

Tristan Carroway, Viscount Dare, nodded back at

him, his solemn face at odds with the twinkle in his light blue eyes. "Ruddick."

Sending her a last, angry look, Victor strode off in the direction of his latest political allies. "Ogre," she muttered.

"I hope you realize I'd rather break my neck than dance a quadrille," Dare said, taking her arm.

"I know."

"I've been commanded to escort you to Georgiana," he said amiably, guiding her around the fringes of the crowd. "She wants to chastise you."

Everyone seemed to, tonight. "And what do you think, my lord?"

"I think that whatever game Saint is playing, you probably don't want to be a part of it."

"I thought you were friends."

The viscount shrugged. "We used to be. Now we play cards together on occasion."

"Why does everyone call him Saint?"

"Besides the obvious? He inherited the St. Aubyn title when he was six or seven. I would guess that 'Saint' seemed better suited to a youth than the mouthful of 'Marquis of St. Aubyn.' Now, though, I imagine he finds it . . . amusing, since he's about the furthest thing from a saint there is without taking hell into account."

"Why?"

"You'd have to ask him—not that I would, if I were you. Which I'm not, thank God, since I'd look dreadful in an evening gown."

Evie chuckled, though Dare's comments were a little surprising. His own reputation as a rake had been well warranted, to say the least, though now that he'd married his heretofore harshest critic, most of the gossip had ceased. If he felt it necessary to caution her about

St. Aubyn, his words were something she should take seriously.

"Thank you for the warning," she said, granting him a warm smile, "but Lord St. Aubyn is merely an obstacle to the commencement of a project of mine. In another few days I'll have little or no reason even to set eyes on him."

"Well, until that time, just don't turn your back on him, Evie."

That didn't leave her feeling the least bit better about any of this. At the same time, all of the rumors and finally meeting St. Aubyn face-to-face made her nothing if not more curious. As things were, however, she'd be better off leaving her questions about him unanswered.

She spent the next morning organizing questions and points to look for during her tour of the orphanage. Thankfully Victor stomped off to one of his meetings early, leaving her with one of his perturbed glares that wondered why she even breathed when he hadn't instructed her to do so. The longer she could put off a confrontation over her waltz with St. Aubyn, the more likely he was to forget about it—especially if he needed her to go to a tea party or charm one of his fat, bald compatriots.

If he discovered her plans, he would forbid her to have anything to do with the orphanage. And if that happened, she wasn't certain what she would do. Best, then, if he didn't find out.

The only places she could go without a chaperone were Lucinda's, Georgiana's, or her Aunt Houton's, so she told the butler that Victor would be able to find her at her aunt's. That seemed the location least likely to raise his ire or his suspicions. It was ridiculous, to have to lie about doing good deeds, but she didn't want her plans ruined before she even had a chance to begin them.

When Phillip stopped the coach on Great Titchfield Road, she sat inside for a long moment, making certain she had her pencil and papers and notes so she wouldn't look like a fool in front of her escort—or the children. "Please wait for me," she said as she emerged. "I may be a short while."

The driver nodded. "It's all that heavy traffic between Ruddick House and Lord and Lady Houton's," he said, shutting the door behind her and climbing back up to his perch.

Evelyn smiled at him, more grateful than she could express. Since Victor's return from India, all the servants had aided her escapes from his frequent political diatribes. They had to know that if he discovered their activities, any or all of them would be summarily dismissed.

She hurried across the street. As she knocked at the orphanage doors, Evie frowned. St. Aubyn hadn't said who would be leading her about the orphanage. She hoped it wouldn't be that dreadful housekeeper. Evie couldn't imagine she would be the least bit helpful or understanding.

The door creaked open. "Yes?" the housekeeper asked, her broad shoulders filling the doorway.

Drat. "I had an appointment this morn—"

The housekeeper bobbed an awkward curtsy. "Oh, . . . you're Miss Ruddick," she stammered, bobbing again. "Please come in. You're expected, miss."

Evie walked past her into the foyer, not certain whether to be alarmed or relieved at the housekeeper's sudden politeness. Any further contemplation, though, halted as she caught sight of the figure leaning against the stair banister.

Even in the middle of the morning on a pleasant summer's day in London, the Marquis of St. Aubyn had about him the aura of a figure of the night. It was probably his reputation, but even without that, Evie would have known that he didn't belong in a place of plain, graying white walls and tallow candles. Chandeliers and rich wall coverings and dim, curtained bedchambers seemed much more his natural habitat.

"You're staring, Miss Ruddick," he said, straightening.

She started. "I'm merely surprised to see you this morning," she countered. "I mean, I appreciate your personally bringing word that I'm to have a tour, but you might have sent a note."

He nodded, coming toward her with that panther's stalk of his. "I have to admit, usually when I see this side of morning it's because I haven't yet gone to bed."

Evie wasn't quite certain how to answer that. "Ah. Well, if Mrs. . . . ." She trailed off, at a loss.

Saint glanced at the housekeeper. "What the devil is your name, anyway?"

"Mrs. Natham," the housekeeper answered. From her tone, it wasn't the first time she'd supplied him with the information.

"Thank you," Evie said, offering the woman a half smile. They'd simply gotten off to a poor start; there was no reason to assume they couldn't deal together. "If you don't mind, Mrs. Natham, I would like to begin the tour."

"I . . . but . . . ah . . ."

"She isn't conducting your tour," the marquis said, cynical humor touching his voice. "I am."

"You?" Evie blurted, before she could stop herself.

"Yes, I. Shall we?" He led the way to a door on the right side of the foyer and held it open for her.

"But . . . don't you have more important things to do?"

"Not a one." His mouth curved in that sensuous smile of his. "You asked for a tour. I am providing one. Decline, and you're free to walk out the door. But you won't be allowed back again."

So that was it. Another of St. Aubyn's attempts at control through intimidation. This morning, however, she wasn't in the mood to be intimidated. Today she could begin doing something useful, and no jaded, arrogant marquis was going to make her run away.

Saint had a difficult time not laughing. His guest looked like a deer surrounded by a pack of wolves, not knowing which direction to run. Undoubtedly she'd thought to spend the morning gossiping with the troll, Mrs. Whatever. The idea that Miss Ruddick would actually have to confront some of the orphanage's inhabitants and view their living quarters must have been horrifying to her.

Her expressive gray eyes studied him and the doorway beyond as though she were weighing her chances of going in and coming back out alive. It would have been amusing, if it wasn't so predictable.

"Very well, my lord," she said, gesturing for him to lead the way.

Saint exited the foyer, swiftly covering his surprise. With her falling in beside him, they entered the downstairs hallway. Hm. Perhaps she wasn't quite as predictable as he'd thought. That made her an exception among females. So far. "These were for the most part administrative offices. This used to be an army bar—"

"Barracks for George the Second's Coldstream Guards," she finished. "What do you use them for now?"

"You've done some research," he said grudgingly.

"Surprised?" she asked coolly.

And becoming more so by the moment. "I'll let you know." He returned his attention to the long corridor. "The orphanage uses the rooms for storing old furniture and for the odd accountant."

Nodding, she made a note of some sort on the top page of the stack of papers she cradled in her left arm. "How many offices are there?" she asked. "And how large are they?"

So now the timid Miss Ruddick was all business. He gazed at her profile. "As for quantity, about a dozen. Size, I don't know. Let's go inside one and explore, why don't we?"

She swallowed, looking up from her scribbling. "I . . . don't think that's necessary. I don't have anything with which to measure, anyway."

"Ah." And now she became the timid virgin once more. "Would you care to go to the music or drawing room, then? Or perhaps the ballroom. You would find that more pleasant, I'm sure."

Evelyn stopped so abruptly that Saint had to turn around to face her. For a long moment she glared at him. Women didn't do that very often, and he had to admire it for that reason. In a moment, though, she would no doubt begin crying, and he detested that.

"Let me make something clear," she said, her voice quavering a little, as it had when she'd accepted his invitation to waltz. "I am not afraid of seeing something unpleasant. I couldn't very well do anything helpful for an establishment that didn't require any assistance. What I don't want is for this venture to ruin my reputation. Being escorted by you is a risk in itself, but at least in the hallway we have witnesses. Going into a storage room with you would be both stupid and useless on my part."

He took a slow step back in her direction. "It might be stupid," he murmured, "but it wouldn't be useless. I could teach you a great many things. Isn't that why you're here? To learn?"

Color flooded her cheeks. Saint studied her expression, her stance, the language of her slender, petite body. Despite his experience with women, he wasn't all that familiar with virgins. He'd made it a point not to be; their clinging hysterics complicated things far too much.

This one, though, made him curious.

She turned on her heel. "Good day, my lord."

"Giving up already?" he asked, forcing himself not to stalk after her. He wasn't finished with her yet, but neither would he allow her even the momentary advantage an apology would give her. That wasn't how he played the game.

"I am not giving up. I'll continue the tour with Mrs. Natham. At least she won't attempt to seduce me in the broom closet."

Apparently she'd heard the rumor about himself and Lady Hampstead. Nearly everyone had. "Continue with me. I promised you a tour, and you shall have one."

Evelyn faced him again, the stack of papers she carried clenched so tightly that the edges curled. "A tour of the orphanage, my lord. Not of your . . . private parts."

"Agreed—for today."

She assessed that statement, then turned to the nearest closed door. "Storage?"

"Yes."

Disliking the idea that she might yet change her mind and scurry off, Saint kept his distance as she opened the door and stepped inside. A moment later she reemerged to scribble further notations in her book. "Are they all the same size?"

Saint stirred, beginning to feel a bit uncomfortable as she continued to make notes. Good God, an innocent chit asking innocent questions and attending to an innocent task, and he was going hard. "Relatively."

"Excellent. Shall we continue?"

So she meant to take him at his word. Another surprise, and with even more agitating results. Part of him thought continuing the tour was useless, since he'd given his word not to seduce her. The other part, though, was practically pointing the way down the hall. "What are you scribbling there?" he asked in an attempt to distract himself, as they continued toward the far end of the hallway.

"Notes."

"About storage room size?"

"I prefer not to say until I present my plan in its entirety, Lord St. Aubyn. I believe you have enough preconceived notions about me without my providing you more."

"Saint," he said, ignoring the rest of her commentary.

She looked up at him, her cheeks still glowing with the attractive half blush from which she seemed perpetually to suffer in his presence. "I beg your pardon?"

"I said you should call me Saint. Nearly everyone does."

Evelyn cleared her throat. "Saint, then."

He gazed at her until she looked away. Apparently she wasn't going to grant him permission in turn to use her Christian name, but that wasn't likely to prevent him from doing so.

"So . . . these are all unused rooms?" she offered into the silence.

"I thought we'd covered that." He stifled a grin. "Or have you run out of questions already? You might have spared me the bother of conducting a tour if y—"

"I am clarifying," she said sharply. "And I didn't ask *you* to conduct this tour. That was your idea, my lor— Saint."

Now she was arguing with him. Saint wondered what her reaction would be if he pinned her to the plain white wall and kissed her. Nor would he stop there. Once he got his hands on her and pulled off that abysmally prim bonnet and those buttoned kid gloves, he would continue his exploration of her slender naked body until he'd figured out why she aroused him, and until he'd purged the virginal female from his thoughts.

Perhaps that was it: With her bonnet and her gloves and the high-necked, conservative gown she'd worn for the tour, the thought of her smooth warm skin beneath all that material was causing his imagination to run rampant.

"Aren't you going to say anything?" Evelyn asked, facing him again.

"I would, but I gave my word that I would behave myself." And he hoped she appreciated that, because he didn't do it very often. Almost never, in fact.

"And so I should be grateful?"

"Not particularly. I know I'd be much more grateful if I *weren't* behaving. Do you wish to see the kitchens or the orphans next?"

"The kitchens, I think." Her pert nose wrinkled, as though she'd thought of something unpleasant. "I wish to have a basis of reference before I interview the children. I'm *not* avoiding them."

"I didn't say a word."

She looked at him sideways, amusement touching her gaze. "You were about to."

For a moment Saint was too mesmerized by her smile to reply. Rising this early in the day had made him mad. Nothing else made sense. And certainly nothing else explained why he was beginning to enjoy conducting a tour of the damned Heart of Hope Orphanage for a proper chit like Evelyn Marie Ruddick.

Chapter 4

'Tis pity learned virgins ever wed
With persons of no sort of education,
Or gentlemen, who, though well-born and bred,
Grow tired of scientific conversation:
I don't choose to say much upon this head,
I'm a plain man, and in a single station,
But—Oh! ye lords of ladies intellectual,
Inform us truly, have they not hen-peck'd you all?

—Lord Byron, *Don Juan, Canto I*

Evie kept forgetting to write notes to herself, and she knew precisely whom to blame for her absentmindedness.

She'd begun the day nervous about her ability to appear competent. With Saint as her guide, her anxiety increased a hundredfold. Men were nothing new; she'd talked with, flirted with, and been courted by dozens of them since her debut. They rarely moved her to more than a chuckle or a frown. The Marquis of St. Aubyn, however, wasn't like any of those men. He was, in fact, precisely the sort of male both her mother and her common sense told her to avoid at all costs. In her first attempt to escape her brother's staid version of what her life should be, however, it made sense that she would be confronted with St. Aubyn.

For some reason he'd been polite since she'd set the rules of behavior this morning, and uneasy as it made her to have the panther at her side, even with claws sheathed, she would use the circumstance to her own best advantage. She glanced over her shoulder at him as he stood, arms crossed, in the entry to the girls' dormitory. He was gazing at her again—or rather, still—his light green eyes seeking or seeing something she assumed had very little to do with propriety.

"Miss Evie, I thought you was to bring us pudding," Molly said, her plaintive tone shaking Evelyn back to her senses.

"I said I would, and I shall, but today I'd just like to chat with all of you, if I may."

"Is *he* coming in?" another of the girls whispered, prompting some low-voiced giggling.

"I wish he would," another of them said with a coy smile. "I heard his estate at St. Aubyn is paved with gold coins."

Evie frowned. "How old are you?"

"Seventeen, Miss Evie. In another eight months I'll be gone from here, living with some fancy man in Covent Garden, I imagine."

"Good heavens, I hope not," Evie muttered, looking more closely at the flock gathered around her. *Is that what they all expected of their lives?*

"Well, I'd rather live in a house with gold floors than on dirt in Covent Garden."

"As if he would marry the daughter of a seamstress, Maggie. You're not even fit to clean his floors, much less stand on 'em."

Maggie swirled her tattered cotton skirt around her

hips, flipping the ends at Molly. "I didn't mean we should marry, halfwit," she murmured.

Molly stuck out her tongue. "That would make you a who—"

Hoping St. Aubyn hadn't overheard that part of the conversation, Evie stepped between the two girls. No one would be kicking or punching or verbally assaulting anyone while she was present. "I'm sure Lord St. Aubyn isn't worth all this fuss, whatever his floors are made of. I don't want to know about him, anyway; I want to know about all of you young ladies."

"I'm not a young lady. I'm a little girl." Rose came forward, holding her scruffy doll by one foot. "And we're all orphans."

"Not all of us are," another of the two dozen girls— Iris, she thought—interrupted. "William and Penny's papa got transported for seven years."

Alice Bradley grinned. "And Fanny's papa's in Newgate for cracking a bottle over a tavern keeper's gourd."

"That rum cove deserved it," Fanny shot back, knotting her hands into the front of her dingy brown dress. Evie couldn't even tell what the material was any longer, though it had likely been of inferior quality to begin with.

"Stop telling tales, Alice, you stupid sot, or we'll tell her what your mama did to end up in Newgate."

"You will not!"

Oh, dear. "Now, now. How about if I ask a question, and those of you who wish to may answer it?" She sat again, smoothing her skirt.

Rose leaned against her knee. "I like the way you talk," she said, scratching at her bottom with the hand not gripping her doll.

"Thank you, Rose."

"What's the first question?"

Evie took a deep breath. She certainly didn't want to do or say anything to make the girls upset with one another or with her, and neither did she intend to leave herself open to barbs at the hands—or rather, tongue—of St. Aubyn.

"My first question is, how many of you can read?"

"Read?" Penny burst out. "I thought you were going to ask what kind of sweets we like."

"Yes, sweets. You're the one who brung candy here before, ain't you?"

Evelyn tried to ignore both the poor grammar and the smug, cynical look aimed at her from the doorway. She wished he would go away so she could concentrate, but he obviously had no intention of doing so.

"But what about my question? Do any of you—"

"Sweets!"

The room erupted in a loud, cacophonous candy dance. This was terrible. She'd taken less than ten minutes to lose control of the situation entirely. No one was going to answer any of her questions now.

"*Out!*"

St. Aubyn appeared at her shoulder. At his bellow, the girls screeched and scattered for the exits, the candy dance disintegrating into yips and yelps of surprise.

In only a moment she and the marquis were alone in the dormitory. "That wasn't necessary," she grumbled, stacking her papers so she wouldn't have to meet his amused, cynical gaze.

"They were making my head ache," he rumbled. "Miniature clucking hens. Finished with this nonsense?"

She shook her head. "Not yet."

"Miss Ruddick," the marquis said in his deep, jaded voice, "while I have to admit that you've lasted longer than I expected, you obviously aren't going to accomplish anything here."

Evelyn took a shallow breath, refusing to give in to frustrated tears. St. Aubyn would *not* see her cry. "And so I should go home and embroider, I suppose?" Being indignant was good. At least if she was indignant, she wouldn't cry.

"My original offer stands," he said in a lower voice, taking the pencil from her hand and pulling her to her feet. As they touched, a pulse of lightning shot down her spine. "You would find sharing my bed much more satisfying than this."

He ran his thumb along her lips, the touch warm and soft, and Evelyn stopped breathing. Moving slowly, as though they were in an intimate boudoir rather than a large, open-doored dormitory, he took her notes and set them on one of the beds.

"What are you doing?" she whispered, her voice unsteady.

"I'm going to kiss you," he answered, as calmly as if he were discussing the care and cleaning of silverware.

Her eyes focused on his mouth, on his sensuous and slightly parted lips. Evie shook herself, willing herself not to give in to his knowing gaze and the strength of his tall, hard body. She could learn so much from him, she knew, but the lessons would ruin her entirely. Other women had fallen for him before, and where were they now?

"S . . . so you think you're Richard the Third?" she managed, backing away until her calf hit the edge of the bedframe.

His brow furrowed. "Explain."

"Richard the Third seduced his sister-in-law over the dead body of his brother."

"I know that," he said brusquely, closing the distance

between them with one long step. "How does that make me ugly and hunchbacked and a pretender to the throne?"

"You are none of those, my lord. What I—"

"Saint," he corrected, brushing hair from her forehead.

She felt distinctly as though he wanted to and intended to eat her alive. Another shiver ran up the backs of her legs. "Saint," she amended. Good God, if he actually meant to kiss her—if someone saw them kissing—she would be banished to West Sussex for life, if Victor and her mother didn't disown her entirely. "What I meant to say was, you tell me I'm incompetent and useless, and then try to use my subsequent despair to seduce me."

The expression in his eyes changed for a heartbeat, and then darkened again as he chuckled. "You're not useless. You've merely stepped beyond the bounds a chit should properly observe."

Apparently women believed him sometimes, or he would never have ventured to say something so ridiculous. And he still had power to attract her, even when she acknowledged that his statement was ludicrous. She wondered whether he could hear her heart beating. His looks and his presence remained seductive, but it reassured her to some degree that she'd managed to stand against him thus far. "And a chit's proper place is in your bed, I assume?"

He nodded, leaning closer, his gaze on her mouth. "Yes."

"Your bed must be very crowded, then," she said, stepping sideways and retrieving her papers. "I don't think there's room for me there."

"Evelyn—"

"I would like to see the boys' dormitory now," she exclaimed, striding for the door and trying not to break into a run.

Until this moment she never would have thought she could feel so angry and so . . . exhilarated at the same instant. No notorious rake and scoundrel had ever pursued her before, and now the worst of the lot, a very handsome and experienced one, was trying to kiss her—and more. It was even a little heady, despite his obvious and utter disdain for the quality and capabilities of her mind.

Evie slowed, frowning, as she crossed into the hallway. It was either a seduction or he was trying once again to intimidate her into leaving without enough information to put together her proposal. "How did you become involved with the orphanage, anyway?" she ventured, not sure whether she preferred the idea that she was being seduced or that she was being distracted.

"Very bad luck," he returned, catching up to her.

"I thought someone like you didn't believe in luck."

"There are some things skill can't compensate for. And *that* is bad luck."

"What sort of bad luck led you here, then?"

He smiled, no humor in the expression. "Pretend curiosity all you want, but when your little plan comes to nothing but sweets and sing-alongs, we'll both know why you're really here."

"And why is that, my lord? Because of you? You might consider that no self-respecting female would want to be seen in your company, and that in addition, under your direction this is one of the sorriest establishments for the underprivileged that I've ever seen."

It was the only establishment she'd seen up close, but he didn't need to know that. Saint said something under his breath that Evie preferred not to interpret. Before she could renew her questioning of his motivations, he grabbed her arm and guided her against the wall.

He didn't push or pull her or use any obvious force, but at the same time she couldn't have gotten away from him if she'd tried. And at the moment she was too startled to try.

"Don't forget," he murmured, bending his face to hers, "that you *are* in my company, and that when you intentionally provoke me, you have to expect certain consequences."

Drawing even closer, he brushed his mouth against hers, soft and warm and intimate, then straightened again.

"Now, shall we?" he said, his mouth curving in that faint, cynical smile of his, as he gestured for her to continue down the hall.

Her mind spun. "You . . . you, sir, are a . . . a scoundrel."

St. Aubyn stopped, turned on his heel, and stalked up to her again. She tried to draw a breath to say something even more indignant and insulting, but he captured her mouth in a hot, hard kiss. Shoving her back against the wall, Saint tilted her head up to deepen their embrace. Dimly she heard her stack of papers hitting the floor as she wrapped her fists into his black jacket.

Experienced or not, jaded or not, the Marquis of St. Aubyn knew how to kiss. On a few occasions the more daring of her suitors had kissed her. The sensation had been pleasant, she supposed, but she'd had no real basis for comparison—until now.

Heat ran down her spine, and her toes positively curled in her shoes. *Stop kissing him,* she shrieked at herself, trying to force her fingers to let go of his lapels.

Even so, it was St. Aubyn who broke the kiss. Looking at her from inches away, he ran his tongue through his lips as though he'd just eaten something he'd enjoyed.

"You taste like honey," he said, his voice a low drawl.

She felt as if she'd been standing in a field of cannon— her ears rang, her legs felt limp and shaky, and she had the desperate desire to flee somewhere, anywhere, safe. "St . . . stop that," she squeaked, shoving at his chest.

"I already did." Her pushing didn't budge him an inch. Instead his gaze lowered to her mouth again. "Curious," he murmured, as if to himself, brushing her lips once more with his fingers.

Evelyn tried to breathe. "What's curious?"

Saint shrugged, backing away. "Nothing. Shall I escort you to the boys' dormitory now?"

"I believe I already suggested the dormitory," she bit out, bending down to pick up her notes. Naturally he didn't offer to retrieve them for her. Her fingers shook, and she grasped the pages quickly, snatching them to her bosom.

He led as they continued along the hallway, and Evie took those few moments of relative solitude to straighten her bonnet and attempt to gather her scattered wits. As a proper, upstanding female she should have slapped St. Aubyn and stormed out of the building—though of course she shouldn't have been at the Heart of Hope Orphanage to begin with.

She decided, however, that he had kissed her precisely so she *would* flee. His insults hadn't worked, so he'd attempted an even more personal assault. If she'd run, he would then have had his excuse never to allow her back in again—and she wouldn't have the chance to prove to herself that she could accomplish anything useful. It might have worked, except that the beckoning, seeking sin of his lips had stirred . . . something inside that almost made her wish he would do it again.

Saint opened the door to the boys' dormitory, reflecting that he probably should have begun the tour there, rather than easing her into the place through the storage rooms and the kitchens and the girls' rooms. He was getting soft, figuratively speaking. This was the encounter that would send her fleeing, and if he'd brought her here first, he wouldn't have had to resort to kissing such a proper female. No wonder his insides felt twisted; no part of him knew how he was supposed to react to a virgin.

He glanced over his shoulder. "Coming?"

"Yes, of course."

As Evelyn brushed past him, he leaned in to smell her hair. Lemons. Honey on her lips and lemon in her hair, and her skin probably tasted of strawberries. Evelyn Ruddick was a veritable dessert, and he wanted to feast. Badly.

Self-restraint had never been among his best-loved or most-mastered traits, but he supposed simply falling on her wouldn't get him what he wanted. That would probably make her faint, which would be no fun for him at all.

Most of the two dozen boys were gathered at the far end of the room, crowded into a semicircle bound by one wall. Even through the chatter and shouts, he could hear the distinct clink of coins.

"What—" Evelyn began, then stopped.

"They're pitching pennies," he said, slowing to look at her.

"Wagering? In an orphanage?"

Saint stifled a sigh. Proper chits were more trouble than they were worth. "Any coins on the floor by the time I get there," he said in a carrying voice, "belong to me."

The boys yelped, diving onto the floor to gather up stray pennies, while the onlookers formed a ragged, imperfect line of attention. They didn't see him down here very often, and none of them looked any more pleased about it than he was.

"This is Miss Ruddick," he said, gesturing at Evelyn. "She wants to know about you."

"Thank you, Lord St. Aubyn." With a slight, nervous twitch of her fine lips, she stepped into the center of the line. "First of all, please call me Evie."

"Give us a kiss, Evie," one of the older boys called.

Saint grinned. Since she'd let him kiss her, he supposed the boy had half a chance, as well. Crossing his arms, he leaned against one of the support beams that ran down the center of the dormitory. This should be interesting.

"If you want a girl to kiss you," she said sharply, facing her heckler, "perhaps you should take a bath first."

The other boys laughed, while the taunt of "dirty Mulligan" circled the room. Saint allowed it; she obviously hadn't been talking about him. He'd bathed this morning. And shaved.

"Now, now," Evie continued, patting Mulligan on the shoulder. "I'm not here to make fun. I just want to know you. Do you stay in here all day?"

"The Iron Mop said we had to stay indoors today for an inspection," one of them answered.

"The Iron Mop?"

"Mrs. Natham, I mean, Miss Evie."

"I see."

Saint thought a faint smile might have passed her lips, but it was gone too swiftly for him to be certain. He frowned. Proper ladies didn't have a sense of humor; his god-awful reputation was proof enough of that.

"How do you generally spend your days, then? In school?"

" 'In school?' " another of the boys mimicked. "Did you come here from Bedlam, Miss Evie?"

"Are ye one of them religious ladies, come to pray for our heathen souls?" Mulligan put in.

"No, of course n—"

"The Reverend Beacham comes here every Sunday to try to save us," another lad said.

"No, he don't. He comes for the Iron Mop!"

Evelyn shot Saint a frustrated glance, and he lifted an eyebrow. "Perhaps you should offer them pudding," he suggested.

"I'm a heathen!"

"I'm a Red Indian!" one of the younger boys whooped, starting a war dance.

"Interesting, Evelyn," Saint murmured, just loud enough for her to hear. "Does chaos follow you everywhere?"

She scowled at him, then quickly wiped the expression from her face as she turned back to the boys. "Do you know about Indians?" she cut in, squatting down to the brave's eye level. "Would you like to know about them?"

"Randall told me about them. They scalp people."

She nodded. "And they can move through a forest without making a sound, and follow a bear's trail over rocks and through rivers."

The boy's eyes widened. "They can?"

"Yes. What's your name?"

"Thomas Kinnett."

Evie straightened. "You know, Mr. Kinnett, when you introduce yourself to a lady, you should bow."

The boy's brow wrinkled. "Why?"

"So you can look up her skirt," Saint commented dryly.

This was typical; a female attempting to teach babies etiquette before she knew whether they had enough to eat. Abruptly he felt disappointed. For a moment, he'd thought Evelyn Ruddick might have a bit of sense in addition to her tempting body.

"Lord St. Aubyn!" she snapped, flushing. Snickers and giggles erupted around her.

"Yes, Miss Evie?"

"I don't believe—" she began sharply, then stopped. With a look around her, she excused herself from the circle and stomped up to him. "I don't believe," she repeated in a quieter, equally fierce voice, "that these boys need a poor example set before them. You have not done them a good turn."

He leaned forward, holding her gaze. "Neither have you. Bowing lessons for seven-year-old pickpockets are, in a word, useless, Evelyn."

Her fair complexion paled, and for a bare, surprised moment he thought she might slap him. Finally, though, she nodded. "At least I am making an attempt to do something for them. I very much doubt you can make the same claim."

Good God. She was *baiting* him. Women didn't do that unless they wished to end up either publicly humiliated or, better, naked beneath him. "Evelyn Marie," he whispered, unable to stop the smile from touching his lips, "I've only laid claim to one thing today, and that is your mouth. And I mean to collect on the rest of you."

She blinked and then, stammering something to herself, backed away. "Scoundrel," she muttered.

Saint sketched a bow. "Ready to service you."

With another stunned, furious look, she turned on her heel and fled. Saint stood in the midst of the laughing boys and watched her leave. That should take care of things. She'd be a fool to approach either him or the orphanage again after that. Neither thought, however, left him in a particularly good humor.

"You stupid sots," the youngest boy complained. "I wanted to learn about Indians."

Saint stifled a scowl as he left the dormitory. The comment hadn't been aimed at him, of course, because no one—not even infants—were allowed to speak that way to him. And this wasn't about what little boys wanted, anyway. It was about what was best for him—and for Evelyn Ruddick.

Chapter 5

Saint Peter sat by the celestial gate,
His keys were rusty, and the lock was dull,
So little trouble had been given of late;
Not that the place by any means was full.

—Lord Byron, "The Vision of Judgment"

"**Y**ou're joking. Aren't you?" Lucinda stopped
beside the Barrett coach as her maid piled a
half dozen boxes and parcels onto one of the plush seats.

"Do I look as though I'm joking?" Evie returned,
handing over her own parcel to be added to the stack. It
was a sad commentary on the state of her nerves when
she could only find one item to purchase on a shopping
excursion.

"Hm. I've never heard anything good—or rather, *re-
peatable* and good— said about St. Aubyn, but for him
to publicly question your competence seems uncalled
for. Your uncle is the Marquis of Houton, after all."

"I'm certain he doesn't care a fig who my relations
might be," she said, wishing Luce would tell her something about St. Aubyn or his reputation that she didn't
already know.

"No, he probably doesn't care," Lucinda admitted.

"Oh, I heard that Luckings just received some new hats. Shall we?"

Evelyn actually wanted to work on her proposal, but Victor was home today, and if he caught her holed up in the library on such a fine morning, she wasn't certain she would be able to deflect his suspicions. "Absolutely."

They strolled down Bond Street toward the milliner's, Lucinda chatting and smiling at acquaintances as they went, and pretending that she hadn't noticed how distracted Evelyn seemed to be. That was one of the nicest things about Lucinda Barrett; calm and practical, she would patiently wait until a friend was ready to confess what a muck he or she had made of things, and then she would offer what was invariably sound and logical advice to correct the problem.

Confessing that she'd allowed the Marquis of St. Aubyn to kiss her, however, would only make Evie feel more like an idiot than she already did. She doubted Lucinda would be able to say anything to alter her opinion. As for her proposal and her plans for the orphanage, she still intended to do something, kiss or not. For that task, though, she didn't want to admit that she was already falling short of her own expectations.

"Evie?"

She shook herself. "I'm sorry. What were you saying?"

"I was just asking whether your brother had decided on a political platform. Georgiana's going to dinner with the Duke of Wycliffe tonight, and she offered to extol Victor's virtues if you wanted her to."

"I'm not certain Victor has any virtues. And Georgie certainly doesn't need to spend the small time she has with her cousin talking about *my* brother."

The space between Lucinda's delicate eyebrows furrowed. "That's considerate, but not terribly politically savvy of you, my dear."

Evie sighed. "I don't want to be politically savvy—and especially not on someone else's behalf. I want to be a part of something meaningful."

"Like the Heart of Hope Orphanage?"

"Yes."

Lucinda stopped. "You know, I have an idea." With a quick smile, she took Evelyn's arm and turned them back in the direction of the coach. "You're right; it's not the Duke of Wycliffe you need. It's the duchess."

"The duchess? What—"

"She used to be a girls' school headmistress. Who would know better about helping young people than a headmistress? And who would be more discreet about it than Emma Brakenridge?"

Slowly hope began to push aside yesterday's frustration. Saint might have sent her fleeing before she could complete her interviews, but that didn't mean she couldn't go elsewhere for information. "Lucinda, have I mentioned lately how very fond I am of you?" she asked, squeezing her friend's arm.

"I'm glad to be of assistance, my dear."

Saint sat back in his chair. "It's only a suggestion," he said, tapping the ashes off the end of his cheroot. "Take it or not."

The scowl on the face of the large gentleman seated across from him didn't lift. "I have to consider public opinion, you know, even if you don't."

"It's not as though you're doing something underhanded. A new, larger park for the public, part of the Prince Regent's grand plan for the improvement of London."

"Yes, Saint, but it would involve *razing an orphan-age.*"

The headache lurking in Saint's temple began to throb again. "The orphans won't be in it, for God's sake. I'll see them all relocated, at my expense."

Someone scratched at the office door and cracked it open. "Your Majesty?"

"Not now, Mithers," the prince grunted. "I'm engaged in business."

The narrow face in the doorway paled. "Bus . . . business, Your Majesty? With . . . with . . ."

"Yes, with me, Mithers," Saint finished with a soft grin.

"Oh, dear. Oh, dear, oh, dear, oh—"

"Mithers, go away," Prince George ordered, pitching a glassful of expensive Madeira in his secretary's direction.

The door closed.

"Damn me," the Regent continued, "in five minutes he'll have half the ministry in here."

Clenching his cigar between his teeth, Saint refilled the prince's glass. Mithers was right to go fetch reinforcements, which didn't leave him much time. "Before they throw me out, just consider. I'm *giving* you the deed to several acres of land, to use as you see fit. It borders the project you're working on now, and the only cost to the taxpayers will be tearing the damned thing down and planting a few trees."

His chair creaking at the shift of his substantial weight, Prince George leaned forward. "But what, my dear Saint, is in all this for you?"

Saint studied the prince regent for a short moment. Prinny couldn't keep a secret to save his life, but the plan he'd concocted over the past few months—while it was rather underhanded, despite what he'd told the prince—wasn't illegal. "It's simple," he said through a puff of cigar smoke. "My mother's will stipulated that my family—meaning me—maintain an interest in and supervisory position over the Heart of Hope Orphanage. If the Crown were to take over ownership and tear down the place, my obligation would be removed."

"So your mama had an affection for the place?"

"She liked to embroider table runners for holiday meals and call it 'aiding the unfortunate.' I won't be saddled with continuing such nonsense. Not when you're building a perfectly good park just across the road."

Swirling his glass of Madeira in chubby yet elegant fingers, the prince chuckled. "I'll have my staff look into it, but I'm not agreeing to anything you propose without first finding someone more reputable to confirm the facts."

Saint smiled back without humor. "I expect nothing less." He could be patient. After all, he'd inherited care of the damned place six years ago. He'd managed to bide his time, looking for an opportunity, for this long. He could wait another few weeks.

"Now," the prince continued in a more conspiratorial tone, "tell me, my boy. Is it true that Fatima, Lady Gladstone, makes certain . . . sounds while in the throes of passion?"

"Mews like a kitten," Saint answered, draining his glass. "Anything else, Your Majesty?"

Chuckling again, the prince shook his heavy jowls. "Be off with you. It amazes me, Saint, that you can own so few redeemable qualities and still be so likable."

Saint stood, sketching a bow as he backed away. No

sense in offending the Regent now, when he finally looked to have a chance to be orphanage-free. "It's a talent, Your Majesty."

"Would that more of us possessed it."

As Saint left Carlton House and called for his horse, he reflected that his conversation with Prince George had actually gone more favorably than he'd anticipated. Considering that he was willing to pay for both the razing of the building and the planting of the park, a tentative "I'll look into it" before he had to offer either was good news, indeed.

He turned Cassius toward Boodles's for luncheon, and several minutes passed before he realized both that he seemed to be taking a roundabout route to reach his club, and that this particular direction was for a reason. With a slight scowl, he slowed before the white house on his left.

Ruddick House wasn't large or grandiose by anyone's definition, but the small garden appeared nicely kept, and the stable was full. Victor Ruddick's business in India, conducted on the Marquis of Houton's behalf, reportedly rendered the brother, sister, and mother a healthy income.

Rumor had it that Victor had recently developed some political ambitions, something that his uncle no doubt approved. Those ambitions explained Evelyn's approach of Fatima last week—the look of distaste on Miss Ruddick's face had been the most amusing part of the evening. He wondered how she would react if he went up and knocked on her front door.

That same door opened. Saint straightened, anticipation running through him. It was only the mother, though, dressed for some luncheon or other. He waited in the shade of the elms that lined the far side of the street, but only a maid followed. No Evelyn Marie.

He had an appetite, and she'd definitely whetted his hunger. He'd probably been too forward with the delicate miss, and now she'd abandoned her orphanage project for a nunnery or something. Saint shrugged, turning Cassius back toward Pall Mall. If she didn't appear at the board meeting the day after tomorrow, she wasn't worth hunting, anyway. Even so, he couldn't keep from looking over his shoulder at the house as he turned the corner. He could wait until Friday to find out. Anticipation appealed to him—as long as he could see it satisfied.

"I'm more familiar with lesson planning for already-educated females between the ages of twelve and eighteen," the Duchess of Wycliffe said, leaning down to dangle a cookie in the direction of the nearest end table.

"Any assistance you could give me would be wonderful, Your Grace," Evelyn returned, only half listening as the end table rocked.

"Emma, please," the duchess said, grinning as she slid off her chair to kneel on the carpet, cookie still before her. "Crawling about on the floor doesn't seem very regal." She turned her attention to the unseen object of the cookie bribe. "Elizabeth, Mama can't fit under there. Please come out."

A giggle answered her.

Emma sighed. "This is because your papa told you that silly story about the magic faerie who lived in a cave, isn't it?"

More giggling came from beneath the end table.

Straightening, Emma popped the cookie into her own

mouth. "Very well, the magic faerie's papa can explain why she can't live under the end table."

A servant scratched on the door, and the duchess returned to her more elegant perch on her chair. "Did you find them, Beth?"

"Yes, Your Grace." The maid set a short stack of papers and books on the table, and jumped at the subterranean giggle that erupted a moment later. "Dear me!"

"Please see if you can locate His Grace, Beth. Last I heard, he was in the billiards room with Lord Dare."

The maid curtsied. "Yes, Your Grace."

Evie sent a glance at Lucinda, who seemed to be enjoying her afternoon immensely. Miss Barrett, though, didn't have to explain that she wanted to devise a plan to teach orphans to read. Nor did she have to worry about the reaction she might receive from the Duke of Wycliffe or Viscount Dare if they were to learn of her recent activities. And even their disapproval would be nothing compared to Victor's. For a moment she wished Georgiana was here to intercede on her behalf with the male members of her powerful family, but the viscountess was having luncheon with her aunt. And besides, no one would intercede if Victor found out anything. No, she needed to learn to stand up for herself.

"Now, where were we?" the duchess asked, wiping cookie crumbs from her fingers. "Ah, yes." She lifted the books onto her lap, flipping through them, and then handed one to Evie. "This is a basic primer, which might at least give you a direction for starting some of the younger children on their letters. I would recommend beginning with vowels and their sounds—fewer letters to cause confusion."

"Oh, thank you," Evelyn said feelingly, opening the

book. "I've felt so frustrated, wanting to do something and having no idea how to begin it."

"You have ideas," Lucinda said stoutly. "You just worry too much, Evie. And no one could—or should—fault you for wanting to make a positive difference in anyone's life."

Evie smiled. "Thank you, Luce."

Emma gave her a speculative look. "Are you going to be doing all of the instructing yourself? I might warn you, teaching is very rewarding, but it will occupy every waking and sleeping hour you possess."

"I would like to do some of it, but . . ." Evie hesitated. She knew she could trust the Duchess of Wycliffe with her secrets, but confessing aloud how restricted she felt in all this meant admitting it to herself.

"Your family duties take up much of your time," the duchess finished for her. "I understand. Believe me."

With a smile, Evelyn picked up another of the books. "I do intend to oversee the hiring of instructors, and the courses of education. These are wonderful, Emma. Thank you so much."

"My pleasure. Take whatever you wish, for as long as you need them."

"You summoned me?" a deep voice came from the doorway.

Tall, broad-shouldered, and tawny-haired, the Duke of Wycliffe strolled into the room, Lord Dare on his heels. Evelyn grimaced, hoping they hadn't been lurking in the hallway. In all fairness, "lurking" didn't seem quite their style, unlike a certain marquis who'd been troubling her dreams over the past few nights.

"Yes, I did. A magic faerie has taken up residence under the end table and is refusing to emerge for her bath."

The large duke lifted an eyebrow. "A faerie, eh?" He knocked on the smooth mahogany surface. "Is there a faerie under here?"

A shrieking cascade of laughter answered him.

With a grin that made Evelyn smile in return, the duke removed the candy dish and tea tray from the table, handing them to Dare. That done, Evie expected Wycliffe to lower himself to the floor as the duchess had done and extricate young Elizabeth. Instead, he simply lifted the table up and set it aside.

"My Samson," the duchess murmured with a warm smile that made Evie blush.

Bright auburn hair in short curls all over her head and gowned in yellow and white, Lady Brakenridge gave another shriek and trundled toward the writing desk. In one long stride the duke caught up, scooping her into his arms. "Hello, Lizzie," he cooed, hefting the infant up to his shoulder.

With another blurbled word, Elizabeth wrapped her fists into her father's jacket and giggled again.

"Did you hear that?" the duke asked with a wide grin, turning to Dare. "She said 'papa.'"

The viscount returned the candy dish and tea tray to the relocated end table. "I distinctly heard 'baboon.'"

"Hm, well, you're distinctly deaf."

"I heard that."

Laughing, Emma shooed the two tall men toward the door. "Go away. We're chatting."

Immediately Dare came to a stop. "About what?" His glance took in Evelyn, and she remembered his earlier warning about Saint. Well, she hadn't turned her back on the marquis; he'd kissed her right on the mouth.

"French fashions and jewelry," the duchess answered without a pause.

"Gak. I say we teach Lizzie to play billiards," the viscount returned, grimacing.

The duke nodded, motioning him out the door. "It's suggestions like that which make me glad I encouraged you to marry my cousin."

" 'Encouraged' me? As I recall, you threatened to shoot me if I didn't."

The argument faded down the hallway, while Evelyn sat back, listening in wonderment. These two men had at one time been well known for their black reputations and bedchamber escapades. Now, however, one of them cradled an infant as though it were the most natural thing in the world, while the other would be in a similar situation within six months.

"Evelyn?"

She shook herself. "My apologies, Emma. What did you say?"

The duchess smiled. "I just asked whether you needed any help in putting your organizational plan together."

"Thank you, but no. I would like to attempt to do it on my own."

It wasn't that she couldn't use the help, but Saint seemed to think she was an imbecile good for nothing but warming his bed. If she received help, he would know it, and he would undoubtedly say something about it—in front of the rest of the board of trustees. No, this was her project, and she would put it together herself.

"Of course. But please remember, I'm available if you have any questions."

After some cursory chatting about French fashions and jewelry, Evelyn and Lucinda left Brakenridge House. She'd made a small beginning already, but now, with her stack of borrowed books beside her, she felt as though she had half a chance of putting together something acceptable. The only problem was, acceptable wasn't good enough. The plan needed to be perfect, and she needed to have it ready in two days.

And the proposal wasn't the only part of this that needed to be ready; she was determined that the Marquis of St. Aubyn would not send her fleeing again. Nor would she allow him to kiss her again. Whatever amusement he was after, she wouldn't be the one to provide it.

Saint narrowed his eyes. "I am not nearly drunk enough to approve funds for you to tally up the contents of the storage rooms, Rutledge."

Timothy Rutledge gave him a black look, his earnest posture taking on a distinctive defeated slouch. "There is sixty years' worth of accumulated furniture, paintings, re—"

"If you're so curious," Saint interrupted, "tally it yourself." He sat forward. "But if I find you've sold one stick of it, I'll be very . . . unhappy."

"I—"

"Give it up, Rutledge," Sir Edward Willsley said gruffly, downing the remains of his glass of port. "I would never have approved it, either."

"Your thefts will have to be more creative than that, if you wish them to get past me." With a dismissive glance, Saint refilled his own glass, then Sir Edward's. All this was a great deal of nonsense, anyway. The only merit to Rutledge's prattling was that it kept Saint occupied while he waited to see whether Evelyn Marie would appear.

He doubted it, but not enough to forgo the board meeting altogether. Waiting, however, didn't sit well with him under most circumstances; here, he felt distinctly territorial and defensive of his inherited territory—no doubt to Rutledge's dismay.

"So do we have any other new business to discuss?" Lord Talirand asked around a puff of cigar smoke.

Sir Edward cleared his throat. "The leftmost window in the older boys' dormitory is coming loose from the casement again."

Saint offered a faint grin. "How else would they slip out at night?"

"What?" The baronet sat forward. "You knew?"

"I'm not blind, Willsley."

"Ha. You'd turn this establishment into a thieves' rookery if it was up to you."

Lord Talirand exhaled another cloud of smoke. "At least then we'd be making a profit."

Saint only sipped his port, reflecting that the only thing worse than being on the Heart of Hope Orphanage board of trustees was having to attend the meetings.

Someone scratched at the door, and he was on his feet before he registered the wish to remain seated. A slow heat ran under his skin. Damnation, that had best be her.

"Expecting someone?" Talirand drawled, eyeing him.

"Eager to escape," he countered, strolling to the door and pulling it open. "What is it?"

The housekeeper jumped backward. "My . . . you said . . . it's Miss Ruddick."

"Show her in, Mrs. Housekeeper."

"Natham, my lord."

He ignored her squawking as Evelyn came forward, and ignored the shuffle of feet as the board stood behind him. She wore a pale green muslin, high in the neck and very plain for one of the diamonds of Mayfair. Her auburn hair, coiled severely at the back of her head, gave her the appearance of a governess; no doubt she intended to look demure and businesslike.

She curtsied. "Good afternoon, Lord St. Aubyn, Lord Talirand, gentlemen," she said, passing by Saint and keeping her gaze turned away from him.

"How brave of you," he murmured, motioning her toward his vacated chair. "And you've brought gifts." Wanting to touch her, he settled for tapping his fingers against the stack of papers she held in her arms.

"Supporting documents," she returned, setting them on the chair.

"What brings you here today?" Rutledge asked, coming forward to take her hand and draw it to her lips.

Saint felt her glance, but ignored it, making his way over to lean against the writing desk. He wanted a vantage point from which to observe her, where the others couldn't see him doing so. Informing anyone of her anticipated arrival smacked of servitude, and he hadn't been keen on giving any of the other males in the room advance notice, anyway.

"I . . . am here to present a proposal for improvements to the orphanage," she said, her voice only a little unsteady. "Lord St. Aubyn seemed to feel that I should be allowed to donate my time and money only if I could account for the wheres and hows."

Talirand favored her with a smile as the board seated themselves once more. "How delightful. Please tell us your plans, Miss Ruddick."

At that she launched into a presentation concerning education, clothing, food, building improvements, and several vast social issues. Saint didn't note much of it. Instead, he caught himself studying the way her hands moved, the turn of her head, and the earnest, enthusiastic expression on her mobile face. Whatever she was after, she seemed to think this was how she would achieve it.

He didn't doubt that he could wear her down, bring her to the point where she would beg for his caress, for his kiss, for his hands on her bare skin. The question was why he seemed to be obsessed with her. Fatima, among others of his former lovers, would laugh if she knew he was hard for a virginal chit.

At the sound of polite applause, he shook himself. Whatever she'd said, his fellow board members had liked it—though they'd probably decided to give over their support as soon as she'd mentioned donating money.

"I find your enthusiasm quite admirable," Willsley said. "If you need any assistance or advice in managing your project, I hope you'll feel free to come to me."

Rutledge nodded, as well. "You'll no doubt find this management business far too dull and complicated for someone of your tender sensibilities. I am at your service."

Scavengers, Saint thought. Let them have the remains; he wanted the main course.

Evelyn smiled with the smooth expression he'd often seen her use to charm her dance partners, angelic and a little aloof. "Thank you very much, gentlemen. Does this mean I have your approval?"

Even Talirand was standing now, the scent of a weak-witted female with funds practically making him salivate. "Shall we take a vote? All in favor say aye."

The eager chorus of ayes was nauseating.

"Well, St. Aubyn, what about you?" Rutledge asked. "Surely you have no objection to Miss Ruddick's proposal. Aye or nay?"

Saint remained in his relaxed slouch, deciding his own position. He could refuse; he didn't need her meddling while he was trying to dispose of the place. Evelyn would be angry and stomp home and slight him at soirees for the remainder of his life. That was well and good, except for one thing—he'd never have her spread beneath him, moaning his name.

He pursed his lips, gazing at the object of his interest. "I assume this little experiment will remain under my supervision?"

Evelyn's confident smile faltered just a little. No doubt she didn't know what to do with a male who didn't fall to his knees at the sight of her smile. "If you insist," she hedged.

"I do insist."

She lifted her chin, the fine blush of her cheeks deepening. "Then yes, my project may be placed under your supervision."

He gave her a slow smile. "Then my answer is aye."

Chapter 6

Though the day of my destiny's over,
And the star of my fate hath declined,
Thy soft heart refused to discover
The faults which so many could find.

—Lord Byron, "Stanzas to Augusta"

"**E**velyn!"

Evie froze halfway out the front door of Ruddick House. Before she could decide whether to risk a dash out to the waiting coach or not, Victor stomped down the last flight of stairs. Crossing his arms and glowering, he came to a stop in front of her.

"Good morning," she said, favoring him with a bright smile.

"I stopped by Aunt Houton's yesterday," he snapped. "She hasn't seen you in over a week."

"That's where—"

"You missed the Tuesday West Sussex Ladies' Tea."

"I didn't mean—"

"And you have failed to explain to me why you agreed to waltz with St. Aubyn."

"Victor, if you would—"

"That's it, isn't it?" he went on, then took a slow breath. "Before I returned from India you could do

71

whatever you wished. Evie, once I'm voted into the House you can go back to shopping and soirees and whatever else gladdens your heart. Until that happens, please show some restraint and common sense."

She hid a frown. This was obviously not the moment to confess anything. Instead, evasiveness seemed the most logical defense. She decided to offer up the explanation she'd been working on for the past several days. "I am not trying to damage your campaign, Victor. I think you would make a splendid member of Parliament. I do have several commitments of my own, however. If I were to neglect them, it would reflect badly on both of us."

"Ah." Her brother reached over her head, pulled the door from Langley's surprised fingers, and shut it. "What 'commitments,' pray tell?"

Drat. If she told him she was preparing to essentially take over the supervision of an orphanage where St. Aubyn was head of the board of trustees, he would lock her in her room. "Lady Dare and the Duchess of Wycliffe have taken an interest in education of the poor. They've asked me to help."

"You?"

She tried to ignore the skepticism in his voice, as though he could never conceive of anyone asking *her* for assistance or advice if they had any choice in the matter. "Yes, me. I help you, too, if you'll recall."

"That remains to be seen. And the waltz with St. Aubyn?"

"He asked. I . . . feared if I refused him, the scene would have been worse than if I accepted."

She could see the reluctant agreement in his expression as he nodded. "You're probably right. But stay away from him, Evie; don't give him the opportunity to ask you again."

"I won't."

Victor took a step closer. "And remember that your 'commitments' are secondary at the moment. You can't neglect your duties to this family—which means to me. Mama has agreed to accompany you to the next tea. We need to redouble our efforts. Plimpton's after the Alvington votes."

"Mama's going?"

"She's very committed to my cause. And so should you be, Evelyn."

"I already am, Victor." *Wonderful.* Now she would have to go to the tea, and she'd have to spend the entire time there listening to how wonderful Victor was, and how their mother had encouraged her to marry before Victor's return from India, because now that he was home, no one would be good enough for Evie. And it wasn't because she was perfect; it was because Victor's standards were so high.

"Where are you off to now?" Her brother took the top book from the stack in her arms before she could stop him. "A reading primer?"

"The duchess asked me to familiarize myself with it."

With a snort, he returned it. "Have your fun, then. Does the duke know you're supporting his wife's cause?"

"Of course he does." Thankfully, lying to Victor was fairly simple, since he remained consumed with his campaign.

"Make certain he knows that you have my approval, then."

"I will."

"Well, hurry up. You don't keep a duchess waiting."

No one kept the Marquis of St. Aubyn waiting, either. As soon as Victor vanished into his study, Evelyn hurried out the front door. "To the orphanage, with all possible speed," she whispered up to Phillip.

"Very good, Miss Ruddick."

This project would have been so much easier without Victor or St. Aubyn about. One misstep in front of either of them would ruin everything. As Lucinda had pointed out, other charities existed, all of them without Saint and at least one of them probably tame and ladylike enough to be acceptable to Victor and his political ambitions.

The Heart of Hope Orphanage, though, was the establishment that had caught her attention, the one that most seemed to need her, and the one that she most needed. If she could make a difference there, then she would truly have accomplished something. No one would stop her from doing that; she wouldn't allow it.

The Marquis of St. Aubyn eyed the clustered group of females inside the orphanage's main entry. He had no idea where they'd come from or why they'd decided to visit the Heart of Hope this morning, but they were a wholly unremarkable lot, as far as he was concerned. If they hadn't been muttering Miss Ruddick's name, he never would have allowed them entry. At least they'd provided him with a few moments of amusement, when he'd tried pacing back and forth and they'd scurried away from him like a terrified flock of hens. Apparently even the lower classes knew of his reputation.

Frightening poorly coiffed spinsters was well and good, he supposed, but he hadn't risen at the ungodly hour of nine in the morning for their sakes. He pulled out his pocket watch and flipped it open again. Miss

Ruddick was late. If she didn't appear in the next ten minutes, she would find these odd females booted out to the street and the doors locked behind them.

He supposed he didn't need to wait; the more objects he placed in Evelyn's path, the more likely she was to give up this nonsense. At the same time, he found himself curious as to what she intended to do here. In his experience, no one volunteered their time or their money without reason; whatever she was up to, he would figure it out. He would figure *her* out, and then take all of his building frustration out on her, again and again and again.

The front double doors opened. He half thought it might be another of the hens, but at the electricity creeping up his arms, he turned. Miss Ruddick hurried into the foyer, her bonnet blown back from her auburn hair, and a stack of books and papers clutched to her heaving chest. *Delicious.*

"Good morning, my lord, ladies," she panted. "My apologies for being late. I was unavoidably detained."

"By whom?" Saint asked, leaving the sanctuary of the stairwell and not stopping until he stood in front of her. Slowly he reached out to untie the bonnet strings from around her throat.

Gray eyes met his, startled, then darted in the direction of the huddled females. "By my brother. Please stop that."

He finished untying the knot and drew the strings and the bonnet slowly across her shoulder. "I've been trapped here for twenty minutes," he murmured, tucking a stray strand of her windblown hair back into its clip. "Be thankful I don't end this little farce of yours right now."

She squared her shoulders. "This is not a farce," she

stated. Snatching the bonnet back from his fingers, she faced the fright-faced females. "I assume that you are all here in answer to the advertisement I placed?"

They shuffled into curtsies. "Yes, ma'am."

Saint stepped still closer, leaning across her shoulder. "What advertisement?" he asked, breathing in the lemon scent of her hair.

She began flipping through her papers. "The one I placed in the *London Times*. For instructors, to answer your next question."

His jaw clenched. *Bloody wonderful.* If Prinny or his gaggle saw that the orphanage was hiring instructors, he'd have a hell of a time explaining what he was up to. "Consult me first, next time."

She nodded the back of her head at him. "Very well. Ladies, I will take three of you at a time into the adjoining room for interviews."

"And what about the rest of the flock? I'm not going to entertain them."

Evelyn faced him. "You are not required to be here."

"Yes, I am. Without me, you have no project."

"The board voted otherwise, my lord."

He gave her a slow smile. "*I* am the board, Miss Ruddick. Don't forget that. Now, what other little surprises do you have planned for today?"

"I have a small group of workmen coming at noon to begin clearing out the downstairs rooms." She lifted her chin, looking him in the eye again. "And you will not discourage or dissuade me."

Partly because he admired the way she always met his gaze straight on, he refrained from pointing out that this was only her first day here, and that he made a habit of getting what he wanted while doing as he pleased. She'd find that out soon enough. "Why are you cleaning out the storage rooms?"

"To make classrooms." Her fine brows furrowed. "Did you listen at all to my proposal?"

"No."

"No? But—"

"Evelyn Marie," he said in a low voice, wishing the flock of chickens was elsewhere so he could taste her honeyed mouth again, "you're not here because of your proposal."

Her scowl deepened. "Then why—"

"You're here because of my proposition."

"I told you that you wouldn't frighten me away, my lord."

"Saint," he corrected. "Have you ever seen a man naked and aroused with wanting you?"

A deep blush stole up her cheeks. "N . . . no."

"You will." Unable to stop himself, he reached out to touch her cheek. "The things I will teach you, Evelyn, aren't lectured about in classrooms. And you'll beg me to teach you more."

Her mouth opened and closed again. "Go away," she finally commanded in a quavering voice. "I will not be seduced by you."

"Not today," he agreed, glancing beyond her at the flock. "Where would you like the storage items to go?"

"I . . ." He watched as she struggled to return to their previous conversation. Good. She was confused. "To the old stables," she managed after a moment. "I'll need to go through everything and take an inventory of whatever might be useful."

Saint sketched a bow. "As you wish."

"You actually mean to help?"

With another smile, he turned on his heel. "Help, yes. Volunteer, no. Nothing is for free."

The workers Evelyn had hired turned out to be stock boys and footmen from some of the less reputable gentlemen's clubs. The mix smelled of Lord Dare—though, straitlaced as Tristan had become since his marriage, Saint couldn't imagine that Evelyn had given him the real reason she needed help.

Dare had used to be an amusing companion with a pleasingly cynical sense of humor, until female propriety had ruined him. Damned shame, that was. Now they barely exchanged greetings except at Parliament or one of the rare respectable gatherings he attended during the Season. Saint wished him luck, but it certainly wasn't a life he wanted for himself.

Once he directed the workers regarding which rooms to empty and where to deposit the ramshackle items, he didn't have much to do. Pulling the flask from his pocket, he leaned against the far wall and took a swig of gin.

Evelyn thought he was being helpful—though of course she questioned his motives. He had some questions about hers, as well. At least he knew what he was doing, and why. Once Prinny agreed to expand his park onto the orphanage site, they'd have to empty the building before they tore it down, anyway. Gaining favor with Evelyn and getting a head start on a demolition schedule seemed a productive way to spend the day.

The spinster herd at the far end of the hallway had dwindled to a handful by early afternoon, and a half dozen of the storage rooms were empty of everything but cobwebs and dust. For the past hour or so he'd been aware of young pairs of eyes peering around the far corner at the activity, but he ignored them. He kept food in their stomachs and a roof over their heads; this little flurry of activity was Miss Ruddick's idea, and she could explain it to them.

A whisper of lemon curled around him. "You might tell them what we're doing," Evelyn said, coming to stand at his elbow.

"What *you're* doing," he corrected. "I'm here in an attempt to avoid boredom."

"It's still good work."

She looked terribly pleased with herself. "Miss Ruddick," he said, "whatever it is you're up to, don't think I'm a blind follower. My eyes are wide open, and whatever I do, you may assume it's for *my* reasons, and not for yours."

"I'm not 'up to' anything, except trying to help these poor children. I assume that is why you chair this board of trustees, as well."

"You assume incorrectly." Pushing away from the wall, he faced her. "My dear mama stipulated in her will that a member of the Halboro family remain involved with the Heart of Hope Orphanage for the duration of its existence. *I* am the only remaining member of the Halboro family that I've been able to locate, so here I sit."

He'd tried not to place overmuch emphasis on the "duration of its existence" part of his speech, but she seemed happy to concentrate on other portions, anyway.

"Halboro," she said softly, as if to herself. "I had no idea."

"Good God, we're not related, are we?" he asked, scowling. He made a point of not mating with relations, no matter how distant; any thickening of his family's bloodline, intentional or otherwise, couldn't be good for anyone involved.

"No." She shook herself. "I just realized that I didn't know your family name. Nor do I know your Christian one."

"Ah. Michael."

"Michael," she repeated, and he found himself watching her mouth. That wasn't unusual, except that it wasn't because he wanted to kiss her, though he did. Very few women had ever called him by his Christian name, and he didn't like when they did so. It implied a familiarity they hadn't earned. Sex hardly gained them the right to fawn or coo over him. To his dismay, however, when the angelic, virginal Evelyn Marie Ruddick murmured his name, his pulse stirred. Odd, that.

"Yes. Dull and common, but so was my mother's imagination."

"That's unkind."

He shrugged, growing less fond of this conversation by the minute. "It's honest. I thought you'd appreciate that."

Evelyn continued to gaze at him. "This makes you uncomfortable, doesn't it? Talking about your family, I mean." She wasn't certain what made her ask the question; he had been nothing less than arrogant and dismissive and cynical toward her, but for some reason it seemed important.

"Nothing makes me uncomfortable, Evelyn," he murmured, taking a slow step closer. "I have no conscience, or so I've been told."

Evie took a step backward, both because of his advance and because of the predatory gleam lighting his green eyes. The workers she'd hired for the day could no doubt hear every word of their conversation, and Lord Dare had only vouched for their willingness to work. He hadn't said anything about their willingness to keep from gossiping if they happened to witness St. Aubyn kissing her. "You're just baiting me," she replied, trying to sound amused in a jaded sort of way.

He shook his head. "I'm warning you. As I said before, I don't do any good deed for free. I will expect payment for my work today."

"I didn't ask you to help," she retorted before she could stop herself. Good heavens, she knew better than to throw challenges at him. St. Aubyn hadn't backed down from anything so far, and making pronouncements had only gotten her kissed or ridiculed, depending on his mood.

"No, what you've asked for, my dear, is my indulgence. And for the devil knows what reason, I've been willing to indulge you." A slow, sensuous smile curved his lips. "But the devil and I are good friends, Evelyn Marie. You shouldn't tempt either of us too far."

Still moving with that deceptive ease of his, he reached toward her cheek again, his gaze lowering to her mouth. Evelyn swallowed, but before she could protest his impropriety and inform him that he was *not* going to kiss her again, his fingers flicked in a feather-light caress against the base of her throat, trailed up to the back of her neck—and came away with her favorite pearl pendant necklace.

She hadn't even felt him open the clasp. "You . . . how—"

"You should see me unfasten a gown," he murmured, lifting the single suspended pearl to examine it. "My payment for today's work. If you want it back, you may ask me for it at the Dundredge soiree this evening. I assume you're attending?"

"I . . . am."

"Then so am I, apparently. Good day, Miss Ruddick.

Inform Mrs. Housekeeper when you're finished playing."

"I am not playing," she snapped, her voice annoyingly unsteady, as he vanished around the near corner.

Even if he'd heard her, he probably didn't care. Outrage was difficult, anyway, when her mind was still stuck on his gown comment. Once he said it, she couldn't help but imagine his fingers gliding down her back, her gown falling loose beneath his skilled touch. And then his hands would . . . "Oh, for heaven's sake," she muttered, pushing the vision from her mind. As if she would ever succumb to his seductions. He was only trying to shock her and to amuse himself, after all. He'd as much as said so.

Devilish and charming as she sensed he could be when the whimsy possessed him, he was also dangerous, and as Lady Gladstone had said, very, very bad. And if she ever wanted to see her necklace again, she was going to have to approach him at the ball tonight. No doubt he would ask her for a dance, and no doubt he would see to it that she couldn't refuse.

Evelyn frowned. Victor was absolutely going to kill her. If the Marquis of St. Aubyn didn't ruin her first.

Chapter 7

We are entwined—let death come slow or fast—
The tie which bound the first endures the last.

—Lord Byron, "Epistle to Augusta"

"**I**f he stole your necklace, you should inform the authorities and have him arrested," Lucinda said in a hushed voice, her indignant gaze searching the Dundredge crowd, no doubt for any sign of St. Aubyn.

Evelyn had been looking for him, too, and with no more success than her friend. "Having him arrested would kill two birds with one stone, I suppose," she whispered back, pretending to nibble on a sugared orange peel. "Rid me of St. Aubyn, and do in Victor with the apoplexy the gossip would give him. Really, Luce."

Lucinda chuckled. "Just trying to help."

"Then be more helpful. What am I going to do? Simply walk up and ask him to give it back? What if he's with that awful Lady Gladstone?"

"Then you could tell Victor you were recruiting her for his election campaign."

Evie started to reply, then closed her mouth again. "You know, that might work." As she contemplated the idea, though, reality crashed down again, as it had been doing all evening. "No, because then Lady Gladstone would demand to know why Saint had my necklace, and she'd claw my eyes out before I could answer."

"Whose eyes are getting clawed out?" another female voice asked from behind her.

Her abrupt breath left in a relieved sigh. "Georgie," she said, taking her friend's hand and squeezing it, "you frightened me half to death."

Georgiana's tall husband nodded sympathetically. "Happens to me all the time." Snatching a handful of chocolate balls, he gave one to Georgie and popped the rest into his mouth. "How were the slaves I sent you?"

"Shh," Evie said, though likely no one but she and Georgie could interpret Dare's chocolate-mangled question. "It's a secret."

The viscount swallowed. "Yes, so I gathered. And why was I secretly sending stock boys to an orphanage?"

His wife scowled at him. "None of your affair, Tristan. Go bother Emma and Greydon now."

"Yes, my love." With a grin and a swift kiss on the cheek, Lord Dare strolled off into the crowd.

As soon as he was gone, Georgie lowered her voice to the conspiratorial whisper Evie and Lucinda had been using. "All right, whose eyes are getting clawed out?"

"Mine," Evie returned, unable to help a grin. Georgie and Lucinda were quite simply the most marvelous friends she could ever have hoped for. Whatever she told them would remain a secret, and she could tell them anything. That, though, didn't serve to explain why neither of them knew yet that St. Aubyn had kissed her. Nothing, however, could explain that—or why she continued to think about it so often.

"And why is that?"

"The Marquis of St. Aubyn stole Evie's necklace this afternoon," Lucinda explained, "and we're trying to form a strategy to get it back that won't involve bloodshed."

"You're certain he stole it?" The amusement in the viscountess' eyes vanished.

"He took it off my neck," Evie said, "and told me that if I wanted it back I could ask him for it tonight."

"Well, he's obviously trying to make trouble for you. From what I've heard, he delights in that sort of thing." Georgiana joined Lucinda and herself in searching the crowd for the marquis. "You know, Evie, this may have passed the point where you can safely participate."

It had passed that point the moment she'd learned of St. Aubyn's involvement with the orphanage. "I will not be cowed by someone else's poor behavior," she stated. "And especially not that scoundrel's."

"Poor behavior, hm?" Luce repeated in a thoughtful tone. "And here you are, Evie, without a student for a lesson in—"

Georgiana blanched. "No, no, no! We could never send our Evie after St. Aubyn. He'd ruin her in a second if he realized what she was doing. We'll find someone more malleable to whom she can deliver her lessons."

"I—" Evie began, her heart skipping a beat.

"Yes, you're right," Lucinda interrupted, sparing a sympathetic glance for Evelyn. "A subject must at least have the remnants of a soul. I'm afraid, Evie, that Georgiana's correct; this orphanage plan of yours has become too risky. I'm sure we can find somewhere safer for you to volunteer your time."

"And a safer student for you to instruct," Georgie added.

Evelyn looked from one of them to the other, the

noise of the ballroom dimming to a dull background roar. Her friends, her dearest friends, expected her to fail before she'd barely begun, and to make a muck of her reputation at the same time. More than likely they'd thought her orphanage plan a disaster as soon as they'd heard about it, and the marquis with his awful reputation had merely provided a convenient excuse enabling them to spare her feelings. Well, just for once if she was going to be considered inadequate, she would like to make an attempt to succeed first.

"You're right, Luce," she said quietly, wondering if they could hear the fast thudding of her heart.

"Don't fret, Evie. We'll begin looking for a more suitable charity for you first thing tomorrow."

"No, I mean you're right that St. Aubyn is the perfect candidate for a lesson in polite behavior toward females. And that I happen to be in the perfect position to deliver it."

Lucinda's eyes widened. "No, Evie, I was very, *very* wrong. If you take this on, you wouldn't just be working at improving a questionable orphanage, you would be working on—"

"On improving St. Aubyn. I know. I don't think I could ask for a grander challenge than that. Do you?"

Georgiana took her hand again. "Are you certain? You don't have to prove anything."

"Only to myself," she returned, though that wasn't quite true. "And yes, I'm certain. I'll be either a spectacular success on both fronts, or a catastrophic failure."

Her friends continued to argue with her, trying to convince her that she was taking an unnecessary risk and that both the orphanage and St. Aubyn were simply beyond her depth. They were wrong, however, and whatever they were saying ceased to make any sense, anyway, as Saint strolled into the crowded room.

For the first time, she noticed how many women gazed at him from behind their husbands' backs and from the fluttering shelter of their ivory-ribbed fans. He couldn't possibly have that many clandestine lovers; there weren't that many nights in a lifetime, when one added in the single, less reputable females also known to consort with him. Even so, the looks reminded her of what Lady Gladstone had said, that Saint didn't have to be good because he was so bad.

They all seemed to want him, or at least to want to watch him. His smooth panther's stalk was magnetic even when he wasn't hunting. With an entire room full of willing game, then, why was he after her? Or was he just amusing himself, as he'd claimed? Perhaps he had a pocketful of necklaces waiting to be reclaimed by damsels he'd accosted during the day.

"Evie," Lucinda whispered urgently.

She shook herself. "Beg pardon?"

"He's here."

"I know. I saw."

Her friends exchanged glances, which she pretended not to notice. "What are you going to do?" Georgiana asked.

Evelyn took a breath, trying to calm her racing heart. "Ask for my necklace back."

"But—"

Before she could lose her nerve, Evelyn walked away toward the refreshment table. Saint looked to be heading in that direction, and a chance meeting there would raise fewer questions than if she stalked up to him, hand outstretched.

When she reached the rendezvous point, however, Saint was still several yards away, requesting a drink from a footman. She studied him from behind the shelter of an ice sculpture, the glassy swan wings twisting and elongating his broad chest in his stark black jacket, but leaving his lean face unobscured.

Michael Halboro. She wondered what his middle name might be. Knowing so little about him made every possible bit of information more . . . significant than it probably was. Dark hair obscured one eye, giving him a vulnerable, raffish expression. Then his gaze flicked up to meet hers, as though he'd known where she was all along, and her heart stopped.

Whatever game or amusement he had in mind, it was aimed at her. With a slow smile, he dismissed the footman and made his way past a half dozen other young females, not even sparing them a glance.

"Good evening, Miss Ruddick," he drawled in his low baritone voice, the sound reverberating down her spine. "You came."

"Did you think I'd be hiding under my bed?" she returned. Her voice sounded composed and steady, thank goodness.

"When I think of you, it's not *under* a bed. Ask your question."

Heavens. Standing in the middle of the ballroom as they were, no doubt dozens of guests could overhear every breath of their conversation. And she could think of no way to phrase her question without it sounding as though she'd done something tawdry or improper. No doubt he counted on precisely that. Whatever she said next, he could use it to ruin her. She *should* have hidden under her bed tonight.

Best to get it over with, then. "Lord Dare mentioned

that you'd found a necklace at the Hanson soiree. I think it might be mine. May I see it?"

His lips twitched. "Yes, I discovered it in the punch bowl," he said smoothly, and reached into his pocket. "Would this be it?"

Evie felt faint with relief. "Oh, thank you so much, my lord," she gushed, before he could even produce the thing for her inspection. "It's my favorite piece, and I thought I'd never find it." She held out her hand.

Saint stepped behind her. "Allow me."

Before she could do more than gulp and flush bright red, the marquis slid the cool chain around her throat and fastened it. His fingers brushed the hairs at the back of her neck as he leaned closer. "Well done, Evelyn Marie," he murmured into her hair. "Now smile and say 'thank you, Saint,' or I'll kiss your ear."

If her heart beat any faster, it would burst from her chest. She gave a friendly smile to the air. "Thank you again, Saint. That was quite thoughtful of you."

"You arouse me," he whispered, "and you'll pay for that." Then he released her and stepped back.

The lesson, she reminded herself frantically, closing her eyes for just a moment to steady herself. "Lord St. Aubyn, have you met my mother?" she asked, turning. "I'm certain she'd like to thank you for your good deed, as well."

He froze for a heartbeat, then faced her. "You want me to meet your mother?" he repeated, surprise touching his eyes.

It was the first time she'd ever seen him off balance. "Yes. Why not?"

"I can name a thousand or so reasons," he returned, then shrugged. "But why not, indeed? The evening's been fairly uneventful so far."

Yes, except for her near ruination and nearer fainting spell. "This way, then, my lord."

"Saint," he reminded her softly, falling into step beside her and, to her horror, offering his arm.

"But—"

"If I'm being civilized, then so must you be." Not waiting for her response, he took her hand and draped it over his black sleeve.

As they left the ballroom for the salon where most of the matrons had gathered to gossip and nibble on sweets, Evie realized what a mistake she'd just made. "Saint," she whispered, as her mother came into view, "she doesn't know I'm working at the orphanage. *Please* don't say anything."

For a moment she thought he hadn't heard her, that he was occupied with noting the shocked expressions and gasps of the matrons as they realized who'd wandered into their midst. Then he glanced at her, green eyes amused and cynical. "For a kiss," he murmured.

"B . . . beg pardon?"

"You heard me. Yes or no?"

With the rest of the matrons edging away from her, Genevieve Ruddick pasted a mortified smile on her thin face. "Evie! What in the world are you—"

"Mama, I would like to introduce the Marquis of St. Aubyn to you. He found my missing necklace in a punch bowl at the Hanson ball, of all places. My lord, my mother, Mrs. Ruddick."

"Mrs. Ruddick," he said amiably, taking her hand. "I should have introduced myself days ago, I suppose, since your daughter and I—"

Oh, no. "Yes," Evie hissed.

"—waltzed at the Hanson soiree," he finished smoothly. "She's a brave young lady."

Her mother's expression darkened into a frown, which looked much more natural on her pale countenance. "An impulsive one, anyway."

Evelyn held her breath, waiting for the marquis to turn her mother's comment with some insinuating remark of his own. Instead, though, he only offered a brief, enigmatic smile. "Indeed."

Well, that was good. It might very well have been his first attempt, but he'd managed to be polite for nearly three minutes. And that was probably pushing her luck far enough for one evening. "Oh, is that the quadrille?" she asked brightly. "I promised this dance to Francis Henning. Excuse me, Mama. Would you care to escort me, Lord St. Aubyn?"

He didn't say anything further, so Evie decided it would be more prudent to leave and hope that he followed. She'd barely made it through the door when a hand clamped down on her shoulder and nudged her into the nearest alcove.

"What was that all about?" Saint asked, regarding her darkly.

"Nothing. I only wanted to see if you would do it. Now, if you'll excuse me, I have a—"

Saint put out an arm, blocking her escape. Very aware that only part of a curtain screened them from the hallway and the ballroom beyond, Evelyn swallowed. Her friends had warned her how dangerous teaching St. Aubyn a lesson would be, but she was well aware of that anyway. In an odd way, though, it only seemed fair that if he meant to try to ruin her, she should attempt to improve him.

"Please move."

"Kiss me."

"Now?"

With one step he closed the small distance that remained between them, so that she had to lift her chin to meet his gaze. "Yes, now."

Evie sighed to cover the sudden speeding of her pulse. "Very well."

He stayed where he was, gazing at her. She wondered what he saw that made him keep teasing her like this. A petite female with reddish brown hair and gray eyes, her face darkened by yet another blush. Anything else? Did he think her as naive and useless as her friends did?

"Well?" she whispered after a moment. "Get it over with."

Saint shook his head. "You will kiss me." His eyes half closed, he ran a finger across her skin, just above the low neckline of her gown. "Kiss me, Evelyn, or I'll find something more intimate for us to do."

Her skin where he'd touched her felt hot. Abruptly she realized what the problem was—she *wanted* to kiss him. She wanted to feel the sensation again that she'd experienced when he'd kissed her at the orphanage.

He slowly slipped her gown from one shoulder, his caress soft and warm as he slid his fingers beneath the material. "Kiss me, Evelyn Marie," he repeated in an even softer voice.

Trembling and scarcely able to breathe, she raised up on her toes and touched her lips to his. Heat blazed through her as his mouth responded to her soft touch, deepening the embrace with a thoroughness that left her floating. No one's kiss had ever made her feel like this, humming and shivering inside.

"How in the devil am I supposed to watch her every damned minute?" her brother's angry voice snapped from very close by.

She gasped, and Saint flattened himself against her,

pressing her back against the wall. Hiding the two of them behind the curtain's scant shelter was her only hope; if anyone saw her there, alone with St. Aubyn and even with space separating them, she would be ruined.

"I don't expect you to," her mother's voice, equally sharp, returned. "But you escorted her here, Victor. I think she's lost her mind, introducing me to St. Aubyn."

"I half think she's trying to ruin my political career so I'll go back to India. There's Lady Dare. Ask her if she's seen Evie. I'll go look for St. Aubyn."

The voices faded, but Evie couldn't relax—not with Saint's lean, hard body pressed against hers. She should be grateful, she supposed, that he hadn't simply tossed her out of the alcove to the wolves. If they remained any longer, though, her fading luck was bound to leave her completely.

"Saint—"

He lowered his mouth to hers again, his hands flat against the wall on either side of her head. This time he was hard and ruthless and very thorough. A helpless moan left her before she could stop herself, and her hands lifted to slide around his waist.

Before she could actually touch him, though, he broke the kiss, backing to the far side of the alcove. "So sweet, you are," he said in his low voice, wiping a hand across his mouth. "You'd do best to stay away from me, you know. Good night, Evelyn Marie."

Leaning against the wall and trying to regain her breath and her senses, Evelyn thought her mother might be right. She must be going mad; now even St. Aubyn himself had warned her to stay away, and all she could think of was that she would see him again tomorrow.

With a last deep breath she yanked her sleeve back up, straightened, and returned to the hallway. A mirror hung just outside the ballroom door, and she took a moment to check her hair and make sure he hadn't removed any other articles of her clothing, or her necklace again.

Evelyn froze, gazing at the reflection of her throat. A single diamond in a sterling silver heart pendant winked back at her. Slowly, her hand shaking, she reached up to touch it. It wasn't just her imagination. The Marquis of St. Aubyn had taken her pearl necklace this afternoon, and replaced it with a diamond this evening. An exquisite one. "Oh, my," she whispered.

If nothing was for free, what would he expect in return for this? After that last kiss, a part of her wanted to find out.

"St. Aubyn."

Saint didn't look up from the gaming table. He'd managed to slip into the Dundredge card room via the servants' stairs, though at the same time he was dodging Victor Ruddick he had to wonder why he bothered. Almost no one called him out any longer; the survivors had warned the rest of the populace about the danger of questioning his honor, warranted or not.

Evelyn Marie, however, had actually asked him not to ruin her. That had surprised him into complying, along with the additional thought that if he *did* ruin her reputation, she would be removed from his grasp. It was all a good lesson in reasons not to dangle after proper, virginal females, but it didn't lessen his obsession with her in the least.

"St. Aubyn."

With a sigh, he looked up over his shoulder. "Yes?"

"Have you . . ." His square jaw clenched, Victor Ruddick glanced at the crowded room and lowered his voice. "Have you seen my sister?"

"First of all," Saint said, gesturing for another card, "who the devil are you?"

Evelyn's brother grasped the back of his chair and leaned forward. "You know who the devil I am," he muttered, "and you know who my sister is. She may be appallingly dim, but she's a good girl. Stay away from her, St. Aubyn."

Saint's estimation of Mr. Ruddick rose a notch or two. Direct threats took guts, especially when aimed at him. "I'm out," he informed the rest of the players at his table, dumping his cards into the discard pile.

On the other hand, though he knew relatively little about Evelyn, he had gathered that she wasn't the least bit stupid. He stood, sliding his chair back so that Victor had to move aside or get knocked over. The rest of the room had quieted to an eager buzz of muted conversation; but then, probably everyone knew he'd waltzed with Evelyn last week.

"Shall we?" he asked, gesturing her brother toward the door.

"I prefer not to be seen conversing with you," Victor stated, scowling. "You're no good for anyone's reputation. Just leave my family alone."

"Then cease sending your sister to chat with my particular . . . friends," Saint returned. "Do your own dirty work, Ruddick."

With that, he strolled out the door and back into the ballroom. Damn all brothers and husbands and fathers. This had been a perfectly nice evening before Victor Ruddick had stepped into it. Interesting, though, that no one in Evelyn's family knew she was dabbling in charitable works at the Heart of Hope Orphanage. He could use that to his advantage.

Saint smiled darkly. He seemed to be holding all the

cards in this little game. Whatever Evelyn was up to, it centered around the orphanage—which meant it involved him. Tomorrow he would just up the ante a little and see if she still wanted to play.

Chapter 8

Then bring me wine, the banquet bring;
Man was not formed to live alone:
I'll be that light, unmeaning thing,
That smiles with all, and weeps with none.

—Lord Byron, "One Struggle More,
and I am Free"

Saint awoke with a start, hurling the nearest object to hand—his boot—at the shadowy figure lurking at the foot of his bed.

"Ouch! It's me, my lord! Pemberly!"

"I know that." Saint lay back again, pulling the blankets over his head. "Go away."

"You instructed me to awaken you at half past seven, my lord. It is precisely half past—"

"Pemberly," Saint growled, wakefulness beginning to steal like a pounding hammer into his skull, "fetch me a drink. Now."

With a mumbled curse, the valet fled the room, narrowly avoiding the second boot aimed at his backside. At the door's subsequent slam, Saint uttered a curse of his own and clutched at his temple.

This was ungodly. And if half past seven was the time at which good, proper-minded folk rose, he was glad not to be one of them. He sat up again, more slowly this

97

time, and lit the lamp Pemberly had left on his bedstand.

Considering that he'd only returned home three hours earlier and that he'd slept alone—again, and for the thirteenth day in a row—Saint decided he had every reason to be in a piss-poor mood. At nearly thirty-three years of age, he'd settled his life into a certain pattern that most people found decadent and sinful, and probably secretly envied. He happened to enjoy it, himself. For the most part, anyway.

He scowled, shoving sheets and blankets aside and sliding to the edge of the bed. The orphanage matron, whatever her name was, had showed him Evelyn's schedule for the week. Today had been designated as "painting day," or some such nonsense, but it was to commence at nine o'clock in the morning.

Obviously he didn't need to be there to watch workmen spread paint on the walls, but Evelyn would be there.

Running a hand through his tousled hair, he yawned and gave a tentative stretch. In the long parade of mistresses and lovers with whom he'd shared a bed or a broom closet, he couldn't recall one who'd made him work this hard.

Nevertheless, giving up on the proper miss was out of the question. If he didn't get her on her back soon, though, he was going to explode. Or part of him was, anyway. Saint looked down. "Poor fellow," he muttered. "Be patient."

He was pulling on his trousers when Pemberly cracked the door open and peered in. "My lord? I've brought whiskey and coffee."

"Then get in here. And bring me today's *London Times*. I need to know what social nonsense is going on this week."

Already in the past two weeks he'd attended more proper social functions than he'd visited all last year. Putting up with the two-faced hypocrites was just another thing for which he would make Evelyn pay.

Saint half closed his eyes, conjuring the lemon scent of her hair and the feel of her soft, smooth skin beneath his fingers. This when he'd had so many lovers he couldn't even name them all, and when most of the time he felt little more than bored. It was maddening, to want Evelyn Ruddick so badly that he practically came to a point every time he set eyes on her, and to know that he was a fool to do so. She didn't know how to play this kind of game, obviously, and teaching her was going to take time. Lifting her skirts and taking her against some wall wouldn't be enough any longer; no, Miss Ruddick needed a very thorough education.

Sitting at his dressing table to shave, he also realized that if he meant to seduce her, he needed to begin getting a better night's sleep. Seduction rarely involved frightening one's intended partner half to death with one's red eyes and scarecrow hair. "Jesus," he muttered at his reflection. Pemberly's whiskey coffee had best be the strongest ever brewed.

When Pemberly returned, it was with both the newspaper and yesterday's mail. Saint flipped through it, setting the few invitations he received aside instead of relegating them to the trash as he usually did.

"What's this?" The missive, closed with the Prince of Wales's official seal, surprised him. Prinny generally took weeks to decide anything. Three days was extraordinary.

He opened it, skimming through the closely spaced contents. Prinny invited him to Brighton again, apparently because nothing inflamed Queen Charlotte more than Prince George gathering disreputables like Saint around him.

The next paragraph, though, made him scowl. "Damnation." Prince George had ordered a study to be made regarding a proposed park expansion. A study commissioned by the Prince was one step shy of an open debate in Parliament. "Damn, damn, damn."

Undoubtedly the Regent had been encouraged to gain Parliamentary approval because of his financial troubles, but Prinny himself had been the one to mention the possible negative publicity involved in razing an orphanage. He obviously took his scant popularity seriously, damn it all.

Saint rose quickly, heading down to his office to scrawl out a reply. No time remained for subtlety; he needed to scuttle this before it reached open debate—and the ears of his fellow trustees. The idea that Evelyn might discover his plans before he was finished with her darkened his mood even further. Writing hurriedly, he offered to cover all expenses involved in finding and transporting the orphans to a different location, destroying and removing the old building, and planting the additional area of the park.

"Jansen!" he bellowed as he folded and sealed the letter, addressing the outside.

The butler hurried into the doorway. "Yes, my lord?"

"See that this gets to Carlton House immediately. Make certain they know it's from me."

"I'll see to it at once, my lord."

Saint sat back, wiping ink from the tip of his pen. Just what he needed—another complication. His uncertain timetable for disposing of the Heart of Hope Orphanage had just accelerated to immediate, and he had a civic-minded young lady painting classrooms in the bloody place.

He saw only one course of action: Make her give up, quickly, and seduce her at the same time. With a grim smile, he returned to his bedchamber and finished dressing. Perhaps he could make himself her next project, and cure himself of his odd desire for her before she realized what he was up to. He certainly had tensions only she could ease. Educating Evelyn was going to be very pleasurable, indeed.

"I don't want to go to school!"

Oh, dear. "It's not school, Charles, it's only a few classes," Evelyn explained, keeping the determined smile on her face. Preparing classrooms, buying books, and hiring instructors was well and good, but if no one participated, the project would be a failure. And so would she.

"A few classes in what?" one of the older boys demanded.

"Reading, first of all. And writing. And arithmetic."

"That's school!"

"If someone hires you for work and agrees to pay you a certain wage, wouldn't you like to know if he's paying you what he promised?" she countered. "Wouldn't you like to be able to read the newspaper and know if any jobs are available? Wouldn't you like to be able to read stories about pirates and Red Indians and brave soldiers?"

The reluctant, muttered agreement gave her hope. The Duchess of Wycliffe's advice had helped, but Emma had taught at an upper-class girls' school, where the students wanted to learn and to succeed in Society. These children wanted food in their stomachs and clothes on their backs, and so different tactics became necessary.

What Evie couldn't tell them, but what she'd begun to realize almost immediately upon meeting them, was that facts and figures could only make up part of her program. Even more than letters and numbers, these children needed to see that someone cared about them. That was why she was taking so much care in hiring instructors, and in making the classrooms clean and cheery and pleasant.

She'd tried to explain her thoughts to the board of trustees, but they seemed as willing and able to pay attention to her as her own family was. Well, she'd offered money, and that had convinced them to say yes. The rest was up to her. And that was how she wanted it, anyway.

The hairs on the back of her neck pricked, and she looked up. The Marquis of St. Aubyn leaned against the doorjamb, gazing at her. Heat ran down her spine, warming her in delicious places she was certain she could never tell him about. It was one thing to be attracted to the scoundrel; to admit to it would be as good as announcing that yes, please, she wanted him to strip her naked and run his hands all over her body.

As always he was in dark colors, as though he disdained the light of day. Nighttime seemed much more suited to his pursuits, anyway. Evie stood, shaking herself. "Good morning, my lord," she said, curtsying. His real self was enough trouble without her inventing fantastic, even more seductive imaginings.

Saint returned the gesture with a careless, elegant bow. She wanted an example for the boys to follow, and little as she wished it to be the marquis, he seemed to be the only one available. The rest of the board apparently avoided actual contact with the orphans whenever possible. The girls around her began muttering and giggling, and she stifled a frown. She definitely would have preferred someone more reputable, for everyone's sake. Beggars, however, couldn't be choosers.

"It reeks of paint in here," he said, scowling. "Up to the ballroom, everyone. And open the damned windows."

In a happy, cacophonous rush they were gone, clattering up the stairs like a herd of cattle, before she could even protest. "We were chatting," she stated belatedly. "Now it'll take me another quarter hour to settle them down again."

Saint arched an eyebrow. "Did you have somewhere else to be today? A tea or a music recital, perhaps?"

Actually, if she didn't appear for Aunt Houton's tea this afternoon, her family would know for certain that she was up to something. "That is not the point. I'm trying to gain their trust. You're not supposed to stomp in here and disrupt everything."

"Chaos is my forte," he said, grinning.

For a moment her breath stopped. The light touching his green eyes was genuinely amused, and the transformation to his lean, cynical features was . . . remarkable. "I have noticed that," she ventured, just to say something.

He moved away from the door. "Where's your necklace?" he asked, coming toward her.

Evie reached up to touch her throat. "You still have it, I believe," she returned, wishing he'd stayed across the room. "And I wish to return the other one to you. I can't accept it." She pulled it from her pocket, holding it out to him.

He ignored the gesture as he stopped in front of her. "Can't, or won't?"

As his gaze swept down the length of her and back

again, she abruptly realized how very alone they were. The children were all on a floor above them, and the workers a floor below. "Both, my lord. You—"

"Saint," he interrupted. "Keep it."

"No. I—"

"Then throw it away, or sell it for bread to feed the dockworkers. I don't care."

She lifted her chin. "Yes, you do."

"No," he returned, taking the bauble from her hand and slowly sliding it back into the pocket of her pelisse, "I don't."

His hand lingered there, brushing against her thigh. "Then . . . why did you give it to me?"

He put his right hand in her other pocket, using the material to tug her up against him. Evie instinctively put her hands against his chest to keep from slamming into him. "Because I wanted to. Ask me another question."

"I . . ." She searched her brain wildly for something that wasn't insipid. "Don't you have other things to do today? Women to seduce, clubs to get drunk at?"

He smiled again, less amused and warmer at the same time. "What do you think I'm doing right now?" he murmured, lifting his hands.

The material of her pelisse, and her gown beneath, lifted as well. He slid his spread fingers along her thighs and up to her waist, raising her dress past her knees. At the same time he leaned down and kissed her, teasing at her mouth with his lips and tongue.

Knees wobbling, Evelyn gasped and wrenched backward. "Stop that!" She shoved her dress back down where it belonged.

Frustration crossed his gaze for just a moment, as though he'd forgotten he was teasing. If he had been teasing. "One day very soon, Evelyn Marie," he said in his low drawl, "you'll beg me to continue."

"Doubtful." She conjured a scowl, which wasn't very difficult considering that she was torn between running away and demanding to know what he would do next.

"Hm." He gazed at her for another moment, then returned to the doorway. "Stay here if you wish, then. I'm going up to the ballroom."

He vanished into the hallway. With a frustrated sigh, Evie looked at the vacated space around her and the scant quarter page of notes she'd been able to make. She needed to just ignore him, or better yet, to tell him he was wasting his time and that his seductions would never work on her.

Except that they were working on her. She rubbed her arms, trying to subdue the goose bumps his touch had caused. She knew the names of at least half a dozen of his rumored lovers, and yet when he looked at her she couldn't remember anything but how exciting and tantalizing it felt when he kissed her.

Slowly she gathered her books and papers in her arms. She'd heard about his confrontation with Victor last night, and she also knew that he'd been outright banned from Almack's and even a few of the less forgiving households in Mayfair. However much he deserved it, and however much he pretended not to care, it had to bother him. Even if he enjoyed living on the fringes of Society, it had to hurt, knowing that he couldn't move back to the center if he wanted to. No one could *like* being a pariah.

And heaven forbid he should find a woman he actually cared for and wanted to marry. With his reputation, no woman of good standing would care to be courted by him—just his interest could ruin her. She knew first-hand that even his haphazard teasing and taunting was dangerous.

Evelyn left the dormitory for the stairs. Saint waited there for her, looking completely composed, as though he hadn't just been lifting her skirts halfway to her waist and slipping his tongue down her throat. Such things probably happened daily where he was concerned. Per-haps he really did need her lessons and her decorum as much as the orphans did. Yes, choosing him as her stu-dent was a fine idea, whatever Lucinda and Georgiana might think her chances of succeeding might be. And it had nothing to do with the way his touch and his kisses made her shiver.

"After you, my brave Evelyn," he said, motioning her to precede him up the stairs.

She remembered Dare's warning about not turning her back on him, but face-to-face was obviously just as dangerous. And if he was ever going to learn how to be-have properly, someone was going to have to set an ex-ample.

With each step Evelyn took up the stairs, her shoes and her ankles appeared for just a moment beneath the hem of her gown. Saint hung back a little, fascinated by the glimpses of her legs.

He was utterly mad. That was the only explanation. For God's sake, he'd seen more women's bare legs in his lifetime than he could count. Dainty virginal ankles were new, but they were attached to parts of which he well knew the workings.

In near desperation he raised his gaze, but the sight of her swaying hips and bottom didn't make his trousers feel any looser. It made no sense. Even lovers who knew exactly how to pleasure a man didn't leave him feeling this way. No one had aroused him like this in a very long time.

"We opened the windows!" one of the boys yelled from the top of the stairs. "They ain't here for us, are they?"

Evelyn glanced over her shoulder at Saint, a frown furrowing her brows. "Who is here, and for whom?"

"You'll see."

"I'm not sure I want to," she muttered, and he grinned. Anything that kept her thinking of him and distracted her from teaching could only help his own cause.

They topped the stairs, and he drew even with her as she reached the wide double doors of the old ballroom. Paint and wallpaper peeled from the walls, and two of the now-open windows were cracked, but the hardwood floor remained in fair shape. Evelyn wouldn't be looking at any of that, though. Her attention would be on the seated figures at one end of the room, noisy children milling around them.

She faced him. "An orchestra?"

"I thought it might be a nice treat," he said in his most innocent tone. At least he hoped it sounded innocent; he hadn't attempted that adjective in a long while.

"Well, it's a surprise," she conceded. "But how am I supposed to talk to any of the children with an orchestra playing? You shouldn't have—"

"Make 'em play, Lord St. Aubyn!"

Saint stifled his smile. The more frustrated Evelyn became, the better for him. "You heard the boy," he said, raising his voice to be heard over the gaggle of orphans. "Play us a waltz."

"A waltz? You can't—"

The music began with a loud flourish. The children

squealed and began leaping and twirling about the room. It looked like a scene from purgatory. *Perfect.*

"Music soothes the savage breast, does it not?" he asked, watching the frustration and disappointment play across Evelyn's expressive face.

"These aren't savages," she snapped. "They're children."

"I was talking about myself, actually." Saint gazed toward the gyrations going on across the room. "But are you certain about that?"

"Yes. Now make them stop playing, or I will."

He shrugged. "As you wish. I think I should warn you that you may find yourself rather unpopular, however."

To his surprise, tears welled in her light gray eyes. "Fine," she said with a dainty sniffle. "You're right; they deserve some fun. Heaven knows, clomping about is more interesting than arithmetic."

Damn. Women used tears on him all the time, and he considered it selfish and manipulative. Evelyn was fighting hers, though, and she turned away so he—and the orphans—wouldn't see them.

"Perhaps we might teach them to count to three," he suggested, taking her shoulder and turning her to face him again. "Dance with me."

"What? No! You—"

"Come, Evelyn Marie. Show them what fun arithmetic can be."

Before she could conjure another protest, he slid his hand about her slender waist, captured her hand, and swung her into the waltz. She would have pulled away, so he began counting the time aloud, sweeping them among the children.

She danced well, and when her concerns were for something besides the potential scandal of being seen in his company, she relaxed, sinking into the waltz with a spirited enjoyment that he couldn't help appreciating.

"One, two, three," she chanted with him. "One, two, three. Come on, everyone! Join us!" Evelyn smiled up at him, and his heart gave an odd, unpleasant skip. "Dance with one of the girls," she said, spinning out of his grasp. "We'll teach them all."

Before he could protest that he intended on dancing only with her, she caught up one of the younger boys. As Saint watched, the lad stepped on her toe. Evelyn only laughed.

This was wrong. The orchestra was there to disrupt whatever plans she'd made for the day, and to give him another opportunity to have her in his arms. And now, because her tears had bothered him, he'd apparently inspired her to teach the waltz to half a hundred orphans who'd never even seen a sheet of music, much less danced to the tune.

She whirled by him again, a boy on each arm now. "Come, now, my lord, don't be shy," she taunted, laughing. "Choose a partner!"

"I did," he muttered under his breath. Outwitted by a proper chit. It was embarrassing. With a sigh, he collected one of the female infants and taught her the waltz.

"No, the point, Donald, is that proposing any sort of legislation is useless if we don't have the votes to carry it."

Victor Ruddick sat back in the crowded coach, keeping on his face the placid, interested look that he'd been practicing for weeks. He'd wanted an audience with Prince George since he'd returned from India, but accompanying the Regent along with five other hopeful representatives of the House of Commons while Prinny went to an appointment at Hoby's wasn't what he'd envisioned. At least no one seemed to be throwing rotten vegetables at the vehicle today.

"But if we propose the legislation, Victor," Donald Tremaine returned, sweat glistening from his domed forehead, "then at least we'll be giving notice of our determination to see it succeed."

He resisted wiping his own brow; the day was warm enough without being crammed into the closed vehicle with an overweight prince and his nervous entourage. "And our weakness in seeing it fail."

"Such spirit," the Regent applauded. "If only damned Pitt would succumb, we would be a sight to see."

If only support from Prince George could assure a vote, we might succeed, Victor amended silently. More likely it would sink his career to be seen in the old fool's company, but if a prospect didn't court the Prince, he had very little likelihood of serving in the House.

Screams and music flooded through the coach's tiny open window. "Driver, stop!" Prinny demanded, banging on the ceiling with his cane. "What is that ruckus?"

"Don't know, Your Majesty," came the muffled reply.

At the Prince's command, Tremaine opened the door, hanging out in an attempt to locate the source of the sound. "Do you think it's a riot?" Prince George asked, worry crossing his round face.

"I doubt it, Your Majesty," Victor soothed. "I haven't heard of any unrest at all this Season." Not in London, anyway, though he refrained from adding that part. Giving the prince an apoplexy would be akin to political suicide.

"It's coming from there," Tremaine said, pointing. "The . . . Heart of Hope Orphanage. All the upstairs windows are open, and it looks as though they're having a soiree of some kind. I can see children leaping about in the room."

The Prince visibly relaxed. "Ah, no worries, then. That'll be St. Aubyn, no doubt auctioning off some furniture before he tears the place down."

Victor scowled. That damned marquis again. "If I might ask, Your Majesty, why would St. Aubyn be destroying an orphanage?"

"He's the chairman of the board of trustees there. Offered me the land for free, if I'd agree to let him knock the place down. Don't know what's in it for him yet, but I'll figure it out. Can't outfox me, St. Aubyn." The Prince chuckled again. "Let's carry on, eh?"

Victor sat back as the coach lurched into motion again. The information wasn't at all surprising, but he was happy to have it, nevertheless. Whatever little game Evie thought she was playing, trying to get back at him for something by encouraging St. Aubyn's presence, once his soft-hearted sister found out her marquis was throwing orphans out of their home, she'd have nothing more to do with him. And that was fine with him. Better than fine. It was perfect.

Chapter 9

In secret we met—
In silence I grieve,
That thy heart could forget,
Thy spirit deceive.

—Lord Byron, "When We Two Parted"

Despite the interruption of the impromptu ball, Evelyn decided that she had made definite progress. In some ways, St. Aubyn's surprise soiree had even helped her cause: A dozen of the girls had afterward asked her to teach them the waltz.

She'd hesitated for a bare moment, since, as much as she might wish them to have the experience, the odds of these girls ever being invited to an actual soiree were abysmally remote. Almost immediately, though, and despite Saint offering her a cynical look from across the room, she'd realized that the dance lessons were secondary. The girls wanted her attention, which, thanks to her project, she could provide in abundance.

"That shall be one of our classes, then," she announced, "beginning tomorrow and for anyone, boy or girl, who wishes to learn."

"But what about today?" little Rose asked, looking crestfallen.

Evelyn had the feeling she'd lingered too long already. She genuinely liked her Aunt Houton, but not even the marchioness would wish Victor or Lord Houton's wrath aimed at her, any more than Evie wanted to face it. "Tomorrow is only a few hours away."

"Miss Ruddick has important things to attend to," the marquis added in his low drawl.

"And we ain't important," one of the older boys— Matthew, she thought—said, echoing Saint's cynicism and tone to near perfection.

She desperately needed to improve Saint's demeanor, if he was to be the boys' role model. "Of course you're important," she stated. "I made a prior promise to attend to something this afternoon. I keep my promises. Rose, you will be my first partner tomorrow, and Matthew, you shall be my second."

From the jostling and whistles, she'd made an impact, anyway. Little Rose pranced up and hugged her around the legs. "Thank you, Miss Evie."

"You're welcome," she said, smiling. Today had been a good day. She glanced at Saint's dark expression. Whatever he'd intended with his orchestral distraction, he hadn't achieved it—which in all likelihood was for the best. "We should thank Lord St. Aubyn as well, for arranging all this."

He accepted the thanks with a nod, which the children seemed to understand was their signal to clomp back downstairs to the dormitories or out to the old courtyard to play. Well, she'd managed to squeeze in a lesson for him, as well, that a lady appreciated a kind deed—whatever his motivations for performing it.

"That was very nice of you," she said, picking up the books and papers she'd set aside.

"One of them stole your brooch, you know," he said, drawing even with her at the doorway.

She reached up to feel her collar. "I didn't notice! Are you certain?"

"The tall boy with the red scarf."

"Don't you even know his name?"

"Don't you?"

"Randall Baker. Why didn't you stop him?"

He shrugged his broad shoulders. "This is your game, not mine. I'll get it back for you."

"If he stole it, then he needs it more than I do."

Saint lifted an eyebrow. "Aren't you the martyr?"

"No, I'm not. I don't need it."

"You wanted your necklace back."

"*You* didn't need that. And this is not a game to me. Can't you see that by now?" No one could be that jaded. Not even St. Aubyn.

"I'm sure you love having them look at you as their savior in green muslin, Evelyn," he returned, "but you're nothing new."

"Beg pardon?"

He glanced over his shoulder at her as he started down the stairs. "Whenever you get tired of being worshiped, you'll go, too."

"I am not here to be worshiped."

He ignored her retort. "My mother used to visit here, on the first Tuesday of every month."

"She did? The marchioness was quite civil-minded, then. You should be proud that she made an effort to think of someone in need. What—"

Saint snorted. "She and her sewing circle provided table doilies for holiday dinners."

"She still contributed something," Evie offered to his

back as she followed him down the stairs. If he was implying that she behaved in the same way, she didn't like it.

"Yes, she did. Rumor has it that two or three of the former inmates here belonged to her husband, which might have had something to do with her interest. I suppose that means my father contributed something of himself to this bloody place as well."

Heat rose in Evie's cheeks. Men weren't supposed to have such conversations with ladies of good breeding. "Are any of them yours?" she asked anyway, surprised at her boldness.

Apparently he was, as well, because he turned around and looked up at her. "Not that I know of," he answered after a moment. "I'm not likely to contribute to my own misery."

"Then why are you here?"

"Today? Because I want you."

Oh, dear. "I mean, why are you on the board of trustees?"

"Ah. I told you. My mother's will stipulated that two thousand pounds a year and a Halboro family member go to the Heart of Hope Orphanage."

"But—"

"I was tired of seeing the other trustees buying carriages and keeping mistresses with the family proceeds."

"Surely not."

"We all get something out of it," he went on with a cynical smile. "Father got sex, Mother got to tell her friends how charitable and tragic her life was, and the rest of the board gets to pocket whatever funds they can siphon off and be thanked annually by the lord mayor of London for it."

"And what do you get?"

"I get to pay penance. I'm helping orphans, after all. Doesn't that keep me out of hell? What are you getting out of this, Miss Ruddick?"

If she told him, he would only laugh in her face. "Don't you get some sense of . . . satisfaction," she asked slowly, "from seeing that these children are fed and clothed? They might very well be on the streets if not for you seeing that their funding is spent where it should be."

"What I get satisfaction from," he returned, "is seeing Timothy Rutledge and the other vultures trying week after week to put some moneymaking scheme or other by me, and my slapping them down." He climbed the steps separating them. "Perhaps you should look more kindly on me after all, Evelyn. At least I don't steal from the brats."

"I don't believe anything you've said," she declared with all the conviction she had remaining. "You're only trying to shock me, and to convince me to leave."

"No. I'm only trying to convince you that if it's satisfaction you want to feel, there are other, more pleasant ways to go about it. Whatever you do here won't make any difference. It never does. If nothing else, there'll always be another peer contributing to the unwashed populace."

"That is not true!"

Saint reached out to touch her cheek in a careless, intimate gesture. "Why don't you try to save me instead?" he murmured.

If he only knew. "It seems to me," she said, so angry and frustrated by his jaded interpretation of everything that her voice shook, "that the way to rescue you would be not to indulge your base urges. So please feel free to think that I *am* trying to save you." She brushed past him. "And now good day, my lord."

His low, confident chuckle made her spine stiffen. "I kissed you, Evelyn Marie. And you kissed me. You're not as proper as you think you are."

She paused at the bottom of the stairs. "And despite your dislike of this place, you still feed these children, Michael. So perhaps you're not as awful as you think you are."

Saint watched her down the hallway. "You're right," he muttered. "I'm worse."

Evelyn barely made it inside the front door of Ruddick House in time to hear the clock strike one. With a hurried breath, she traded Langley her morning bonnet for her afternoon bonnet and parasol, and faced the stairs.

"Good afternoon, Mama," she greeted Genevieve Ruddick as her mother began her descent down the squared staircase. "Are you ready for our political tea?"

"You spend far too much time with Lucinda Barrett, you know," Genevieve complained, licking her finger to spiral a last fashionable blond curl against her forehead.

"I know, Mama. I lost track of the time. I do apologize," Evie said with a bright smile.

"Yes, well, be thankful Victor's not home. I shudder to think how he might react if you missed another tea."

"Don't worry. I have no intention of missing another tea. Shall we go?"

Her mother stopped in the doorway to peer suspiciously at Evelyn's face. "Your color is very high, Evie," she said. "Are you certain you're well?"

"I'm only a little out of breath from hurrying." *And a little unsettled after her last conversation with Saint.*

"I hope that's all it is. I couldn't tolerate it if you made a scene by fainting or something."

Evie took her mother's arm to guide her to the waiting coach. "No fainting. I promise."

"Good. Because we must make the best of impressions today, for your brother's sake. Your Aunt Houton's political teas have become quite famous, you know. Many a career has been made or destroyed over tea and biscuits. And you must not speak about your own theories on educating the poor. This is not the time, nor the place."

"Yes, Mama." That particular demand was actually a little easier to agree to today. She didn't need to talk about it, because she was doing it. "No discussions about anything progressive, unless it directly benefits Victor."

"Precisely."

Even with her newfound confidence, the afternoon was nearly intolerable. Most of the ladies reminded Evelyn of Saint's description of his mother—compassionate and caring, so long as it took no effort and meant no inconvenience on their part. That raised another question: If the attitude was so common, why did it seem to bother Saint so much, especially when he claimed that nothing bothered him?

"You're quiet this afternoon." Lydia Barnesby, Lady Houton, sat on the couch beside Evelyn, her skirt settling around her in a gentle, graceful wave. "You always are, at these things, but you're not even stammering with indignation today."

"Or stammering, period," Evie returned with a slight smile. "It always makes me nervous, that my slightest *faux pas* could sink all of Victor's political ambitions."

"You shouldn't think that, my dear. I doubt you could

single-handedly bring about Victor's ruination. I wouldn't allow it to happen at one of my teas, for one thing."

"That's reassuring," Evelyn admitted. "Since the only use he has for me is being charming to his political gentlemen friends, I feel a bit . . . secondary here, anyway." She lowered her voice. "I don't think anyone here even notices me."

Her aunt leaned closer. "That isn't entirely true. I, for instance, wanted to mention that you have a smudge on your skirt. A handprint, it looks like. A small one."

Evelyn blanched. "Oh! Well, Luce and I went walking this morning, and we came across three adorable children and their gov—"

"You visited that orphanage again," Aunt Houton interrupted in a low voice. "I warned you how dangerous that could be. They have all sorts of diseases, and according to your brother, most of them are criminals."

"It's not . . . dangerous, for heaven's sake." *Well, not unless one took St. Aubyn into account.*

"If you were married, your husband might allow you to make some sort of monetary contribution to the institution. For a young single lady of your standing, and at a facility for complete commoners and outside of Mayfair—it's just not done, Evie."

Evelyn tried to look chagrined and ashamed, rather than annoyed. "I know."

"Promise me that you won't do it again."

Drat. "I promise." But she crossed her fingers beneath her teacup, just in case someone was paying attention.

As Saint strolled into the main chamber of the House of Lords, the resulting murmur of comment sounded like a wave, growing louder as it approached and crashed over him. True, it had been nearly a month since his last appearance, but they all knew he came by from time to time—if he didn't, without fail someone tried to have him declared dead or unfit and confiscate his considerable properties for the Crown.

For a moment he considered taking his usual seat with Dare and Wycliffe, the least offensive of his peers. Both of them knew Evelyn, however, and Dare at least seemed to have been needled into helping the paragon of propriety. He paused. On the other hand, both of them *knew* Evelyn.

"What did I miss?" he asked in a low voice, sitting beside Dare.

"Today, or in the last month?"

"Be quiet, you young good-for-nothing," old Earl Haskell hissed, turning to glare up at them.

"You have spittle on your chin, Haskell," Saint drawled back at him. "Do you have any teeth left at all?"

The earl's face turned beet-red. "You young bastard," he growled, lurching to his feet. The peers on either side grabbed his shoulders and yanked him back down again.

"We're discussing Prinny's debts again," Wycliffe rumbled.

Damn. He probably should have stayed away, then. If Prinny or one of his advisors had been gossiping, things could get nasty. "The usual nonsense, eh?" he returned, borrowing a billet from Dare to doodle on the back of it.

"Seems so. If not for the occasional spray of spittle, I'd be asleep in my chair." With a faint grin, the viscount sat forward. "I'm glad you're here, actually. Saves me the trouble of hunting you down."

"I thought you didn't associate with me any longer." Saint realized the face he was sketching had begun to look familiar, and he quickly added a mustache and beaver hat. Evelyn Ruddick gave him no peace even when she wasn't present. "That whole marriage claptrap and all."

The viscount's smile only deepened. "Domestication has its good points." He dropped his voice still further. "That's why I was looking for you, actually. I'm to ask you to stop teasing after Evie Ruddick."

It was far from the first time he'd been warned away from a female, but usually it was after things had become more complicated than amusing, anyway. This time, though, he was hungry for the chit and extremely frustrated by his lack of success. "Did this warning come from the same lady discovered last year with her dainty hand down your trousers?"

Dare's eyes narrowed, the humor in his expression vanishing. "Are you certain you want to play this game with me?"

Saint shrugged. "Why not? I play it with everyone else."

"You're speaking about my wife, St. Aubyn."

"And my cousin," the large Duke of Wycliffe muttered, his expression tense and annoyed.

"I see." With feigned carelessness, he pushed to his feet. Dare and Wycliffe together were formidable enough that he didn't want a brawl in the House of Lords, though anywhere else would have suited him fine. "Why don't you ask Miss Ruddick whether she wants me to leave her alone or not? Until then, I bid your domesticated backsides a good day."

Across the aisle Lord Gladstone sat glaring at him.

Several husbands seemed none too happy to see him, as a matter of fact. As he left, it occurred to him that Fatima, Lady Gladstone, would likely be at home accepting visitors at this time of day, and that if he wanted some of his tensions eased, she would no doubt be eager to accommodate him.

At the same time, he knew he'd indulge in no such thing; he was concentrating on different, more difficult prey. When one wanted pheasant, one didn't settle for chicken.

His pheasant was at some political tea or other, from what he'd been able to glean from her. Women only, and they'd be mostly old, wrinkled ones. Not many chits who still could find other ways to amuse themselves went to political teas.

Not being a chit interested in politics, he went home. "Jansen," he asked his butler, as he shrugged out of his jacket, "do I have anything here with which I might amuse myself?"

"Ah, are you referring perhaps to . . . female company, my lord? No one of that persuasion has come calling today, I'm afraid."

"No, not females," he returned, scowling. "You know, things people—men—use to pass the time when they're not bedding some woman or other."

"Oh." The butler glanced over his shoulder, but if any other servants had been in earshot, they'd already vanished. "Well, you do have a library upstairs, and—"

"I do?"

"Yes, my lord."

"With books?"

By now Jansen had begun to realize that he was being toyed with, but he seemed to accept it with his usual equanimity. No doubt he considered it better than being bellowed at or having things thrown at him. "Yes, my lord."

"Hm. I don't really feel like reading. Anything else you might suggest?"

"Billiards, perhaps?"

"Billiards. Do you play, Jansen?"

"I . . . I don't know, my lord. Do I?"

"You do now. Come on."

"But the d—"

"Gibbons or someone can mind the door."

"You don't employ anyone named Gibbons, my lord."

Saint paused halfway up the stairs, hiding a grin behind another frown. "Fancy that. Remind me to hire someone named Gibbons, then."

"Yes, my lord."

"And don't think you're getting out of billiards. Come on."

He tortured the butler for an hour or so, but it hadn't been that amusing to begin with, and despite himself he actually began to pity Jansen. Evelyn's influence, no doubt. She seemed to have the ability to make a statue soft-hearted. Well, he wasn't a statue, and a kiss or two certainly wasn't going to turn him into a mirror of Dare or Wycliffe. For God's sake, it was seven in the evening, and he was at home playing billiards with his damned butler.

"Have Wallace saddle my horse," he said, tossing the cue onto the table.

Jansen nearly sagged with relief. "At once, my lord. Will you be returning for dinner?"

"No. I won't be returning at all tonight, with any luck."

He dined at the Society club and sat for a game of faro

with Lord Westgrove and two gentlemen he'd never met. That suited him fine; most gentlemen he knew hesitated to wager with him any longer.

"I say," the younger, stouter of the two began, "my Uncle Fenston said the Society would be crawling with peers and nonsuches. It seems rather . . . thin, tonight, if I do say so."

Westgrove grunted as he lost another ten quid to the bank. "Almack's tonight. Another flock of fledgling debutantes'll be getting presented. All the bucks have gone to scout out the plumpest pockets."

"Damn me," the other, older, thinner of them mused. "Almack's. Always wanted to go there."

"Why?" Saint scoffed, setting his wager. He'd forgotten it was Wednesday, Almack's Assembly night. His pheasant would be there right now, no doubt, curtsying and smiling and telling everyone how she'd tricked St. Aubyn into letting her meddle with his damned orphanage. Except that she seemed to want that kept a secret.

"Everyone goes to Almack's. Don't they?"

"Tepid lemonade, no liquor, no gaming rooms, old, glaring-eyed patronesses everywhere, and barely a waltz all evening. That's Almack's. You're not missing anything."

Westgrove chuckled, the sound turning into a hacking cough. "Don't mind him, lads. He's only saying that because he's been banned."

"Banned? Really? Why?"

"Too much intelligence," Saint muttered, wishing Westgrove would shut up. He wasn't there to entertain two country buffoons after some town bronze.

"For engaging in intercourse with Isabel Rygel in the storage room, as I recall."

"In— Really?"

"No." Saint glanced up, then placed his next wager. "It was hardly intercourse. Fellatio, perhaps, but not intercourse."

"Stop my cork!" the young, large one exclaimed. "Who did you say you were?"

"I didn't."

"That, my lads," the viscount supplied, "is none other than the Marquis of St. Aubyn."

"You're *the Saint*? They say you killed a man in a duel. That true?"

"Probably," Saint answered, nodding at the dealer to close him out. "But I'm sure he deserved it. Good evening, gentlemen."

"But—"

The cold night air felt good against his face as he and Cassius went looking for less talkative game. At this hour of the evening, the party at Almack's would be its most crowded, with probably half a hundred men all waiting in line to be charmed by Evelyn Marie Ruddick.

Without really meaning to, he turned his mount north. A few blocks later he stopped outside the nondescript brick building to look toward the lighted windows. Music drifted out on the chill breeze, not quite covering the twittering of conversation beneath.

She was in there. He knew it, and it frustrated him. Evelyn could get into places that he couldn't. Proper, stuffy, self-righteous, boring places, but for once he couldn't convince himself that he liked it that way. He'd been banned from Almack's for five years, and until tonight it had never bothered him. Until tonight.

Evie pushed aside the curtains, trying for a breath of cool, fresh air. Whatever the temperature outside, Almack's always seemed stifling. A horse and rider stood in the dimness across the boulevard, and for a moment she thought one of them looked vaguely familiar. Before she could be certain, though, they rode off. Still . . . She shook herself. Saint wouldn't be found dead in the vicinity of a proper place like Almack's. And he'd have no reason to be lurking outside tonight, anyway.

"Evie, are you listening to me?"

She blinked and let the curtains slide back through her fingers. "I'm sorry, Georgie. What was it?"

"I said that St. Aubyn nearly caused a brawl in the House of Lords today. That's what Tristan told me, anyway."

"Oh, please, Georgiana. He's always doing things like that. What do I care?"

"You might at least acknowledge that I put myself in harm's way on your behalf, Evie," the deeper voice of Viscount Dare came from her other side.

Georgiana stiffened. "No, you didn't. Go away now."

"No, I didn't," he repeated amiably, and nodded. "Good-bye."

"Wait!" Evelyn caught his arm. "What do you mean, on my behalf?"

"I . . . ah . . ." He glanced over her head at his wife. "I don't mean anything. I have a mental disability."

"Please, Dare, tell me what's going on. I'm trying to work with him, you know, and I really, *really* don't want you making things more difficult."

The tall viscount sighed. "I only suggested that he stop pestering you. You're not the usual type of female who attracts him, so I can only assume he means you no good."

"I don't think he's ever meant anyone any good," she muttered. "I appreciate your concern, but as I said, if I'm to continue my work, I need his cooperation. Please don't speak on my behalf anymore."

He nodded his dark head. "Just don't say that I didn't warn you, Evie. He's done things that make *me* look like an angel."

"Yes, as difficult as that may be to believe," Georgiana added, tucking her arm around the viscount's. "And blame me, Evie. I asked Tristan to say something to him. I'm worried about you."

"Don't be. I can take care of myself."

No doubt they disbelieved her; obviously even her closest friends thought her helpless and incapable of anything but smiling and uttering pleasantries when the occasion called for them. Saint was no better, but at least he had no reason to think otherwise. He might be able to coax a kiss or two from her, but if that was his price for allowing her to help with the orphanage, she was willing to pay it. And if she could coax a pleasantry or two from him, she would consider the venture a success.

The orchestra began one of the few waltzes of the evening, and without much difficulty she convinced Georgie and Tristan to join the other dancers on the floor. Lucinda wasn't in attendance tonight, and Evie found herself in the unusual circumstance of being alone.

Unfortunately, it didn't last. "Evie," her brother said, strolling up to her in the company of an elderly gentleman, "have you met the Duke of Monmouth? Your Grace, my sister, Evelyn."

"Charmed," the duke rumbled, and she curtsied.

"I was just telling His Grace of your fondness for chess, Evie."

Chess? She detested chess. "Yes, it's true, though I'm afraid I have more affection than talent for it."

The duke nodded, a strand of his white hair standing straight up from his head. "I've often said that chess is beyond the faculties of females. Glad to see at least one of you young ladies realizes that."

Evie smiled through her clenched jaw. "How kind of Your Grace. I assume you are a skilled player, then?"

"I am the champion of Dorsetshire."

"How splendid!" Whatever contribution Victor thought Monmouth could provide for his campaign, it had best be a good one. Good heavens. An ancient chess player with ill-styled hair.

"His Grace specifically sought an introduction to you, Evie," Victor said with an indulgent smile. "I suggested you might take a stroll about the room with him, since neither of you is fond of the waltz."

Evie stifled a sigh. Chess and no waltzing. Apparently she was dull as cotton. "It would be my pleasure, Your Grace."

At least she didn't have to worry about keeping up her half of the conversation. The duke not only knew the game of chess, but also the best material for chessboards, the origins of the game, and the most expensive set ever made—which he apparently owned.

She gave pleasant nods and smiles at the appropriate times, all the while sending silent curses in her brother's direction. He'd done this before: found a potential supporter, discovered their favorite pastime or hobby, and made it hers. She'd always detested it, but disliked it even more now that she felt like she had better, more important things to do.

She was so busy nodding and smiling that it was a moment before she realized he was bidding her good evening. "Thank you for a most interesting discussion, Your Grace," she said with a final smile and a curtsy. As soon as his upright hair vanished into the crowd, she went to find Victor.

"Well done, Evie," he said, offering her a glass of lemonade.

She refused it with a grimace. "You might at least have warned me. I don't know the first thing about chess."

"I'd teach you, if I thought you'd give it even an ounce of your attention."

Evie cleared her throat. She put up with this for a reason. Maybe, if she tried to convince him . . . "Victor, I've been doing some research," she began. "Do you have any idea how many parentless children live in London? What if—"

"No, no, no. I'm campaigning, not reforming. And you're supposed to be helping me."

"That's what I'm trying to do."

"Then stop speaking to St. Aubyn, and stop your little research projects. If children interest you, get married and produce some."

"That's mean."

"I'm not here this evening to make friends with you. By the by, you shouldn't look like such a wallflower. Your popularity reflects on me."

"But I thought I didn't like the waltz," she retorted, wishing she had accepted the lemonade. Even tepid, it would have been a blessing in the stifling assembly room.

"You don't like the waltz when Monmouth is present," he said, sipping his own lemonade. "Nor when St. Aubyn is anywhere near."

"Humph. At least St. Aubyn doesn't lie to everyone about everything so he can influence people."

Immediately she realized that she'd said the wrong

thing, but it was already too late to take it back. Victor set aside his lemonade and took her by the elbow, guiding her to one side of the room.

"I have been as patient as I intend to be about you and St. Aubyn," he murmured. "I'm sure you think you're being clever and independent or something, but as your brother I must inform you that you're only making yourself look like a hypocrite and a fool."

Frustrated tears welled in her eyes, but Evie blinked them away. She would not give him the satisfaction of knowing he'd made her cry. "You've always thought I was foolish," she retorted, "but I am *not* a fool, or a hypocrite."

"Ah. So you've given up your quest to aide the lower classes, the orphans, and the beggars of London?"

Ha. If he only knew. "No, I have not. I never will."

Her brother gave her a grim smile. "Then you should know that the scoundrel you've been flaunting in my face is currently in negotiations with Prince George to tear down an orphanage and put a park in its place. You can't cling to both your hobbies, Evie, not without being a hypocrite. *And* a fool."

Unable to draw a breath, Evelyn stared at Victor. Her brother was lying. That was the only explanation. "That is not true."

"Of course it is. I heard it from Prinny himself. The Heart of Hope, or something like that. No doubt St. Aubyn'll make a tidy profit in the deal, too. He's not exactly known for his altruism."

She yanked her arm free of his grasp. The pain of his grip was nothing compared to the aching, gaping hole his words had opened in her chest. Why would Saint do such a thing? On occasion, he almost seemed . . . nice. And those children were under his protection. If he intended to tear the building down, why had he allowed her to clean out the storerooms? And . . .

Evelyn scowled. Of course he'd let her empty the rooms downstairs. It would save him the trouble of having it done later. As for painting the walls, well, that would only be a minor inconvenience, and he hadn't had to pay for it. And it had certainly kept her and the children from suspecting anything.

"Perhaps from now on you'll listen to me when I attempt to advise you," Victor said. "I do have your best interests at heart, you know." He leaned closer. "Now go dance with someone and stop standing there with your mouth hanging open. You've done well tonight. Have a little fun."

She snapped her jaw closed. Damn St. Aubyn. He was not going to destroy her only hope of contributing something worthwhile. She wouldn't allow it.

Chapter 10

In flight I shall be surely wise,
Escaping from temptation's snare;
I cannot view my Paradise
Without the wish of dwelling there.

—Lord Byron, "The Farewell to a Lady"

She arrived early at the orphanage, entering the dining room just as the children were finishing their breakfast. In light of what she'd discovered, she could acknowledge that they were well fed, but that the fare was simple and prepared by the minimum necessary staff.

The walls, the roof, the building itself, all became pieces of the puzzle to which Victor had given her the key. Everything was adequate, and nothing more. Damn, damn, damn. How could she have been so blind? Everyone had warned her about St. Aubyn—she hadn't listened, because the warnings had been about safeguarding her own reputation. They'd all said the same thing, though, that he did nothing without good reason, and that he never did anything for free.

"Miss Evie!" Rose squealed. She and Penny charged forward, hugging her about the waist. "I made a picture for you."

"Did you? I can't wait to see it!"

"It's all of us dancing. I'm wearing a green dress, because green is my favorite color."

Evie made a mental note to see that Rose received a green gown. They all needed new clothes, something more than the worn, nondescript clothing supplied by the orphanage. Unfortunately, she'd already used this month's pin money for the paint and the instructors. Perhaps if she could convince Victor that she could aid him better in a new gown or two, he would advance her a bit more.

"Do we get to waltz again today?" Penny asked.

Even the more cynical Molly couldn't quite keep the excited smile from her face. Evelyn smiled back, fighting the sudden urge for tears. The children were beginning to trust her, and the Marquis of St. Aubyn meant to ruin everything. Or at least he meant to try.

"We don't have an orchestra, but I will show you the steps. Anyone who wants to learn to dance is welcome to join me in the ballroom."

"Does that include me?" Saint's low drawl came from the doorway.

She stiffened. Yesterday she'd found the marquis enigmatic and enticing, all at the same time. Today she wished she'd never met him at all. "Good morning, my lord," she said through clenched teeth, not trusting herself to face him. "Say good morning, children."

"Good morning, Lord St. Aubyn," the chorus of younger ones sang.

"Good morning. Why don't all of you head up to the ballroom? Miss Ruddick and I will join you in a moment."

"Oh, nonsense," she returned with a forced chuckle. "We'll all go up together."

To make sure that St. Aubyn wouldn't intercept her, she joined hands with Rose and Penny. She needed—and wanted—to confront him about his treachery and his duplicity, but not until she decided what she wanted to say. And not until she could do it without bursting into tears or, as satisfying as it would be, punching him.

Saint fell in behind as the gaggle of orphans and their beloved Miss Evie climbed the stairs to the third floor. Apparently the orphanage's entire populace wanted to practice the waltz.

Hanging back to watch suited him for the moment, anyway. Considering the heated dreams that had tortured his sleep for the few hours he'd managed to close his eyes, Evelyn's greeting this morning had been like a bucket of cold water dumped over his head.

She'd probably heard about his confrontation with Dare and Wycliffe in Parliament and was attempting to punish him for his poor behavior. Since he hadn't maimed anyone, however, he didn't think he'd behaved all that badly.

Evelyn stopped in front of him, and he blinked. Her gown this morning was a soft rose muslin that somehow deepened the gray of her eyes. All she needed was a pair of wings to complete her angelic appearance. Him, lusting after an angel. No doubt both God and the devil were laughing at him.

"Will you partner with Molly?" she asked, her gaze somewhere past his shoulder.

"Which one is Molly?"

Gray eyes met his, then darted elsewhere again. "Don't you know any of their names?"

Considering her mood, it probably wouldn't be wise

to mention that he'd spent more time at the orphanage in the past two weeks than he had over the last entire year. "I know your name."

"I'm not a resident of an establishment under your supervision. Molly is the green-eyed girl with the short red hair. She's skittish around men, so be nice."

She would have walked away, but Saint grabbed her arm. "Don't give me orders, Evelyn," he said in a low voice. "I'm here because I choose to be."

Evelyn shrugged free. "Yes, well, the children aren't."

His sense of humor, already damaged from too much gin and not enough sleep, dwindled even further. "And do you think a few dancing lessons will improve their lot in life?"

A tear ran down her cheek. Evelyn swiped it away with an abrupt, impatient gesture. "And do you think tearing down their home will? Don't you dare dictate your nonexistent moralities to me."

Damnation. "Who told you?"

"What does that matter?" she retorted, her face pale. "You are a despicable man. It makes me ill to look at you."

Saint gazed at her. Anger swept along his muscles, anger and frustration, because now he would never have her. And if he couldn't have what he wanted, neither could she. "Leave," he snapped.

"You—What?"

"You heard me, Evelyn. You are no longer welcome here. Get out."

Another tear ran down her cheek. "May I at least say good-bye?"

Her crying still bothered him. Whatever was wrong with him lately was her fault, he decided, but her damned tears still troubled him—even when he was angry enough to strangle her. He nodded stiffly. "You have fifteen minutes. I'll be waiting downstairs."

"Very well."

Saint took one step closer. "And just remember, whatever you tell them, you're not going to change anything. So I suggest you consider your little darlings' feelings and keep your mouth shut," he murmured.

"Bastard," she muttered at his back.

Without a backward glance, he descended the stairs. When she looked around again, all of the children were staring at her. Whatever they knew, they had no power to change any of it. And she had no more control of this situation than they did. Only three or four people aside from St. Aubyn even knew she was here. So much for her supposed convictions about changing the world.

"What's wrong, Miss Evie?"

She hurriedly wiped her eyes again. "I'm afraid that I . . . have to go," she said. It was the most difficult sentence she'd ever uttered.

"That's all right," Penny said, skipping forward to take her hand. "You can waltz with us tomorrow."

Oh, dear. "No, Penny, I can't. I've . . . I've . . . been asked to leave."

"St. Aubyn don't want you here anymore, do he?" Randall Baker scowled.

"No, that's not . . ." Evie stopped. She was tired of defending everyone and standing up for everyone when they so obviously didn't deserve it. She was not going to lie to these children—and certainly not on St. Aubyn's behalf. "No," she began again, "he doesn't."

"Why not?" Rose, tears in her own large brown eyes, grabbed Evie's other hand.

"Because you wouldn't let the bastard under your skirt, I'll wager." Matthew Radley pulled a cigar from his pocket.

She blushed. "You shouldn't say such things, Matthew."

"We all know it, Miss Evie." This time it was Molly who stepped forward. " 'E never used to spend much time here until you came." Her lower lip quivered. "And now he's making you leave."

"We should lock St. Aubyn in the dungeon and let the rats eat 'im."

Matthew's suggestion met with cheers from the other children. Evie could understand the sentiment, but flights of imagination and plots of devilish revenge only took away from her remaining time with them. And she knew St. Aubyn would come to get her if she didn't leave when he specified.

"Unfortunately, Matthew, you are children and I am a woman, and he is a marquis. And we don't have a dungeon. Penny, why don't you fetch a book, and I'll read one last story to all of you?"

"We do have a dungeon," young Thomas Kinnett insisted. "With chains and everything. And we have rats, too."

"What are you talking about?"

Penny tugged her toward the back stairs. "Come on. We'll show you."

Whatever they thought they'd seen, it seemed important to them. And if St. Aubyn or any of the other board members had set up some nefarious chamber of horrors, she could alert the authorities and maybe even stop demolition of the place. Dark as St. Aubyn was, dungeons didn't quite seem his style, but at the moment she was so angry that she wouldn't put anything past him.

The children, unusually quiet for them, led her to the back of the building and down four flights of older, even more decrepit stairs to the large larder. The cellar was crowded with old boxes and bedding and new supplies for the orphans—sacks of flour, barrels of apples, and the like. In the musty, windowless dimness it did seem rather . . . dungeonlike, but she had to admit that she saw nothing horrific or remotely illegal.

"Yes, it's very scary in here," she agreed, so as not to hurt their feelings, "but unless we pelt the marquis with apples, I don't see anything useful."

"Not here, Miss Evie," Randall said with a slight, superior grin. "Over there."

Together he and Matthew and Adam Henson, another of the older boys, shoved aside a stack of old bedding. Once the dust settled, she made out the outline of a door in the wall the old mattresses had concealed. Randall elbowed it open while Molly produced a candle.

Inside, a short, narrow set of steps led to another door, this one slightly ajar. A small window inset with bars decorated the top portion of it. "Randall, let me go first," she said, lifting the candle.

"But there's spiders," Rose whispered from behind her.

Spiders? "All right, but be careful," she said shakily, motioning the tall youth to precede her.

He grinned and pushed the heavy door open the rest of the way. "Right."

As soon as she entered, she realized what the small room must be. "This is the old soldiers' brig, I would imagine," she whispered.

Two sets of shackles, two each for wrists and ankles, hung from the walls. A small stool and a bucket were the only furniture, other than a pair of sconces for candles on either side of the door.

"You see?" Thomas asked, lifting one of the leg shackles and dragging it halfway across the room until the chain went taut, "we could lock Lord St. Aubyn in here and no one would know."

"Well, it's a very nice thought, my dears, and I do appreciate it, but kidnapping a nobleman is not a good idea."

"But if we made him stay in here, you could keep visiting us every day." A tear ran down Penny's cheek.

Her brother, William, put a skinny arm around her shoulder. "Don't cry, pretty Penny."

"But I wanted to learn how to read."

"Aye, so did I," Randall said in a grimmer voice. "And I heard him tell Mrs. Natham once that he should just tear down this place and be done with us."

"Oh, Randall, don't—"

Matthew chuckled around the stub of his unlit cigar. "'E couldn't tear it down if he was locked underneath it, now, could 'e?"

Evie stared at the towheaded boy. They were just bandying stories; they had no idea the marquis actually meant to reduce the orphanage—for some of them the only home they'd ever known—to a pile of rubble.

"You're tempted, ain't you, Miss Evie?" Randall said in a lower voice. "We'll make you a bargain: You promise to come back in a few days, and we promise you won't have to worry about St. Aubyn trying to stop you."

Her heart began to race. Saint had warned her that some of the orphans here were already master criminals, but she had to wonder if he had any idea just how far they would go if they felt threatened. Whatever she told them, once she left today they might very well attempt to lock the marquis in here, and someone would more than likely get hurt—or worse. And even if they did manage it, they could never let him out. Abducting a nobleman, even one with as scandalous a reputation as St. Aubyn's—was still a hanging offense.

On the other hand, if Saint could be forced to become acquainted with them, to see how badly these children needed someone to care about them, and how desperately they needed this family they'd formed for themselves at the Heart of Hope Orphanage, maybe he would change his mind.

She blinked. And maybe he would learn what it was to be a gentleman, and a man in the best sense of the word.

Oh, this was insane. But if she turned her back or even attempted to warn St. Aubyn, the children would end up in a worse position than if she'd never come to the orphanage at all. If she kept control of the situation, though, made the rules and guided the plot, maybe, just maybe, she could save everyone. And even make a difference.

"All right," she said slowly, sitting on the stool, "we all have to agree to this. And we all have to agree that I'm in charge. What I say, goes. Agreed?"

Matthew pulled the cigar from his mouth and saluted. "Aye, aye, Captain."

"Good. I have to tell you something first. And we must work quickly."

Chapter 11

Brightest in dungeons, Liberty! thou art;
For there thy habitation is the heart.

—Lord Byron, "Sonnet to Chillon"

Saint paced the length of the foyer. He should have given her five minutes to pack up her books and her instructors and leave, and nothing more. Apparently the tears of Evelyn Ruddick were his Achilles' heel, however, and now all he could do was check his pocket watch every two minutes, and curse.

"She thinks I'm despicable," he muttered, mimicking her indignant tone. "My presence makes her ill."

No one said that to his face and got away with it. And certainly not someone he found interesting. Not that she interested him that much—it was just that he seldom spent time around anyone who seemed so . . . pure.

Too pure to wish to taint herself with his presence, obviously. Well, he would see about that. He would see her begging for him before he was finished with her. The angel would find herself considerably tattered—and everyone would know it.

He flipped open his pocket watch again. Two minutes

left. If she didn't appear soon, he would go up and get her. Saint snapped the watch closed. In fact, why wait?

"Saint?"

He whipped around. Evelyn stood at the staircase, her cheeks flushed and her chest heaving. "Get your books," he snapped. "Time is up."

She didn't move. "I've been thinking."

Suspicion washed through him. She didn't look incapacitated with tears as he'd half expected, and she wasn't pleading with him either to let her continue reforming the orphans or to stop his plans for destruction of the damned place. "About what?" he asked anyway.

"About . . . about how you said you never do anything for free."

Evelyn was nervous—and that wasn't all; he could practically smell the charged air between them. "And?" he prompted, all of his senses coming to attention.

She cleared her throat. "And I was wondering," she said in a voice so quiet he had to strain to hear her, "what price you would ask to keep the orphanage open."

Saint hadn't stayed alive for this long by being a fool. The angel was up to something. On the other hand, if it involved the two of them being naked, he was all for it. Still . . . "I thought I made you ill."

"Yes, well, I was angry."

"And you're not any longer?" He didn't attempt to hide the skepticism in his voice.

"I don't understand how you could close the orphanage," Evelyn said slowly. "Your mother—"

"For God's sake," he interrupted, "if we're talking about a seduction, don't mention my mother."

"My apologies," she said with a nervous grimace. "I'm new to this."

"To what?"

"You . . . you're going to make me say it?"

He strolled up to her, abruptly in much less of a hurry to see her gone. "Yes, I am," he replied, and kissed her.

She was going to make him promise things, no doubt, and if she timed it right, he would agree to whatever she said. Just talking to her about it left him hard and aching. Of course, he would also listen very carefully to how she worded her requests. Long experience had taught him there was more than one way to bed a woman—and more than one way to be rid of an orphanage.

He lifted his head, but Evelyn pursued him, raising up on her toes and twining her dainty fingers through his hair. She pulled his face down for another kiss. Almost of their own accord, his hands slid around her slender waist. He tugged her up against him.

"You still have to say it, Evelyn Marie," he murmured. Her damned classrooms were the closest private place he could think of. The doors didn't lock, but all the brats thought she'd gone. "Say it."

"I . . ." she began breathlessly, her gaze on his mouth, "I want to know if you'll stop your plan to tear down the orphanage if . . . if I . . ."

Sweet Lucifer. Angels could be a frustrating, pitiful bunch. "If you take me inside you," he whispered, pulling a clip softly from her hair. Auburn waves of lemon cascaded over his hands.

"Yes."

Saint shook his head, removing the second clip. "Say it."

Her cheeks flushed and, her lips already swollen from his attentions, her breasts pressed hard against his chest, the pristine angel moaned. "If I take you inside me," she whispered.

Difficult as logical thought was becoming, he was nevertheless aware that her choice of phrase regarding the orphanage left him a fair amount of room to maneuver. "That is a deal, Evelyn."

"Not here, though," she said, gasping as he brushed the outside of her breasts with his thumbs. "The children—"

"How about one of your little classrooms?" He captured her mouth again, only partially aware that he didn't usually react like this. Of course, he'd been suffering through a nearly three-week drought, but this lust, this hunger, was new. And it was hunger for *her*—not some nameless, faceless female to satisfy his needs.

"No. Oh, Saint. More private. Please?"

She wasn't even able to utter full sentences any longer. "The boardroom."

"The cellar," she countered. "It's after breakfast, and—"

"The cellar," he agreed, grabbing her hand and pulling her to the stairs. A clean patch of dirt would have suited him at the moment.

"But my hair," she protested.

"We'll go down the back way. No one will see you."

Because of its history as a barracks, two sets of stairs descended into the cellar; the ones from the kitchen, and the ones through the old administrative office for keeping a tally of supplies as they arrived.

Saint grabbed a lamp from the hallway and pushed the office door open. "Are you sure this won't do?" he asked, yanking her up against him for another kiss. Thank God she'd decided to give in, because he wasn't certain how much longer he would have been able to keep his hands off her without going stark, raving mad.

"Windows," she managed, clinging to his lapels.

"I'm going to make you scream with pleasure," he whispered against her mouth.

If they paused here much longer, he, who prided himself on his self-control, wouldn't be able to walk. Saint took her hand again to lead her through the far door and down the stairs.

As soon as they reached the cellar floor, he pressed her back against the stone wall, meeting her upturned mouth with a hot, openmouthed kiss. Finally, just the two of them, with no one to interrupt for at least an hour, until the kitchen help began luncheon preparations.

"Evelyn," he groaned, kissing her throat, peeling back the collar of her gown to kiss her shoulder.

"I'm sorry, Saint," she whispered, her breath coming already in hard, fast gasps.

Sliding one arm back around her waist, he pulled her up against him. "What are you sorry for?" he breathed, kissing her again.

"It's for your own good."

"What—"

A footstep sounded behind him. Saint whipped around as something blunt and heavy crashed down against the side of his skull. He uttered a half-articulate curse and collapsed.

Evelyn stared down at the Marquis of St. Aubyn as he lay slumped at her feet. She couldn't move, couldn't speak, couldn't think of anything. They couldn't change their minds now, and yet in the hot, sensual place Saint had awakened inside her, she almost wished they had been alone in the cellar, and that he'd fulfilled his promise to make her scream with pleasure.

Randall lowered the oak bedpost. "I've been wanting to do that for a year, now."

Shaking herself out of her nervous, aroused, and shocked stupor, Evie sank to her knees. "He's still breathing," she exclaimed, sagging further with relief. Aggravating as St. Aubyn was, she didn't want him dead. Even the thought left her feeling oddly . . . empty with imagined loss.

"A course he's still breathing," Randall said in an annoyed tone, obviously disgusted that she could doubt his expertise in the field of head-bashing. "Let's get him in the brig before Nosy Nelly comes down to steal apples."

"Nosy Nelly?" Evie repeated, brushing hair from Saint's forehead as another half dozen children materialized from the gloom around her. A trickle of blood ran past his ear, and she checked again to make sure his heart still beat. He looked so . . . innocent, with his face relaxed and the cynicism gone from his expression. Innocent, and beautiful. The most beautiful man she'd ever seen.

"One of the cook's helpers. Come on, lads. Heave 'im up. If we drag 'im, we'll leave tracks."

Randall seemed to know a great deal about kidnapping. Evie stood, stepping back as the six oldest boys grabbed legs, arms, and waist and, with much groaning and complaining, lifted St. Aubyn off the floor.

"Be careful with him," Evie cautioned, lifting a candle to guide them to the narrow, half-hidden door.

"Now you say that," Matthew grunted. "Just think what he'd be doin' to us right now if he was still awake."

Evelyn shuddered. Even knowing his seduction would be stopped, she still felt dazed and a little resentful. Saint was going to be furious. According to rumor, he'd killed people in duels over slights to his honor; this must fall somewhere far beyond that.

They'd thrown a fairly decent mattress and clean

blankets in the far corner, batted down the spiders and cobwebs, and stolen two lamps for the wall sconces. With less than fifteen minutes to prepare, they'd actually done an impressive job of readying the room for a resident.

The boys tossed St. Aubyn onto the mattress with less care than she would have liked. The marquis groaned.

"Cripes! Get the shackle on him!" Adam Henson yelped, jumping backward.

"Wait!" Evie broke in, struggling free of the haze that had enveloped her. "Don't hurt him!"

"Too late now, Miss Evie. He'll see us all on prison barges or transported to Australia."

"Or hanged," Randall added, squatting to fasten the shackle.

"Do we at least have a key for that?" she asked, beginning to feel light-headed.

"Aye. And for the door."

"Give them both to me, if you please."

Matthew obediently handed the brass keys over to her. Evelyn pocketed them and sat heavily on the stool. Good heavens, what was she doing? Kidnapping a marquis was worse than insanity. On the other hand, without her involvement, Randall and the other boys might have chosen a more permanent and deadly solution to the problem of St. Aubyn. With her in possession of the keys, she could at least protect him to a degree.

"He's waking up," Adam announced.

"All right, everyone out. I don't want him to know who hit him. And close the doors, but leave a candle on the stairs. Don't do or say anything out of the ordinary."

Randall grinned. "We'll make a criminal of you yet, Miss Evie."

She didn't seem to need their help with that. "Go. Hurry."

Seconds after they closed the barred door, Saint came awake with an abrupt start that made Evie jump. With a low, almost inaudible groan, he rolled onto his hands and knees.

"Are you all right?" she asked, her voice shaking as badly as her hands had begun to.

"What the hell happened?" he grumbled, putting a hand to his temple. It came away bloody.

"It's a long story. Do you need medical assistance?" They couldn't summon a doctor, of course, unless Saint's injury was life-threatening. If pressed, she could probably sew up a wound, though even the thought made her distinctly queasy.

"No. What I need is a pistol. Who hit me?" Slowly he straightened up onto his knees, looking across the room at her where she perched on the stool.

"I can't tell you that. Saint—"

As his gaze sharpened and focused, he began looking at their surroundings. "Where are we? Are you unhurt?"

"Me? I'm fine. I need to—"

Staggering, one hand pressed against the wall for balance, Saint climbed to his feet. "Don't worry, Evelyn. I'll get us out of here."

Oh, dear. Now he wanted to be chivalrous. "Saint, you don't understand. I'm not a prisoner. You are."

She watched as he slowly absorbed what she'd said. Then, faster than she could draw a breath to explain, he sprang across the room at her. "You damned—"

The chain snapped taut, and he went down almost at her feet. With a shriek, Evelyn fell backward off the stool. Saint reached for her, and only missed her ankle because she jerked her knees up to her chest.

"Stop that! You'll injure yourself!" she gasped, rolling to crawl away from him as fast as she could. Her gown was going to be ruined, but if he got his hands on her, her clothes would be the least of her worries.

The keys fell from her pocket with a thunk. Evie squirmed around as Saint lunged for them. The chain pulled him up just short. He clawed into the hard-packed earth, stretching out his fingertips, trying to reach them as she snatched them up and scooted backward again.

"Give me those damned keys," he growled in a dark, angry voice.

This was the St. Aubyn everyone feared, she realized, the man he was with the veneer of civility torn away. And she'd managed to awaken him alone in a dungeon, with no help in earshot—not that she dared call for any.

"Calm down," she ordered, backing away still farther, even though there was no way he could possibly reach her.

He drew up into an alert crouch, green eyes glittering with a fury that made her blood chill. " 'Calm down?' " he snarled, swiping again at the dirt-mingled blood running down his cheek. "I'm shackled to a wall, God knows where, and—"

"We're in the orphanage cellar," she interrupted. "The old brig, I would assume." She sat up straighter, pocketing the keys again.

His eyes followed every move she made. "Why am I shackled to the wall in the goddamned orphanage cellar, Evelyn?" he asked in a low, dangerous-sounding growl. "And who hit me?"

He obviously wasn't going to be able to listen to reason at the moment. If anything, trying to speak in a rational manner with him would only make him angrier.

Evie reached behind her for the wall and pulled herself to her feet. "I think you should calm down a little, Saint," she suggested, wishing her voice would stop shaking. "I'll bring you some water and a cloth for your head." She edged toward the door.

He straightened, pacing her at the end of his chain. "You are not going to leave me here, damn it. Evelyn, this is ridiculous. Give me those keys. *Now.*"

"I can't do that. And I'm not leaving you. I'll be back in a few minutes."

He gazed at her levelly. "If you don't give me those keys now, you'd best hope I never get out of here," he said in a low, hard voice. "Because the first person I come after will be you."

And she'd been worried he might want to see her arrested. Evie swallowed. "If you ever want to get out of here, you'd best not say such things," she said grimly, and slipped out the door.

Chapter 12

Though pleasure fires the maddening soul,
The heart—the heart is lonely still!

—Lord Byron, "One Struggle More,
and I am Free"

Saint froze as Evelyn closed the door. A lock clicked, and through the narrow-spaced bars he heard the tap of her shoes as she climbed six, seven, eight steps. A second door squeaked open and then closed, leaving him in utter silence.

He stood there for another moment, listening. Nothing. Dust coated his jacket, trousers, and waistcoat. The inside of his mouth and his nails felt caked, as well. He spat into the dirt, then clanked back to the mattress in the corner and sat.

They'd—and he knew Evelyn hadn't done this without assistance, whatever she might say—locked the shackle over his boot, just above his ankle. It was a snug fit, and the rust-coated iron was already doing a splendid job of ruining the leather of his expensive Hessians.

Experimentally he tugged at the clasp, then at the ring that joined the shackle to the chain. Nothing budged. Link by link he worked his way back to the iron ring sunk and bolted into the wall. All the work was as solid as if it had been installed last week, rather than last century.

Sitting back again and crossing his legs as best as he could with the left one chained to the wall, he began going through his pockets. Some money, a handkerchief, his pocket watch, a button that didn't belong to him—Fatima's walking dress, he thought—but nothing remotely helpful in aiding his escape.

Saint fingered the cut on his temple again. He'd been an absolute idiot. Why had he thought Evelyn meant to spread her legs for him? Because he'd wanted to think that. She'd acted odd and distant all morning, then had lashed out at him in fury, and he'd accepted that she would twenty minutes later offer her body as a bribe because he wanted it to happen.

He'd underestimated her, which in an odd way pleased him. As dicey as were some of the situations in which he'd found himself, no angry husband or jealous lover had ever managed to lock him into a dungeon.

"Damnation." He gave the chain another hard yank, but only succeeded in cutting his finger on a sharp-edged link.

Whatever lesson Evelyn thought she was teaching him, he wasn't having any of it. No chit bested him at anything. All he needed was to discover what she thought she wanted from this, and then use that to free himself. And revenge where she was concerned was going to be very sweet, and it was going to take a very long time.

If not for his pocket watch he would have thought much more than thirty-seven minutes passed before the door at the top of the eight steps creaked open again.

Saint lurched to his feet, clutching at his head as another wave of dizziness hit him.

The key turned in his door, and he leaned back against the wall, crossing his arms over his chest. Maybe she would forget how far his chain reached, and she'd wander into his grasp.

"Saint?" she said in a low voice, peeking her head around the door.

He didn't answer, instead measuring the distance between the end of his reach and the door—a good six feet, by his guess. Whoever had built the brig had wanted to be sure no one got out until or unless they were supposed to.

"I'm glad to see you've calmed down a little," she ventured, her color still high and her expression nervous. She'd dusted off her gown and put her hair back up, though she still looked as disheveled as he felt. "Will you listen to me now?"

"Yes. I'd love to hear how beating me over the skull and kidnapping me is—how did you put it?—'for my own good.'"

Evelyn winced. "Lady Gladstone told me once that you were so bad you didn't need to be good."

Fatima had more intelligence than he'd given her credit for. "And you disagree, I take it?"

"Yes, I do." She stepped back into the doorway and reemerged with a tray. "Water and a cloth, as I promised."

Saint continued to observe, curious as to how she intended to give them to him without coming within reach. He tensed, ready to move at the hint of a mistake on her part.

She set the tray down, though, well beyond the reach

of his shackles. Reaching back through the door to her unseen helper, she returned with a broomstick, which she used to push the tray toward him.

"You haven't by any chance done this before, have you?" he asked, not moving.

"Of course not."

"When I said I intended to be your first, this wasn't what I meant."

Evelyn flushed, hurrying over to whisper something outside and close the door. "I understand why you're angry," she said, turning the stool back upright and sitting down again. "You've been injured, and someone has taken away your freedom, all against your will and your wishes."

"Not someone," he corrected. "You."

"Well, someone had to."

Saint narrowed his eyes. Normally he enjoyed the give and take of their conversations, but normally he wasn't chained to a wall and forced to endure them. "Get on with your speech, Evelyn."

"Very well. I took your freedom before you could take something from me."

"Your virginity?" he suggested cynically. "You offered it to me."

"No, I didn't! That was a ruse."

"Hoyden."

"Stop it. You're trying to take the home away from these children. And you're trying to take away my ability to do something worthwhile. My chance to make a difference. You're just like all of the other men in my life, you know."

Whatever she meant by that, it sounded insulting. "No, I'm not."

"Yes, you are. Victor sends me to talk to disgusting

old men because they think I'm charming. He doesn't care if I have to lie to them about how interesting I find them, or whether the stupid political teas he makes me attend are useless and worthless and make me very . . . nervous. And you—you're worse."

"Do tell."

"You only let me into the orphanage because you thought it would give you the chance to lift my skirts. You're handsome, and exciting, and . . . enticing, but I do have a mind, you know. You don't know me, and you don't know these children who depend on you for their lives. All you care is that it's inconvenient."

His angel certainly had a mouth on her. He would never have expected it, but at the moment he didn't much appreciate it. "Are you finished?" he snapped.

"Not yet. As of this moment, nothing is inconvenient for you. You now have all the time in the world. And someone else gets to judge whether you should be let loose into Society again or not." She stood. "And ponder this, Lord St. Aubyn. If you never reappear, will anyone even miss you?"

A cold chill went down his spine. "Evelyn, think about what you're doing," he said slowly, beginning to realize just how deep the hole he'd dug for himself was. "If you don't let me go right now, do you think you'll ever be able to do so?"

She stopped, one hand on the door handle. "I hope so. You're a very intelligent man. I think you could also be a good man. It's time for you to learn something."

Evie closed and locked the door, then sagged against the heavy closure. She'd never spoken like that to anyone in her life, and it actually felt good to finally say those things aloud.

On the other hand, the situation terrified her; she could never allow harm to come to him, but neither could she allow him to swear out a statement against the children. "Please understand," she whispered, a tear running down her cheek.

The encounter had actually gone better than she expected, considering that she hadn't known precisely what she was going to say until she'd begun speaking. The dark, predatory speculation in his eyes bothered and excited her still, but she supposed a hard look was better than yelling and attempted attacks.

Eventually he might even appreciate the lengths to which she was going in her attempt to turn him into a true gentleman. Evie sniffed, wiping her cheeks. Kidnapping hadn't been part of the lesson plans she and Lucinda and Georgiana had concocted. Straightening, she managed a grim smile. Last year they'd worried that Georgie's maneuverings were going too far. Lord Dare had had it easy.

Upstairs she gave another lesson in the waltz, then ran through a few last-minute instructions for the older children as they were all called down for luncheon.

"Do we have to feed him?" Molly asked, scowling.

"Of course we do. And be nice to him. He doesn't like being in there, and we need to show him how to care for people besides himself."

"And if that don't work?" Randall asked, squinting one eye.

"It will work," Evie returned, with more confidence than she felt. Dangerous as it could be, her plan wouldn't succeed unless St. Aubyn could be made to interact with the orphans under his care. "He'll probably be mean at first. We'll have to show him better manners."

"I'll show him some fine manners," Alice Smythe cooed.

She'd been afraid of that; she knew firsthand how charming Saint could be. She would never fall for his kisses again, but these girls—these young ladies—could be very susceptible to him. "Just remember how important this is. He's very devious, so no one is to go in to see him alone. And I'm keeping the key to his shackle with me. If he knows you don't have it, there's no reason for him to try to take it from you."

"Seems like there's an easier way to take care of this." Randall pulled a small whittling knife from his pocket.

Oh, good heavens. "No. Having Lord St. Aubyn as an ally is much better than having him . . . dead. Promise me that none of you will harm him."

"You want a promise? From us?"

"Yes, I do. And I expect you to keep your word."

Randall jabbed his knife into a bedpost. "All right. We promise."

The rest of the children echoed him, and finally Evie could breathe again. They had lessons to learn, just as Saint did. And for some reason she seemed to have been chosen to deliver them. "I will see you first thing in the morning. Good luck."

When Evelyn reached Barrett House she was only twenty minutes late, but she couldn't rid herself of the feeling that she'd lost more time than that, and that somehow everyone could see right through her and know that she'd kidnapped St. Aubyn and was holding him captive in the cellar of the Heart of Hope Orphanage.

"Evie," Lucinda said, rising to clasp her hands. "We were getting worried about you."

Evelyn forced a careless laugh and went to the couch to kiss Georgiana on the cheek. "I'm not that late, am I?"

"No, but you're usually never late at all."

"I was playing with the children."

"And your gown?" Lucinda asked.

Evie looked down. She'd tried to clean up, but patches of dirt still sullied her dress where she'd fallen to the floor. "Oh, dear," she said, forcing a chuckle. "I suppose I should play less enthusiastically."

"And your hair?" Georgie fingered one of the strands that had come loose from her haphazard bun.

Blast. "Some of the girls and I were doing our hair. Is it too hideous?"

Lucinda chuckled. "I'll have Helena make general repairs before you leave."

They chatted about the week's events, as they always did, and Georgiana regaled them with an anecdote about Dare's youngest brother, Edward, who had just turned nine. Evie slowly began to relax, though she couldn't escape the vision of Saint chained alone in a cellar while she nibbled at tea cakes and laughed with her friends.

"How goes your other lesson?" Lucinda asked, sipping her tea.

"Which other lesson?"

"You know—St. Aubyn. Or have you decided to take our advice and select a more reasonable student?"

"I haven't seen him today," Evie blurted before she could stop herself. *Blast it, she sounded like an idiot.* "And . . . I have to confess," she went on, pretending not to notice the look her friends exchanged, "he's more of a challenge than I expected."

"So you'll forget him, then, yes?" Georgiana took her hand. "It's not that we doubt you, Evie. It's just that he's so . . ."

"Awful," Lucinda finished. "And dangerous."

"I thought the idea was to choose someone awful," Evelyn countered. "You kept telling us that Dare was the worst man in England, Georgiana. I thought that was why you chose him."

"I know." The viscountess gave a small smile. "I had personal reasons for wanting to teach him a lesson. You both knew that. You have no such connection with St. Aubyn."

She did now. "Nevertheless," Evie said aloud, "I am determined to teach him how to be a gentleman. Think of all the maidenly virtue I might be saving."

Lucinda put an arm around her shoulder. "Just protect your own. Be careful. Promise us that, anyway."

"I promise," Evelyn repeated obediently, beginning to wonder whether Saint was having a greater influence on her than she was on him. She never used to be able to lie with any success at all. "I'll be careful."

"Good. And if you need a distraction tonight," Luce went on with a smile, "I'll even dance with your brother."

Evie frowned. "Tonight?"

"The Sweeney ball, my dear. Even St. Aubyn's been invited to the mayhem, from what I hear."

Her insides turned to ice.

She'd hoped to have a few moments to go check on St. Aubyn before the ball, but by the time she returned home and changed, Victor was pacing in the foyer.

"Heavens," she said, taking her wrap from Langley and pulling it on herself when Victor declined to offer his assistance, "you don't want us to be the first arrivals, do you?"

"Yes, I do, actually," he returned, taking their mother's arm and leading the way down the front steps. "I've been trying to have a word with Lord Sweeney for over a week. He's spent time in India, as well. I won't have a better chance to recruit him than this. He may even get me an audience with Wellington."

She stifled a sigh. "And what are Mama and I to do while you're recruiting, then?"

Victor glanced at her like she was a child's porcelain doll who'd suddenly developed the power of speech. "You're to chat with Lady Sweeney, of course."

For a moment she considered mentioning that she had a rude, arrogant marquis locked in a cellar, and a second set of manacles ready for another occupant. Instead, she smiled. "I'll do my best."

Saint didn't know what time it was, because he couldn't see his pocket watch. He was fairly certain it was first thing in the morning, though he was mainly judging by the rumble of hunger in his stomach and the scratch of his whiskers.

Neither did he know how long he'd been awake, though it seemed like hours. What little sleep he'd managed had been interrupted by restless dreams in which he took his vengeance on Evelyn Marie Ruddick's naked body again and again, until he awoke aching and hard.

"Idiot," he muttered into the darkness, the sound hollow and dull in the small room. She'd kidnapped him, probably concocted the entire plot, and he still lusted after her. Whatever lesson she'd meant to teach him about desiring a stubborn, devious virgin, he hadn't learned.

For a time he'd considered what she'd said, about the consequences if he never reappeared in Society again. His servants were used to him vanishing for several days without a word, and he'd just made an appearance in Parliament, so no one would begin to miss him there for weeks. Because of Evelyn he was between mistresses, so no woman would be crying about missing him from her cold bed.

As for friends, he really didn't have any left. While they'd mended their ways and married, or died of their bad habits, he'd simply sunk deeper into the black heart of London. Even that, though, wasn't as black as this prison had become when the last candle went out. So that was it. No one would miss him at all.

He shuddered. He didn't fear dying; he remained surprised that he'd lasted as long as he had. Rather, it was the idea of being completely forgotten that bothered him. No one to mourn him, no one to wonder where he'd gotten to, no contribution he'd made that would make anyone regret his absence.

The outside door squeaked, and he sat up straighter. A moment later a small trickle of light crept through the bars at the top of the door, touching the upper part of the wall behind him.

A key rattled in the lock, and the door pushed open. Candlelight flooded the room, and he squinted against it. A moment passed before he could make out Evelyn behind the light.

"Oh, I'm so sorry about the lamps," she exclaimed. "I thought—"

"These are foul accommodations," he interrupted. "I don't suppose you have any coffee, either? Or a newspaper?"

He heard a boy's voice on the far side of the door utter an admiring curse. At least he'd impressed someone. Saint lifted an eyebrow.

"I have coffee," she said, setting the candle on the sconce. "And buttered bread and an orange."

"At least you've spared no expense to see to my comfort," he said dryly.

She brought the tray in, setting it on the floor and pushing it to him with the broom handle. Saint was too hungry to be stubborn, and he leaned forward to drag the tray closer.

"Didn't they feed you last night?" Evelyn asked, sitting on the stool beyond his reach.

"Someone cracked open the door and lobbed a raw potato at my head, if that's what you mean," he replied, digging into his scanty breakfast. "I decided to save it for later."

"I'm so sorry," she said again, watching him eat.

"Evelyn, if you're sorry, then let me go. If you're not going to do that, then for God's sake stop apologizing."

"Yes, you're right. I suppose I'm just trying to set a good example."

"For me?" Saint paused between mouthfuls of bread. "You have an odd method of teaching manners."

"At least I have your attention," she retorted.

"You had my attention before."

"For my looks, yes," she said slowly. "But now you have to listen to me." She folded her hands primly in her lap as though she were sitting in an elegant morning room and not in a dirty, stone-walled brig. "So what shall we chat about?"

"Your prison sentence?" he suggested.

She paled so alarmingly that for a moment he thought she might faint. He almost took his statement back, but stopped himself. She might think she was in complete control here, but he did have some power remaining. It was best that she remember that.

"I'm sure we can come to some sort of agreement eventually," she returned after a long moment. "After all, I have all the time in the world to convince you."

She was learning the rules rather quickly herself. "So how did you pass your evening, then?" he asked.

"I attended the Sweeney ball, actually," she said. "Oh, and you should know that my brother credits your absence to his warning you away from me."

He grunted. "I should have listened to him."

She was silent for a moment, and when he glanced up, he caught her studying his face. Evelyn blushed and made a show of straightening her skirt. "I have a small bargain for you."

"And what might that be?"

"I will bring you a chair to sit on, if you will read to some of the children."

He could refuse, of course, but his back was already aching from sitting on the hard floor. "A comfortable chair," he returned. "With padding."

Evelyn nodded. "In return for a comfortable chair with padding, you must also teach them their vowels."

"By writing in the dirt?"

"I will provide you with a writing board. And an instruction book."

Saint moved his coffee cup aside and stood, bringing the tray up with him. While she rose from the stool, watching him warily, he walked to the end of his chain. "And another candle." With a clatter he dumped the tray at his feet.

She hesitated for a moment, then nodded, gray eyes meeting his. "Done."

"It's a shame you don't like me," he said in a quieter voice, conscious of the little brats waiting for her just outside the door, "because I could use some company right now."

A small smile touched her mouth. "I'll see what I can do about that."

She turned and strolled back to the door. "I'll come by again before I leave. Behave yourself with them."

"They're not the ones you should be concerned about." He gazed at her steadily, making certain she understood his meaning, before he toed the tray beyond his reach.

Whatever she'd said about not liking him, she still felt attracted to him. He didn't need to be a soothsayer to sense that. And she hadn't left him there alone in the dark again, a salvation he was feeling more grateful for than he probably should. Still, all he needed from her was one false step. If she thought he wouldn't take advantage, she was greatly mistaken.

Chapter 13

He, who grown aged in this world of woe,
In deeds, not years, piercing the depths of life,
So that no wonder waits him; nor below
Can love, or sorrow, fame, ambition, strife,
Cut to his heart again with the keen knife
Of silent, sharp endurance: he can tell
Why thought seeks refuge in lone caves, yet rife
With airy images, and shapes which dwell
Still unimpair'd, though old, in the soul's haunted cell.

—Lord Byron, *Childe Harold's*
Pilgrimage, Canto III

"**N**ow who are you?"

The little girl rolled her eyes. "Rose. And that's Peter, and that's Thomas. And we're supposed to tell you that we don't have any keys."

Saint pursed his lips. Evelyn had sent the babies to him, evidently deciding they were the ones he was least likely to harm. "And you don't have my chair, either."

"Miss Evie said you have to show good fate first."

"Good faith, you mean?" he corrected.

"I don't know, because I'm only seven years old. Are you going to read to us now?"

The older of the two boys, Peter, shoved a storybook

at him. Obviously Evelyn had instructed them not to get too close, because all three had plunked themselves in the dirt in the corner beside the door.

He picked up the book and opened it. "Did Miss Evie say why I'm supposed to read to you?"

"So you can have a chair," Thomas answered.

"And so you'll like us," Peter continued.

"So I'll like you?" Saint repeated. That made sense. She was trying to convince him not to destroy the orphanage by acquainting him with the orphans. She wanted to soften his heart; a shame, then, that he didn't possess one. "Let's begin, shall we?"

Odd as it felt for him to be catering to children, he had to admit, as he read and showed them the pictures, that it was better than being in the brig alone. Infant company was better than none at all.

"Isn't this nice?" Evelyn's voice came from the doorway. "Is Lord St. Aubyn a good storyteller?"

Rose nodded. "He makes the scary bits very scary."

"I'm not surprised at all." She entered the brig. "It's time for you to go up to luncheon. Remember to take the back stairs and go around through the dormitory."

"We remember. And we're not to say anything about him."

"That's right."

The children scampered out the door. "Lovely," Saint noted. "Teaching them to be criminals in infancy. Saves trouble later, I suppose."

"I'm only asking them to keep a secret for the benefit of all the children here."

Saint closed the book and set it aside. "You're only delaying the inevitable. Could you kill me, Evelyn Marie?"

She swallowed. "I have no intention of harming you. Not for any reason."

That actually surprised him. "Then this orphanage will be turned into one of the Regent's parks."

"Not if you change your mind."

"I won't. Who are my next pupils to be?"

"Just one. Me." Evie looked over her shoulder. "But first I promised you a chair."

She moved aside as Randall and Matthew hauled a heavy cushioned chair, obviously liberated from the board's meeting room, into the cell. Their wary attention on St. Aubyn, they dragged the chair to the edge of his reach.

"That's good enough. Tip it forward, and he can drag it the rest of the way."

"Aye, aye, Captain," Matthew said, grinning as he kicked the chair over backward.

Evelyn wished they weren't enjoying this so much, especially in front of St. Aubyn. The marquis's expression didn't change, however, and he kept his gaze on the two boys until they left the cell, closing the door behind them. "One of my fellow board members warned me that I would turn this place into a thieves' rookery," he said in his low drawl. "It seems you've beaten me to it."

"I don't consider working toward one's self-preservation to be thievery," she retorted. "And besides, the chair is orphanage property. We've only relocated it."

Standing, he heaved a sigh. "My backside's too tired to waste time with arguing semantics." With no apparent effort, he righted the chair and dragged it into his corner beside the mattress.

He looked tired and disheveled, and in desperate need of a shave. His fine clothes were covered with dirt, and a dark smudge of the stuff ran across his cheek, where it had mingled with his blood. It was odd, because attractive as she'd always found him, he looked even better to her now. The polish was gone, but the man underneath remained as enticing as ever.

"Trying to think up your next torture for me?" he asked, sinking into the chair with a sigh of relief that couldn't possibly be faked.

"You need a shave," she said, feeling her cheeks warm.

"Well, all I have for the task is my watch fob, and it's not very sharp."

"I'll see what I can come up with." Evie sat on the small stool. "I think it's time I explained my position to you."

He sat back, closing his eyes. "I thought you'd done that. I'm in here because I've stepped between you and your only chance to make a difference in the world."

"Rose has lived here since she was two, you know. And so has Matthew, and Molly since she was three and a half. This is their home."

"They can just as easily make a home in another orphanage. One without me on the board. You could even volunteer there, and save the world from King's Cross Road or somewhere."

"That's not the point. They've become brothers and sisters, and you want to break them apart because it's inconvenient for you to be here."

Green eyes opened, gazing at her. " 'Inconvenient' doesn't begin to describe it, Evelyn. My mother and her little waifs. It was ridiculous. She was convinced they would give her some horrid disease. Her way of showing bravery and conviction was to line them up for inspection once a month."

"You told me that."

He nodded. "And then, when she contracted measles,

she blamed the brats for it. And still in her will I was to look after the Heart of Hope Orphanage. She didn't have time to change it." Saint gave a short, humorless laugh. "The darlings did kill her, after all, and now she's stuck me with them."

St. Aubyn's dislike of the orphanage ran deeper than she'd realized. Evelyn looked at him for a long moment. "They aren't brats, or darlings, Saint. They're only children, without anyone else to watch over them."

Crossing his ankles, the chain clanking as he did so, Saint closed his eyes again. "They have you, Evelyn. Only you're too ashamed to tell anyone else that you're even here, aren't you?"

"I am not ashamed. This . . . doesn't fit in with my brother's ideas of my duties, and so I've had to be secretive about it. That's all."

"Do you ever ask yourself what bloody good it is teaching them how to dance or how to read, Evelyn?" he went on. "Once they turn eighteen they leave, and other than the females dancing in some bawdy house waiting for someone to pitch them a penny to lift their skirts, I can't think of a single practical bit of instruction you've handed out yet."

Evelyn clenched her hands together, determined not to let him see how much his words upset her. "The dancing and the reading are a means to an end, my lord," she said stiffly. "I'm here to provide a little kindness, to show them that the entire world is not populated by heartless, self-centered, arrogant men like you."

"Those are brave words while I'm chained to a wall, my dear," he murmured, eyes glittering through half-closed lids. "Perhaps you might show me a little kindness and bring me some luncheon."

He'd had little enough to eat this morning that he was probably starving. "The children will bring you something when they return for their afternoon lesson in vowels." She stood, dusting off her skirt, then paused. "Do you have a heart at all, really?" she asked.

"If I do, you're not likely to convince me of it here." He straightened. "If I teach them their consonants, might I have a pencil and some paper?"

"Yes. Of course. I'll come see you before I leave."

She left him sitting in his chair. She'd known that convincing him not to dispose of the orphanage was going to be a monumental task under any circumstances; having him locked in the cellar made the situation more difficult still. At least she still had one thing on her side. Time. Time, and patience. And, she hoped, a great deal of luck.

When she returned to his cell at the end of the day, he was no more cooperative than he'd been earlier. She couldn't blame him; if she'd been locked alone in a dungeon in the dark all night, she would have been far closer to hysterics than anger. For that reason, she provided him with a candle and flint so he wouldn't have to go through that again. Still, she hated leaving him and going home when he couldn't. He'd done it to himself, she kept repeating as she returned to Ruddick House and changed for dinner.

"Evie, you haven't listened to a thing I've said all night." Victor set his glass of Madeira down hard enough to make the scarlet liquid slosh over the side. A footman immediately appeared to sop up the wet and re-fill the glass.

"I told you that I just have a bit of a headache," she returned, blinking. She'd hardly touched her dinner, and she would need her strength for her next round of verbal combat with St. Aubyn. Grimacing, she went back to work on the roast pheasant.

"Even so, I would appreciate if you would make an effort to pay attention. Lord Gladstone has invited you and me over for dinner tomorrow night. I've accepted on your behalf."

She choked on the mouthful of bird. "You—"

"Apparently Lady Gladstone mentioned me to him, and she thought you were charming. Please make sure that you are. Plimpton's been courting them ruthlessly, so this may be our last opportunity."

"Don't you wish Mama to go in my place? She's so much better at polite conversation than I am. And—"

"No, I wish you to go with me. You're the one Lady Gladstone knows." He took a bite and chewed. "Thank God I sent you over to make her acquaintance. You made an impression, after all. Thank you."

"You know," their mother said from the far end of the table, "Lady Gladstone and that awful St. Aubyn are rumored to be lovers."

"That's another thing," her brother took up. "Do not mention that scoundrel in Gladstone's house. He's likely to have an apoplexy, and then where would we be?"

"But you don't mind me being friendly with Lady Gladstone?"

Victor frowned at her. "She's the reason we've been invited."

"Even though she's rumored to have taken a lover behind her husband's back? I thought you were campaigning for morality."

"People like to say they support morality. And I won't have you saying anything different. St. Aubyn's been panting after you as well, as I recall. Or was it you panting after him, to annoy me?"

"Neither," Evelyn answered stiffly.

"I wonder that anyone tolerates him at all," Mrs. Ruddick noted around a slice of bread.

"Probably because he doesn't pretend to be anything other than what he is," Evie returned.

"Would that we all had that luxury." Her brother sighed. "This is only for a few more weeks, Evie. Please come with me."

She lowered her head. "Yes, Victor."

Evie excused herself early, then went to lurk in the library until Victor disappeared into his office, closing the door behind him. A few minutes later, Hastings, her brother's valet, went down by the servants' stairs to collect tomorrow's shirts and cravats.

"Steady, Evie," she said to herself, and darted up the hallway to her brother's bedchamber.

Already laid out on his dressing table and ready for Victor's morning ablutions, she found his razor, shaving soap, and shaving brush. She took everything, including the cup.

Bundling them into the handkerchief she'd brought along for the occasion, Evie listened at the hall door for a moment, then hurried out to her own private rooms. Once she was certain she was alone, she laid the items on her bed to study them.

Of course she couldn't allow St. Aubyn access to the razor, because once he had a weapon, she'd never be able to get close enough to release him. That meant she would somehow have to shave him herself. She knew the mechanics of shaving a man, though she hadn't actually done it since she'd been seven and her father had let her smear soap on his face. Shaving Saint, though, was not going to be the problem.

"Hmm," she mused, strolling to the fireplace and back again. The brig had come equipped with manacles, but convincing him to put his wrists in them would be impossible without some sort of leverage.

And leverage where Saint was concerned meant either her body or a pistol. A low thrill went through her at the thought of what he might request from her in return for this. At the same time, he would remember her previous ruse, and he wasn't likely to fall for it again. St. Aubyn might be lustful and decadent, but he wasn't a fool by any means.

A pistol, then, though he had to know she would never shoot him. One of the boys would be a better choice, but the thought of Randall or Matthew with a firearm filled her with dread.

Slowly she lay back on the bed, dusting the dry shaving brush across her chin. Of course, if Saint *thought* she'd armed the boys, she probably wouldn't actually have to provide them with ammunition.

Evie smiled. Once she procured one of Victor's pistols, Saint would find himself clean-shaven in the morning. Perhaps she might even beg some cold pheasant from Mrs. Thatcher, the cook, for his breakfast.

Saint tossed another pebble into his bucket. He'd already done sketches of Evelyn, himself, the grim reaper, and his students on the scant half dozen sheets of paper she'd provided for him. And he'd read the book Evelyn had left with him enough times to have it memorized, despite the fact that it was a ladies' etiquette book called *The Mirror of Graces,* by "A Lady of Distinction." It sounded like something Evelyn and her fine friends would author. She'd failed if she meant it to enlighten him, but the thing had at least given him a chuckle or two.

He hated being bored. In fact, he'd spent a great deal of energy in his life avoiding that very thing.

As Evelyn had pointed out, at the moment he had nothing but time. And the problem with that was it lent itself to all sorts of unhealthy things—like thinking.

He sent another pebble into the bucket. Even with a tallow candle for his personal use, the silence and solitude of the night seemed to last forever. Concentrating on physical discomforts was easier than dwelling on whether his servants had done anything more than note his absence for a second night in a row, or whether anyone else in London missed his presence at all.

To be sure, the physical annoyances of his enforced stay were mounting; his clothes, his skin felt grimy, his left ankle alternated between throbbing and numbness, and his face itched. Worse than anything else, though, was a sensation he'd never before been conscious of—he felt lonely. He, the Marquis of St. Aubyn, felt lonely.

Absently scratching at his chin, he reached for another pebble, then froze as the upstairs door squeaked open. He started to pull on his discarded jacket, then decided it was a useless gesture. At this point, nothing was going to make him look friendlier or less dirty.

He did check to make certain the lengths of his chain he'd buried beneath his mattress remained well hidden. With any luck, someone—Evelyn—would forget how much room he had to move, and he'd be able to liberate the shackle key.

He scented lemons as the door opened, and even before she stepped into view, he knew Evelyn had come again to see him. However insane her little plot was, at least she seemed genuinely concerned that he remain in good health. That was more than he could say for most people of his acquaintance.

"Good morning," she said, eyeing him warily. He didn't blame her; he hadn't been nice yesterday, but then she hadn't deserved anything else.

"Good morning. You've brought my ration of bread and water, I hope?"

"Actually, I managed a pheasant sandwich and hot tea."

His mouth began to water. "Really? What do I have to agree to in order to receive this delicacy?"

"Nothing."

Matthew something-or-other carried the tray into the cell and pushed it toward him with the broom handle. Trying not to act as starved as he felt, Saint stood up, retrieved his breakfast, and sat in his nice, soft chair to eat. Two other children replaced his spent wall candles with new ones, and Saint licked his thumb and forefinger to pinch out his reading candle. No sense wasting light.

Evelyn cleared her throat, and he realized he'd been wolfing down his sandwich in a fairly uncivilized manner. "My compliments to the chef," he muttered, taking a swallow of tea. He preferred more sugar, but he wasn't about to complain. At least the potato they'd shoved at him last night had been boiled.

"Thank you," she answered, smiling.

Saint stared at her softly curved lips until their amused expression faltered. He arched an eyebrow to cover his discomfiture. Solitude was obviously making him insane. "*You* made my breakfast?"

"It's actually my lunch, but I thought you'd appreciate it more than I. And yes, I made it."

"Then I thank you," he said, venturing a smile of his own. He no doubt looked like a half-starved escapee from Bedlam, but she didn't run away screaming in terror. Evelyn, he was beginning to realize, was a great deal braver than he'd given her credit for.

"You're welcome." She turned away, walking back to the door, and he lurched forward so abruptly he nearly dropped the tray.

"Are you leaving?" he blurted, grabbing the remains of his sandwich before it pitched onto the floor.

Evelyn stopped, looking over her shoulder at him. "No. I brought you another present. Two, actually."

"One of them isn't a key, I suppose?" he suggested. "Or perhaps they involve you removing your clothes?"

She blushed prettily. "You're hardly in a position to be saying such things."

"I'm shackled; not castrated. Unless that's your surprise."

Evelyn's mouth twitched, but she only disappeared behind the door for a moment, returning with a small, laden table and Randall. Saint kept his attention on the youth; he couldn't prove anything, but he was fairly certain Randall had been the one to put the club across his skull.

"First," Evelyn said, putting down the table, "I must ask for your cooperation."

That didn't sound promising. Saint swallowed his last mouthful of sandwich. "My cooperation in what?" he returned slowly. The tray wasn't much of a weapon, but it would at least serve as a distraction if necessary. He gripped the edge of the flimsy thing.

Evie looked nervous. "I need you to . . . to stand up and slip your right hand into that manacle there."

Saint just stared at her.

"Now, please."

Several responses came to mind, but Saint dismissed them all as perfunctory and inadequate. "I may look a bit bedraggled," he spat out finally, "but allow me to assure you, Evelyn, that I would sooner chew off my own foot than allow you to chain me to that wall."

She paled. "You misunderstand. It's only for a few minutes, so . . . so I may shave you."

Well. That was unexpected. Anger began to slide into something warmer and less tangible, though he had enough pride remaining that the entire situation infuriated him. "Let me shave myself."

"I won't provide you with a razor, Saint."

"Smart chit. I don't feel particularly civilized, however, and I don't see the point of letting you fool yourself into thinking you've made me more comfortable by removing my damned whiskers."

"That isn't the point," she insisted. "I am attempting to bring out your better qualities. I believe it's easier to behave like a gentleman when you look like a gentleman."

He folded his arms. "But I'm not a gentleman."

"Nevertheless," she returned, "please cooperate."

"Aye," Randall echoed, pulling a pistol from behind his back, "do as Miss Evie says, m'lord."

"Hmm," Saint mused, every sense alert as he slowly set the tray aside and stood, "I suppose even the devil could pretend to be a gentleman if someone aimed a pistol at him."

Evelyn didn't appear to be surprised at the appearance of the weapon; she'd probably provided it to the lad. Saint wondered whether she had a real idea of how many laws she was breaking in the course of her little experiment.

"It's just a precaution, Saint," she said in a soothing voice. "Please do as I ask."

She didn't let out the breath she'd been holding until he took a slow, deliberate step toward the wall. She'd known that he would rebel against further restraints, but it would have meant something if he'd cooperated without the need for the pistol. Of course, Randall hadn't given him much time to consider his options.

His jaw clenched and his eyes hard and cold, he lifted the right-hand manacle from where it hung along the wall. The look he sent her said she would pay for doing this, but she was already so far in trouble that adding more to the pile hardly signified. With a deep breath he put his right wrist against the clasp and snapped it closed with his left hand.

Evie glanced at Randall, noting the practiced and steady grip the young man had on the pistol. Thank goodness it wasn't loaded. With an unsteady breath of her own, she crossed into Saint's domain within the cell.

His right wrist hung suspended about level with his shoulder. His left hand, however, was still free, and he looked angry enough that she couldn't be entirely certain the threat of a pistol would prevent him from grabbing her. She could just forget the entire thing, let him grow a beard down to his knees, but her argument was serious. She needed him to be a gentleman, and he therefore needed in his own mind to have the appearance of one. Besides, even if she changed her mind now, she would still have to approach him to unlock his wrist.

"Frightened of me, Evelyn?" he murmured, apparently reading her thoughts.

"Just cautious," she returned, closing the distance between them.

With his jacket removed, his shirtsleeves pushed up, and his cravat dirty and wilted, he somehow seemed even more masculine and virile than before. Evelyn was abruptly and forcefully reminded that even with the amount of time spent in his company, they hadn't touched in three days. And the last time they *had* touched, he'd been removing her gown and sticking his tongue in her mouth.

"Your fingers are shaking," he noted, lowering his left hand.

"Be careful now, Marquis," Randall cautioned.

"You don't need to make this so difficult," she said, stopping in front of him. Holding her breath, she reached down and took his wrist in her fingers.

"Yes, I do." Saint lowered his voice so it was barely more than a whisper. "I know what you want."

He didn't resist as she raised his arm and closed his left wrist in the manacle. "And what is it that I want?" she asked, feeling bolder now that he was secure.

Saint gave a faint grin, lopsided and dark through three days' growth of whiskers. "It's not for me to be a gentleman, Evelyn Marie." He glanced past her at Randall. "Tell him to leave. You don't need him right now."

If she had any sense, she would do no such thing. With Randall there, though, St. Aubyn would never converse with her about anything serious or important. And besides, in the deep, dark part of her that whispered this was all an excuse to touch Saint again, she knew she didn't want Randall present, either.

She half turned. "Randall, hide the pistol in the cellar where none of the children will find it. You're scheduled for a reading lesson with Mrs. Aubry right now, aren't you?"

The boy nodded his lanky blond hair. "Aye. Don't you let him go without me here, though."

"Of course not. Will you come back in thirty minutes?"

"You sure you want to do this?"

"Yes. It's necessary."

"Whatever you say, Captain. He better start bein' convinced soon, though."

"He will be."

The boy left, closing the door behind him.

"Be careful about him," Saint said in a low voice, his face turned toward the door as though he were listening for something.

"Randall?"

He returned his attention to her. "If you don't help his cause as he likes, there's nothing to stop him from locking you in here with me."

She looked up at him, a small, uneasy thrill running through her. "Are you worried about me?"

"I think you're in a great deal more trouble than you realize, and I think any mistakes on your part might get me killed."

So he was still only thinking of himself. "You've threatened to take his home away from him. How is he supposed to react? How are any of them supposed to react?"

He scowled. "I remain unconvinced. And at the moment, Evelyn, you are very precious to me." Saint rattled the chains imprisoning his wrists. "So be careful. I don't wish to end up as a skeleton in the cellar of an orphanage."

"You won't." This was ludicrous. Even in the middle

of a mercenary proclamation, he could say she was precious to him and it made her pulse speed. It was only because he showed such little concern for anyone else; when he did so, even in passing, it was as spectacular as a stroke of lightning.

"Evelyn?"

She started, her gaze darting back to his enigmatic green eyes. If he knew what she'd been thinking, he didn't say. Evie blushed anyway. No one made her blush as he did; probably because no one said things that made her self-conscious, made her think outside her prim, proper life as he did. "My apologies. I was considering your warning. I will keep it in mind."

"Good."

"And now I believe you need a shave."

"To be honest," he returned, his expression softening a little, "my face itches like the devil."

Evie wished that he would remain angry; wry and charming, the Marquis of St. Aubyn stirred into life far too many unaccustomed sensations.

Taking another breath, she backed up to retrieve the little table. Fortunately she'd escaped Ruddick House before Victor rose and found his things missing. No doubt she would hear about the theft when she returned home, and all during the evening with Lord and Lady Gladstone. "Oh, bother," she muttered, mixing the shaving soap with water.

"I did offer to do this myself."

With a grimace she dunked the brush into the soapy water. "You're not the bother. My dinner appointment is."

"Tell me why."

She paused, the brush halfway to his chin. "Why do you want to know?"

"Why not? It's not as though I have anything to do but listen to your scintillating tales."

"It's nothing. My brother and I are invited to dinner with Lord and Lady Gladstone."

His expression didn't change, even though he and the countess were known by everyone to be lovers. "I don't suppose you'd give my regards to Fatima?"

"No, I won't." Evie knocked the brush against his chin, and more lather than she expected splattered onto his face, his neck, and his wilted cravat. "Apologies."

"Don't apologize; tell me why you don't like dear Fatima."

"Humph. Tell me why you do like her."

"Lovely soft breasts, long, slender legs, and a willingness to s—"

"Stop!" she demanded. "She's someone else's wife!"

He shrugged, the manacles clinking against the rough stone wall. "I take her marriage vows as seriously as she does. As they all do. You can't be that naïve."

"I don't consider my opinion naïve. I like to think it's honorable."

Saint gave a short, humorless laugh. "You are unusual, Evelyn. I'll give you that. Now, are you going to shave me, or just throw soap on me?"

"You're awful." Evie lowered her hand, just staring at him. How could she feel . . . attracted to this man?

"I never said I wasn't awful. It's not my fault if you view me as something other than what I am, my dear."

For a long moment she kept her silence, considering. "I prefer to think that I view you as what you could become, under your cynicism and your whiskers." Slowly she raised the brush again, sliding it up along his cheek. "And I intend to reveal that person."

"He died a very long time ago, I'm afraid. And no one, including myself, mourned his passing."

"Stop talking. I'm trying to do this right." Dipping the brush into the soap again, she lathered his other cheek. She liked touching him when he couldn't do anything about it, when the contact was entirely on her terms.

"Have you decided how long my sentence is to last?" he asked when she set aside the cup and picked up the razor.

"I prefer to think of it as your enforced education."

"If our positions were reversed, I could think of several ways to educate you," he said with the hint of a smile. "I'm at your mercy, Evelyn. Is shaving me the wildest, wickedest thought you could come up with?"

His low, sensual drawl made her shiver. Her fingers trembling, she backed away for a moment to collect herself. "Behave," she commanded.

Saint shifted his gaze from her face to the razor. "At least kiss me good-bye before you cut my throat with that."

"Shh." Pressing the fingers of her free hand against his chin to hold him steady, she slowly, carefully ran the sharp blade of the razor down the side of his face. "This would be easier if you weren't so tall," she complained, letting out her breath.

"Use the footstool," he suggested, clanking the chains again as he indicated her seat on the far side of the room.

He seemed awfully helpful suddenly, and as she retrieved the stool and stepped up onto it, she realized why. Evie found herself at eye level with St. Aubyn, her face only inches from his.

"I—"

Lurching forward against the restraints, Saint captured her mouth in a hard, soapy kiss.

She felt it all the way to her toes. All she had to do was back away a few inches, and he wouldn't be able to reach her any longer. The knowledge made her feel . . . powerful, even as his hard, demanding mouth against hers left her breathless and aching for things she didn't dare express aloud.

Evie kissed him back, tangling her free hand into his dark, disheveled hair and boldly running her tongue along his teeth. Saint moaned, and a hot, tingling sensation ran down her spine and started a low warmth between her thighs.

Oh, he was right. There was so much more she'd rather be doing with him than shaving his face. She kissed him again, hot and openmouthed. The chains around his wrists rattled as he pulled against them, trying to embrace her. He was hers, and she could do whatever she wanted with him. Whatever she wanted.

"Stop," she hissed, more to herself than to him.

"Why, Evelyn?" he murmured, seductive as the devil. "Touch me. Put your hands on me."

She wanted to, so badly that it hurt physically to step backward off the stool to the floor. "No."

He scowled, soap smeared across his face and one cheek smooth. "You want me as much as I want you. Come here."

Evelyn shook her head, trying to clear her mind of the warm, intoxicating haze his presence inspired. "This isn't about what you or I want; it's about what's best for those children."

"Don't flatter yourself," he retorted, making a last lunge toward her against the chains and then falling back against the wall. "Did you really think shaving me would turn me into your version of a hero? You wanted to touch me. You still do; you're trembling for it."

"I am not." She tucked her hands behind her back.

"Let me go, Evelyn. Forget this nonsense, and I'll take you somewhere with satin sheets and rose petals." He lowered his voice still further, to that soft, sensual drawl that left her heart racing. "I want to be inside you, and that's where you want me."

"You're fooling yourself," she retorted, pacing to the door and back again. "Yes, you're handsome, and I'm sure you're . . . skilled at your seductions." Oh, he was infuriating, and even more so because his words created images in her mind that enticed and aroused her. "You'd best remember, though, that you're not chained to a wall because your better qualities outweigh your poor ones."

He lifted an eyebrow. "And?"

"And so you'd best stop trying to seduce me and start listening to what I'm saying." She grabbed the stool, moved it back half a foot, and tromped onto it again. "Now hold still."

"As long as you're holding a blade to my throat, my dear, I'll do as you ask. But I'm not here because I want to be convinced of something. I'm here because you lied to me and locked me up. You're the one with a task. And I don't plan on being here much longer, so you'd best get on with it."

At least he'd made her angry enough that she wasn't thinking about kissing him any longer. Saint wasn't a coward, to bait her while she held a razor in her hand. Still, if she expected him to become civilized, she would have to lead by example.

Evie took a deep breath. "I have no doubt, given your . . . keen sense of self-preservation, that you will try to escape." She slid the razor down his other cheek, trying to ignore the sharp green eyes watching her every move. "For that same reason I also believe you will listen to the argument I present to you."

A slow, wicked smile curved his mouth. "Before you start presenting your argument, you should wipe the soap off your chin, Evelyn Marie."

Chapter 14

His love was passion's essence—as a tree
On fire by lightning; with ethereal flame
Kindled he was, and blasted; for to be
Thus, and enamored, were in him the same.

—Lord Byron, *Childe Harold's*
Pilgrimage, Canto III

Saint hoped someone was tending his horse. Evelyn had mentioned that they'd put Cassius into the old barracks' stables, which made sense; whether his peers missed him or not, someone was bound to notice a prize bay Arabian tied outside the Heart of Hope Orphanage for a week. Feeding the stallion was a different part of the equation, but considering Evelyn's compulsion to rescue children, he assumed she would be equally diligent about feeding his animal.

A damned, bloody week. She'd even brought him a copy of the *London Times* yesterday, just to prove that no one had come forward to say they were missing a marquis. He paced to the end of his shackle and back again, as he'd been doing for the past hour. It hardly counted as stretching his legs, but he needed to do something for exercise.

He'd been playing along with her, learning all the orphans' names, teaching the infants their letters and numbers. It passed the time, if nothing else. He knew what Evelyn was looking for: some sign that he'd grown a conscience and had fallen in love with the little brats. The stubborn, prideful part of him refused to go along with that scenario, even to fool her. Admittedly, some of the orphans were brighter than he'd expected, and a few of them seemed actually to have a share of wit. And yes, having them about was better than pacing alone in his dungeon.

The two or three oldest boys bothered him, not so much because of the hard looks they had for him, but because of the way they seemed to treat Evelyn's orders as a game. He knew several of them were members of the local thieves' rookery, and without his intervention, they might very well have begun hiding stolen items or even their older fellows in the orphanage. If Evelyn stumbled across one of them, her keen sense of righteousness and honor would not protect her for an instant.

The board of trustees would have met yesterday. In his absence, he had no idea what scheme they might be contemplating now to fleece the orphanage of the current month's funds, since of course they had no idea he was planning to pull the proverbial orphanage rug out from beneath them and their purses. Even more frustrating, he had no idea which of them might have stepped in to assist Evelyn's little education project in his apparent absence. They would be oh, so helpful, and flatter her intellect even though they believed her to be nothing but a pretty innocent with feathers for brains.

His door rattled and opened, and he stopped his pacing, startled. His students were early for their afternoon session, and he hadn't heard the door at the top of the stairs open. Damned Evelyn distracted him even when she wasn't about.

"What's this?" a female voice said, and the house-keeper's head edged around the door. "Saints preserve us," she gasped as she saw him.

Thank God. "You," he demanded, striding to the end of his chain, "fetch me an axe or a hacksaw at once." Evelyn still had the key to the shackles, and he needed to get out before any of the children realized what was going on and could warn her and whoever she'd given that damned pistol to.

"What are you doing here, my lord?" she asked, taking in the shabby room and the mattress and the books stacked against the wall.

"I'm being held prisoner," he snapped. *Wonderful. Rescued by a bloody imbecile.* "I don't have a key to the shackle, so I need an axe. Hurry, if you please."

"I was wondering what the children were doing, creeping down here at all hours. I thought maybe they'd taken in a stray dog or something. Bless me, though, they've captured a nobleman."

"For God's sake, Mrs. . . . Housekeeper, get—"

"Natham, my lord," she interrupted. "Natham. For four years, it's been Mrs. Natham. I heard the wee ones whispering that you were going to sell this place. That would put me out of work, you know."

"We can discuss your employment later. In fact, freeing me will earn you a reward. Fetch me—"

"Hmm. I'd best talk this over with Miss Ruddick, I think. She's been down here, too, if I'm not mistaken. It's been awful pleasant upstairs, the past few days. And she's given me a salary increase, too. Nice lady, Miss Ruddick."

"Yes, she's wonderful. Now—"

"Good day, my lord." Slipping her head back out of the cell, she slammed the door closed. A second later the key turned in the lock, and a moment after that he swore he heard her hoarse chuckling as she climbed the short set of stairs.

Saint dropped into his chair, growling curses in several different languages. Evelyn had probably sent the hag down here to prove her point that his friends and allies were few and far between.

He knew that already. He'd known it practically since he was seven years old. They'd sent a solicitor to the family estate to tell him that his father had died in London and that he was now the Marquis of St. Aubyn. He'd barely known the old marquis, who had whored and gambled until his fiftieth year, then married and fathered an heir. That task finished, he'd gone back to whoring and wagering until it killed him. Saint intended to model his life after the man. It made more sense than the rest of the hypocrisy leveled at him once he donned his black mourning jacket and half-pants.

His mother had been so busy with huge mourning dinners and soliciting male support from her many new admirers that she hadn't returned to St. Aubyn for more than six months. The servants in residence at St. Aubyn Park had fawned over him in her absence, hoping to be retained if the family should relocate upon the widow's probable remarriage. When his mother and new papa *du jour* suggested he go away to boarding school, he'd been relieved to escape the pandering.

His instructors and his fellow students, though, had carried on the new tradition of bowing to his every whim. Rules didn't apply to a twelve-year-old marquis with a bottomless income, and he had long ago realized that he could get away with anything short of murder. He'd come into his majority before his mother died, and once he had control over her income, she'd been as fawning and sycophantic as anyone else.

He didn't trust anyone any longer, nor had he for years, and so he'd become someone no one would want to trust. He knew then why anyone sought his company; with his reputation as he'd carved it out, the contact couldn't be for friendship, so it had to be that they'd been drawn in by the smell of power and money. Those fools, he knew precisely how to deal with.

Deciphering Evelyn took considerably more time and effort. She'd told him what she wanted: to save the children, the orphanage, and him. The most difficult part of the puzzle was that she seemed to be telling the truth. She had no ulterior motives that he could discover, and nothing he'd said or done or offered seemed to have swayed her an inch. And that was remarkable, especially considering that the foe to all three of her goals was the same exact person—him.

Her existence, then, was simply . . . impossible. No one was that pure; no one's motives were that noble. And no one *ever* tried to change him. They changed themselves to become more amenable to what he wanted, so they could have what they wanted. Period. *Ergo facto finito.* And no one locked him up when he refused to play their game. They went away and bothered someone else.

Saint kicked one of the few pebbles remaining on his side of the cell. So he'd been missing for a week and no one had noticed. His solicitors paid his staff at his London home and his various estates, so none of the servants would fret over his absence. Hell, they were probably enjoying it, drinking his expensive French wines and smoking his American cigars.

With a scowl and another curse at Mrs. . . . . *Natham,* damn it all, he stood again, yanked off his shirt, and tossed it onto the pile with his discarded cravat, waist-coat, and jacket. This morning Molly and Jane had brought him a washing cloth and a bowl of clean water. What he wanted was a bath, but that seemed unlikely at the moment.

Plunging the cloth into the water, he wrung it out over his head, letting the cold water course down through his hair and past his shoulders. The upstairs door squeaked open, but he ignored it. He knew precisely what he was doing, as he always knew; he was feeling sorry for himself. His afternoon class could damned well wait until he was finished washing and sulking.

He didn't see the point of him teaching etiquette to anyone, much less to a herd of orphans. Of course, it was part of Evelyn's plan to civilize him. Well, he'd feel more civilized if he was clean.

The lock turned and the door opened. "Lord Saint," Rose's plaintive voice came, "girls don't bow, do they?"

"On occasion," he grunted, going to work on his torso with the cloth, "though there's generally a man in-volved and the chit's facing away from him and grabbing her ank—"

"Enough!" Evelyn roared.

He whipped around to face the door. She looked the vision of fury, fists clenched and stone gray eyes glinting. The muscles across his abdomen tightened. "Good after-noon, Evelyn."

Her gaze trailed down his bare chest and snapped up to his face again. "Children," she bit out, "I'm afraid that Lord St. Aubyn's lesson for today is canceled. You have free play this afternoon."

Grumbling turned into cheers, and the half dozen youngsters filed out of the cell again. Saint held Evelyn's gaze. "Who do you think you're punishing—them or me?"

"Put on your shirt."

"I'm wet."

She turned on her heel. "Fine. I'll have someone bring you dinner tonight." Breezing back out, she slammed the door behind her.

Something tight and uncertain ran up from his stomach and tightened his throat. Dinner was a good six hours away. "Evelyn!"

Her feet continued stomping up the stairs. Saint glanced at the candles. Two hours of light remained, at the most.

"Evelyn, I apologize!"

The top door squeaked open.

"Evelyn, for God's sake, don't leave me down here alone again! Please! I'm sorry!"

Silence.

Cursing, he grabbed up the water bowl and hurled it against the door. It shattered, porcelain shards and water spraying everywhere. "Is that your lesson for today, then, that you get to do what you want to do, and I get to sit on my ass in the dirt, in the dark, until you decide otherwise? I've learned that one already! Teach me something I don't know, Evelyn Marie, damn it!"

"Saint?" Evelyn's voice came from the other side of the door. "Calm down, and I'll come in."

Breathing hard, he realized what was happening. He was panicking. Him. The heartless, ruthless, soulless Marquis of St. Aubyn was afraid of being left alone again in the dark. "I'm calm," he snapped.

No one who had the power of thought could possibly have believed him, but Evelyn obviously had more compassion than sense, because she opened the door.

Saint started to say something that would convince her to remain for at least another few minutes, but he stopped when he saw her face. With a nearly audible groan, his mind angled around from thinking of his own terrors to wondering what he'd done to hurt her now. "Why are you crying?" he said in what he hoped was a more reasonable tone.

Wiping at the tears flowing down her pale cheeks, she sniffed. "Because I don't know what to do."

He raised an eyebrow. "You? You always know what to do."

Evie looked at him. Water still ran in slow, angled drips down his shoulders, down his bare chest, down his muscled abdomen, and soaked into the waist of his trousers. Damp hair hung across his left eye, and her fingers twitched with the abrupt desire to brush it back from his face. He looked so . . . innocent. And that wasn't all. She absolutely wanted to devour him.

Wiping at her face, she made a show of positioning the stool and plunking herself down on it. *He knows what he looks like,* she told herself fiercely. *He knows what to say.* This was just another part of his game, to make her wish to stay and keep him company, or better yet, to make her feel so sorry for him that she would let him go. When she felt slightly more in control of her base, counterproductive, lustful emotions, she looked up at him again, to find him still standing there, gazing at her. Evie swallowed. "I wasn't feeling sorry for you," she said.

"Of course you were," he returned, his own voice

calmer and deeper, more in control. "You feel sorry for everyone."

For her own safety, and her own sanity, she knew she had to stay one step ahead of him, one inch further in control. "I'm mad at you, not sorry for you."

"You're mad at *me*," he repeated. "And yet you're the one with the keys, my dear. Imagine my own feelings."

"Perhaps you're right." She sniffed again. "It's not you I'm mad at; it's me."

"Now we have something in common," he drawled, shaking out his hair.

Droplets flew, several of them landing on her arms. Goose bumps raised, though she thought the shiver running along her nerves was due more to the idea of being alone in a room with a very handsome half-naked man than from a few drops of water.

"For a week I've tried to show you what good you can accomplish and how kindness begets kindness. I've had your undivided attention. And yet, nothing's come of it."

Saint looked at her for a moment, an emotion she couldn't read crossing his face. "I'm a hopeless case," he finally said.

"But you can't be."

"And why not?" Saint sank onto his haunches. Reaching out, he could just bat the toe of her shoe with his fingertips.

Oh, good heavens. Now she had a handsome, desperate, half-naked man literally at her feet. "You . . . no one is as awful as you are."

"And yet, here I am."

"That's not what I mean. It's . . ."

He tilted his head, his gaze taking in, measuring, her

every expression. "You may as well be blunt. Honesty looks well on you."

"Is that a compliment?"

"Don't change the subject. We're talking about me."

"Yes, we are," she agreed. "I mean that no one—*no one*—can be as much a scoundrel as you are and still be as charming and interesting and even likable as you are."

"You've lost me."

"You're faking it, Michael."

His gaze dropped for a moment. "That's very nice of you to say, I suppose, but believe me, I am a self-serving, hedonistic bastard."

"Perhaps, but that's not all you are."

To her surprise, his mouth curved in that damned sensuous smile of his, instantly transforming him from innocent to so . . . enticing her mouth went dry. She swallowed again.

"You are a very interesting female," he murmured. "But is it for my sake or your own that you claim to see some sort of redeemable qualities here?"

"Both of us, probably."

"Honesty again." He batted her toe again, absently, like a cat playing with a ball of yarn. It was the first time he'd touched her without demanding more, a kiss or his hand up her skirt. A warm tremor went through her.

She took a breath, trying to retain her sense of logic. "Why do you behave as you do?"

"Because I can? I don't know. How, though, will you ever know if you've saved me or if I'm merely playing with you?" He straightened, making her abruptly aware that she was sitting too close.

Before she could fling herself backward, he seized her by the ankle and tugged. With a grunt, she fell forward off the stool, bumping her bottom against the hard dirt floor.

Even as she opened her mouth to scream, she realized no one was close enough to hear her. Before any sound came from her throat, Saint leaned across her, placing his hand over her mouth. "Shh," he whispered, slipping his free hand into her pelisse pocket and retrieving the shackle key. "I suppose we'll find out right now whether you've redeemed me or not," he said. "Care to wager on the outcome?"

"But—" She grabbed for the key, but he evaded her grasp, planting himself on her skirts to keep her from rising while he shoved the rusted key into the rusted lock and twisted it. With a snap the shackle opened, and he was free.

He stood to fling the restraint against the wall, and Evelyn scrambled, half crawling, for the door. If she could get it closed, the key remained in the lock, and she would still have him imprisoned.

With several long, limping strides, he beat her to the door. "It's not going to be that easy, my dear," he said.

For a moment she thought he meant to escape and lock her inside the cell, and white cold panic hit her. "Saint—"

The marquis reached around the door, pulled the key free, and closed it. "I told you this wouldn't last much longer." He smiled, catlike. "And I also said that you would be the first person I came after."

And next would be the children, and the orphanage. She couldn't allow that. Evie lunged for the door key, but he lifted it above his head, out of her reach. Unable to stop her forward momentum, she slammed into his bare chest, pushing them both back against the wall.

"Interesting strategy," he murmured, twining his free

hand into the back of her gown and drawing her closer against him. He met her gaze for a heartbeat, then leaned down to kiss her.

It was a hot, deep, openmouthed, plundering kiss, the kind that knew they had no witnesses, nor anyone likely to come looking for them—for her—for hours. She needed to get out of there, to lock him up for the sake of the orphanage. But if he was kissing her like that, some part of her reasoned, he couldn't be thinking of escape.

Evelyn kissed him back, heat searing down her spine and out along her fingers and toes. Her hands, already reaching up for the key, sank into his damp, dark hair. She wondered whether other women felt so intoxicated, so overwhelmed by his attentions. He nudged her chin up and began a series of slow, warm kisses along her jaw-line, and her breath became a fast, ragged pant. She couldn't get enough air, couldn't get close enough to him.

"You're trying to distract me," she accused breath-lessly, pressing herself against his bare, damp chest.

Saint shook his head, looking away just long enough to throw the door key across the room. "You're distract-ing me," he growled, slipping his fingers beneath the ma-terial at her shoulders and peeling the gown down her arms with aching, slow relentlessness.

His mouth and tongue and teeth followed, and he turned them so that she was the one pressed back against the wall. In a second he had her pelisse open, and he reached beneath the material to cover her breasts with his palms. Even through the thin muslin of her gown she felt the warmth of his touch, the pressure of his embrace, and she gasped.

"Saint, please," she practically whimpered, seeking his mouth again.

"Please what?" he rumbled, pulling her forward

against him to yank the pelisse off her arms and down to the floor. Like a skilled harpist playing the strings, his fingers ran down her back, and her gown loosened. Nudging her back again, he stripped the material down to her elbows, imprisoning her arms in the muslin. Before she could answer or even do more than gasp again, he took the shift, the only thing covering her front from his glittering gray gaze, in both fists and ripped it open.

"Oh! Saint, please—"

"Michael," he breathed back, glancing into her eyes before his gaze returned to her breasts. "Call me Michael."

"Michael," she managed, then couldn't even breathe.

He ran his fingertips across her breasts, light but utterly ruthless, circling closer and closer until his thumbs crossed her nipples. They hardened beneath his touch, budding as he passed his nails back and forth across them.

"Good hea . . . heavens."

"Your skin is so soft," he murmured, then lowered his face. "So soft."

With one hand he continued to tease and mold her left breast, while he ran his lips and the tip of his tongue around her right one, following the path his fingers had blazed. When he took her nipple in his mouth, she thought she would faint right there.

Evelyn lifted her chin and closed her eyes, overwhelmed by sensation as he suckled first one breast, then the other. She couldn't move, didn't want to move, as heat spread down her body and deep between her legs. With her arms half pinned, all she could reach was his waist, and she clung to him, trying to draw him closer, wanting to be part of him.

His mouth and hands left her breasts, and she opened

her eyes again. "Don't stop," she begged, embarrassed at the keen wanting she heard in her own voice.

"I won't," he returned almost soundlessly, taking the arms of her gown and drawing them down her elbows, freeing her hands and then pushing the material down to her feet.

Kneeling, he continued his slow destruction of her shift, ripping it inch by inch to her waist. Every inch of her skin that he exposed, he covered again with his mouth. Downward, past her navel, past the dark patch of hair at the apex of her thighs, traveling down her hips, her thighs, to her knees.

"Lift your foot," he instructed, and he slipped off her thin shoe, the gown with it. Repeating the action with her other foot, he trailed his hands and mouth up again, up the insides of her thighs. And then he slipped a finger inside her.

"Oh, God," she whimpered, her legs trembling.

"You're wet," he murmured. "For me."

"Michael."

"Shh," he continued in the same husky tone, standing, gliding his hands up along her body to her shoulders so he could push off the ruined shift, sending it to the floor with the rest of her clothes. "I want you, Evelyn Marie. I want to be deep inside you."

Lifting her in his arm, he carried her the few feet to his mattress and rumpled blankets, and knelt to lay her down there. He sat, turning sideways to pull off his boots, wincing as the left one came free. "You're hurt," she said unsteadily, trying to blink back to reality.

"My ankle's swollen," he answered, facing her again. "You'll pay for that in a minute."

"I—"

"You've caused swelling elsewhere, as well." He unbuckled his belt and with swift fingers unfastened his trousers. Shoving them down, he came free, erect and hard and very, very large.

"Oh, my."

"Now you've seen a man naked and aroused with wanting you," he continued, leaning over her, taking her breast in his mouth again and suckling hard.

He settled between her knees, kicking off his trousers and spreading her legs as he brought himself closer to her, until the swollen length of him pressed against the inside of her thighs.

"Michael, please," she managed, reaching up around his hard, muscled shoulders to pull him closer, her heart pounding so hard and fast she thought she would die from it.

"Please what? Say it, Evelyn Marie. I want to hear you say that you want me inside you."

"I want you inside me." She had no idea what to do to make that happen, but her body knew. Arching her hips, she lifted toward him. "Please," she said again, "please, now."

Lifting onto his hands, he covered her lips with his again, teasing her mouth open with his tongue. She felt him slide slowly inside her, between her legs. "It will hurt," he murmured against her mouth, his own breath not quite steady.

"How—"

He pushed his hips forward. She felt him reach her barrier, then with a fast, tearing pain, break through and fill her.

She shrieked, squeezing her eyes closed and arching against him, bending her knees harder. That brought him in deeper as he followed her retreat with his body. Slowly the pain eased, and when she opened her eyes he was looking down at her from inches away, his face hard with tension. "Pain for pain," he whispered, and pulled his hips away again.

"No, don't leave," she protested.

"I'm not." Slowly he pressed forward again, deeper and deeper, until he was fully buried. "And now, pleasure for pleasure."

He repeated the motion, thrusting against her, into her, slowly and deeply. Evelyn couldn't think any longer, couldn't manage a thought other than how satisfying it was to have him moving inside her. She felt heady and tense, her body tightening around him as though it knew before she consciously did that more was to come. She moaned in time to his deepening thrusts, raising her hips to meet him and clutching her fingers into his back.

"Michael, oh, Michael," she gasped, then with a pulsating rush she shattered, crying out his name.

His hips moved harder and faster, his pace more urgent. He lowered his head, kissing her deeply, then shuddered, holding himself tightly against her. "Evelyn," he murmured, tucking his face against her shoulder.

He lowered himself against her, breathing hard and hoping he wasn't crushing her. From the tightness of her grip around his waist and the slowly relaxing spread of her legs beneath him, he didn't think she minded. Good God. If that was what bedding a proper virgin was always like, he'd been missing out.

He'd meant to draw it out longer, punish her with his mounting, but when she'd come, pulling him in and pulsing so tight around him, he hadn't been able to hold back. He didn't lose control like that; not him, and not after all this time. No female made him feel that way. But she did. And he wanted to feel that way with her again.

"Michael," she whispered, and he lifted his head to look down at her.

Her cheeks were flushed, her lips swollen from his kisses. Saint kissed her again, slowly and deeply. "Yes?"

"Is it always that . . . nice?"

He could truly punish her now, if he wanted to, tell her whatever he chose. Instead, he shook his head. "No, it's not. You are exceptional, Evelyn."

With a reluctant scowl, he withdrew from her warmth and turned onto his side, keeping one arm across her slender waist and pinning her between himself and the wall. His mind didn't want to function yet, but he knew he didn't want her getting away from him. Not until he'd figured out some things. And not until he'd figured out what he needed to do next, besides make love to her again. Repeatedly.

He braced his head on one crooked elbow, looking down at her. She smiled, delicate fingers reaching up to trace his scraggly jaw. "I knew you had a good heart," she whispered.

"What does my heart have to do with this?" he asked, trying to ignore the rush that her gentle touch roused in his chest.

"Remember? You said if I took you inside me, you wouldn't close the orphanage. That's why we . . ." She frowned, obviously reading the suspicion in his expression. "Isn't it?"

Saint sat up. "Are you saying that you whored yourself for those brats?" That was unacceptable. She'd wanted *him*, not something from him. If not, that would make her just like everyone else—and she wasn't like everyone else.

"No! I wanted to . . . do that with you. But you made

a deal. That's why you wanted to be with me, isn't it? So you could keep your word?"

"I wanted to be with you because I wanted to be with you, Evelyn," he grunted, an odd, painful feeling continuing to grow in his chest. Perhaps his heart was giving out. They said that was what had happened to his father, in the end. "It doesn't mean anything other than that."

She sat up beside him, lovely and soft and still utterly naive about his empty soul, despite what he'd taught her about her body. "But you gave your word."

"And you kidnapped me. Remember that, my love?" He shifted his bruised, raw ankle for her inspection, and she gasped.

"I didn't mean to hurt you."

"I know that," he grumbled, grabbing his trousers.

"Please . . ." she began, then changed whatever she'd begun to say. "If you're going to have me arrested," she managed, "just please tell them it's all my doing. No one else's."

Trying to ignore her pleas, which continued to cause some painful commotion in the vicinity of his chest, he gritted his teeth and yanked his ruined boot back on. His other boot followed, and he picked up his dirty shirt and pulled it on over his head. He needed to get away from her, away from her soft skin and honey-tasting lips, so he could think.

"Michael," she continued anyway, putting a hand on his arm, "Saint. Don't blame the children. Please. They have no one to speak for them."

He gazed at her, pulling his arm free and standing. "They have you," he murmured, and slipped out the cell door.

Though she expected him to lock her in, he left the

door open and continued upstairs and into the main cellar, leaving her in candlelit silence.

"Oh, no," she whispered, a horrified sob breaking from her chest. They'd all be arrested, Victor's political career would be destroyed, and the children would lose the orphanage in favor of prison—and all because she'd failed. Again. All she had to do was convince him that he had a heart, and that he should listen to it. All she had to do was think of a way to keep him from razing the orphanage.

She'd failed, miserably. And now, thanks to her own stupid lust and desire and hope for a terrible, heartless man, she was ruined. Everything was ruined.

Chapter 15

For he through Sin's long labyrinth had run,
Nor made atonement when he did amiss,
Had sigh'd to many though he lov'd but one,
And that lov'd one, alas! could ne'er be his.

—Lord Byron, *Childe Harold's*
Pilgrimage, Canto I

Jansen pulled open the front door as Saint reached the top step at the entry of Halboro House.

"My lord," the butler said, bowing, "we'd begun to wonder where—"

"I want a bottle of whiskey, half a chicken, and a hot bath, all in my private rooms. Now."

"Yes, my lord."

He knew he looked the worse for wear, arriving unshaven, dirty, shirt untucked, and with his jacket, cravat, and waistcoat missing. At the moment he didn't give a damn what he looked like. He'd spent seven days shackled to a wall in a cellar and no one had noticed. No one but Evelyn Marie Ruddick. And she'd made the mistake of thinking she could change him—improve him, even. *Ha.* Well, he'd shown her.

His bedchamber upstairs looked as it always did, dark mahogany furniture, dark wall hangings, and dark, heavy curtains closed against the daylight. With a scowl, he limped to the nearest window and shoved the dark blue material aside, then flipped open the latch and pushed open the window. He repeated the action with all five windows, not pausing as footmen began struggling in with heavy buckets of steaming water. After a week in the dark, he certainly had a new appreciation for sunlight.

His valet hurried into the room, only to stop dead in the doorway. "My lord, your—" Pemberly gestured at Saint's attire. "The—"

"Yes, I know," Saint grunted. "Get out."

"But—"

"Out!"

"Yes, my lord."

If there was one thing he didn't need, it was his valet spreading rumors about his battered appearance, and especially about his ankle and the scratch marks Evelyn had left across his back. Once his luncheon and the whiskey arrived, he slammed his door closed and dropped into his dressing chair. The shirt was easy to remove, but his boots were something else entirely. With a grunt he pulled off the right one, tossing it to the floor, then went to work on the left.

The polish and smooth black leather were worn away, and after having the boot off and putting it on again, the swelling in his ankle had worsened. After several attempts and some cursing, he hobbled to his writing desk, pulled out the knife he used for sharpening quills, and sliced the boot open.

His ankle was black and blue, the skin raw and swollen. It hadn't seemed as painful an hour ago, but he'd been preoccupied then. Shedding his trousers, he stepped into the tub, hissing at the sting, and slowly sank into the hot water.

Reaching over the side of the tub, he dragged up a chair and lifted his plate of food onto it so he could tear into a drumstick. He eyed the whiskey, but now that he was in the hot bath, the need for it didn't seem as pressing.

Evelyn Marie Ruddick. Given his lifestyle, he frequently found himself in possession of information that could ruin marriages, fortunes, or his fellows. For the most part he kept the secrets, because the notion amused him. This was the first time in his recollection he had information that could send a woman to prison and probably see her transported to Australia. The children, especially the older ones, could face worse—except that Evelyn would shoulder all responsibility for their criminal actions.

And there he sat, soaking in a blissfully hot bath: not summoning a solicitor to prepare a case, not swearing out a statement against any of them—and not going to see Prince George and finalize the plan to destroy the orphanage, and not informing all and sundry that proper Evelyn Marie Ruddick had lifted her heels for him. Saint dunked his head and reached for the soap.

He'd escaped. He'd satisfied his damned lust where she was concerned, he'd freed himself from his shackles, and now he could do as he pleased, with whomever he pleased. Except that what pleased him, what occupied him at the moment, was the idea of having her in his arms again. Saint submerged in the water once more.

After this past week, and especially after today, he held more information about her than he could possibly use for any plan that might occur to him. He sat up, snorting and blowing. "Jansen!" he roared. "Bring me my mail!"

He'd missed attending a week of London's social events with her. He wasn't going to miss any more.

"Evie! We're going to be late!"

Evelyn jumped, dropping her earring for the third time. "Just a moment, Mama."

She'd tried to explain that she didn't feel well enough to attend the Alvington ball. Given her pale complexion and the way her hands shook, she'd thought convincing her mother and Victor would be simple. Victor apparently wanted her to dance with Lord Alvington's idiot son Clarence, however, and so of course he expected her to rally enough to do her duty to the family.

All day she'd waited for Bow Street Runners to knock on the front door of Ruddick House and arrest her for marquis-napping. All afternoon she'd waited for one of her mother's or Victor's friends to come calling with news of St. Aubyn's reappearance and his extraordinary tale of how she'd spread her legs for him and practically begged for his touch.

As she bent down and retrieved her earring, a sudden, hopeful thought occurred to her. Given her family's— and her uncle the Marquis of Houton's—standing in Society, the authorities might hesitate to arrest her in public. All she needed to do, then, was attend the Alvington ball and every other event for the remainder of the Season, and hide in a very dark hole between parties.

She sighed shakily. "Everyone warned you. *He* warned you. Idiot."

"Evie! For heaven's sake!"

Grabbing up her reticule, she hurried out her bedchamber door and sent up a silent prayer that by the end of the evening she would still have a shred or two of dignity remaining. "I'm coming!"

As the three of them took their seats in the coach, her mother reached over to straighten Evelyn's shawl. "You should at least attempt to look as though you're enjoying yourself."

"She will," Victor said, giving her an appraising look. "Pinch your cheeks. You look too pale."

Oh, for God's sake. The idea of prison didn't seem so awful when she compared it with this. They had no idea anything troubled her. "I'll do my best," she said, sinking lower into the corner.

"And don't forget to save the first waltz for Clarence Alvington."

"For heaven's sake, Victor, perhaps you should pin your instructions on my dress so someone can read them to me if I forget."

Her brother scowled at her. "Complain all you want in private. Just be charming in public."

His campaign must have been going well if he couldn't even be bothered to yell at her. Dinner with the Gladstones had been an interesting sort of torture, but she couldn't shake the feeling that Fatima Hynes knew something about her attraction to Saint. At any rate, Lord Gladstone had thrown his support to Plimpton. Victor, though, never ran out of ideas, or alliances.

Evie suppressed another shudder. Once St. Aubyn contacted the authorities, Victor would do far more than yell at her, because no alliance would withstand a scandal of this magnitude. She hoped if she could convince everyone that he'd known nothing of her activities, and if he worked quickly to disown her, he would survive her downfall, though she doubted it. She should probably tell him what had happened so he could devise a strategy to protect himself, but disaster already stalked her. She didn't feel up to waving her handkerchief and attracting attention.

At least in kidnapping St. Aubyn she'd had pure motives—or so she thought. Certainly having him seduce her hadn't been on her list of things to accomplish. But what she'd done with him this afternoon had had nothing to do with concern for others. She'd wanted Saint, wanted to put her hands on him and feel his embrace and know what it was like to be with him.

The terrible thing was, she'd satisfied her curiosity about the mechanics of sex, but not her yearning to repeat the deed with him. And though St. Aubyn seemed content with numerous lovers, she only wanted one— him. And the next time she saw him, he'd probably laugh at her and have her arrested on the spot.

Evie entered the ballroom behind her family, unable to keep from glancing about for uniformed soldiers—or worse yet, and as unlikely as his presence would be this evening, Saint himself. Thankfully none were in sight. A hand gripped her arm and she whipped around, a shriek rising in her throat.

"Evie," Lucinda said, kissing her on the cheek. "I heard that Clarence Alvington is prowling for you."

Evelyn forced herself to breathe again. "Yes, I'm supposed to waltz with him."

Lucinda wrinkled her nose. "Lucky you." She wrapped her arm around Evie's, guiding her toward the refreshment table. "I also heard that St. Aubyn has vanished from London. Perhaps your lessons were too much for him."

Evie managed a laugh. "Perhaps so."

"How are the orphans?"

"Shh. Please, Luce."

"I'm being very discreet," her friend returned, frowning. "But I hate that your brother can make you feel guilty about helping children. Propriety be damned."

Oh, she felt guilt about so much more than the orphanage. And it was time she acknowledged that she could be harming her friends by her mere presence. Evelyn extracted her arm from Lucinda's grasp. "At least I helped a little," she said. "But I should find Clarence before Victor finds me."

"Are you well, Evie?" Lucinda asked, her brow still furrowed. "What do you mean, 'helped'? You've finished?"

"No. Of course not. It's just that I wish I could do more."

"You've already done more than most. Don't look so solemn."

"I have a bit of a headache." She forced a smile. "I imagine surviving Clarence will perk me up. Will you do me a favor and chat with Victor while I find Mr. Alvington?"

Lucinda grinned. "I'll even dance with him."

As her friend vanished into the ballroom, Clarence Alvington emerged from the crowd by the doorway. Someone had poured him into a black coat and trousers, or sewn it onto his person, because there seemed no earthly way he could have dressed in the normal fashion with the material stretched that tightly. As he bowed, she was certain she heard threads groaning with the strain.

"Lovely, lovely Evie Ruddick," he drawled, taking her hand and drawing her knuckles across his lips. "So very pleased to see you tonight."

"Thank you." His tightly curled hair had been dampened and brushed straight, though the blond ends, now drying, had begun turning upward so that his body looked as though it were topped by a large blue-eyed flower. An upside-down daisy, she decided as he creakily straightened again.

"Will you favor me with a waltz tonight?" he continued, pulling a snuffbox from his pocket and tapping the silver lid with soft fingers.

"It would be my pleasure, Mr. Alvington."

"So polite, you are. I insist that you call me Clarence."

Evie favored him with her practiced dimpled smile. "Of course, Clarence. Until then."

"Ah. Yes. Until then, my dear." With another seam-popping bow, he strolled away.

At least the preliminary torture had been brief. "Thank goodness," she breathed, and turned around to look for an out-of-the-way place to skulk until the waltz. And stopped dead.

The Marquis of St. Aubyn stood no more than a dozen feet from her, shaking hands with one of the numerous nobleman acquaintances who didn't dare cut him in public. As she noticed him, his gaze shifted and met hers, and she dimly heard him excuse himself from Lord Trevorston.

She couldn't breathe. Her feet were frozen to the floor, her heart stopped, and she was going to expire in the middle of the Alvington ballroom. He approached, slightly favoring his left foot, and the stupidest thought occurred to her: *At least she wouldn't have to dance with Clarence.*

"Good evening, Miss Ruddick," he said, nodding at her.

He, too, had dressed in black, but unlike Clarence Alvington, no breath-strangling seams or false padding were necessary, or evident. He looked lean and hard and simply . . . deadly. And utterly desirable.

"Cat got your tongue, Evelyn?" he continued softly, taking another slow step closer. "Wish me a good evening."

"I'm going to faint," she muttered.

"Then do so."

Closing her eyes, she concentrated on breathing. He wouldn't come to her aid; he probably wouldn't even keep her from falling flat on her face. Her heart continued to beat wildly, but after a moment the cold dizziness faded. She opened her eyes again, to find him still gazing at her, the expression on his face unchanged.

"Better?"

"I don't know yet."

Brief appreciation touched his hard gaze. "No, you don't, do you? Wish me good evening."

"Good . . . good evening, Lord St. Aubyn."

He glanced past her. "If I were you, I wouldn't bother with kidnapping Clarence Alvington. It's just a rumor, but I hear that the Alvington family coffers are nearly depleted."

"Please don't say such things."

"And besides, you already have someone to share your bed. You certainly can't want him."

For a surprised moment, she wondered if that was jealousy she heard in his voice. But Saint couldn't be jealous, because he claimed not to have a heart. "My brother wants me to be nice to him. But what are you doing here? I thought you preferred darker haunts."

He pursed his lips. "I'm here because of you, my love. You thought the constabulary might hesitate to make an arrest at the Alvington ball, yes?"

Oh, no. "If . . . if you're going to have me arrested," she whispered, the blood draining from her face, "then do so. But please don't let them bring the children or my family into it."

"You already asked me that. Would you pay the price I would ask to keep silent?"

Her pulse hammered. "But I—we—"

"I want you again, Evelyn." He tilted his head, eyes studying her face. "Don't you want me?"

So much she could barely keep from leaping on him, despite dozens of potential witnesses. A tear started, and she brushed it away before anyone could see it. He couldn't possibly care for her. She was such a fool, and she'd made such a muck of everything, and she was so blasted confused. "I was only trying to help."

"I know. And I have no intention of seeing you arrested, my dear one."

"You . . ." It took two tries to force out the words. "You don't?"

Saint shook his head. "That would be too easy. I'm going to blackmail you."

"Blackmail me?"

With one stride he closed the scant distance between them. "You belong to me now," he said in a low, intimate voice, "and for that you can thank yourself."

"I will not be—"

He brushed a second tear away with his thumb. "But I'm afraid you'll have to wait until morning to discover what it is I want from you. So go smile and dance with your fop, and dream tonight about what may come."

"Saint, just promise me—*please*—that you'll blame no one but me for what happened."

The marquis smiled, the expression warm and dark and utterly desirable. "Don't worry on that count. I blame you entirely."

"You blame my sister for what, St. Aubyn?" Victor appeared from the direction of the refreshment table.

If Evie hadn't been driven far beyond the point of fainting, her brother's arrival would have sent her to the floor. By now, though, she'd begun to consider claiming insanity. She'd be locked away in Bedlam, but then at least no one could reasonably hold her responsible for her actions.

"I blame Evelyn for convincing me to speak to Prinny about naming you to his Cabinet," Saint said smoothly. "The consensus seems to be that several ministries will open before the end of the Season. Two ambassadorships as well, I believe."

Victor looked nearly as skeptical as Evie felt. "And why would I want your support in anything, St. Aubyn?"

"Wait here."

The marquis headed in the direction of the Alvingtons' drawing room. As soon as he was out of earshot, Victor grabbed her by the elbow.

"Did I or did I not warn you to stay away from that man, Evie?" he growled. "I can't believe . . ." He shook his head. "Is concentrating on your duties to me for one damned evening so difficult? I've tried to excuse your flightiness on account of your youth, but I'm beginning to think you're merely dim and st—"

"Mr. Ruddick," Saint's voice came from beyond them, "it's my pleasure to introduce the Duke of Wellington. Your Grace, Victor Ruddick."

Evelyn wasn't certain who was more amazed—Victor or her. Her brother certainly recovered first, stepping forward to shake the duke's hand. "It's an honor to meet you, Your Grace."

"Saint informs me that you've spent time in India," Wellington said, gesturing Victor to join him. "Tell me, did you ever make the acquaintance of Mohmar Singh?"

The two men strolled into the crowd, leaving her standing with St. Aubyn. "How in the world did you manage that?"

"I can be quite persuasive." Saint gazed at her for a moment. "And it seemed the most efficient way to dispose of your opinionated brother. But don't think I've done you a favor, Evelyn. Wellington may . . . consort with the occasional whore, but he's death-defyingly conservative. If he were to discover that his new friend Victor Ruddick was brother to a ruined, nobleman-kidnapping lunatic, he'd—"

"He'd see Victor's career destroyed," she finished quietly.

"Just remember that this is between you and me, Evelyn. You began this game; I've just altered the rules. And we play till the end. I will see you tomorrow, my sweet one."

Obviously her actions had been enough to gain her the jaded St. Aubyn's complete, undivided attention. It worried her, mostly because he excited and aroused her so much. But if he wanted to continue the game, as he called it, then she still had a chance to save the orphanage. And Saint. And herself.

It wasn't how he'd meant to end the conversation. Several occurrences, though, had put him more than a little off kilter. Firstly, he'd been . . . absurdly pleased and gratified to see her. Secondly, the small part of her brother's tirade he'd managed to overhear had infuriated him. And thirdly, he'd wanted to swat Clarence Alvington like an insect for putting a hand on her. He'd been her first, and now she was his. No one else was allowed to play this game.

She'd obviously wandered far out of her depth in this little escapade, but in their acquaintance he'd found her anything but stupid or self-centered. She thought more with her heart than with her head, but as far as he'd been able to determine, her motives had been as pure as an angel's.

At the same time, she'd caused him a great deal of annoyance, and he owed her for that and for the amount of soul-searching the long, solitary hours had forced upon him. Evelyn Marie wanted to turn him into a gentleman. Well, he wanted to turn her into his mistress. And he had far more experience at being devious than she could ever dream of.

As for whether she might be better off with someone else—of course she would be. Saint scowled. It didn't matter whom she might be better off with, because he refused to relinquish his hold on her. She'd begun this, but he would end it, in the manner of his own choosing.

"Saint." Fatima glided up to him. "I knew you would never leave town during the Season, whatever the wags might say."

"Do the wags say anything else of interest?"

She favored him with a coy pout. "They say you've found a new lover." Sliding her fingers along his lapel, she practically purred. "It's that Evie Ruddick, isn't it? You've been hunting her for three weeks."

"She seems a bit proper for me, don't you think?" Saint drawled, capturing her hand and drawing it away from him. He didn't have time for dueling with jealous husbands of past, forgotten lovers at the moment; he had other plans to put into action.

"I had Gladstone ask her and her lovely brother to dinner the other night, you know," she continued. "You've tasted her. A woman can tell these things."

"Can a woman tell when a man is about to push her into the punch bowl?" Saint returned. "I told you, I enjoyed your company for a while, when you were amusing. Now you're annoying. Go away."

Her eyes narrowed. "You will pay for the awful things you've done, Saint. I've already given Gladstone's backing to Plimpton, so Miss Ruddick's brother certainly has nothing to gain by your acquaintance."

"Sterling of you. I imagine when the time comes I'll be in the queue for Hades right behind you, Fatima. Good evening."

The countess looked as though she wanted to slap him, but she wisely seemed to think better of it. For the moment she would leave him alone, until she thought of something vindictive she could do without any danger to her own reputation, or until she found someone else who better catered to her whims. He'd been through that God knew how many times before—so often he could almost mark the schedule for attempted retribution on a calendar. Before she tried anything, though, she would be wise to consult with other of his former lovers about their own lack of success.

Music began for a waltz, and without thought he strolled back into the ballroom. Evelyn was already on the dance floor, Clarence Alvington trying to pull her closer than propriety allowed. She held him off with nothing more than a smile and a word.

He wondered what Clarence's reaction would have been to finding himself leg-shackled in a dungeon for a week. The dandy's first action would probably have been to wet himself, and if he managed an escape, his second would most likely have been to swear out a statement against Evelyn Marie and then to have the orphanage torn down with the brats still inside.

And in so doing, he would have lost every point of leverage he held. Saint smiled. Some said that revenge was sweetest when it was served up cold and logical; where Evelyn was concerned, heat and lust were the emotions he still wanted satisfied. Proper females didn't kidnap people. And no one had ever bothered trying to deal with him before. He held all the good cards, and she couldn't walk away from this game. Not until he let her.

Chapter 16

There be none of beauty's daughters
With a magic like thee;
And like music on the waters
Is thy sweet voice to me.

—Lord Byron, Stanzas for Music

Pemberly tossed the third ruined neckcloth of the morning onto the floor. "My lord, perhaps if you could inform me of the style you wish to achieve, I could be more helpful."

Saint scowled at his reflection in the dressing mirror. "If I knew, I would do it myself. Just something more . . . dull."

"Dull? You wish to be poorly dressed, my lord?"

"No! Plain. Not ostentatious. Harmless-looking. Whatever it says under 'proper gentleman' in the thesaurus."

"Ah." The valet muttered something under his breath.

Saint narrowed his eyes. "What was that?"

"I—nothing, my lord. My—" He cleared his throat as Saint continued to gaze at him. "I only said that if your intent is to appear harmless, perhaps you should send someone else in your stead."

221

The valet had a point. "Do your best, Pemberly. I don't expect a miracle."

"Very good, my lord."

If Saint hadn't already decided that he felt keen anticipation at putting his plan into motion, he would have thought himself nervous. That, of course, made no sense, because he was never nervous.

As he descended the stairs to the main floor of his home, he noticed that the tenderness in his ankle was nearly gone. Other pains remained, however, especially an unpleasant ache located somewhere beneath his ribs that only seemed to ease when he was in Evelyn's presence. Someone really needed to post a warning about proper chits. "Is the phaeton ready?" he asked Jansen, accepting his hat and driving gloves.

"Yes, my lord. And the . . . rest, just as you instructed."

"Good." He stepped through the front door as the butler pulled it open, then paused. "I expect to return home this evening. If I don't, you may consider me missing and in peril."

The butler chuckled. "Very good, my lord. Best of luck with your peril, then."

Saint sighed. It was simply no use to assume that anyone would care if he vanished again or not. "Thank you."

He went down the front steps and climbed up to the phaeton's high seat. His liveried tiger jumped onto the narrow back behind him as he sent the team into the street.

Hundreds of carriages, carts, horses, and pedestrians crowded the streets of Mayfair. Eleven o'clock in the morning had seemed a civilized hour to call on someone, but as he joined the slow-moving crush he couldn't help wondering if an earlier hour might have been better. If she'd gone out already he was not going to be pleased. But he'd warned her that he would call on her this morning. By his pocket watch it would still be morning for another fifty-three minutes. That answered that. She had best be home.

He arrived at Ruddick House with thirty-seven minutes to spare. His tiger held the horses while he lifted a bundle from the seat and made his way to the front door.

From the butler's blank, efficient expression, the man had no idea who he was. "I'm here to see Miss Ruddick."

"May I say who is calling?"

"St. Aubyn."

The butler's professional countenance collapsed as his jaw dropped open. "St. Aubyn? Y . . . yes, my lord. Pl . . . please . . . ah . . . wait here, and I shall inquire whether Miss Ruddick is . . . home."

The door closed in Saint's face. Evidently even wearing Pemberly's version of a plain neckcloth didn't make him look harmless enough to be admitted to the foyer. On another occasion he might simply have opened the door and followed the butler in. Today, however, he would wait.

After five minutes of standing on the portico, he was ready to change his mind. As he reached for the doorknob, though, the door opened again.

"This way, my lord."

Saint followed the servant down the hallway and into the morning room. The news of his arrival had spread already, judging from the number of maids and footmen who suddenly had business in the hall.

"Lord St. Aubyn," the butler said, throwing open the door and then escaping.

Saint strolled into the room—and stopped. Evelyn sat in one of the deep green couches tucked into the cozy room, but she wasn't alone. "Miss Ruddick, Lady Dare, Miss Barrett," he said, nodding, though he kept his gaze on Evelyn, trying to analyze and explain away the raw heat that ran through his veins as their eyes met.

She'd tried to outmaneuver him, then, by providing witnesses. Not a bad strategy, considering that if anyone else learned of the kidnapping or her subsequent indiscretion, he wouldn't be able to hold it over her any longer. And her brother thought her stupid.

"Lord St. Aubyn," Evelyn said, not moving, "how nice of you to stop by this morning."

He smiled. "I feel somewhat sheepish," he drawled, cursing her silently. *Didn't she realize by now that he had no idea how to be a proper gentleman?* A little warning would have been nice, so at least he might have practiced propriety before venturing out with the act in public. "I'd hoped to take you on a picnic today." He held out the bundle in his hand. "I brought you roses."

"They're lovely, aren't they, Evie?" Miss Barrett said, with far too much enthusiasm.

"Yes, they are. Thank you."

Evelyn knew he wanted to see her alone. She also knew he wouldn't simply hand her the bouquet of roses, wish her a good day, and leave. The only defense she could think of in the short time she had between last night and this morning, though, had been to invite her friends over for a chat.

"We heard you had to leave town for a few days," Georgiana said, favoring Evie with a quick glance that clearly said, *What the devil is he doing here?* "I trust everything is well?"

He nodded, strolled over, and without being asked, seated himself on the couch beside Evelyn. "I had a few knots to unravel," he returned conversationally, his friendly tone surprising her even with the accompanying innuendo. He was *never* so nice—not without reason.

Oh, he was impossible, and even worse now that she knew how very good and wicked he could make her feel. In fairness he probably heard such compliments from females he'd bedded all the time, so he never saw any reason to alter his behavior. Evie scowled. She wasn't jealous, of course; she merely felt sorry for all of those poor ladies.

Her friends had been correct: She should have chosen another orphanage, and another student to reform—one who didn't cause such havoc with her insides. It was too late now, however, to do anything but attempt to minimize the damage she'd stupidly caused.

Belatedly she realized that everyone was looking at her. *Say something,* she told herself. "Would you care to join us for tea?"

"Thank you, but no. My tiger and phaeton are waiting for us."

He handed her the bouquet, brushing her fingers with his as he did so. Evie waited for the resulting jangled thrill of nerves at the skin-to-skin contact. She swallowed. Her own lack of discipline and restraint frustrated her, but she wasn't entirely certain whether to blame it on him or herself.

Lucinda cleared her throat. "I, ah, wasn't aware that you enjoyed picnics, my lord."

"Evelyn has told me I should spend more time in the daylight," he answered. "This is my first attempt. Shall we, Miss Ruddick?"

Oh, he was clever. He might not know of the pact she and her friends had made, but he'd guessed enough to know she would have mentioned her dismay at his poor behavior.

"I can't abandon my friends," she said, wishing her voice didn't sound quite so shrill. "Perhaps another time, my lord."

Green eyes met hers, and she felt her cheeks warm. "Today," he murmured, leaning close to her shoulder, "or I'll use the time to go see Prinny and finalize my transaction."

"You wouldn't."

His teeth showed as he grinned. "I've had my cook prepare pheasant sandwiches," he continued in a more conversational tone. "You're particularly fond of them, I believe."

Lucinda and Georgiana remained silent, watching the exchange with interest even though they couldn't hear all of it. They wouldn't volunteer to leave unless she signaled that they should, but the events of the morning obviously had them baffled. They had her baffled, as well, and even more flustered.

"Evie?" Victor leaned into the room. "Langley tells me that St. Aubyn is . . . Ah, St. Aubyn. Good morning."

Even knowing the strength of her brother's political ambitions, she couldn't quite believe it when he entered the room and offered his hand to Saint. Still more astonishing, the marquis stood to shake it.

"Good morning. I've been attempting to kidnap your sister for a picnic. I'm afraid she worries that you won't approve."

Evelyn choked, and hoped everyone would attribute her discomfiture to her dislike of Victor's strictness rather than to the marquis's choice of phrase. Saint seemed supremely confident that he now made the rules—and he had no problem with reminding her of that fact, damn him.

From his tight expression, Victor *didn't* approve of Saint's presence, or his suggestion. On the other hand, he'd been trying to make Wellington's acquaintance since his return from India, and he had to be supremely grateful that the marquis had provided him with the introduction.

"I believe I can spare Evie for one afternoon," her brother said slowly. "With an appropriate chaperone, of course."

Of course. Saint couldn't say anything to incriminate her in front of her maid. She wished she'd thought of that. Drat. She really needed to work at being more devious.

Saint also seemed to realize that his opportunity for private conversation or private anything else was vanishing. "I've brought my tiger."

Victor shook his head. "I'm grateful to you for last evening, St. Aubyn, but I'm not foolish. She may go only if her maid accompanies her."

"Very well, then."

Well, he hadn't quite outmaneuvered her, but he'd come close, and they were still in the drawing room of her own house with three other people present. And if she protested now, Victor would be angry, which would put her at further disadvantage, and Saint might very well carry through with his threat to dispose of the orphanage once and for all. Lucinda and Georgie obviously realized who'd won, because both of them stood.

"I should be going anyway," Lucinda said, for appearance's sake. "Georgie, did you still want to see the new lace at Thacker's?"

"Yes." The viscountess kissed Evie on the cheek. "Are you all right?" she whispered as she did so.

Evie nodded. "I just didn't expect him to reform so quickly," she improvised.

Lucinda squeezed her hand. "We'll see you at Lydia Burwell's recital tomorrow, yes?"

"Actually," Victor cut in, escorting them to the door, "Evie has a political tea to attend tomorrow at our Aunt Houton's."

"We'll see you tomorrow evening, then."

"Oh, yes. I wouldn't miss that."

"Miss what?" Saint asked as Victor showed her friends from the room.

"*As You Like It* at Drury Lane," she answered.

"Interesting title." She waited for him to say something more, but he only lifted an eyebrow. "Go fetch your maid, Evelyn," he continued after a moment. "Let's not waste the day, shall we?"

Heat ran down her spine. He seemed to be willing to keep her secrets thus far, but she had no doubt this polite demeanor was merely a mask for some new game of his. "You may fool them," she said quietly over her shoulder, "but you haven't fooled me."

"I don't need to fool you," he returned in the same low tone. "I own you, remember?"

Not for the first time, Evie contemplated the merits of running away from home as she climbed the stairs to get her gloves and fetch Sally. Usually she wanted to escape because of Victor and his high-handed pronouncements of how he understood politics when she never would. Today, however, any flight would actually be to protect her brother. If she vanished, though, no one would be able to stop Saint from destroying the orphanage—and what remained of her reputation.

Unless he was bluffing, of course, but it wasn't a risk she was willing to take. Not when she still had a chance to convince him to help the children.

She and Sally made their way back downstairs to find Saint and her brother standing in the foyer, both looking as though they desperately wished to be somewhere else. If she hadn't been so nervous, she would have been amused.

"All right, then, my lord, shall we?" she said, deciding to act as though she had already anticipated every move he might make and that nothing he did or said could possibly surprise her.

"We shall. Ruddick."

"St. Aubyn. I expect her back by four o'clock."

Victor *was* grateful for the introduction to Wellington, if he'd allotted Saint four hours with her. The marquis was gazing at her, though, so she only nodded and stepped past him to collect her bonnet and parasol.

Saint took her gloved hand, wrapping it over his arm as they descended the front steps to the short drive. "If I saw him elected to Parliament, would he grant me unsupervised overnight visitations to your bed?" he murmured.

Probably. She almost said it aloud, but thankfully her common sense took hold of her tongue before she could do so. "Sally and I won't both fit in your phaeton," she said instead.

"Yes, you will."

"No, we won't," she returned, unable to stifle a brief smile at his scowl. "Not with your tiger there, as well. And no, Sally will not perform the services of a groom so you can leave him behind. She's terrified of horses."

Sally was no such thing, but the maid seemed to understand the part she was playing, because she edged away from the spirited black team.

The word Saint muttered under his breath didn't seem the least bit polite, and neither was the look he sent Sally. "Fine. We'll walk."

"Walk?"

"Yes, walk. Felton, take the carriage back home."

"Yes, milord."

Saint strode to the back of the phaeton and hauled down a large picnic basket. Thrusting his arm through the handle, he stalked back to her side. "Anything else you'd care to put in my path?"

"No, I think that'll do for now."

"Splendid. Come along."

He offered his arm again, and after a hesitation she took it. With an escort present, the touch was perfectly acceptable, and the small, naughty part of her knew that she did like touching him. Very much.

"Have you really never been on a picnic before?" she asked.

"Not with a guard present, in a public setting, or with sandwiches in a basket."

"Then what . . ." She trailed off. "Never mind. I don't want to know."

"Yes, you do," he returned, glancing over at her. "You just think you're too proper to ask."

"*You* just think you have to be improper enough to shock everyone with every sentence. Don't you get tired of that?"

"Are we attempting to reform me again, or is this a mere chastisement of my usual poor behavior?"

Evelyn sighed. "Didn't you learn anything?" she

whispered, so that Sally, walking several feet behind them, couldn't hear.

"I learned a great deal. I learned that you like to chain men up and kiss them when you're the one who can dictate the action. I learned—"

"That is not so!" she snapped, her face heating.

"No? You did like making love with me, Evelyn. I know that." He hefted the basket, obviously annoyed to be reduced to performing manual labor. "Have you touched anyone else like that?"

"No."

"I didn't think so."

"You, however, have obviously . . . touched several women before, my lord. I fail to see why you continue to torment me about my . . . slip of propriety."

He chuckled, the sound low and so seductive that several women they passed on the street turned to look at him and then titter to one another. "My dear, you said you wanted to turn me into a gentleman. Don't I have the same right to attempt to turn you into a wanton?"

"That would ruin me, Saint," she said, trying to remember her strategy of not allowing herself to be shocked by anything he said. Honesty would work—at least it had seemed to with him before. "And I don't wish to be ruined."

"It would only ruin you if someone else knew about it. All we need do is be discreet. I could make sex a condition for keeping your little escapade a secret, now, couldn't I?"

"I suppose you could. Reminding me of some awful thing you might do, however, hardly predisposes me to want to be seduced by you."

This time he laughed outright. It was the first time

she'd ever heard him do that, and the hearty, merry sound resonated down her spine. *My goodness.* If he weren't so terrible, she'd be halfway to being infatuated with him.

"What's so amusing?" she asked, reminding herself that desirable and charming as he could be, he was still blackmailing her.

He leaned closer to whisper in her ear. "I already did seduce you, my love. And I think you like me *because* I'm awful."

The gesture reminded Evie of the night all this chaos had begun, when she had found him whispering naughty things into Lady Gladstone's ear. Only now she was the hoyden welcoming his scandalous attentions. And she did welcome them, and the heat and craving he awakened in her.

"Perhaps I do," she admitted, noting that Lady Trent nearly ran into a lamppost, she was so busy gawking at proper Evie Ruddick walking arm in arm down the street with the Marquis of St. Aubyn. "But perhaps I'd like you even better if you were nicer."

Saint hefted the picnic basket again as they reached the western boundary of Hyde Park. *Nicer.* "I've invited you to join me for a picnic," he returned. "I think that's very 'nice' of me."

Evie chuckled, leaning a little against his arm as she did so. "Yes, if we overlook the fact that you threatened the orphanage if I didn't join you."

"Would you have come otherwise?"

Coming from him, it sounded like a childish, naive question, but he was dismayed to realize that he wanted to know the answer. And Evelyn would tell him the truth; she always did.

"I don't know," she said slowly. "I . . . I know you said you wouldn't have me arrested, but I—"

"You want my word that I'll leave the orphanage be," he finished, somewhat distracted by the warmth of her hand over his arm. "Yes?"

Earnest as she was, she'd never join him in bed again if he didn't give his word. And when he did, she'd expect him to keep it. Saint took a breath. He'd waited six years for an opportunity to be rid of the place. He could wait a little while longer, until he'd purged himself of the desire for her.

He nodded. "Then I give you my word. You have . . . four weeks to convince me to leave the Heart of Hope Orphanage standing. But I warn you, I will take a great deal of convincing."

From her expression, now that he'd acquiesced, she didn't know what to do next. That suited him; he'd just given himself four weeks to learn why he'd become so obsessed with her, satisfy that torment, and end their affair. If he didn't, she would, because in four weeks the Heart of Hope Orphanage, brig and all, was becoming part of the Prince of Wales's newest park.

"This is nice," Evelyn said, slowing beneath a stand of old English oaks.

Saint glanced at the crowded riding path just fifty feet away, and at the equally busy footpath half that distance in the opposite direction. "Too many witnesses," he said, urging her deeper into the park.

She pulled free of his grip. "This is a luncheon, is it not? What do you care if people see us?"

Because she was the dessert he wanted. "Here," he said dubiously. "In the middle of everything."

"It's pleasant and pretty."

"But I can't kiss you here without ruining you. And you insist on not being ruined, as I recall."

With an overloud laugh, Evie took his arm again. "Be quiet," she muttered. "Talking about it is just as bad as doing it."

"But not nearly as much fun." Beginning to wonder whether he'd wandered into someone's idyllic nightmare, Saint relented. "You ask a great deal, you know."

She smiled at him. "It's not so difficult once you get used to it. Did you bring a blanket?"

He set the heavy basket on the grass. "I don't know. I told them to pack me a picnic."

"Let's see, then."

Evelyn seemed amused, undoubtedly at his expense. Since good humor made her eyes light and set tiny dimples into her cheeks, he could tolerate it.

The basket did contain a blanket, blue and neatly folded and completely unfamiliar. Saint took it from Evelyn and snapped it open, letting it settle onto the cool grass. "Now what?"

"Put the basket in the center of the blanket, and we sit down."

Saint directed a thumb at the maid. "And the propriety shackle? Where does she go?"

A soft blush climbed Evelyn's cheeks at his choice of words, as he knew it would. He liked when she blushed. It made her seem so . . . pure.

"Sally will sit on one corner of the blanket," she directed, following him onto the material as he moved the basket where she indicated. She knelt beside it, her green muslin gown flowing out around her.

Saint gazed at her for a moment, at the pert, perfect coil of auburn hair atop her head, at the soft curve of her neck as she peered into the basket and drew out a bottle of wine, at the long, curling lashes concealing her eyes from him. He swallowed, his mouth abruptly going dry. Good God, he wanted her again, wanted to peel the gown from her shoulders and kiss every inch of her soft, smooth skin.

She looked up at him. "Are you going to sit?"

He sat, folding his legs in front of him. *What was he doing with this goddess of grace? And what was she doing with him?*

"You're being very quiet," she said, and handed him the wine bottle. "And that's a fine cabernet."

"It goes with the pheasant." Saint reached into his pocket. "I do have a flask, if you prefer gin."

"Wine is splendid." Pulling two glasses from the basket, she raised up and leaned toward him. "Now you pour."

He shook himself. Sweet Lucifer, he was behaving like a gawky village idiot. The Marquis of St. Aubyn did not moon over females or their fine bosoms, particularly *after* he'd bedded them. With a twist of his fingers he uncorked the bottle. "A cabernet tastes better on naked skin," he drawled, "but since we're not discussing that, I suppose glasses will do."

The glasses wavered a little in her hands as he filled the fine crystal. "You've . . . picked a lovely day for our outing," she said crisply.

"Are we talking about the weather now?" Saint set the bottle in the grass and took one of the glasses from her, making sure that he brushed her fingers as he did so. It seemed imperative that he touch her every few moments.

"The weather is always a safe topic."

He took a sip of wine, gazing at her over the rim of the glass. "A 'safe' topic. Fascinating."

Her eyes lowered. "No. It's dull."

Evidently he'd said the wrong thing. Being proper was even more difficult than he'd imagined. "No, really. This is new territory for me. Usually by now on a picnic I'm unclothed. Are there other 'safe' topics?"

She looked up at him again, suspicion in her clear gaze. "The weather is the safest, being that everyone knows something about it. Fashion is controversial, unless one laments the new decadence of style, and—"

"Decadence. I like decadence."

Evelyn smiled. "I know. And bemoaning the waltz is safe with the older generation, for the same reason. Also, no one likes Bonaparte, and the Americas are very gauche."

"So it's safest to like nothing."

She hesitated for a moment, taking far too large a swallow of her wine. "And to approve of nothing, and to do nothing."

"My, my, Evelyn. I had no idea you were a cynic." He tilted his head, trying to read her expression. "That's not it, though, is it? That's just what you say to your brother's odd selection of political Bedlamites. Because you, my dear, are far more interesting than the dull creation you describe."

To his surprise, her eyes filled with tears, though the apology for whatever he'd said wrong this time faded on his lips at the sight of her warm smile. Some very uncomfortable things began happening to his nether regions.

"That, Lord St. Aubyn, is a very nice thing you just said."

He reached into the basket to cover his sudden discomfiture. "How very unusual of me," he muttered, and produced a sandwich. "Pheasant?"

Chapter 17

Nor was all love shut from him, though his days
Of passion had consumed themselves to dust.

—Lord Byron, *Childe Harold's
Pilgrimage, Canto III*

The sun was edging the trees by the time Evie asked
Saint to consult his pocket watch.

"Twenty minutes of four," he said, shoving the expensive silver-etched timepiece back into his pocket as though it had done something he didn't like.

She wasn't terribly pleased by the news, either. Aside from the fact that she'd been enjoying the afternoon, she hadn't even mentioned the children or the orphanage. He'd given her less than a month to convince him, and she'd just wasted nearly four hours. If she returned home late, though, Victor would make seeing Saint again more difficult than it already was.

"We need to go."

With a scowl Saint climbed to his feet and offered her his hand. "I suppose kidnapping you is out of the question." He pulled her upright, leaning to whisper in her ear. "That's right, we tried something like that already, didn't we?"

"Stop that," she whispered back, protesting more because his intimate tone made her shiver than because of what he'd said. She'd begun to realize that he wouldn't tell anyone their secret; if he did, he would lose some of the advantage over her that he valued so much.

He tossed the remains of their luncheon back into the basket, crumpled the blanket and dumped it on top, then hefted the basket up again. "I don't suppose you'll let me drag you into the shrubbery for a—"

"Saint!"

He glanced at Sally. "For a handshake, before we go?"

Of course her maid knew what the marquis meant, but Sally also knew his reputation and, Evie hoped, thought he made such scandalous propositions without provocation.

"No handshakes."

She tucked her hand around his arm as they left Hyde Park. Even with Saint behaving himself, as he'd done to a remarkable degree this afternoon, she still felt like a kitten in the company of a sleek black panther. Claws sheathed or not, he was still a force to be reckoned with.

"I only have so much self-restraint, Evelyn Marie."

The lustful expression in his eyes started heat between her legs. Heaven knew, at least a half dozen times during the picnic she had to stop herself from leaning over and kissing him. More than anything, she wanted to feel again the way she'd felt in his arms. If he knew that, though, she would lose what little control she had over him. It was a balancing act, and she kept teetering on the edge of disaster.

"Who else does your brother want to meet?" Saint asked, apparently realizing that she wasn't going to jump into an alleyway with him.

"Wellington was his main target for a Cabinet post, but since we seem to have lost Gladstone's support, Alvington is the one who can probably do the most to get him the West Sussex seat in the House. How did you manage Wellington, really?"

He shrugged. "I'd heard your brother wanted to meet with him, and I wanted to see you. Wellington likes fine sherry, and I own several cases of the finest."

"My brother would make a fine member of Parliament, you know."

Saint looked down at her. "And?"

"And so you did a good thing."

"Yes, I did. I took you on a picnic."

Evie grimaced. "You know perfectly well what I mean. Why do you refuse to admit that you did something nice?"

"Why do you think it was nice? I wanted something, and I did what was necessary to get it."

She shook her head. "No. I refuse to believe that your only motive for sending Wellington into Victor's path was to gain a picnic with me."

He only smiled. "Tell me who else your brother needs in order to put together his campaign, and I'll arrange it."

She stopped, and he came to a halt beside her. Sally also stopped a few feet behind them, and in full hearing of whatever she might say. "And what would you expect in return for that?"

"More time with you."

Her first impulse was to shout at him that she was tired of being parlayed to men in exchange for political influence. At the same time, though, she realized that Saint had only seen what Victor had been doing for weeks, and had decided to use it to his advantage.

"You might just have said that you were being help-ful, with no ulterior motives."

"That would have been a lie. I was under the impres-sion that you valued honesty."

Evie continued, walking beside him for a long mo-ment in silence. Saint *was* honest. He'd never made any pretense of what he wanted from her. Even his honesty, though, wasn't for its own sake; he used the admission of his mercenary qualities to gain her approval. Every-thing was so complicated, but if she meant to continue delivering her lessons to him, she needed to figure out how to convince him of the merits of doing a deed for its own sake.

"My lady," Sally hissed from behind them, "Mr. Ruddick."

She looked up. Victor stood on the front portico, his open pocket watch in his hand and a scowl on his face. "Oh, dear."

"We're not late," Saint said, following her gaze. "He acts like a procurer. Shall I remind him that you're not someone's whore?"

The tone was mild, but Evie heard the steel beneath. Saint was angry at Victor—and on her behalf. A low thrill ran through her. "You will do no such thing. It would only put him in a foul mood, and it certainly wouldn't benefit me."

"Perhaps not, but it would greatly improve *my* mood. I don't enjoy being told how long I may spend with someone."

"Saint," she muttered as they turned up the short drive.

"I won't enlighten him tonight," he murmured back, "but please remember what I said about my flagging self-restraint."

He was teasing. Evelyn wanted to kiss him on the cheek—or better yet, on the mouth—but then Victor would faint. "I'm not likely to forget."

"I trust you had a pleasant afternoon," Victor said, pocketing his timepiece as he came down the front steps.

"Yes, it was lovely," she answered.

He took Evie's free arm, and she abruptly worried that Saint would refuse to relinquish her and the two men would tug her in half. The muscles along Saint's arm tightened beneath her fingers.

"Your sister is delightful," the marquis drawled.

"Yes, she's always quite charming."

Evie cleared her throat. "My goodness, so many compliments. I thank you both. And I thank you for a lovely picnic, my lord."

With a stiff nod, Saint relaxed his arm, letting her pull her hand free. "Thank *you*, Miss Ruddick," he returned. "And you were correct."

"About what?" she asked, turning to keep him in view as he took a step back down the drive.

"About daylight. It's exceptional. Ruddick, Miss Ruddick."

"St. Aubyn."

As the marquis and his picnic basket returned to the street and whistled down a hack, Victor tightened his grip on her other arm. Evie made herself look away from Saint and face her brother.

"What was that about?" Victor asked, towing her up the steps and back into the house.

Langley closed the door before she could give in and see whether Saint looked back at her again or not. It wasn't important, but she was vain enough to want to know if he thought about her, spared her a single thought, even, once she was out of his sight. "What was what about?"

"The comment about daylight."

"Oh. I told him that he should attempt to emerge into the sunlight on occasion."

"Ah." Victor released her, heading upstairs to his office, where he'd probably spent all afternoon plotting.

"You might try it yourself," she called after him.

He looked back at her from the top of the stairs. "Try what?"

"Sunlight."

"Just because St. Aubyn introduced me to Wellington, don't think you've talked me into a friendship with the scoundrel. He did me a favor, and so I allowed you to be seen with him on a picnic. Don't get used to it. I don't owe him anything more."

Evie sighed. "In case you were wondering, he was a perfect gentleman today."

"So long as you were a lady. I suppose I should congratulate you on your determination to upset me. Evie Ruddick, advocate of the unwashed masses, dining with a man set to tear down an orphanage."

Not if she had any say in the matter. "Yes, Victor," she called, strolling into the morning room, "thank you for reminding me."

Saint took a seat at the main faro table at the Society club. "What the devil is a ladies' political tea?"

Tristan Carroway, Viscount Dare, finished placing his wager, then sat back, reaching for his glass of port. "Do I look like a dictionary?"

"You're domesticated." Saint motioned for a glass of his own, despite unfriendly looks from the tables' other players. "What is it?"

"I'm not domesticated; I'm in love. You should try it. Does wonders for your outlook on life."

"I'll take your word for it, thank you. But if you're so in love, why are you here, and where is your wife?"

Dare drained his glass and refilled it. "A political tea, I believe, is an arena for ladies to discuss how they might best support and further the political aims of their . . . men." He pushed back his chair. "As to your other question, it's none of your damned affair where my wife is, and I suggest you stay the hell away from her."

With a glance Saint took in the tense expression on Dare's face, the half-full bottle still gripped in the viscount's hand, and the wagers being discreetly exchanged at neighboring tables. "I've set my sights elsewhere than your wife, Dare. If you wish a fight I'll be happy to oblige you, but I'd prefer to share a drink."

The viscount shook his head. "I'd prefer to do neither with you, Saint. Evie Ruddick is a friend of mine, and you seem to have nothing good in mind for her. Agree to stop bothering her, and I'll drink with you."

A few weeks ago Saint wouldn't have thought twice about informing Dare and anyone else who cared to listen precisely how much of his attentions Evelyn Marie Ruddick had enjoyed. Tonight, without caring to examine too closely why he declined to speak about it, he stood. "Neither it is, then. For tonight."

He left the Society in a roar of speculation behind him. Let them wonder what he had in mind for innocent Evie Ruddick. She wasn't quite so innocent any longer, but that was none of their business. Nor did they need to know that he still craved her body, her voice, and even her warm, sweet smile. He supposed a ladies' tea, political or not, would be off limits to someone of his sex, but there was still Shakespeare at the Drury Lane Theatre.

He would see Evelyn again tomorrow, no matter who didn't want him to.

As he rode home, still fresh enough from imprisonment that even the cold, foggy evening felt good on his face, he ran the day through his mind again. If a month ago someone had told him he would be going on a picnic with a proper chit, he would have laughed in the prophet's face. But not only had he done so, he'd enjoyed it, and more than he felt comfortable admitting.

By his usual standards, the evening was still young. As had happened over the past few nights, however, he wasn't quite sure what to do with himself. His usual haunts—the gaming hells, the bawdy houses, the hellfire clubs' lurid soirees—would only just be beginning their fun in earnest. Where once any attractive, semi-interesting female would have served, though, Saint didn't want to ease his frustrated lust on some other woman.

The low, flowing heat in his veins was for one woman in particular. The sensation invigorated him, made him feel more aware—more alive—than he could remember feeling in years. In her presence, seeing her and talking with her and being unable to touch her as he wanted, the torture was exquisite, and only bearable because he'd already promised himself that he would have her again.

Cassius slowed and stopped, and Saint realized he'd managed to detour around to Ruddick House yet again. Only one window upstairs glowed with candlelight, and he wondered whether Evelyn's night was proving as wakeful as his. He hoped so, and he hoped she was thinking of him.

With a quiet cluck he sent the bay forward again. Whatever it took, he would have Evelyn Ruddick as his mistress. He didn't want anyone else, and he wouldn't accept that she might choose to decline the offer. By now he knew what she liked, and he would simply convince her.

Evelyn managed to evade both Victor and her mother, and left Ruddick House for her aunt's political tea early enough to accommodate a stop at the Heart of Hope Orphanage.

It seemed far longer than two days since she'd last set foot in the glum old building, and from the children's enthusiastic greeting any observer would have thought she'd been away for a year.

"Miss Evie, Miss Evie!" Rose cried, flinging her arms around Evie's waist. "We thought you'd been hanged!"

"Or beheaded!" Thomas Kinnett added, wide-eyed, still scaring himself with his proclivity for gruesome tales.

"I'm fine, all in one piece and very happy to see all of you," she answered, hugging Penny with her free arm.

"So'd he escape, or did you let him go?" Randall asked from the deep window sill, where he sat whittling.

She remembered Saint's warning about the older boys, but Saint was jaded and cynical. These boys had risked more than any of the other children in helping her, after all. "He escaped. But I also have his word that he will give me another four weeks to convince him to spare the orphanage."

"Four weeks ain't much time, Miss Evie. And if you couldn't convince him in chains, what makes you think 'e'll change his mind now?"

"He agreed to the four weeks without argument. I think that's a very good sign."

"Should we give him back his pictures?" Rose asked, finally lifting her face from the folds of Evie's gown.

"What pictures?"

"The drawings he made." Molly went to her bed and pulled a handful of papers from beneath the mattress. "We hid them so no one would know."

Know what? Evelyn began to ask, then stopped the question as Molly handed her the papers. She'd seen Saint scribbling a few times, and he'd asked for additional paper twice, but she'd thought he was merely doodling to pass the time, or drafting letters to his army of solicitors about his imprisonment.

"You look very pretty," Rose said, taking a seat beside Evelyn as she sank onto the edge of one of the beds.

Pages of children's faces, caricatures of St. Aubyn turning into a skeleton in his cell, but mostly pencil sketches of her, covered every inch of free space, front and back. "My goodness," she whispered, her cheeks warming.

He'd caught her eyes, her smile, her scowl, her hands, her tears, all with remarkable skill on these coarse, smudged, wrinkled parchments. Looking at them, she felt as if he'd seen into her and drawn her secrets.

"You're certain, now, Miss Evie, that you didn't just let 'im go?" Randall asked again, lifting his knife from the wood. "'Cause it seems from them that you was sitting down there letting him do portraits of you."

"I wasn't," she returned, hearing the accusation in his tone. After seeing the drawings, she couldn't blame him. "He must have drawn them from memory. And look, he drew pictures of all of you as well. That means he was paying attention, and thinking of you."

"So he'll let us stay, do you think?" Penny asked, sitting on Evie's other side. "Because I don't want to have to live on the street and eat rats."

"Oh, Penny!" Evelyn hugged the slender girl. "That will never happen. I promise."

"I hope you're right, Miss Evie," Randall drawled, "because there's still ways to make sure it don't happen."

"Randall, promise me you won't do anything rash," Evie said, a cold chill running down her spine. "And that you'll consult me first."

"No worries, Miss Evie," he returned. "I ain't likely to forget that you're a part of this, too. None of us will."

After the tense atmosphere of the orphanage, Aunt Houton's political tea seemed woefully tame. Evie helped create silly political slogans to rhyme with the favored candidates' names, but her thoughts were on the papers she'd carefully rolled up and stuck into the band of her stockings. They scratched her leg uncomfortably, reminding her how much she wanted a few minutes alone to sit and look at them again without a gaggle of curious children gazing at her.

"Your brother sent over a note," Aunt Houton said, sitting beside her as she scribbled out rhyming words for "Fox." "He's in raptures because Wellington has finally agreed to sit down to a quiet dinner with us on Friday."

Saint, again. "My goodness," Evie exclaimed for effect, though she wasn't the least bit surprised by the news. "Just us and Wellington?"

"Not quite. The Alvingtons and . . . St. Aubyn will be joining us as well."

"Hm. Interesting. I hadn't thought St. Aubyn was political."

"I hadn't thought so, either. Victor attributed his sudden interest to some sort of conspiracy to sink his career, but—"

"Nonsense!"

"—but he's willing to take the chance in exchange for another meeting with Wellington." The marchioness turned away to answer one of the other ladies' questions, then faced Evie again. "Do you know why St. Aubyn is so suddenly interested in your brother's career?"

She was truly going to go to Hades for this, and it was all Saint's fault. "He asked me out on a picnic, but I can assure you that he didn't mention this. I have no idea what he might be thinking, but there is certainly no 'conspiracy' between Saint and myself."

" 'Saint'?" her aunt repeated, lifting an eyebrow.

"St. Aubyn. He asked me to call him Saint. Everyone does, I believe." He'd also asked her to call him Michael, but apparently no one did that, and she wasn't about to confess to that or to the circumstances that had brought it about.

"Well, whatever his interest in *you*, make certain you don't encourage it. The Marquis of St. Aubyn is a dark, dangerous man, and no one you need in your life. Especially now."

The words caught Evelyn's attention, but before she could ask her aunt to clarify, Lady Harrington and Lady Doveston began an argument over whether "perfect" was an acceptable rhyme for "Ruddick."

Evelyn shifted in her chair, and the drawings rustled against her leg again. This meeting was such a waste, when she needed to be planning the next step in her education of Michael Halboro. But given what he'd sketched, perhaps he was beginning to be more convinced than she'd realized. And given the way he'd sketched her, she couldn't help hoping that perhaps he would call on her again very soon.

Chapter 18

I want a hero.

—Lord Byron, *Don Juan, Canto I*

"**Y**ou rented an entire box for just the three of us?" Evie asked as her brother offered her one of the two front chairs and her mother sat behind. The orchestra seats below were already filled, and it didn't look as though a single box or chair would be empty this evening. The extravagance of an oversized box surprised her; if Victor was anything, it wasn't frivolous.

"Not exactly. I invited some friends to join us," Victor answered, taking another of the rear seats.

Suspicion ran through Evelyn as she gazed at the empty chair beside her. "Which friends?"

"Ah, good evening, Ruddick," Lord Alvington's booming voice came as he pushed aside the curtains at the rear of the box. "Good of you to have us tonight. Looks to be a sad crush, and I'd already loaned out my box to my demmed niece and her family."

"That was exceptionally generous of you," Victor complimented, shaking the viscount's hand.

"Lady Alvington," her mother exclaimed with achingly sweet glee, rising to kiss the plump viscountess on both round cheeks. "Have you heard that Wellington's to join us for dinner on Friday?"

"Yes, I had. Such a fine gentleman, he is."

Evie rose as well, though everyone ignored her until Clarence Alvington strolled into the box. That explained the empty chair. She was being bartered again. Hiding her disgust behind a smile, she dipped a curtsy as Clarence took her gloved hand and bowed over it.

"You are a vision this evening, Miss Ruddick," he drawled.

"Indeed," said Lady Alvington. "Wherever did you get that necklace, my dear? It's exquisite."

Reaching up to touch the silver heart with the diamond inside, Evelyn was tempted to tell them all precisely where the necklace had come from. She couldn't quite convince herself, though, that it would be worth the ruin just to see the looks on their faces. "It's an old family heirloom," she said instead, and caught her mother's quick frown. "One of Grandmother's, isn't it?" she asked.

"Yes. Yes, I believe so." Barely sparing her a glance, Genevieve Ruddick sat again. "Tell me, Mr. Alvington, how have you been occupying your days?"

"How kind of you to ask, Mrs. Ruddick. I have recently begun designing a completely new style of neckcloth." Clarence tilted up his pointed chin, revealing a cravat tied in so intricate a manner that he and his valet must have begun working on it when he arose that morning. "You see?" he indicated, trying to view his audience with his chin still pointed skyward. "I call it the Mercury Knot."

While everyone gushed over his neckcloth, Evelyn

nodded and turned to the more interesting distraction of looking at the occupants of the other boxes. Two farther back from the stage, Lord and Lady Dare had taken seats together with Dare's two aunts and all of his grown brothers but Robert, the one who had been wounded at Waterloo and who rarely appeared in public at all these days. On the far side of the stage Lucinda sat with her father, General Barrett, and an assortment of his distinguished military and political friends.

The lights dimmed, and with a quick wave and smile at Luce, she took her seat. As the curtains rose, the flash of an opera glass caught her attention, and she glanced toward the massively expensive boxes closest to the stage to see who was staring at her. The pair of binoculars aimed in her direction lowered, revealing the lean, amused countenance of the Marquis of St. Aubyn.

Her breath caught. His family had owned a Drury Lane box for ages, but as far as she knew, he *never* attended such tame events as these. But there he was— and he wasn't alone. Sitting with him were a handful of his raffish male and female acquaintances, including one overly-made-up blond woman with a very large bosom, which she seemed intent on pressing against Saint's arm.

A keen ache shoved its way into her chest. So, despite his recent attentions to her, he considered her no different than any of his other fallen female conquests, a woman to be bedded, taunted for it, and forgotten. Fine. That was fine. She'd only been curious to discover what being with him would be like, anyway.

"What play is this?" Clarence whispered a few moments later, leaning over and giving her a whiff of his very strong cologne.

"*As You Like It,*" she returned, more tartly than she

intended. The title was on the playbill he held in one hand, for heaven's sake.

"Ah. One of Shakespeare's."

"Yes, I believe so."

Someone nudged the back of her chair. Victor, no doubt, warning her to behave. She looked across Clarence's massive neckcloth at Saint again. If he could still be . . . content in the company of his box fellows, and if he could practically flaunt that woman with the large bosom in front of her, then he hadn't learned anything. Evie frowned. Or was she the one who hadn't learned her lesson, despite what practically everyone she knew, including Saint, had told her about him?

Victor's cheek brushed her ear. "Stop scowling," he whispered almost soundlessly.

Oh, she needed to get away for a moment, away from where everyone in the theater could see every expression on her face, every tear in her eyes. "My stomach is unsettled," she whispered back. "I need to get some water."

"Then go. But hurry back."

With an apologetic murmur, she stood and made her way through the heavy curtains at the back of the box. She wanted to sag against the wall and cry, but footmen wandered from box to box in the corridor, delivering drinks and opera glasses and whatever else the occupants required. At her whispered query, one of them directed her to a nearby curtained alcove, and she slipped inside just as the first tear ran down her cheek.

Saint shifted his chair, trying to put more distance between himself and Deliah's eager bosom. He shouldn't have invited anyone along tonight, but he would have looked like an idiot sitting in a six-person box all by himself.

He looked back at Evelyn again, as he seemed to need to do every two minutes or so, to find her chair empty. He stood.

"Saint, bring me a brandy," Deliah cooed.

Ignoring her, he exited the box and headed along the wide corridor toward the Ruddick family's seats. No sign of Evelyn. Deciding she'd probably gone back in, he muttered a quiet curse and turned around again. And paused as he heard a sniffle coming from behind the nearest privacy curtain.

"Evelyn?" he whispered, hoping to God it wasn't Fatima or some other female of his acquaintance.

"Go away."

Thank Lucifer. "What are you doing?"

"Nothing."

He pushed aside the curtain to see her facing the wall, her hands over her face. "If you're hiding, it's not working," he murmured. "I can see you."

"I saw you, too. Enjoying yourself?"

"Not really. I keep hoping Deliah will lean so far she'll fall out of the box, but it hasn't happened yet."

Lowering her hands, she faced him. "Why are you here?"

With a glance up the corridor, he stepped into the alcove and pulled the curtain closed behind him. "Why do you think?" he asked, and covered her mouth with his.

He pressed her into the corner, kissing her, tasting her again. Evelyn was breathing hard and fast, meeting his lips with hers. Gloved fingers slipped over his shoulders, pulling him hard against her.

"Someone will find us," she panted, moaning as he lifted his hands from her hips to cover her breasts.

"Shh."

As soon as he saw her there, Saint had gone hard, and

he absolutely was not going to give her a chance to escape. Kissing her again and again, hot and open-mouthed, only made his aching for her worse. No woman had ever aroused him as she did. Reluctant to let go of her but very aware that they had little time, he released her breasts and guided her hands down to his trousers.

"Here?" she gasped against his lips.

"I want you," he returned, moving her fingers across the hard bulge in his trousers. Then he slid his own hands down her skirt, gathered handfuls of the material and lifted, drawing her dress up past her knees. "Do you feel how much I want you, Evelyn Marie? Do you want me?"

If she said no, he probably would have expired on the spot, but thankfully she began unfastening his trousers with anxious, shaking fingers. "Hurry, Saint," she begged, silent but for the whisper of breath against his mouth.

She freed him, and he lifted her in his arms, pulling her legs around his hips. With a groan he entered her, keeping her pinned between himself and the wall as he strongly pumped his hips against her. Her tight warmth welcomed him. Her harsh, fast breathing brought him to the edge of reason. This was perfection, being inside Evelyn, the joining, becoming one with her.

He felt her come, and captured her moan against his mouth, letting her ecstasy pull him forward into his own. With an almost animal growl he joined her, pressing her so hard against the wall he feared he'd cut off her air.

Breathing hard, he held her, her arms around his neck and her ankles and dainty slippered feet locked around his hips. Even now, still inside her, with the scent of her hair surrounding him and her warm, lithe body in his arms, he craved her, didn't want to let her go.

"Saint?" she whispered unsteadily, licking his jaw.

"Hm?"

"What is your middle name?"

He lifted his face away from her bare shoulder to gaze into her light gray eyes. "Edward."

She smiled. "Michael Edward Halboro," she murmured, running her fingers along his cheek with a surprising gentleness, "is it always like that? So . . . good?"

"No, it's not." Saint kissed her again, slowly, relishing the touch of her soft lips against his.

"Evie?" her mother's hushed voice came from out in the corridor. "Where in the world are you?"

Evelyn stiffened in his arms, stark terror crossing her face. "Oh, no, no, no," she breathed. "Let me go."

Obviously now was not the time to argue. Saint lifted her away from him so she could put her feet back on the floor and lower her skirt. "I'm here, Mama," she said in a low voice. "I'll be right out. My stomach is unsettled."

"Well, hurry up. Your brother is furious. He thinks you're trying to avoid Mr. Alvington."

Saint fastened his trousers again while Evelyn attempted to straighten her dress. Taking a breath, she nodded and reached for the curtains.

Before she could escape, Saint grasped her elbow and turned her to face him again. Shaking his head to let her know that he wasn't letting her escape completely, he ran a finger along the low neckline of her gown, then leaned down and kissed her once more.

"Evie!"

"I'm coming," she said, putting a hand against his chest to push him against the far wall. She half opened the curtains, leaving him concealed in the shadows, and stepped back into the dimly lit corridor.

Saint stayed in the alcove, listening as the Ruddick

ladies' footsteps receded toward their box. He'd kept her secret for her—again. No one knew they'd become lovers; no one but the two of them. As many mistresses as he'd had over the years, it was heady, knowing that he was the first and only man to make love to her.

But what had her mother said? Something about Evelyn not avoiding Clarence Alvington. So that was her brother's scheme. Lord Alvington had little money, but he did own several properties in, and therefore had a great deal of influence over, the voting in West Sussex. That made the calculation simple: In exchange for handing Ruddick a seat in the House of Commons, the Alvington family would acquire Evelyn and her purse.

Saint glanced up and down the corridor, then slipped out of the alcove. He wondered whether Evelyn realized she'd been sold. And if she thought it difficult now to devote time and money to orphans, once her income belonged to Clarence Alvington, any charity at all would be impossible. Her entire stipend would undoubtedly go to neckcloths, racehorses, and wagering.

Of course, Saint would be finished with her by then, so it wouldn't signify. And it wouldn't bother him that thin-necked, thick-headed, high-shirt pointed Neckcloth Alvington would have nightly access to her bed and to her sweet body.

"Saint, where's my brandy?" Deliah asked as he dropped into the seat beside her again.

"Get it yourself."

He sat and stared at the stage for the next hour, though the actors might have been reciting nursery rhymes, for all the attention he paid. With Wellington captured for the dinner party, Victor Ruddick owed him at least one more outing with Evelyn. She'd probably try to make a few more visits to the orphanage, as well, so he could intercept her there. Considering he'd only given the place four more weeks of existence, his chances to see her in private would then end.

Saint glanced over his shoulder at the Ruddick box. The fop was whispering something at Evelyn that she was plainly trying to ignore. As Saint watched, her gaze lifted to meet his, and then she quickly looked away again.

This was intolerable, wanting her so much that he couldn't sleep, and barely being allowed to look in her direction, while the entire time someone else plotted to remove her from his grasp entirely. If he knew anything about his Evelyn, whatever he might wish, she would not consent to be his mistress once she was married, no matter how miserable she might be.

So he needed to get rid of Clarence Alvington, which meant *he* needed to be the one to secure a seat in Parliament or a Cabinet position for Victor Ruddick. And he needed to see Prinny and delay the destruction of the orphanage, because once it was gone, she would never look at him again.

"Saint?"

He started. "What is it, Deliah?"

"Intermission."

The lights had gone up, and he was staring at a curtained stage while the boxes around him emptied and members of Society wandered out to mingle and be seen. He stood. "Good. I'm leaving."

Deliah stood beside him, tugging down the front of her dress to better display her wares. "Lovely. I thought you might be wanting a taste of something," she murmured, running her tongue along her lips.

"I've already eaten. Good evening."

*   *   *

Oh, no. She'd become one of those harlots everyone heard rumors about, the ones who had sex with St. Aubyn in broom closets, on terraces, on chairs while their husbands dozed beside them.

Evelyn put her hand across her eyes as the Barrett barouche emerged into the sunlight between the shops of Regent Street. And even worse, she enjoyed being his harlot, his mistress, his lover. He was so . . . direct. Everyone knew that he took what he wanted—and he obviously wanted her. Being the object of his attentions was so incredibly arousing, she could hardly stand it when they were apart. Perhaps she could stop by the orphanage this afternoon. He might meet her there.

"Well, I never thought it would happen," Lucinda was saying, and Evie jerked to attention.

"I'm sorry, but what were we talking about?"

"Your apparent success with St. Aubyn. An entire picnic during which, as you reported, he was a perfect gentleman, and now last night he stayed for the entire first half of *As You Like It*. I can think of no other explanation but your lessons in civility and propriety."

Yes, she and Saint were both so proper and civilized that they'd disappeared to have standing-up sex behind a curtain. "I tend to think it's just circumstance and coincidence."

"Does he continue to say shocking things to you?" Lucinda asked, her cheeks dimpling as she grinned.

"At every opportunity," Evie said, relieved to be able to speak the complete truth for once.

"But no more stolen items?"

Only her virginity. "No. Nothing I've discovered, anyway."

Lucinda gave a loud sigh. "Evie, what's wrong? Really? You can tell me anything, you know."

"I know." Frowning, she searched for something she was prepared to tell her friend, without Lucinda thinking she was a complete and utter fool. "He's given me four weeks to convince him about the orphanage. I've already tried . . . everything. I have no idea what to say that will change his mind now, when nothing else has."

Lucinda's brow furrowed. "But Evie . . ."

Cold fingers wrapped around her heart. "But what?"

"I'm not entirely certain, so please keep that in mind," Lucinda said, taking her hands and squeezing them, "but I heard yesterday that Parliament has approved Prince George's expansion of the new park."

A roaring began in her ears, louder and louder until she could barely hear Lucinda's words. "No," she whispered. He'd promised. Four weeks. She'd been with him last night, as eager as he was for the joining, and he'd said nothing.

She gave a harsh laugh. Of course he hadn't said anything. If he had, she would never—*never*—have let him touch her again.

And she'd begun to think that perhaps, maybe, he was learning. That he'd changed, at least a little, and that maybe he even . . . cared about her. He said such nice things, sometimes—but now she knew it was all lies. All of it. And she'd thought he always told the truth. That she could trust him. Ha.

"Lucinda," she said, realizing tears had begun running down her cheeks, "will you please do me a very, very large favor?"

"Of course. What do you need?"

"I need you to go with me to St. Aubyn's residence. Right now."

"St. Aub . . . Are you certain?"

"Oh, yes. I'm quite certain."

Lucinda evidently believed her, because she nodded and sat forward. "Griffin, we have a change of plans. Please take us to Lord St. Aubyn's house."

The driver actually turned around to look at his employer. "Miss Barrett? Did you say—"

"You heard me. At once, if you please."

"Yes, miss."

Saint leaned over the railing. "Jansen, have we heard from Carlton House yet?"

The butler emerged into the hallway. "Not yet, my lord. I assure you, I will inform you immediately."

"Immediately," Saint repeated, retreating into his office to pace while he waited for permission to see Prinny. Saving the orphanage was at least something about which he could take action, while he tried to determine how best to undermine Alvington and secure a seat for Ruddick. Thank God, Prince George couldn't do anything without Parliament, someone else's money, and a thousand advisors. And some fine claret. He stalked to the door again.

"Jansen, I need a case of my best claret."

"I'll see to it, my lord."

Leaving the orphanage open would mean keeping him leg-shackled to the damned place. It wasn't forever, he reminded himself, cursing. Just until he'd figured out what to do about Evelyn. Another opportunity would come along, or perhaps he could stall the entire park idea for a few months.

Jansen scratched at the half-open door. "My lord?"

"Did you find the claret?"

"Ah, no, my lord. You have callers."

"I'm not in."

"Female callers."

"Then I'm definitely not in. Get the damned claret. I'm off to Carlton House as soon as I receive permission to visit."

"Yes, my lord."

Usurping Alvington would be trickier. His own influence in West Sussex was negligible. He had no properties there and no acquaintances who did. Neither did he recall any information he held over anyone there that he could use against them if they didn't help.

"My lord?"

"Carlton House?" he barked.

"No, my lord."

"What, then, for God's sake?"

"They won't leave. The one says it is most urgent that she see you."

He sighed. Just what he needed, more female entanglements. "Who are they?"

"They did not give their names. I . . . don't recall seeing them here before, my lord, if that narrows the field somewhat."

Saint sent a glare in his butler's direction. "Fine. I'll give them two minutes. And you'd—"

"I'll notify you at once if the message from Carlton House arrives."

Grabbing his coat off the back of his chair, Saint shrugged it on as he headed for the stairs. Down in the foyer he could just see a bonnet and the tip of the other's shoe. If it was those damned charity ladies who came by from time to time looking for donations for the poor, he'd see them out on their backsides for disturbing him.

"Ladies," he drawled as he reached the bottom of the stairs, "I'm afraid I'm very busy this mor—"

He stopped as they turned to face him.

"Evelyn?"

She rushed forward. His heart pounding, a million disconnected thoughts roiling through his mind, Saint opened his arms to her.

Evelyn punched him in the gut. "You bastard!" she growled. "I hate you, you stupid liar!"

More surprised than hurt, he grabbed her hands to keep her from hitting him again. "What the devil are you talking about?"

She tried to wrench her hands away, but he wasn't about to set her free. "You lied to me. Let me go!"

"Stop attacking me," he countered, glancing over his head at her companion. "Miss Barrett? What is she—"

A slippered foot rammed into his knee.

"Ouch!"

"You said I had four weeks! You didn't even wait four days!"

Saint shook her by the arms, then shoved her backward. "If you come at me again, I will pin you to the floor," he growled, leaning down to rub his knee. "Now, I presume we're talking about the . . ." He looked at Miss Barrett again.

"She knows about the orphanage. Don't lie to me, Saint. Don't you dare lie to me."

"I don't even know what you're upset about," he returned, sinking down onto the bottom stair. "If you must know, I'm waiting to hear from Carlton House so I can call on Prinny and withdraw my offer of the orphanage property."

A tear ran down her pale cheek. "How can you do that," she enunciated, her voice shaking, "when Parliament has already approved the park expansion?"

He blinked. Either she was mistaken or something was dreadfully wrong. "What?"

"Don't pretend you're surprised," she retorted. "I

wanted to do one—*one*—important thing, and you've made it all into a joke."

"Evelyn, I—this—are you certain?"

His question seemed to make her hesitate. "Lucinda heard her father talking about it yesterday. About how the Marquis of St. Aubyn had managed to turn an orphanage into a pot of gold."

"I had no idea. Truly," he said, knowing she had no real reason to believe him. Earnestness wasn't precisely his strong suit.

"I wanted you to know that I know," she said in a slightly steadier voice, "and that I wish I'd never met you. You are the worst person I've ever . . . heard of."

Women had said such things to him before, but coming from Evelyn, it felt as though she'd punched him again. He stood. "I didn't know," he said in a harder voice, "but I intend to find out what's happened." Someone had been maneuvering behind his back. Prinny wouldn't have pressed the project without consulting him, otherwise. "I've never lied to you, Evelyn." He stepped toward her, and she backed away. "I have spent a few days . . . away, but if something's happened, I will find out what it is. And I'll make it right."

She shook her head, backing toward the door. "Don't do anything for me," she shot back at him, swiping tears from her eyes. "It won't make any difference."

Saint narrowed his eyes. He wasn't going to lose his hold on Evelyn because someone else had outmaneuvered him while he'd been looking at her pretty face. "Evelyn."

"I have to go now, to find someplace else for those poor children to live. Good-bye, St. Aubyn. I hope to never see you again."

He let her leave. Obviously she wasn't going to listen

to anything he said today. Cursing to himself, he stalked out to the stable and ordered Cassius saddled. It wasn't over between them. He wasn't ready for that. And so he needed to go see Prince George, whether he was welcome or not.

Chapter 19

And thus, untaught in youth my heart to tame,
My springs of life were poison'd. 'Tis too late!
Yet am I chang'd; though still enough the same
In strength to bear what time can not abate.

—Lord Byron, *Childe Harold's*
Pilgrimage, Canto III

"**I** don't appreciate this interruption," Prince George said as he made his way into the private sitting room where they'd stowed Saint. "I'm meeting with the Spanish ambassador, and I've a huge dinner party at Brighton over the weekend."

"You put the park expansion before Parliament," Saint said flatly. He was attempting to be civil, since shouting would only send Prinny into a faint, but he couldn't remember ever being this furious before in his life.

"I'm in dire straits," the Regent returned. "You know that. Those damned politicians insist on holding my purse strings so tightly that light couldn't escape. It's intolerable, really, but—"

"I've . . . been out of town," Saint said grimly. "Why push the issue while I wasn't here to explain my desire to pay for the thing?"

"It had the backing of your silly orphanage's board of

trustees. Everyone agreed that the government funds saved as a result of razing the drafty old building would best be used elsewhere." The prince pulled a silver snuffbox from his pocket, opened the lid, and took a pinch. "You got what you wanted, so stop glaring at me."

Saint shook his head, using every bit of restraint he had to keep from stalking up to Prinny and punching him. "I've changed my mind. The Heart of Hope Orphanage was very . . . dear to my mother, and I wish to keep it standing."

Prinny laughed. "Who is she?"

"Who is who?"

"The chit who's got you by the balls. 'Dear to my mother.' Ha, ha. Very good. Did you deposit a brat in there, and the female's threatening now to expose it? No one cares, lad. You're the bloody Marquis of St. Aubyn. It's expected."

Saint looked at his Regent for a long moment as it dawned on him that no one would ever believe he did anything without motive. Even Evelyn, who'd tried to convince him that he had the potential to perform selfless acts of kindness, never thought he'd actually done such a thing. And they were right.

"Those children," he said slowly, sinking into a chair, "consider that old building their home. I've . . . had some consultants in, and we've recently begun several programs of education and reform. I think what we're doing there could make a difference in their lives, Your Majesty. I ask that you keep the orphanage standing."

"Saint, it's been voted on. More importantly, it's been in the newspapers. You'll look like a fool."

"I don't care about that."

"*I'll* look like a fool, bowing to the whim of a scoundrel like you. And *I* care about that. Too many hands in the pot as it is. If I have more people stepping in to make decisions and attempting to sway my opinion, this might as well be a damned democracy. I'm sorry, but the orphanage goes."

"And the children?"

"You've already assigned yourself to finding them new housing. I suggest that you do so. Without delay." Prinny made his way back to the door. "And come to Brighton on Saturday. The Turkish consul is bringing belly dancers."

As the prince left, a footman closing the door behind him, Saint rose and went to the window. The Carlton House gardens spread out below him, empty but for a few gardeners and the occasional auspicious visitor. Obviously Prinny wasn't going to do anything now that the newspapers had printed the story and the orphanage's trustees had come up with a plausible reason for its destruction that wouldn't raise the public's ire.

And of course the board had gotten wind of his scheme when Prinny had broached it to his loud-mouthed advisors. With a potential to earn the prince's gratitude by supporting one of his beloved park projects, and with the chance at freed-up government funds sent in their direction, of course they'd jumped at the chance.

Slowly Saint let the curtains slide closed through his fingers. He'd been bested, probably for the first time in his life. And the cost, he was coming to realize, was much more than pride or money. He drew a breath, disliking the tightness across his chest he'd felt since Evelyn had bidden him good-bye.

She'd said she was going to find the children somewhere else to live. Saint strode to the door, collected his hat, and went to find one of his solicitors. Perhaps he could help her with that.

*   *   *

"Evie, we really shouldn't be doing this alone," Lucinda whispered. "Some of these places are—"

"They're awful," Evie returned. "I know. But I need to see them all, before St. Aubyn tries to toss those children into whichever holes will hold them."

The office door squeaked open, and a heavyset man with hanging jowls and small dark eyes stepped behind the small desk and seated himself. "My secretary tells me you're looking for a place to put a child," he said, the smooth tone of his voice making Evie shiver. "We can be very discreet here, given an adequate stipend to pay for the child's food and clothing. Might I ask which of you lovely young ladies is . . . making a deposit?"

"Oh, good heavens," Lucinda yelped, shooting to her feet. "That is the worst thing I've ever heard!"

Evie reached over to take her friend's hand. "There's been a misunderstanding."

"Of course. There always is."

"We are not talking about *a* child," she said crisply, wondering why she bothered to continue when she already knew that she would never leave any of her children in a facility run by this man. "We're talking about fifty-three children, all of whom are about to be displaced. I wish to find them a new place to live."

"Ah, I understand. The Heart of Hope Orphanage, yes? I'd heard the benefactors were closing it. That will never happen at this establishment. It is completely funded by the government."

"And by donated stipends, apparently," Lucinda said caustically.

"You must understand, miss, that on occasion children with . . . imminent parentage are left in our care, and they of course require . . . special treatment."

Like Saint's half-brothers or -sisters, Evie thought, wondering where they might be now. At least they hadn't been left here. "I think we've learned all we need to," she said, standing. "Thank you for your time."

He clattered to his feet. "I do have room for a half dozen or so youngsters under the age of seven. I'd even be willing to donate five quid each for them."

"Why the young ones?" she asked, beginning to feel quite ill. The more she learned, though, the better prepared she would be to help the children.

"They're light. We set them to turn drying bricks at the brickworks. Any older, and they're too heavy—can't walk across the wet clay without smashing it, you know."

"Of course. I'll consider it," she said, following Lucinda to the door. "Thank you again."

"My pleasure, ladies."

Neither of them said anything as they returned to Lucinda's barouche and moved back out into the streets.

"Oh, my God," Lucinda finally exploded. "That's hideous!"

"I'm beginning to think Saint wasn't so awful," Evie forced out. "At least he didn't make the children work, and he kept them fed and clothed without asking for money from their families."

"St. Aubyn did seem surprised by what you said," Luce offered.

"That doesn't matter. Today, or in four weeks, that place"—and she gestured at the low, dark building behind them—"is where he meant for those children to go."

He'd betrayed her. Michael Edward Halboro had completely betrayed her trust, her growing sense of self-worth, and her heart. And whether he'd been lying or telling the truth, in the end it didn't matter. She could never trust him again; he could never redeem himself from this. Everyone had been so right about him, and it hurt so much to realize that she'd been so wrong.

Lucinda offered her a sympathetic smile. "I'd like to meet these children. They seem to have completely captured your heart."

Evie'd been putting off going to the Heart of Hope Orphanage all morning, hoping to have some good news to carry with her. Each establishment she and Lucinda visited, though, seemed worse than the last. And the children needed to know, and to begin to prepare themselves for what very likely lay ahead.

"I'll take you," she said, and gave the direction to the driver.

By now the various attendants at the orphanage were used to her comings and goings. Evelyn was therefore surprised to see Mrs. Natham hurrying down the stairs to meet them.

"Miss Ruddick," the housekeeper said, distress on her hard face. "Is it true? That awful St. Aubyn is going to tear the orphanage down?"

"Yes, I'm afraid so, Mrs. Natham. Have the children heard?"

"Some of them, I think. Oh, I knew I should've thrown away that key the minute I saw him in there."

Evelyn glanced at Lucinda, who was giving the housekeeper increasingly puzzled looks. If even those she trusted as much as her friends knew that she'd kidnapped St. Aubyn, they would lose considerable sympathy for her cause. Mrs. Natham evidently knew about Saint's imprisonment, but she also seemed to think it had been a good idea. She would have to ask Saint . . . Except that she couldn't. Not any longer.

"Yes, I know how conscientious you are," she said. "Thank you for that. Are the children at their lessons?"

"Yes, Miss Ruddick. But what are we going to do?"

"I don't know yet. I'm open to suggestions."

The housekeeper wandered away, shaking her head. Hoping Lucinda wouldn't ask any questions about keys and who had been locked up where, Evelyn took her friend's hand and led her to the classrooms.

"How are you going to tell them?"

"I'll just have to do it directly. They deserve to know the truth." She took a deep breath. "I'd give anything not to have to give them this news," she admitted. "But that would be both unfair and cowardly."

"And I notice which marquis isn't here to assist you," Lucinda commented.

"He wasn't invited."

Evelyn leaned into each classroom and asked the instructors to have the children meet her in the ballroom when their lessons were finished. Lucinda stayed quietly at her side, and she'd never been more grateful for her friend's support.

"Miss Evie!" Penny exclaimed, leading the charge up the wide staircase, Rose on her heels.

She welcomed the girls' hugs, though she felt as if she didn't deserve them. She'd failed—again. And this time she had no solution at all.

Saint felt tired to his bones. Over the past three days he'd slept for perhaps five hours, and those badly.

"My lord, Mr. Wiggins has brought the papers you requested."

Wearily Saint set aside the legal treatise he'd been reading. Rising from the library's comfortable chair, he made his way to the table with its disorganized stacks of books and papers. "Let's see them."

Jansen and another footman carried in two leather-bound stacks of papers. "Mr. Wiggins also wished me to inform you that the owner of the property you viewed this morning will be in London tomorrow."

Saint nodded. "That's good news. Thank you."

The footman left, but the butler hesitated in the doorway. "My lord?"

"Yes?"

"I . . . took the liberty of having Mrs. Dooley prepare some soup this evening. Will you be staying in?"

Something tickled at the back of Saint's mind. "What day is it, anyway?"

He thought he caught a brief smile on Jansen's face before the butler resumed his usual stoic expression. "Today is Friday, my lord."

"Friday." Saint yanked out his pocket watch. Eight-fifteen. "Damnation. I'm late. Send Pemberly upstairs," he said, rising and striding for the door.

By the time he rapped on the door of Lord and Lady Houton's, it was nearly nine in the evening. Eager as he was to see Evelyn after three days, he knew she wouldn't be pleased to see him. That troubled him, because just to spite him she was likely to ally herself with Clarence Alvington, and he needed her to agree to an outing with him tomorrow.

"Lord St. Aubyn," the Marquis of Houton greeted him, standing to shake his hand. "I hope you don't mind that we began dinner without you."

Saint deliberately kept his gaze away from Evelyn. He needed to concentrate for a few moments, and he wouldn't be able to do it with her glaring at him. "Houton. Good of you to have me. I apologize for my tardiness. A late meeting with my solicitor, I'm afraid."

"Yes, we'd heard you and Prince George were closing a transaction on land for a new park," Victor Ruddick drawled, rising as well.

Wincing inwardly, Saint nodded. "Buildings in London are easy to come by; parks, however, are becoming more scarce by the moment."

"Indeed they are," Wellington said, holding out his hand. "Thank you again for that splendid bottle of sherry, Saint. I've never tasted finer."

"My pleasure, Your Grace." He took the seat between Lady Alvington and Mrs. Ruddick, noting that it placed him exactly opposite Evelyn. That would make it rather difficult not to gaze at her, especially when with every fiber of his being he wanted to drag her out of the room and make her understand what had happened. *Contrition.* Another new emotion for him. He was finding bagsful, these days. "So tell me, Your Grace, have you and Mr. Ruddick discovered any mutual acquaintances in India?"

That began the conversation, which he'd interrupted with his arrival, going again, and served to remind Victor that he was the reason Wellington was chatting with him now. Not bad, for one sentence. Taking a breath, he settled the napkin in his lap and raised his eyes.

Evelyn sat chatting with Clarence Alvington, having apparently found the pearl pin in the fop's cravat an item of unparalleled interest. She was being charming again, no doubt on her brother's behalf, but Saint wondered whether she'd yet figured out why Mr. Ruddick kept sending Alvington in her direction.

He'd figured it out, and he didn't like it one damned

bit. "Clarence, I haven't seen you at Gentleman Jackson's lately," he drawled, digging into the roast pork as soon as a footman brought it by.

"No, I'm afraid I've been engaged with writing a poem," the Neckcloth answered, sending a fond glance in Evelyn's direction.

Saint wanted to strangle the bastard. "A poem?"

"A sonnet, actually."

He and Clarence had little in common, and they certainly traveled in different circles. The outlandish intricacy of his neckcloth and the near-to-bursting seams of his waistcoat and jacket, however, gave Saint a fair indication of just how good his poetry was likely to be. As a longtime gambler, he was willing to risk Evelyn's admiration of the piece. "Why don't you regale us with it, then?"

The dandy blushed. "Oh, it's not quite ready yet."

"You're among friends," Saint insisted, smiling his most charming smile. "And the composition of poetry fascinates me."

"You don't need to recite it if you don't wish to, Mr. Alvington," Evelyn said in a low voice, sending a brief glare in Saint's direction.

"Oh, Clarence is such a talent," his mother put in with a chuckle. "While he was away at school, he would send us a composition every week."

"Truly admirable," Saint said, nodding. If this was what proper folk spent their evenings doing, he was glad to be considered a scoundrel.

"Very well," Clarence said, beaming. Clearing his throat, he stood. "As I said, it's still a work in process, but I shall relish hearing your opinion of it."

"Good God," Lord Alvington said under his breath, but Saint pretended not to hear.

"'On a bright summer's morn in London's fair streets,'" Clarence began, "'I chanced upon a sight of dreams and sighs./ Delight and happy thoughts drove me from my carriage seat,/ To look up close upon an angel in earthly guise.'"

A blush began to climb Evelyn's cheeks. She sent another glance at Saint, who returned her gaze, willing her to realize just why Clarence Alvington had begun addressing poetry to earthly angels.

"'I spoke to the maiden and asked for her name,/ But she answered with a sweet, soft blush,/ As pure as the dew the sun tries to tame,/ Silent, and yet still enough to make my heart to hush.'"

"'Blush' and 'hush,'" his mother simpered. "That's so lovely, dear. Do go on."

"'Oh, Evelyn, Evelyn, my soul's delight'—and see, I've used 'delight' twice, so I need to make a different rhyme there," he continued, "'I see thee in every star at night,/ And when the day comes 'round to light,/ I see thee still in the sunshine bright.'"

While everyone applauded, Saint watched Evelyn. Her gaze went from Clarence to her brother and back again, her expression growing grimmer with each passing second. "That's lovely, Mr. Alvington," she finally said, taking a large swallow of wine. "I . . ."

"I thought a sonnet had fourteen lines," Saint said, when Evelyn looked as though she couldn't decide whether to scream or begin pummeling poets. "But I only counted twelve."

"Yes, I've modified the form somewhat, but I think rhyming the last four lines gives it a sense of serene completeness."

"Indeed it does," he agreed, raising his glass in Alvington's direction. "A stunning composition."

"Thank you, St. Aubyn. I have to admit, I hadn't expected to find you an admirer of the fine arts."

"I believe Lord St. Aubyn admires anything which can be used for empty flattery and subterfuge," Evelyn said smoothly, dabbing at the corner of her mouth with a napkin.

Well, at least she was speaking *at* him, if not *to* him. "I'm certain Mr. Alvington didn't intend empty flattery, Miss Ruddick," he returned.

"Of course he didn't," Lady Alvington protested.

"That's . . . that's not what I meant," Evelyn said, her flush deepening. "I only meant that poetry may be *used* for empty flattery, and that is how I imagine Lord St. Aubyn would utilize it."

Saint lifted an eyebrow. "Do you imagine me often, Miss Ruddick?"

"Evie," her mother said sharply, "please refrain from insulting your uncle's guests."

"He's not a guest," she retorted, throwing her napkin onto the table and rising, "he invited himself."

"Evie!"

She glanced at her brother as she stormed out of the room. "I have a headache," she snapped, her voice breaking, and slammed the door open and closed again behind her.

Saint looked after her for a moment. He'd separated her from Clarence, but obviously he hadn't earned any credit for it. And tomorrow she would still hate him, but the idiotic pseudo-sonnet would be forgotten. Giving himself an additional day of her hate was not what he wanted, and it wasn't what he had in mind.

"Tell me, Your Grace," he said into the silence, "have you decided to mentor anyone for the House this Season? Despite my . . . conflict of opinion with Miss Ruddick, her brother is an upstanding fellow—quite the opposite of myself in nearly every way, in fact."

"I refuse to be bartered to Clarence Alvington in exchange for your seat in Parliament!" Evie shouted, striding back and forth before the morning room fireplace.

Victor looked up from his newspaper, then went back to reading. "He's handsome enough, and from good family. Besides, Lord Alvington *guarantees* me enough votes to defeat Plimpton."

"He's an idiot!" she exploded. "And he dresses like a baboon! Don't you care that I'll be miserable?"

"He seems very fond of you, dear," her mother added from across the room, where she was busily addressing correspondence—probably wedding invitations. "And you have to admit, you'd never choose anyone on your own."

"I'd never choose him; that's for certain. Victor, you didn't even say anything to me about it. Instead I have to find out in front of . . . well, *everyone,* when he recited that stupid nonsonnet."

Her brother's eyes lifted above the paper, then vanished again. "St. Aubyn seemed fond enough of it."

"St. Aubyn was making fun of it," she retorted. "'Light, bright, night, delight.' For heaven's sake. I would have laughed at it, too, except I was too occupied with trying not to vomit."

The newspaper snapped down. "That's enough, Evie. Nothing has been decided. Clarence Alvington has merely expressed an interest in you. And he's fairly harmless. An alliance would help me, and marriage to him would do little to upset your social calendar."

"I—"

"As Mother said, you've had five years to find someone. Clarence would maintain and even elevate your status, and at least one of us has a use for him—which is more than I can say for certain other of your male acquaintances. I'm speaking to him again today, though after your . . . performance last night, he may have changed his mind about you."

Evie jabbed a finger in his face. "I will not marry Clarence Alvington. I'd rather have no one," she enunciated, and turned on her heel.

She yanked open the door and nearly ran into Langley as he raised his hand to rap. "I beg your pardon, Miss Ruddick," he said, narrowly missing knocking on her bosom.

"I'm going out."

"Good. So am I."

Only then did she notice the shadowed figure standing behind the butler, waiting to be announced. Saint. Even though she was so angry and hurt and disappointed in him that she wanted to scream, her body still reacted as it always did to his presence. Her heart sped, and her nerves jangled all the way to the tips of her toes. "I'm not going with you."

"But I have something to show you," he murmured, walking around Langley to confront her as though the butler had simply ceased to exist.

He couldn't be attempting to seduce her now. Not after what he'd done. "No."

Saint clasped her elbow, his touch more gentle than she expected. "Come with me," he whispered, leaning forward to brush her hair with his lips. "I hold all of your secrets, remember?"

Someone was absolutely going to get punched in the head today. "I hate you," she whispered back, then faced the morning room again. "Lord St. Aubyn, who introduced you to Wellington and feels you owe him a favor in return, wishes to take me to the zoo. Sally and I will return in time for luncheon."

Victor grunted something that sounded like an assent, so she sent Langley to fetch Sally and stalked off to the foyer, the marquis on her heels. Everyone seemed content to determine the entire course of her life without bothering to consult her about any of it. Her protests, her screams, didn't make any difference.

"Let me guess," Saint drawled. "I'm interrupting the scheduling of an outing with Clarence Alvington, yes?"

So he'd realized what Victor was planning, too. Saint missed very little, so she supposed she shouldn't be surprised. "You may blackmail me into accompanying you," she muttered, "but I will not be conversing with you."

"As you wish, my flower."

Sally hurried down the stairs to join them, and Evelyn led the way outside. Whatever he had planned, her maid's presence would prevent him from attempting further seductions. And as desperately as she wanted to escape that house, even St. Aubyn counted as an improvement.

"I hope you're impressed," he continued. "I brought the curricle so the entire entourage could ride. Are you certain you don't wish to include the butler or the gardener in our party?"

Since she wasn't talking to him, she settled for sniffing and giving her hand to a groom to assist her into the vehicle. Apparently undaunted by her silence, Saint joined her on the low seat and clucked to the matched pair of grays.

She realized that she should have asked him where they were going before she'd decided not to speak to him. With her maid present and with her family knowing she'd return by noon, however, he wouldn't have much time for his mischief-making. She offered him a quick glance. Saint could make a great deal of mischief in a very short time. She'd learned that firsthand at the theater.

After fifteen minutes it became obvious that they weren't going to the zoo or to Hyde Park. "Where are we going?" she finally asked.

"I thought we weren't conversing."

"This is not conversing," she pointed out. "It's a question about our destination. Please answer it."

He gave her a sideways glance. "No. It's a surprise."

Fine. He wanted to be difficult. Well, she could be difficult, too. "You do recall that I said I hated you."

Saint nodded, his gaze hardening. "I recall several unflattering comments you made to me. I will expect an eventual apology for all of them."

"Never."

" 'Never' is a very long time, Evelyn Marie."

"Precisely."

They turned onto an old, tree-lined street, large houses of a long-ago faded gentry on either side. A scrawny black dog trotted across the lane in front of them. His barking made the horses start, but with no visible effort the marquis drew them back under his control.

Half a block farther on, he guided the curricle to the right side of the street and stopped. A coach, large and black with closed curtains, waited opposite them. A faint stir of uneasiness went through Evelyn. She'd kidnapped him, and she could abruptly think of no reason why he wouldn't do the same to her. This quiet old street would certainly be the perfect place for it.

Saint tied off the reins and jumped to the ground.

Coming around to her side of the curricle, he lifted his hand to her. She didn't want to touch him, because when she did, she couldn't seem to remember how much of a scoundrel he was. Neither, though, did she wish to try clambering to the ground in her dress and walking slippers. Taking a breath, she stood. As she did so, however, he stepped closer, sliding both hands around her waist and lifting her to the ground.

"Let go of me," she whispered, her gaze fixed on his plain, neat cravat so she wouldn't be tempted to look him in the eye. Kissing and touching and all kinds of nonsense could follow that, and she was too angry with him to want that to happen.

"For now," he returned, and released her. "Shall we?"

Without waiting for an answer, he strolled across the street and up the short, curving drive of the largest of the old manor houses. Her curiosity outweighing her caution, Evie trailed after him.

At the door they were met by an elderly gentleman with a slight stoop and a limp. "Lord St. Aubyn, I presume?" he asked, offering his hand.

Saint shook it. "Sir Peter Ludlow. Thank you for agreeing to meet with me."

"No trouble at all." He glanced past the marquis at Evie. "Would you and your lady like a tour?"

"N—"

"Yes, we would," Saint interrupted her, offering his arm. "Thank you again."

Well, he was certainly being polite, suddenly. With Sally following, they entered the old mansion. Their quiet footsteps echoed in the large, empty hallway, and Evelyn closed her fingers more tightly around Saint's arm. Whatever he was up to, she wasn't going to let him out of her sight until they were safely back at her home.

"As you no doubt saw yesterday," Sir Peter was saying as he limped into the lead, "most of the furniture and the window coverings are long gone, but the floor's sound, and the walls and roof were patched and repaired after the rain last winter."

"How many rooms again?" Saint asked.

"Twenty-seven. That includes two upstairs sitting rooms, the library, and the morning room downstairs. The ballroom and drawing room are both on the third floor, with the music room, and the dining room is just down this way. A dozen servants' rooms are belowstairs, along with the kitchen and pantry."

"Saint," Evie said, beginning to wonder whether he really did mean to keep her prisoner in the large old house.

"Hush," he murmured. "Let's see the dining room, why don't we?"

A few yards farther down the hallway, Sir Peter pushed open a wide set of double doors. The room seemed closer to a medieval dining hall, with space for perhaps seventy-five guests in its long rectangle.

Saint pulled a scrap of paper from his pocket, scrawled something across it with a sad stub of a pencil, and handed it to Sir Peter. Evie thought the older gentleman's eyes widened for a moment before he nodded.

"Have your solicitor see mine," he said, pulling a key from his pocket. "And you may have this now."

The marquis took the key and, to Evelyn's surprise, offered his hand again. "Thank you, Sir Peter."

"And thank you, lad. I like a fellow who doesn't feel the need to bargain." He tipped his hat at Evie. "Good day, my lady."

As soon as the front door closed, Evelyn released her

grip on Saint's arm. "You obviously wanted me to witness this. So what is going on?" she demanded.

Saint pursed his lips. "Excuse your maid."

"No."

"Then I'm not telling you anything."

He meant it; she knew him well enough to realize that. Scowling, she faced her maid. "Sally, please wait just outside," she instructed, "but return in no longer than five minutes."

Sally dipped a curtsy. "Yes, Miss Ruddick."

Once the maid was gone, Evie turned her attention on St. Aubyn again. Five minutes was both far too long and far too short a time to be alone with him, but she steeled herself to be ready for anything. "All right, we're alone," she prompted. "And whatever . . . nefarious thing you have in mind, just remember that you deserved what I did to you."

Saint gazed at her for the space of several heartbeats. "And you deserve this, I think," he said in a quiet voice, then held out the key. "Congratulations."

She frowned, but took the key from his fingers—both because she would then be able to escape if he attempted to lock her in, and because she wanted to touch him. "You're giving me an old house?" she asked skeptically.

Saint shook his head. "I'm giving you a new orphanage."

Evelyn stopped breathing. *"What?"*

"Fully furnished, eventually, in whatever style you choose. And staffed however you see fit, though I feel compelled to protest the continued employment of Mrs. Natham."

Clutching the key hard in one hand, Evelyn stared at him. It made no sense. He'd finally escaped his obligation to an establishment he detested, only to purchase another one? "Wh . . . why?"

"I talked to Prinny, but he refused to risk losing face by withdrawing his plans the day after he'd announced them. I've discovered that it's difficult to convince a country's ruler, even a Regent, to do what you want once the blasted thing is printed in the newspaper."

"But you hate the orphanage. Why go through all this?"

A small smile touched his sensuous mouth. "I told you I would make it right."

She could breathe again, but now her heart was pounding so hard she feared he could hear it. "So you did this"—and she gestured at the grand old building around them—"for . . . me?"

"Yes."

Oh, my goodness. "I don't know what to say, Saint. This is . . . extraordinary."

He tilted his head at her. "But?" he prompted, old cynicism touching his green eyes. "There's something. I can see it in your face."

It wasn't until then that she realized what had been different about him the last few days—that deep, jaded cynicism had been absent. And that unsettled her more than anything else. "It's only that I had hoped you would have done it for the children, and not for m—"

"Damnation, Evelyn!" he exploded. "Does every deed have to be done for the 'right' reason? Or is it only the right reason if I have no reason at all? I'm very tired, and I'm afraid I'm a little foggy on this, so please, explain why I shouldn't be doing it for you."

"I—"

"Explain to me why you think you don't deserve it,"

he interrupted, taking a step closer. "Isn't that what you were going to say?"

"Saint, it's—"

"Explain why it shouldn't be for you." He put his hands on either side of her face. "And explain why you shouldn't be grateful and why I shouldn't kiss you right now."

He brushed his lips over hers, feather-light.

"I am grateful," she managed, using every bit of flagging self-control she had to keep from wrapping her arms around his shoulders. "So grateful. But—"

"Sweet Lucifer, you torment me," he whispered against her mouth.

Evie couldn't answer any more of his questions. She was too occupied with kissing him back.

Chapter 20

Yet there are things whose strong reality
Outshines our fairyland; in shape and hues
More beautiful than our fantastic sky.

—Lord Byron, *Childe Harold's*
Pilgrimage, Canto IV

The Evelyn that Saint drove back to Ruddick House was a great deal chattier than the one with whom he'd left. For a moment he considered reminding her that she'd vowed not to converse with him, but her enthusiasm was far too exhilarating to put an end to. And besides, if he reminded her of her vow of silence, she would also remember that she'd fled home because her brother was trying to marry her off to that blockhead Clarence Alvington.

"Do you think we might divide the ballroom into smaller classrooms?" she asked, practically bouncing in her seat.

Saint admired her bosom for a moment. "I'm the finances," he drawled. "You're the decisions. Anything you need arranged, ask me, and I'll see to it."

"You do know how much this is going to cost, don't you?"

He gave a faint smile, a warmth he quite liked flowing through him. "Do you?"

"Oh, I know it'll be a great deal of work," she returned, "but if I hire the right people, I think I can manage it."

So she still meant to keep her involvement a secret from her family. For a long moment Saint kept his attention on the team, while he assessed the situation. Angelic, wealthy Evelyn would be a boon to the Alvington family. Her pristine, proper demeanor was a definite bonus to her brother, hence her becoming a part of the bargain. Unless someone disrupted the process, of course. "I'm sure you can manage it," he agreed, "but that's not what I meant."

"What did you mean, then?"

"Everything has a price, Evelyn," he said, glancing at her. "Do you think I'd spend over twenty thousand pounds for no reason?"

"But . . . but you said you did it for me," she faltered.

The hurt in her voice constricted his breathing. "I did," he made himself say. "But nothing is for free."

She raised her chin. "Then what is your price, Saint?"

"Tell your family."

The blood drained from her face, and for a moment he thought she might faint. He steeled himself to grab her if she started to topple from the carriage. Perhaps this wasn't for *her* own good, he told himself, but it was most definitely for his. If she was tainted, he could have her.

"What?"

"You heard me." He glanced over his shoulder at the maid-bodyguard. "Tell your family that you've been volunteering your time and money at an orphanage, and that thanks to your hard work and dedication, the children are being moved to an improved facility where they will receive even better care. And tell them that you intend to continue to devote time to this project."

"Saint, I can't," she gasped. "You don't understand. Victor would—"

"You don't need to mention me, but you will tell them what you've been doing."

"I won't!"

"Then I withdraw my offer."

"You can't do that!"

His lips curved in an unamused smile. "My dear, I can do whatever I please. Haven't you realized that by now?"

"You will destroy my life," she retorted shakily, fists clenching. "Don't you realize that? Or do you just not care at all?"

For a moment he was silent. She was right; he knew her brother well enough to have a very good idea what she would face once she confessed. He shouldn't care. He did things to amuse himself all the time at the expense of others who owed him. This was no different—except that it apparently was.

"Then make me a counter-offer," he said, cursing himself for an idiot. "What would you give me in place of your confession?"

She opened her mouth, then closed it again. "I don't know."

"That doesn't sound tempting at all, I'm afraid."

"May I think about it, at least?"

"You have twenty-four hours, my dear." He looked back at the maid again. "And if you mention this conversation to anyone, I will know it. And you really don't want that to happen, do you?"

The girl's eyes widened. "No, my lord."

"I thought not."

Evelyn was glaring at him, though behind the frown

her expression was one of intense relief. "Please refrain from threatening my maid, Lord St. Aubyn."

They turned up the Ruddick House drive, and he took the opportunity to lean close and whisper in her ear. "I would take you right now if you'd let me, Evelyn. Offer me your body."

"I have twenty-four hours to give you an answer," she said, soft color returning to her cheeks.

"You can't get me out of your thoughts, can you?" he continued in a low voice as the maid and groom disembarked and a pair of footmen appeared. "You crave me."

"Yes," she breathed, then clambered to the ground with the help of the servants. "Thank you for a lovely time at the zoo, Lord St. Aubyn," she said in a louder voice. "I'll convey your greetings to my brother."

Before he could jump down and intercept her she was gone, vanished into the house. It was probably just as well, because after her one-word answer he wasn't certain he could have stood up with any decorum, anyway.

As he left the half-circle drive, a high-perch phaeton took his place in front of the house. Clarence Alvington. *Bloody, bloody hell.*

It made sense politically, he supposed, though it annoyed him that the fop seemed to merit more time with Evelyn than he did, especially considering that he'd literally brought Wellington to the table. Of course, dandy though he was, Clarence was dull enough that his reputation remained fairly unspotted, especially when compared with Saint's own.

Jansen pulled open his front door as he topped the shallow steps. The Hillary ball and several other social events would take place that evening, and if he wanted to survive any of it, he needed to lie down for an hour or so. He could have stayed in tonight and slept, as he dearly wanted to, but then he would miss a chance to see Evelyn.

He shrugged out of his greatcoat. "I'll be in my—"

"My lord, you have a visitor," the butler interrupted, sliding his eyes toward the morning room and back again.

Damnation. "Who?"

"Saint! Thank goodness!"

Fatima Hynes, Lady Gladstone, hurled herself into his arms, all soft curves and warm breath. Reflexively he caught her around the waist to keep from stumbling backward. "What are you doing here?"

"I need to talk to you, my darling," she breathed, taking his hands and pulling him toward the morning room. "I have nowhere else to go."

The "my darling" set his teeth on edge, but he couldn't very well discover what she was up to while standing in the middle of the hallway. He let her lead him into the morning room and close the door behind them.

"Very theatrical," he complimented her, pulling his hands free. "What do you want?"

"Where were you?" she asked.

"None of your affair. What do you want, Fatima? I won't ask you again."

"You were with her, weren't you? Evie Ruddick."

His first instinct was to protect Evelyn, and that surprised him. Generally his first thought was for himself. "Yes, I was engaged in wild, passionate lovemaking with Evie Ruddick, because of all the chits in London she is the only one who could possibly catch my attention."

She gave him a pained grimace. "Saint."

"If you have no other reason for being here than to interrogate me about my whereabouts and what I ate at breakfast, then go. Now."

"There's no need to insult me," she returned, smoothing the front of her deep rose gown, "especially when I've come here specifically to give you another chance."

Saint dragged his mind back to attention. "A chance. At you, you mean?"

"Gladstone is convinced that you and I are still lovers. I don't see why we should waste all of that good suspicion."

"Ah. So Lord Brumley fell . . . short of your expectations, did he?"

She looked at him. "You know everything, don't you?"

"Knowledge is what keeps me ahead of the game," he said dryly. "And ahead of any musket balls that might be flying in my direction."

"What do you say, then, Saint?" she purred, running a finger along his jaw. "We do go very well together."

Surprisingly for him, he wasn't even tempted. "We used to. This time around, I'm afraid I have to decline."

Fatima straightened. "And next time?"

"I don't think there'll be a next time, my lady." Saint smiled. "But thank you for the offer."

Her eyebrows lifted in surprise. "You're welcome. My, my, manners. Where *have* you been—church?"

"Something like that."

"Hm. It'll pass."

"No doubt."

Saint showed her out, then headed upstairs. Whether he could fool Fatima about the particulars of his relationship with Miss Ruddick or not, he couldn't deny that the two of them had a connection. For God knew what reason, Evelyn had crept under his skin, and he pursued her like a starving man after a meal.

It wouldn't last; it couldn't, once Ruddick married her off to Clarence Alvington. And then what would he do? Stand in the shadows beneath her window and moon over her? Making her reputation appear unsavory to the fastidious Alvingtons seemed his best chance to keep possession of her, but as she'd said, her brother would then make her life a misery.

"Damnation," he muttered, falling backward onto his bed. Evelyn, Evelyn, Evelyn. Whatever he did, awake or asleep, thoughts about her consumed him. The only time he felt the least bit like himself was when he was in her presence, and even then he hardly recognized the relatively pleasant, good-humored man he miraculously became. He must be mad. In his right mind he certainly never would have spent twenty thousand quid on an orphanage, and obligated himself as its only benefactor for the foreseeable future.

The new orphanage, though, seemed the only guarantee he had that he would continue to see her on a regular basis. It was either that or marry her, himself.

Saint sat straight up.

It was the most ridiculous thought he'd ever had. Of course, he was obsessed with her; he could acknowledge that. But *marriage*? If there was one thing he'd known since he'd realized how . . . interesting females were, it was that he meant to follow his father's example: Carouse until he was too old to enjoy it, pick a woman, marry so that he could father a legitimate heir, and expire.

He didn't want Clarence Alvington to have her, but taking the step of marrying her to prevent that seemed extreme, to say the least. She wouldn't agree to such a farce anyway—not with him. He didn't have enough fingers to count the number of times she'd called him despicable.

Sex with her was one thing; no one knew about that, and he'd discovered how to seduce her against her better judgment. But obsessed as she was with propriety, to join her name to his and have everyone know that she'd married a scoundrel of his black reputation . . . she'd probably rather join a nunnery, and that would be worse than her ending up with Alvington.

Tiredness merging with supreme frustration, Saint rose from the bed to pace across the expensive Persian carpet in the middle of his bedchamber. What in damnation was he doing, even thinking things like this? It must be because she was practically the only female he'd seen or spoken with or touched in a month. He was simply unused to a monogamous relationship, and the unnatural condition had set his mind and body off kilter.

Obviously, then, he shouldn't have refused Fatima. He needed to visit another female immediately and do anything necessary to purge Evelyn Ruddick from his system. If he was actually contemplating marriage to her, he couldn't risk taking the time to let this obsession run its course. If he didn't recover his old self at once, by tomorrow he might be thinking of having children with her.

"Good God," he muttered, rubbing his temple and sinking into the comfortable chair before the fireplace. He knew he wasn't going anywhere to look for anyone else, however perfect a solution it seemed. The reality was, he wanted Evelyn Ruddick, and spending his energies elsewhere wasn't going to change that. No, he was going to stay home and take a nap like a tired old man, and then he would rush out tonight to whichever of the evening's soirees seemed the most stiff and proper, in the hope that she would be there.

Evelyn held the silver heart and diamond pendant while Sally fastened the delicate chain at the back of her neck. It was a little too elaborate for a small party, but she felt charitable enough toward Saint tonight that she wanted to wear it.

"Charitable" wasn't quite the right term, actually, but she wasn't certain a word existed to describe the way she felt this evening. Saint had saved the children, to be sure, but something of even greater consequence had occurred; he'd acted directly in opposition to his own self-interest. And he'd apparently done it for her.

Her mother knocked, pushing the door open and leaning into the room. "Are you wearing your green silk? Oh, yes, good. It brings out your eyes."

"Why do we want to bring out my eyes tonight?" Evie asked, gesturing Sally to stop pinning up her hair. This morning's battle over Clarence Alvington and his idiotic poetry had been bad enough, but if they wanted more, she would deliver.

"You should always look your best; that's why. It's past time that you remember you are three and twenty, and that most ladies of your age are married and have offspring."

Evelyn kept her silence for a moment. Her mother hadn't mentioned Clarence, and thankfully he would not be in attendance tonight, unless he was even more stupid than she imagined. "I'm not going to find a husband at Lady Bethson's literary dinner," she settled for saying, "so I hardly think it matters what color I wear."

Her mother wrinkled her nose. "I have no idea why Victor still permits you to attend those nonsense bluestocking parties. He's too fond of you, despite your tendency toward poor judgment. Certainly no good can come from a group of silly females and pretentious old men sitting about quoting dead people."

"Didn't you know?" Evelyn countered. The act of being a charming, dim angel irked her enough when it was just for the benefit of Victor's latest potential ally. Apparently her brother thought she really *was* that milksop chit—and so did her mother. She was beginning to realize herself that she had more strength of will and purpose than she could have imagined. "Lady Bethson's cousin is Prince George's chancellor of the Exchequer," she continued. "I'm cultivating her friendship for that reason, to aid Victor. And I'm happy to do so, because she also happens to be a delightful person."

"Ha. You never used to be so opinionated, Evie."

"I never had to be."

Genevieve gazed at her. "And now you shouldn't be. You know it won't do any good. And remember that you and I are to join Victor for an early breakfast at nine o'clock tomorrow morning."

That couldn't be good. A command appearance at breakfast most likely meant that Victor had another ultimatum to hand down. She wasn't going to stand for many more of those. Her mother had it completely wrong. She'd begun to realize that once she'd taken the opportunity to express her convictions and act on them, she'd never felt better. In fact, she wondered what her family would say if she simply told them she preferred Lord St. Aubyn's company to theirs, and that even when she was angry with him, she liked Saint far more than any of the politically motivated connections her brother kept trying to foist on her. He might mean well, but he had a woefully poor idea of who she really was.

Of course, when she thought of Saint, her heart began to hammer. She had less than eighteen hours to think of a way to repay him for his services in procuring the orphanage. She knew how she *wanted* to pay him—he roused such wanton emotions in her that she could scarcely believe it of herself.

That solution, however, was too easy, no matter how satisfying it would be. Whatever she decided to do had to be good for him, had to continue the lessons in being a good person she'd been working so hard to dispense to him.

When Lucinda arrived, she still didn't know how she would best use Saint's latest challenge to her advantage. If something didn't occur to her soon, she would end up naked with him again, because she absolutely could not tell Victor or her mother that she'd practically adopted a houseful of orphans behind their backs.

"Don't fret," Lucinda said, giving her an encouraging smile. "We won't let those children end up in one of those horrid places."

Evelyn blinked. Everything had happened so quickly today that she'd forgotten Luce didn't know. "Actually," she said, "I have good news. St Aubyn has purchased another house for them."

"S . . . St. Aubyn," Lucinda repeated, her expression clearly saying that she thought someone had gone mad.

"Yes. It's lovely. They can all stay together, and I may set up the classrooms and the furniture and decorations however I wish. It will be such a hopeful, cheery place."

"Just a moment, Evie." Scowling, Lucinda sat forward in the coach. "The Marquis of St. Aubyn gave away an orphanage and then went and purchased another one."

"Well, yes. He said he'd tried to change Prinny's mind

about the Heart of Hope, but it had already been in the newspapers, so he couldn't. He found this one, and took me to see it, and then offered Sir Peter Ludlow so fair a price that the baron just shook his hand and gave him the key. And then he gave me the key."

Lucinda looked at her for a long moment. "Evie," she finally said, "if anyone were to hear that St. Aubyn purchased a house for you, you would be ruined beyond repair."

That had been part of what made it so exciting, but of course she could never tell Lucinda that. No one else could know about what she and Saint had done. She shook her head. "He didn't do it for me; he did it for the orphans."

"That's not what it sounds like to me," her friend insisted. "I don't think anyone else would bother to believe that interpretation, either. You heard Lord Dare—Saint doesn't do anything for free. And considering that he bought a house with you present, everyone will think you've become his . . . mistress."

She *had* become his mistress, Evelyn realized. Her heart went cold. When Lucinda said it that way, everything seemed so sordid. What if Saint had planned her ruination all along? When she'd locked him in the brig, he'd said that she would be the first person he went after. He could be devious; she knew that firsthand. But this was beyond devious. This was . . . mean.

"I'm not that naive," she managed, forcing a carefree smile. "After all I've tried to accomplish, if finding a new home for the children involves a risk to my reputation, then so be it."

That had to be it. Of course, in interacting with Saint she would find a certain amount of risk. He'd left the method of payment up to her, and even the one he'd suggested, of Evie confessing her involvement with the orphanage, would only damage her standing with her own family. The rest of society would never know anything about it—and certainly not that he'd bought a house for her.

"I don't understand you any longer," Lucinda said.

"Perhaps that's because I'm not so afraid of making a mistake now. At least I'm trying to do something, instead of just complaining that no one thinks I can accomplish anything useful."

Lucinda looked as though she wanted to continue the conversation, but thankfully the coach rolled to a stop and a footman pulled open the door before her friend could say anything further. She hated lying to Lucinda and Georgiana, but they had the same opinion of Saint as did everyone else in London. They wouldn't understand how important it was that she not act embarrassed or ashamed to be working with Saint. He would know if she did, and then all of her efforts would be for nothing.

Evie hurried to the ground, not sure what to say in response to the next thing her friend might ask. Luce would probably want to know what had caused this change in her, and she had only one answer: Saint.

Whatever fantastical dreams she'd once had of improving society or contributing something memorable and worthwhile, Saint was the reason she'd been able to do more than imagine. She'd accomplished something she could be proud of, and again thanks to Saint, her efforts would now bring about even more telling results.

She could hardly wait to see him again and discuss the next step. A slow heat crept up her cheeks. She could hardly wait to see him again, period. Michael Edward

Halboro, the most interesting, unexpected embodiment of a saint she could ever have imagined.

"Good evening, Miss Barrett, Miss Ruddick," Lady Bethson greeted them, as they joined the small group in the drawing room.

"Lady Bethson," Evie said, catching her mind up to the present enough to smile and give her hostess a fond peck on the cheek.

Unlike her Aunt Houton's political teas, Lady Bethson's twice-a-month literary evenings gave her something to look forward to. None of her aunt's snootier friends would be present, because the evenings were devoted to literary discussions, conversations where one was actually expected to use one's mind.

"Well, I believe we're all here, ladies . . . and gentleman," Lady Bethson said, with a nod to Viscount Quenton, their one regular—and thankfully good-natured—male participant, "so let's begin our reading and discussion of William Shakespeare's *A Midsummer Night's Dream.*"

They all pulled out their playbooks or moved over to share with someone who had one. Despite the scarcity of male attendees, Evelyn had the feeling that Saint would enjoy an evening such as this. No one made pretensions about anything, and without exception all dozen guests were intelligent, well read, and quick-witted. All those who weren't had long ago declined to attend or had ceased to be invited.

They were all laughing over Lord Quenton's rendition of Bottom the weaver when Lady Bethson's butler entered the room to whisper something into the countess' ear.

"How very interesting," the buxom lady breathed,

and nodded to the servant. "Show him in." As the guests watched the butler's exit, Lady Bethson took a sip of Madeira. "It seems we have another participant for tonight's discussion."

As she spoke, the Marquis of St. Aubyn strolled into the room on the butler's heels. "Good evening, Lady Bethson," he drawled, bowing over the countess' hand.

"Lord St. Aubyn. What a surprise."

"I'd heard your literary discussions were amusing," he returned, sending a glance at Evie that raised excited goose bumps on her arms, "so I thought I might impose to join you."

"The more, the merrier," Lady Bethson said with a chuckle. "And you bring an amusing veneer of notoriety with you, as well."

He nodded. "I try to please."

Evie looked away from him. That didn't help, though, because Luce was gazing at her, one eyebrow lifted. "What?" she whispered.

"I'm not saying a word," her friend returned in the same hushed tone.

"Why—"

"Miss Ruddick, might I share your playbook?" Saint stood before her, a slight smile lighting his green eyes. "I seem to have come all unprepared."

Whatever he was up to this evening, he was behaving himself to a remarkable degree. It seemed like far longer than an afternoon since she'd seen him, and as his gaze lowered to her mouth, she half hoped he would kiss her. She wanted to wrap her arms around him and feel the beat of his heart against hers.

"Of course, my lord," she said, shaking herself. *For heaven's sake,* one of them had to show some self-control, and she obviously couldn't rely on him to do it. "We are discussing *A Midsummer Night's Dream*."

"Ah." He seated himself on the couch beside her, managing to brush the back of her hand with his fingers as he did so. " 'He hath rid his prologue like a rough colt;/ He knows not the stop./ A good moral, my lord: it is/ Not enough to speak, but to speak true.' "

Lady Bethson chuckled again. "A literary scoundrel. You are full of surprises, Lord St. Aubyn."

And so was the countess. Evelyn had always admired her forthright manner and self-confidence, but not many—male or female—conversed with Saint to his face about his black reputation.

"I believe it's just that the expectations for me are so low, I can't help but amaze," he returned. Apparently Saint admired self-confidence as well, though Evie had already suspected that.

Lord Quenton cleared his throat. "Despite the presence of a younger male, I refuse to relinquish the part of Bottom."

Saint lifted an eyebrow. "I prefer Puck myself, anyway."

This time Lady Bethson laughed. "Dear me. Puck it is, Lord St. Aubyn. Shall we continue?"

Despite the fact that this was one of her favorite comedies, Evie found it very difficult to concentrate. Saint sat so close that their thighs bumped, and he tugged the playbook over so half was across her knees and half across his. As he leaned over it, reading the part of Puck in his low, cultured voice, she had to stifle the desperate desire to kiss his ear.

She was reading Lysander and Titania, who thankfully had no lines with Puck. Speaking in a normal voice was difficult enough without having to look at Saint. And then he made it even more difficult.

"How are you going to repay me?" he asked, while the other guests interpreted the pairing of Lysander and Hermia versus Helena.

"It hasn't been twenty-four hours yet. Hush."

"Tell me now, or I'll assume you mean to pay me with your soft breasts and your—"

"All right, all right. I will . . ." She paused, desperately trying to think of something when she had been leaning toward making love with him again. "I will procure you an invitation to General Barrett's annual picnic."

"Beg pardon?"

It was perfect. Only the most interesting people were ever invited, and the repartee would immensely appeal to someone of Saint's wit. And it was good company; good for him and the lessons she still told herself she was trying to teach him. "It's quite popular, and very exclusive."

"I know that. How is it doing me a good turn, though, to invite me to a party where I can be muttered about and otherwise ignored?"

"You won't be ig—"

"You will spend the day with me, at my side."

She started to refuse, but Victor would never attend with so many liberals present. "Agreed."

The readings resumed, with Bottom and his companions discussing the performance they were rehearsing for the royal wedding. Saint shifted his hand, hidden beneath the playbook. Keenly aware of him as she was, when his fingers slipped beneath her thigh, gently caressing, she nearly leapt out of her seat.

"Stop that," she murmured, head down. She tried to

move away, but he tightened his grip on her skirt, keeping her there against his thigh.

"Lick your lips," he breathed.

"No."

His fingers crept farther up the underside of her thigh, pressed against her by her own weight. "Are you wet for me?"

With a quick flick she touched her tongue to her lips. "Shall I stand on my head now? Stop it. Lucinda will see."

His fingers stilled, but he didn't remove his hand. "Would she tell?"

"No," Evie whispered, risking a glance at his profile. "But she would ask me. And then I would have to explain you, and I can't."

Everyone laughed at something, and she joined in belatedly. Beside her Saint didn't move, but she could almost see the sudden sharpening of his attention. Her breath caught.

"What would you explain about me?" he murmured, his lips nearly brushing her ear.

Oh, God, she wanted to touch him. "About why I like you," she breathed back shakily. "Don't make me regret it, Michael. Please remove your hand."

His hand slipped back beneath the book, where it belonged, and abruptly she could breathe again. It didn't stop her from yearning to slide her arms around his shoulders and smother his wicked mouth with kisses, but at least she knew she would be able to restrain herself tonight.

"You like me," he repeated. "How interesting." Then he lifted his head, reading Puck's line aloud as though he'd been following the play all along. " 'What hempen home-spuns have we swagg'ring here,/ So near the cradle of the Fairy Queen?' "

Evelyn didn't know how he could possibly be paying attention; she could barely remember there were other people in the room. And that certainly didn't bode well for her continued good reputation.

Chapter 21

It suits me well to mingle now
With things that never pleased before.

—Lord Byron, "One Struggle More,
and I am Free"

Loath to acknowledge that the evening was over, Saint accepted a second slice of cake. If more of Society's events were as interesting as Lady Bethson's, he wouldn't have been so diligent about avoiding them.

Even more interesting, however, had been his hushed conversation with Evelyn Marie. He glanced at her, chatting with Lucinda Ruddick and the countess. With the play, dinner, and discussion finished, maintaining his seat at her side would have been asking too much of her polite sensibilities. But she'd said that she liked him— not because they'd become lovers or because he'd provided a new building for the orphans, but for some reason that she couldn't define.

For the most part, the few compliments he received were on his skills as a lover, or acknowledging that he could be charming or a dead shot with a pistol. They were characteristics he could control and define. The idea of someone actually liking him seemed much more tenuous and precious. And completely unexpected.

With a last chuckle, Evelyn and Miss Barrett rose. Swiftly putting the cake aside, Saint joined them. "I must be going," he drawled, taking Lady Bethson's hand, "or dozens of club proprietors will be sending out search parties. Thank you for allowing me to intrude, Lady Bethson. You host an interesting evening."

The countess' round cheeks dimpled. "The next interesting evening will be on the twelfth, for a discussion of Byron's *Childe Harold*. You will find yourself invited, Lord St. Aubyn."

"And I may very well find myself attending." Saint nodded, offering arms to both young ladies as he caught up to them. "Might I escort you out?"

Miss Barrett's grip was much more tentative than Evelyn's, and he took the contrast as another good sign. She didn't hesitate to touch him, even in public, under the right circumstances. He simply needed to manufacture more of those right circumstances.

"Evie tells me you've made a fortuitous purchase," the dusky-haired lady said, her gaze on the coach as they stepped down to the drive.

She *could* keep secrets, then. "It seemed the . . . proper thing to do," he returned, handing her into the vehicle.

When it came time to release Evelyn's hand, though, he didn't want to let her go. She turned in the coach doorway, looking down at him. "Good night, Saint," she murmured, freeing her fingers.

"Sleep well, Evelyn Marie."

The coach trundled off, and he swung up onto Cassius. As he'd said, the evening had barely begun for night-wanderers like himself, but losing himself in thought would be less problematic over a bottle of brandy at home than over a deck of cards and a hundred quid at Jezebel's.

Jansen blinked as he pulled open the front door. "My lord. We didn't expect to see you so early."

"Change of plans," he muttered, handing over his coat and lifting the brandy decanter from the hall table.

"Shall I send Pemberly to see to you?"

"No. I'll manage. Good night, Jansen."

"Good night, my lord."

Saint trudged up the stairs and down the long hallway to his private rooms. Tomorrow the chaos would begin again, but tonight, by God, he was going to have a few drinks and get a good night's sleep.

Despite the fire crackling behind the fireplace's iron grate, the air in his bedchamber felt cold as he opened his door. Someone had left a blasted window open.

"Hello, milord."

The voice registered immediately, and Saint turned, unsurprised, at the sight of the young man propped up against the bed's headboard, dirty boots leaving mud on the expensive coverlet.

"Randall," he returned, shrugging out of his jacket and tossing it across the back of the nearest chair. "You shouldn't leave windows open."

"I thought I might need to leave in a hurry."

The boy kept his right hand concealed beneath the pillows. Saint mentally measured the distance to the door, the dressing room, and the boy. Randall was the closest. "And why would that be?"

Randall stirred, and a sleek steel muzzle emerged from the clutter, followed by the pistol's barrel, the trigger, and his hand. "Your servants might come lookin' after I make all the noise of putting a ball through your skull."

Nodding, every muscle tense, Saint sank into one of the large chairs between the fireplace and the bed. "Do you just have a taste for murder, or is something in particular bothering you? There are easier targets than me, you know."

"I told Miss Evie we should've buried you in that cellar. I told her no good would come of letting you see daylight again. Miss Evie don't understand that men with money don't care about nothings like us."

"Men with money don't make very good murder targets, either. People who shoot us tend to hang."

The boy shrugged, swinging his feet to the floor and standing. The pistol didn't waver, and Saint doubted Randall would hesitate even for a second to pull the trigger. Thank Lucifer the lad had come after him and not Evelyn.

"If somebody took your home away, wouldn't you shoot 'im? If you'd spent nearly a week listening to the babies crying that they're losing their beds and that they'll have to eat rats and live in the gutter, wouldn't you shoot the man who did it, whether he was a blue-blood noble or not?"

Randall was working himself into a fine lather, and Saint couldn't really blame him. "Yes, I would shoot him," he agreed, "unless he'd already thought of all that and had a solution in mind."

"Say whatever you want; it don't change what you did to us. You might've fooled Miss Evie, but you never fooled me."

"Fooled you about what?"

Randall opened his mouth to answer, and Saint moved. Springing from the chair, he leapt forward. Catching the pistol between his arm and his ribs, he twisted and shoved, throwing Randall to the floor.

He gripped the captured pistol butt with his free hand, but left it aimed at the floor. "Come with me," he said.

The boy sat up, rubbing his wrist. "Damn me. Nobles can't do that. Where'd you learn it?"

"You're not the first fellow to aim a weapon at me," Saint said dryly. "Get up."

"I ain't goin' to jail."

"Now's a fine time to decide that."

"I ain't goin'."

Saint sighed. "No jails, no dungeons, and no chains. I'm not above clubbing you across the skull if you misbehave, however, to return the favor you did me."

Glaring, Randall scrambled to his feet. "Miss Evie thought I'd killed you. I tried, but you've got a hard head."

Saint sent out another silent thanks to whomever might be listening that Randall Baker hadn't turned his rather homicidal attentions in Evelyn's direction. If the boy had hurt or even frightened her, Saint wouldn't have been feeling nearly as charitable as he was this evening.

Keeping Randall in front of him in case the lad decided to try pummeling him with something else, they went downstairs to Saint's office. The servants hadn't wasted any time in going to bed, but that was fine with him. He really didn't want any witnesses seeing him practically holding an infant at gunpoint, anyway.

"Sit there," he said, indicating the pair of chairs facing the desk.

Still eyeing him suspiciously, Randall sat.

Saint took the chair behind the desk, laid the pistol at his elbow within easy reach, and shoved a small stack of papers in Randall's direction. "Has Miss Evie worked a miracle with you, or shall I read the top page there to you?"

The boy scowled. "I read a little."

Hiding his surprise, Saint nodded. Evelyn *had* worked a miracle or two, apparently. "Then read," he said, striking a light and turning up the lamp.

Mouthing the words, Randall went to work. He looked up after an excruciating five minutes. "What's this word?"

Saint leaned forward. "Annualized. It means the property taxes will be refigured once a year." For a moment he watched the growing frustration on the young man's face as Randall tried to decipher what had to be nearly a foreign language to him. "Shall I summarize?" he offered.

"It's about a house. I can see that."

"A large house, on Earl's Court Gardens, with twenty-seven rooms. That," and he flicked the papers with his finger, "is a twenty-three-page agreement for me to purchase the house as a facility for minors without parental supervision."

The confusion on Randall's face cleared. "You're buying us another orphanage."

"Yes, I am."

"Why?"

Saint sighed. "Your Miss Evie is very persuasive."

"You goin' to marry her?"

Attempting to ignore the low flutter in his gut that the boy's question began, he shrugged. "Probably." Saint put the papers back in their neat stack. "Now go home. And I would suggest that you not mention the pistol or the breaking into my house. Considering that Evelyn supplied the weapon, she might find this all a little upsetting."

"Aye. You're not as much a devil as I thought, Marquis. I'm glad I didn't shoot you."

"So am I."

Saint kept the pistol as he showed Randall out the front door. He locked the heavy oak barrier again, leaning back against it. Tonight's incident was far from being the closest call he'd ever had, but it had been more unsettling than previous encounters, nonetheless.

Before, when he had faced a pistol, usually held by some angry chit's husband or other relation, he hadn't really cared about the outcome. Tonight, though, he had cared. Not because he feared being shot, but because death would prevent him from accomplishing the task he'd set for himself—namely, possessing Evelyn Marie Ruddick. In simpler terms, he didn't want to die because he'd found something—someone—for whom he wanted to stay alive.

Pulling the pistol from his pocket, he tilted it to dump the ball into his hand. Nothing happened. Tapping it, he pulled back the hammer, lifting the weapon to examine it in the pale moonlight of the foyer window.

"I'll be damned."

It was empty. From the looks of it, the pistol had never *been* loaded. Evelyn had kept him prisoner with an unloaded gun. Saint shook his head. She'd said she would never injure him, and apparently she'd meant it. No one had ever done such a thing to him or for him before. By God, she had courage.

That, combined with a coachload of good intentions and her determination to see the positive in everything and everyone, made her dangerous. And the only way to protect himself was to make certain he kept hold of her.

What he wanted to do was talk to someone about this strange revelation, but anyone he would consider trusting had closer ties to Evelyn than to him. Saint stayed in the foyer for a moment, listening to the quiet house.

Abruptly, though, the identity of his most likely confidant came to him, and he pushed away from the door,
heading for the servants' quarters.

"Jansen," he called, rapping on the door closest to the
main part of the house. "Come out of there!"

A moment later the door opened. The butler, coatless
and shirt untucked, hurried into the hallway. "My lord!
Is something amiss?"

"Come with me," Saint said, turning on his heel.

"Now, my lord?"

"Yes, now."

"I—ah—very well, my lord."

The muted padding of stockinged feet followed Saint
as he returned to the main hallway. Thank Lucifer the
butler hadn't already removed his trousers. Grabbing a
candle from the hall table, he led the way into the morning room. Jansen paused in the doorway while Saint
crouched before the banked coals in the fireplace and lit
the wick.

"Have a seat," he said, placing the candle on the
mantel as he straightened.

"Am I being dismissed, my lord?" Jansen asked, his
voice stiff. "If so, I would prefer to at least be in my
shoes."

Saint dropped into the chair that faced the doorway.
Splendid. His chosen confidant thought he'd been summoned for termination. "Nonsense," he grunted. "If I
intended to hand you your papers, I'd at least wait for a
decent hour to do it. Have a seat, Jansen."

Clearing his throat and plainly uncomfortable, the
butler trod into the morning room in his white stockings
and perched on the front inch or so of the facing chair.
After a hesitation he folded his hands across his bony
thighs.

Well, this wasn't going to work. Jansen looked like a convicted criminal facing execution, and Saint had enough to ponder without worrying over whether he was giving his butler an apoplexy. "Brandy," he said.

Jansen leapt to his feet. "Right away, my lord."

"Sit down. *I'll* get it. Do you want a snifter?" Rising, he went to the liquor cart standing beneath the window.

"Me?"

Saint glanced over his shoulder. "Stop squeaking. You sound like a mouse. Yes, you."

"I . . . ahem . . . yes, my lord."

Once they were seated and relatively comfortable again, Saint took a long swallow of brandy. "I find myself wanting someone else's opinion on a matter," he began. "And I've chosen you."

"I'm honored, my lord." Most of the brandy in the butler's snifter had vanished, and Saint leaned over to refill the glass.

"Discretion is required. And honesty."

"Of course."

Now came the difficult part. This was so idiotic. He couldn't believe he was even thinking such things, much less considering saying them aloud. To his butler, yet. "I'm thinking," he began slowly, "of making some changes around here."

"I see."

"In fact, I'm thinking of getting—" Saint stopped. The word simply wouldn't come out. It was too strange, too foreign. Clearing his throat, he gave it another try. "I'm contemplating getting—"

"New curtains, my lord? Since you said that you wished my honest opinion, the window coverings, especially in the downstairs rooms, are quite—"

"Not curtains."

"Oh."

Saint finished off his brandy and poured himself another. "This is much larger than curtains, believe me."

"A new home, my lord?" Jansen queried. "Through a fairly reliable source I have heard that Lord Wenston's Park Lane home will be on the market soo—"

"Married," Saint snapped. "I'm thinking of getting married."

For a long moment the butler sat in silence, his jaw hanging open. "I . . . my lord, I simply don't feel qualified to advise you about such matters."

"Don't tell me that," Saint protested. "Tell me whether you can imagine me as a married man or not."

To his surprise, the butler set aside his brandy snifter and sat forward. "My lord, I do not wish to overstep my bounds, but I have noticed a . . . change in your demeanor, of late. The question of whether anyone can imagine you married or not, however, is one I believe must be answered by you. And the lady, of course."

Saint frowned. "Coward."

"There is that, as well."

The clock on the landing chimed once. "Go to bed, Jansen. A bloody lot of help you've been."

"Yes, my lord." The butler padded to the doorway, then paused. "If I may, perhaps the question you should ask yourself is whether you would be happier with a wife or without one."

Jansen vanished into the darkness of the hallway, but Saint sat where he was, sipping at his brandy in the dim, flickering candlelight. At issue wasn't marriage to *a* woman, but marriage to *the* woman. Would he be happier possessing Evelyn, or seeing Clarence Alvington do so? The answer wasn't a simple yes or no, or a resolve to behave or to carry on as he had since before he'd been seventeen, because the question wasn't whether he'd be happy with her, but whether he'd survive without her.

Chapter 22

Though human, thou didst not deceive me,
Though woman, thou didst not forsake.

—Lord Bryon, "Stanzas to Augusta"

As soon as Evie saw the fresh strawberries on the sideboard, she knew what Victor intended. Her brother was already seated at the table, partway through his usual breakfast of toasted bread with honey, and sliced ham. The ever-present morning edition of the *London Times* lay at his elbow, for once unopened and unread.

"Good morning, Evie," he said.

She selected a few strawberries and a slice of fresh bread. "Good morning."

"I trust your evening went well?"

Considering that he generally referred to her twice-monthly literary sojourn as the "bluestocking gossip circle," she felt justified in her suspicions. And considering that all she could remember of last night was Saint sitting beside her and being naughty and pleasant all at the same time, she had no complaints about the evening at all.

"Evie?"

She shook visions of Saint from her mind, though he never went far. "Oh. Yes, it went well. Thank you."

"What did you discuss?"

Evie took her plate to the table and sat. "Where's Mama?"

"She'll be down in a moment. How are the strawberries?"

Evie wanted to throw one at him. He was so obvious, pretending to be polite and concerned so she wouldn't argue when he demanded that she marry stupid Clarence Alvington. And of course she would argue anyway, and storm out of the room, and end up doing exactly as he wanted, because that's what she always did. Well, she'd learned some new games recently, and from a very practiced player. And she had better reasons these days for carrying through with her own plans rather than her brother's. Fifty-three reasons, to be exact, ranging in age from seven to seventeen. "The strawberries are lovely. Thank you for requesting them."

He glanced at her for a moment, suspicion crossing his face, then went back to eating. "You're welcome."

Their mother arrived, sweeping into the room and placing a delicate kiss on Victor's cheek, then Evie's. "Good morning, my darlings. It's so nice when we all breakfast together. We should do it more often."

Don't yell, Evie told herself. *Whatever they say, don't yell.* "Yes, we should. What was it you wanted to tell me, Victor?"

Her brother wiped the corner of his mouth on his napkin. "Firstly, I wanted to thank you for your assistance this Season. You've helped me make some very lucrative connections."

"Yes, I know I have. You're welcome."

Her mother sighed. "Evie, don't be difficult."

"I'm not being difficult. I'm agreeing that I've been helpful."

Victor frowned. "If you'll let me finish? Thank you. You've also made your share of mischief."

She nodded, knowing precisely to what he was referring. "Yes, and St. Aubyn introduced you to Wellington."

Langley stirred in the corner, and for a brief moment Evelyn thought she saw a smile twitch across his stern, professional countenance. At least someone was on her side.

"That isn't the point."

"May I ask what the point is, then? Yesterday we were simply discussing alternatives, or so you said."

He eyed her over the rim of his coffee cup. "The point is, an alliance with Lord Alvington will secure me enough votes to assume Plimpton's seat in the House of Commons. And, as you know, I have been looking for a proper match for you for some time, someone who will nurture your better qualities and who won't stifle your . . . lighthearted manner. I am fond of you, Evie, and I haven't come to this conclusion lightly. If Clarence Alvington hadn't satisfied my requirements, I wouldn't have chosen him for you. And yes, please note that I have not tried to conceal the fact that the decision has benefit for me, as well." He sat forward. "Before you begin screaming about it, hear me out."

Evie clenched her hands together very tightly in her lap. "I'm listening."

"You— All right."

He was too much of a politician to show more surprise than that, but Evie also knew him better than any of his political acquaintances and allies. She'd set him off balance.

Victor cleared his throat. "Mister Alvington has con-
fided in me several times how much he adores you, and
what an asset you'll be when he takes his father's place
as the viscount."

"And what does he think of my friendship with Lord
St. Aubyn?" It was the most defiant question she could
think to ask. Saint's lack of restraint in expressing his
opinion might be refreshing, but she didn't have the
same freedom he did.

"*I* don't think much of it," Victor said in a harder
voice, "which is what should matter. You'd do best to be
more concerned with maintaining your reputation for
propriety. It's not only Clarence and myself who have to
approve the match. The Alvingtons' sense of humor is
nonexistent when it comes to their reputation and good
name."

Oh, really? She'd suspected as much, but hearing Victor say it gave her the inkling of a plan. "So it's all decided," she said in as cool a voice as she could manage,
"between you and the Alvingtons?"

"You need to marry anyway," her mother said. "It
might as well be to someone useful and inoffensive."

Evie wasn't certain she agreed with that assessment of
Clarence Alvington's character, but arguing seemed utterly useless. They'd already decided her fate. She swallowed down a cold lump of stone that had risen in her
throat. She wasn't married yet, but with the next word
she spoke, she needed either to agree to their interpretation of her life or to deliberately begin working against
them toward her own. "All right."

Victor blinked. "What did you say?"

Breathe. "Who am I to argue with my brother and my
own mother? If you don't have my best interests in mind,
no one does."

Her brother's eyes narrowed. "Be serious."

"I am perfectly serious."

"You'll marry Clarence Alvington. Without kicking up a tantrum."

"If he'll have me." But before it came to that, she needed some time to put a plan into motion. "I would like to be asked, though. And if he wooed me, rather than just signing a piece of paper, that would be nice."

"I'll see to it." Victor pushed to his feet. "I have a meeting. I'm taking you at your word, Evie, that you won't refuse this match."

Any response she made would only make him even more suspicious, so she settled for nodding as he picked up the newspaper and left the room. *Ha.* If the Alvingtons were so concerned with propriety, she knew exactly what she needed to do. Clarence Alvington would never ask her to marry him if she didn't measure up to his family's strict standards. Therefore, all she needed to do was utilize a few of the lessons Saint had given her. A little naughtiness should keep Clarence away.

"I'm so proud of you," Mrs. Ruddick said, reaching over to squeeze Evie's hand. "I knew Victor would find you a good match."

"Yes, I'll be so happy, marrying for love like this." Evie finished her last strawberry and stood. "If you don't mind, I'm going walking with Lucinda and Georgie."

"I understand sarcasm, my dear," Genevieve said in a low voice. "I urged you to find someone before your brother returned from India, but you insisted on playing about with your friends. Now you have no choice."

"I might have had a choice if you had stood with me for a change, instead of with Victor. You never asked me if I had any dreams, or ambitions, or wishes. You just assumed that I didn't. I don't mind helping Victor, but I don't understand why I have to be the only one to make a sacrifice."

"Evie—"

"I'll see you for tea with Lady Humphreys, Mama."

Gathering her bonnet and shawl, she escaped out the front door, Sally on her heels. Evie frowned at her maid as they turned up the street. "I'm just going to see Lucinda. You don't need to come."

"Mister Ruddick says I'm to accompany you everywhere," Sally replied with an apologetic smile.

"Did he say why?"

"He only told me to make certain you behave, and to tell him if you don't." The maid dropped a slight, nervous curtsy. "I would never do that, Miss Ruddick, but Mr. Ruddick would dismiss me if he knew."

"Then he will never know. We'll invent something for you to tell him, so you won't get into trouble, and so he won't be suspicious." Feeling more optimistic than she had all morning, Evie patted Sally on the arm. "And thank you."

"Oh, you're welcome, Miss Ruddick. Thank goodness. I didn't know what I should do."

A horse drew up alongside them, matching their pace. "I seem to always come across you in the wrong conveyance," Saint's deep voice said. "I can't very well offer you and your maid a ride on Cassius."

Taking a slow, delicious breath, Evelyn looked up at him. With his blue beaver hat perched at a jaunty angle on his dark, curling hair and his easy seat in the saddle, he looked the image of a perfect, if slightly rakish, gentleman. Sometimes she thought she'd be content just to sit and look at him all day. "Good morning," she said, when she realized she was staring.

He swung down from the saddle, taking the reins in

his left hand, and fell into step beside her. "Good morn-ing. What's wrong?"

"Nothing's wrong. What makes you ask?"

"Don't ever lie to me, Evelyn," he said in a lower voice, though his expression when she glanced over at him was more thoughtful than angry. "Your honesty seems to be the one reliable thing in the world."

"Heavens. I had no idea I was so important," she re-turned, forcing a smile. Damnation, she needed to plan her strategy for avoiding marriage with Clarence. Saint was so distracting she could barely remember her own name when he was present.

He shrugged. "Only to those who know the value of such things. Are you going to tell me what's troubling you, or shall I pull you behind that house there and re-new our acquaintance?"

"Saint, hush," she muttered, indicating Sally follow-ing a few feet behind them.

The marquis only leaned closer. "I haven't been inside you for nearly a week, Evelyn," he whispered in her ear. "I only have so much self-control."

"You practically had your hand up my skirt last night," she murmured back, warmth creeping up her legs.

"And thank God for the book across my lap, or everyone would have known how much I wanted you."

A pair of young ladies passed them in a curricle, and Evie winced. If Saint didn't leave soon, someone would take the tale back to Victor. Which would be all right, except that she didn't have a plan put together yet. She had no wish to be yelled at for no good reason. "You need to stop saying such things," she hissed. "I'm . . . I'm to be married."

Saint stopped so suddenly, she was six feet in front of

him before she realized he wasn't beside her. When she turned around to face him, his expression turned her heart cold.

"Saint?"

"You've . . . someone's asked—you agreed to marry Clarence Alvington?" he growled, hard green eyes daring her to respond.

"My brother informed me that I would be asked and that I was to say yes. With Alvington's support, he is assured of a seat in the House." She shouldn't have said so much; her family's private reasons were not for public consumption, but Saint would know, anyway. He'd known before she did.

"And you agreed."

"He hasn't asked me yet," she hedged, "but yes, I agreed."

"How dutiful of you. And your brother expressed his gratitude, I assume?"

"Stop being so cynical, Saint. They trapped me."

"They treat you like their pet dog," he snapped.

"How dare you?" she said, fighting the sudden wish for tears. "You're only angry because you know once I'm married we won't be . . . friends any longer. Go away, Saint. I thought . . . Go away. You're certainly not helping anything, yelling at me for doing the right thing."

"The right thing?" he repeated blackly.

"Please, just go."

Saint wanted to say more, to demand to know why she hadn't resisted, but neither did he want her to end up hating him. Unless he gave her a good reason not to, she would never deny Clarence's petition, much less marry someone who could damage her precious family's political standing.

"Then I bid you good day," he grunted. Swinging back up on Cassius, he sent the bay up the street at a full gallop.

The idea of never touching her again, of standing in the shadows at soirees and watching other men dance with her, of seeing her and knowing that Clarence Alvington had bedded her and could do so anytime he wished—no one could be expected to tolerate that kind of torture.

"Damn, damn, damn." His first impulse was to find Clarence Alvington, challenge him to a duel, and kill him. Satisfying as that would be, however, it wouldn't get him Evelyn—and it would probably force him to flee England, which would mean he wouldn't even be able to look at her.

He slowed as he neared his destination, forcing himself to think logically again. Evelyn had worded things in a peculiar way, for her. Not that the marriage was set, but that *when* the Neckcloth asked, she would agree. Not that she'd made the decision to marry, but that she'd been *trapped* into it. Not that she wanted Saint to go away, but that he *wasn't helping* by staying there.

He stopped again, swinging down from Cassius and handing the reins to a waiting footman. She obviously didn't love the buffoon, and even worse for her, when she married that idiotic, self-righteous swag, she wouldn't be permitted to continue with the orphanage. The question was, what could he do to make it right?

The tapping of his Hessians echoed down the long corridor. He was late again, but at least he was there. It was all he could think to do, and overall it still seemed the best, most likely plan. Victor Ruddick had made a political match for his sister. If a better one presented itself, he would be a fool and a poor politician to pass it up.

"Saint?" Lord Dare whispered as he made his way up the steps to take his seat. "What the devil are you doing here?"

"My duty," Saint returned, nodding at the Duke of Wycliffe seated beyond. That was it; all he needed to do was make himself the better candidate.

Several rows beneath him, Earl Haskell stood, his face deepening to an alarming shade of red. "I will not tolerate this," he spat. "If you are going to be here, St. Aubyn, I am leaving."

Damn. Saint stood as well. "Lord Haskell, you have sat in this House for twenty-eight years, contributing your knowledge and giving your time. Two weeks ago I insulted you for that. Today, I apologize. If I had a tenth of your wisdom, I would be a better man for it."

The rumbling in the House of Lords was almost deafening, but Saint paid no attention. If he couldn't even sit with his peers for an hour, he didn't deserve much of anything.

"You expect me to believe you're being sincere, boy?" the earl returned.

"No, my lord. I ask you to accept my apology. I am sorry for my behavior." Holding his breath, Saint leaned down, extending his hand to the older man. This was for Evelyn, he reminded himself as the earl glared at him. He could do this for her. He would do anything for her.

"And if I don't accept your apology?"

"Then tomorrow I'll ask you again to do so."

With a sigh, as though deflating, Haskell reached out and shook Saint's hand. Their audience burst into applause, but this wasn't over yet. They both knew Saint could still make a fool of him. The earl had trusted him, as few men ever had before. It was a . . . pleasant, unexpected feeling, to be trusted.

Saint nodded. "Thank you. You are kinder than I deserve." With a slight smile, he resumed his seat. "I shall attempt not to make you regret your generosity."

"You've done well with it so far," the older man rumbled, sitting again.

"Gentlemen," the speaker called, rapping on his podium, "if we might continue?"

"Well, flip my wig and call me Petunia," Dare whispered. "What's gotten into you?"

"I'll let you know when I figure it out," Saint muttered back.

He already knew, though. His mouth dry, he gestured one of the attendants for a glass of water. Abruptly, he knew precisely why he was attempting to make amends, and why he was going to remain in the House of Lords until the end of session today, and why he would attend again tomorrow and the next day and every session for the remainder of the Season. And he knew why he would do anything else necessary that would enable him to marry Evelyn Marie Ruddick. He loved her. Michael Edward Halboro, the man without a heart, loved a lady. And he would stop at nothing to win her.

Saint couldn't help the smile that touched his lips. Good God. He hoped Evelyn would appreciate what she'd done to him. For her, he was going to become a gentleman. And the funny thing was, after five minutes of reform, he was enjoying it.

"Did you manage it?" Evelyn asked, pacing to the window and back.

"Yes, and it wasn't easy, believe me. My father asks too many questions anyway, and convincing him that the Marquis of St. Aubyn should be invited on his picnic . . ." Lucinda sighed, flopping back on the couch.

"He's probably still asking questions, and I'll be called on to provide answers the next time I cross in front of his office door."

"I would explain it to you if I could, Luce." A horseman rode by the Barrett House front gate, and her breath caught until she realized the rider was too stocky to be Saint. She'd told him to leave her alone, though, so she couldn't imagine why he would bother to track down where she'd gone.

"You don't have to explain anything to me. You're my friend." Rising again, Lucinda joined her at the window. "I assume this is another part of your lesson in behavior for your pupil. In fact, all I'm going to say at this point is that you're taking a terrible risk. Your brother is so set on his path that if he thinks you're attempting to place stones in his way, there's no telling what he might do."

"He's already done it."

"What?" Lucinda took her arm, pulling her around so they were eye to eye. "Now, this you have to tell me. What's Victor done?"

"Even without knowing what I'm doing or thinking, my brother has the most remarkable ability to put bricks in front of me," she said, a lone tear escaping to run down her cheek. "I can't imagine anything worse than being married to Clarence Alvington. Can you?"

Lucinda stared at her, then strode to the liquor table at the far end of the room. As Evelyn watched, she poured two glasses of Madeira and returned, holding one of them out.

"Clarence Alvington?" she finally burst out. "Because of the properties his father owns in West Sussex, I presume. For heaven's sake! Doesn't your brother know how poorly you two match?"

Evie sipped her Madeira, wishing it were stronger.

"Clarence is an idiot, and Victor thinks I'm an idiot, so as far as he's concerned, it's perfect." She sighed. "That's not entirely true, I suppose. Clarence is bland and inoffensive, making me unlikely to balk at the match since I'll barely know I'm married to him."

"This is awful. What will you do?"

"I'm still formulating my plan, but it's so difficult—whatever I do, I really don't want to destroy Victor's chances in Parliament." She sighed. "Isn't that stupid?"

Lucinda hugged her. "You're a good sister. I hope he has occasion to realize that eventually. A high degree of blandness is hardly a quality one should look for in his sister's fiancé."

Friends were so wonderful. "Thank you. In the meantime, however, I think I'm going to put to use a few things I've learned from my acquaintance with St. Aubyn. If I've been unable to teach him to be a gentleman, at least he's taught me a few things about being scandalous."

"You can't ruin yourself, Evie. Not even to evade Clarence Alvington."

"No, but I can stray closer to the edge. Michael lives life in a much more . . . exhilarating fashion than I would have believed possible. Far too exciting for Mr. Alvington."

Her friend returned to the couch, setting her glass on the end table. "Michael?" she repeated, her back turned.

Evelyn blushed. *Damnation.* Keeping the way she felt about Saint to herself was difficult enough without using his Christian name in front of other people. "St. Aubyn," she corrected. "He asked—I sometimes call him—"

The morning room door burst open. Georgiana, still untying her bonnet, hurried into the room. "Evie, thank goodness."

"What is it?"

Lucinda went to the door and closed it just as the butler appeared. "Yes, what's happened?"

"You've succeeded—that's what's happened," the viscountess said to Evie, dropping her hat onto a chair. "It's a miracle. I went to your house looking for you, but Langley said you'd be here."

Georgiana was in good spirits, and whatever her own woes were, Evie's heart lifted a little. At least someone was happy. "I have no idea what you're talking about, Georgie."

"I'm talking about St. Aubyn. Tristan just returned from the morning session at the House, and he told me the most extraordinary thing!"

As soon as Saint's name came into the discussion, Evie began to feel light-headed. Sitting in the windowsill, she took a large swallow of Madeira. "What did St. Aubyn do now?"

"He attended Parliament today. And he actually apologized to Lord Haskell for some insult he'd handed him the last time he was there."

Evie lifted an eyebrow. "He *apologized* to someone?"

"Like a gentleman, evidently. Tristan said St. Aubyn also stayed for the entire session, and that he volunteered to sit on a committee for child labor reform."

Both of her friends were gazing at her expectantly. "Oh, my," she offered after a moment.

It was all she could think of to say, when with all of her heart she wanted to run out and find Saint and ask him what he was up to, and then hug him and kiss him because it didn't matter. He had learned something, and even if it couldn't help her, he could do so much good elsewhere. Evelyn shook herself, realizing her friends were still conversing.

". . . marry Clarence Alvington," Lucinda was saying.

"No! Can't he see how completely wrong that dandy is for you?" Georgiana asked, joining Evie at the window.

"Probably not. But he can see how right Clarence is for him. The match assures him a seat in the House of Commons."

"Ha. It would be nice if he succeeded on his own merits, rather than on yours."

Evie smiled. "I wish I'd thought to tell him that."

"Feel free to borrow it any time."

What she abruptly wanted to borrow was Georgiana's life. She had a husband who adored her, an understanding aunt and a cousin with enough power and rank to ensure that no one could ruin them, and a penchant for causes that weren't terribly unfitting for a female.

Evelyn had a scoundrel who by equal turns seemed to like her and to want to ruin her, a family who put their own wishes over hers and cared terribly for everyone else's opinion, and a hopeless dream of running an orphanage for poor young children with wit and potential.

At the same time, Saint had made possible much of what she'd attained thus far. And once she'd proven to him that she wasn't some feather-brain looking for attention, his assistance and advice, though cynical and with a price, had been invaluable.

"What will you do?" Georgiana asked.

"She's going to utilize some of St. Aubyn's methods," Lucinda answered before Evie could open her mouth, "with the hope that a little bit of sin will frighten away Clarence, or at least his parents."

"That's very risky, Evie," the countess said, a grim expression on her face. "Believe me."

"I know. In fact"—Evie took a breath and sent up a quick prayer—"I may need your help."

"In being scandalous?"

Both Georgie and Lucinda looked skeptical. They probably doubted she had the resolve to do anything effective. Well, she would show them. She had a very good teacher.

"No, not in being scandalous," she returned, hiding her scowl. "In pretending as though nothing scandalous is going on." Evie forced a laugh. "For heaven's sake, if *you* frown at me for doing something, I'd be completely ruined."

Lucinda sighed. "I would advise you simply to talk to your brother and tell him how unhappy a match with Clarence Alvington would make you, except that I've seen you try to reason with him before. You may rely on me not to notice anything scandalous you may do."

"I shall do my duty, as well," Georgie agreed. "I only wish you had time to celebrate your success with St. Aubyn instead of worrying about this stupidity." She turned her attention to Lucinda. "However, I would like to point out that if St. Aubyn has truly become a gentleman, you, my dear, are the only one of us who hasn't delivered her lesson."

"Hm. He was only nice for five minutes. I would hardly declare that a definitive victory. Besides, we originally discussed giving a man lessons in how to treat a *female* correctly. Last I checked, there were no females in the House of Lords. Not since Queen Elizabeth, anyway."

While Georgie and Luce continued to banter about whether she'd fulfilled her part of their agreement or not, Evelyn remained occupied with keeping her low, growing excitement in check. Tomorrow she would be Saint's companion for the day, as she'd promised. Tomorrow she would see him again, and she'd given herself permission to misbehave. Silly as it seemed to admit after all the time she'd spent trying to improve him, part of her very much liked that the Marquis of St. Aubyn was a scoundrel—and that from time to time he seemed to be *her* scoundrel.

Chapter 23

She walks in beauty, like the night
Of cloudless climes and starry skies;
And all that's best of dark and bright
Meet in her aspect and her eyes.

—Lord Byron, "She Walks in Beauty"

Saint turned his phaeton onto the meadow grass, joining the long line of horses and carriages rolling out of the city toward General Barrett's traditional picnic site. He had to admit that the meadow the general had selected, on a gently sloping hill overlooking old London town, was picturesque. He also had to admit, as he returned Lord and Lady Milton's astonished stares with a polite nod, that he felt like a fool.

No one invited him to their al fresco luncheons, and when they did, he certainly didn't send replies thanking the host for the invitation and expressing his intention to attend. Nor did he arrive on time and with the idea of staying for the duration of the event.

As he drew his team to a halt and hopped to the ground, he estimated that between forty and fifty guests were in attendance, though with the number of footmen, grooms, valets, and maids the setting required, he found it nearly impossible to determine who was there to play and who was there to work.

"You came."

At the sound of Evelyn's voice, all of the nonsense and atypical behavior and the bee flitting around his beaver hat ceased to matter. "You managed to procure me an invitation," he returned, facing her.

"I thought you might still be angry with me."

"And yet you kept your part of the bargain."

Gray eyes danced as she met his gaze. The yellow of her muslin gown matched the color of the scattered daffodils in the grass, and as she smiled at him, Saint forgot how to breathe.

"It was either see you invited or find myself rendered naked, as I recall," she whispered.

Saint shook himself. "My, aren't we outspoken today?" he murmured, offering his arm. "I'd still be happy to accommodate you regarding the rendering, if you'd like."

She blushed, and he abruptly felt more comfortable. Evelyn might be willing to say something bold to him, but she was still proper, anything-for-orphans Evelyn. To his surprise, however, she took his proffered arm.

"Perhaps I should introduce you to some people first."

This was interesting. Not at all unpleasant, but certainly unexpected. "Arm in arm?" he asked, lifting an eyebrow. "Not that I'm complaining, but I was under the impression that we were only to touch when no one else could see us doing so." He leaned closer, breathing in the scent of her hair.

"I owe you a payment," she returned. "You said I was to stay at your side today, so here I am."

That explained her compliance. She was making good on a promise. His angel would stand by the devil if she'd given her word to do so. "Introduce me, then."

They crossed the grass to where the majority of guests had gathered. Dare was there with his wife, and Saint stifled a scowl. He'd mocked the viscount for becoming domestic, and yet here they were at the same event. And not for the first time.

No, no, no. He had not been domesticated. He was here because he wanted to see Evelyn, and because it might be interesting. A picnic for some of the *ton*'s greatest and most respected wits, and he'd found himself invited.

"General Barrett," Evelyn was saying as she tugged him around, "have you met Lord St. Aubyn? My lord, your host, General Augustus Barrett."

The tall gentleman, eyes the same color as his steel-gray hair, nodded with the precision of a salute. "St. Aubyn. My Lucinda suggested I invite you. Enjoy yourself." He glanced at Evelyn and back again. "But not too much, I trust."

"Thank you, sir."

As he watched the general stride over to greet the next group of arrivals, it occurred to Saint that his host had hit on the key to success. If he wanted to win Evelyn over the dull, idiotic Clarence Alvington, he simply needed to enjoy himself less. Stodginess would win the day—not his usual method of speaking his mind and damn the consequences. It would be difficult, but he could at least tell himself it was a challenge.

"That wasn't so terrible, was it?" Evelyn whispered, gripping his arm more closely.

"No, I suppose not." He looked down at her fingers curled over his sleeve. "What are you doing, by the way?"

"What do you mean? I told you, I made you a prom—"

"In the month or so we've known one another, you have spent most of your time telling me how little you want to have to do with me, Evelyn Marie. What's happened? Or is it that you've decided to continue our . . . friendship after you marry Clarence Alvington?" In front of everyone else, he would behave. She already knew better, and he saw no reason to be less than honest.

Her jaw dropped. "Of course not!"

In reality it was probably the best he could hope for, he realized. To be her lover after she married the man chosen by her family. "Would it be so bad?" he pursued softly. "No one would know. Just you and me, Evelyn."

"Stop it," she snapped. "Don't even suggest such things. I would not be unfaithful to my husband."

"But what if I don't want to let you go?"

She slowed, gazing up at him. "Then do something about it," she whispered, and pulled her hand free.

Saint stopped, looking after her as she walked over to chat with Lord and Lady Dare. What was she trying to tell him? That he should make a bid for her hand? He was quite prepared to do that, but she had to know at least as well as he that her brother would never condone a match with someone of his reputation.

He could kidnap her, of course, as she'd done to him. It was more than intriguing, the idea of keeping her captive at St. Aubyn Park, dressed in silk robes and nothing else. She'd probably even enjoy it for a time, until she realized how completely ruined she was.

A wide empty circle seemed to have formed around him. The same phenomenon happened at most proper events he attended, but it wasn't supposed to happen today; that had been the purpose of keeping Evelyn by his side. People liked her, even if they were terrified of him. Taking a deep breath, he followed her. *Be good*, he reminded himself sternly. *Whatever the temptation, be good.*

"Why the smile?" Georgiana asked, kissing Evie on the cheek.

"It's a pretty day." *And she was going to spend it with Saint.*

Dare took her hand, bowing over it. "Even with the sun and the birds, the notion that I was being forced into a marriage with Neckcloth Alvington would not leave me with the urge to smile."

Georgie elbowed him, none too gently. "Dare."

"Oof. On the other hand, I am happily married, so who am I to naysay another's union?"

"Naysay all you like. I have been." Evie watched as Georgie leaned against her husband's shoulder, their fingers entwined. She felt a distinct stab of jealousy. Georgiana and Tristan's courtship hadn't been easy by anyone's standards, but they were so obviously in love. Sometimes seeing them together made her want to cry. Today she kept trying to shake the image of herself and Saint standing just like that, and how very nice it would be.

"You're not married yet, Evie," Georgiana said firmly. "Your brother may still come to see reason."

"We could always kidnap him and force him to reconsider," Saint drawled from close behind her.

Used to his comments as she was becoming, being near him in itself was enough to send heat to her face and down her spine. "I doubt it would have any effect on Victor."

The marquis shrugged as he stopped beside her. "Sometimes people surprise you."

The same compelling urge she'd felt at Lady Bethson's

to touch him, to run her fingers along his bare skin, left her trembling. And then she remembered that she had decided to be a little naughty today. "Yes, sometimes people do surprise you," she returned, sliding both hands around his arm.

His muscles tensed beneath her fingers, but otherwise he didn't move. "Then a kidnapping it is," he said, his voice not sounding entirely steady.

Dare cleared his throat. "I meant to tell you, Saint, you earned Haskell's respect yesterday—and that of a few others' as well, I'd wager."

"It was either apologize or begin a brawl, and I was wearing my good jacket."

Evie glanced up at Saint's lean, handsome face. He actually looked uncomfortable, as though he didn't know what to make of a compliment. Whatever had happened, he seemed sincere about it. *For goodness' sake.* She felt so proud of him. And she wanted to kiss him so badly that it physically hurt to remain unmoving beside him.

"Evelyn?" he murmured.

"Yes?" Her heart skipped.

"You're going to draw blood if you don't loosen your grip on my arm."

"Oh. *Oh.*" She relaxed her fingers a little.

"What do you think of General Barrett's picnic soiree so far?" Georgiana asked brightly.

"It's interesting. I'm glad Miss Ruddick recommended me for an invitation."

Evie glanced up as Lord and Lady Huntley crossed the grass in front of them, leaving one group of guests for another. The countess was Clarence Alvington's second cousin, and known to be fiercely loyal to her relations' good standing. Neither Evie's brother nor the Alvingtons would be in attendance today, so the Huntleys were her best chance for getting a tale carried to Clarence. She tugged on Saint's arm.

"Let's pick some flowers, my lord," she said in a carrying voice, making an effort to giggle. "The guests always supply the blooms for the serving tables."

From Saint's expression, he thought she'd lost her mind, but he nodded. "Flowers. Of course, Miss Ruddick. Will you join us, Dare, Lady Dare?"

Tugging again, Evie decided it would be easier to move the Tower of London than the Marquis of St. Aubyn if he preferred to stay put somewhere. "Everyone's going. Come on, before they find all the best flowers."

Dare didn't look any too confident about her mental state, either. "Evie, perhaps Saint would prefer to remain—"

"You two go on," Georgie interrupted. "It's perfectly proper. Look, even Mrs. Mullen is gathering daffodils with the general. You don't need a dull married couple for chaperones."

The viscount raised an eyebrow at his wife. "Dull?"

Apparently Saint didn't want to hear the inevitable argument, because he gave way with the reluctance of a tree root giving up its hold on the earth. Evie nearly fell on her backside.

Saint caught her beneath the elbow while she regained her balance. "You might warn a body," she muttered.

His gray eyes twinkled. "Apologies, my gentle little lamb."

"Ha." Gripping his arm with one hand and lifting her skirt free of the meadow grass with the other, she led the way down the slope.

"By the by," he continued conversationally, "are you completely insane?"

"Because I want to pick flowers?"

"Because you want to be seen with me, Evelyn. I said you should stay by my side. I didn't mean we should wander off into the wilderness together. If your brother should hear—"

"Never mind my brother," she interrupted, with more confidence than she felt. She was walking a tightrope, and lustful as she was feeling at the moment, she'd be lucky not to fall off and end with her skirt above her waist. "Just enjoy yourself, Michael."

"If my goal for the day were to enjoy myself, you and I would be in my bedchamber with the curtains drawn. This," and he gestured at the scattering guests, "I am tolerating."

Evie slowed. Perhaps she was the one being mean and self-centered today. Of course he wouldn't enjoy himself here, with everyone looking askance at him. "Do you wish you hadn't come?"

He smiled that dark, sensuous smile of his. "If I hadn't come, I would at this moment be pacing my billiards room and wishing for it."

"Why?"

"Because you're here. Why do you think?"

"I . . . just didn't expect . . ." She felt her face warm as he leaned even closer.

"You didn't expect me to admit it," he finished, holding her gaze. "Why shouldn't I?"

"Saint—"

He shook his dark hair. "Michael."

Oh, goodness. Maybe, if she acted startled or surprised afterward, she could get away with kissing him and not being completely ruined. It would be worth it, just to feel his mouth on hers, just to feel him against her and know that he wanted her as much as she wanted him. Just—

"Look, daisies."

Moving with an awkward abruptness completely unlike his usual grace, Saint practically pushed her off his arm, backed away, then turned and strode toward a small stream. Breathing hard, Evie looked after him. Something was very wrong. She'd wanted him to kiss her, and he hadn't done it. He'd run away, or very nearly.

"These are nice, aren't they?" he called, yanking a few of them from the ground.

Evie blinked, biting the inside of her cheek to keep from sudden laughter. He was *nervous*. "Heavens. Not the roots. Just the stems."

He looked down again, twisted the roots off with an easy strength she couldn't help admiring, and held the stems out to her. "Better?"

She took the poor broken-backed things from him as she reached the stream bank. "Ah. Very nice. Don't you have a knife, though?"

"Yes." He bent over, pulling a narrow, nine-inch blade from his boot.

Evelyn swallowed. "Did you . . ." She stopped, tearing her gaze from the weapon to look up at his amused expression. "Did you have that at the orphanage?"

"And if I did?"

"Then thank you for not using it."

Saint pursed his lips, his gaze far away, as if he were thinking of something else. "I didn't have it with me. And in retrospect, I'm glad of that." He squatted, slicing the stems of another half dozen daisies and handing them up to her. "I think my life would have been very different if I'd been armed."

"So you're . . . glad I kidnapped you and chained you up for a week in an orphanage cellar."

He smiled, a gentle, thoughtful smile she'd never seen before, one that made her heart do an odd flip. "I've finally realized why they called that damned place the Heart of Hope. Because somehow, someone guessed you and I would meet there, Evelyn Marie."

Oh, my. "Michael, I very much want to kiss you right now."

Saint's smile deepened, the wicked light coming into his eyes. "Evelyn, kissing is only the beginning of what I want to do to you right now. However," and he straightened, offering her another handful of perfect blooms, "I am not going to do anything."

She couldn't help scowling at him. "Why not?"

He ran a finger along her cheek. "Because I'm trying very hard to behave."

"But I don't want to behave." His light touch left her trembling.

"A tumble in the grass would be . . . delectable," he murmured, offering his arm, "but someone would see. What I want of you doesn't end today, my dear. And frustrating as being proper might be, if that is what it takes, that is what I shall do."

For a moment she couldn't speak. Saint—Michael— had changed so much she could scarcely believe it. And apparently it was because of her. "You are very nice sometimes," she whispered. Even if there was no hope for the two of them, she wasn't ready to admit it yet to herself, and much less to him. Not today.

As the sounds of flirtatious conversation faded downstream, Lady Huntley craned her neck to peer around the stand of cattails behind which she and her husband had taken refuge. Thank goodness she had decided the cattails would make a lovely centerpiece, or they might not have known until too late. "Did you hear that?" she whispered, elbowing her husband.

"Sounds as though St. Aubyn's tomcatting after that Ruddick chit," he grunted, climbing to his feet and brushing damp grass from his knees before he pulled her up after him.

"Oh, it's much worse than that, I'm certain. I think she's already been caught. And orphans, and someone was kidnapped, and God knows what else. We must inform Alvington."

"Alvington? Why?"

"She's the girl Clarence is set on marrying, for heaven's sake. Do keep up."

"I'm trying, my dear."

Evie decided later that she should have realized an ambush was coming. At Victor's most boring, stodgy dinner party of the year, however, she was more concerned with keeping her eyes open than with looking for traps. After the most wonderful day she could ever remember spending, her brother's political acquaintances and strict propriety only reminded her how much she'd come to enjoy having Michael Edward Halboro in her life.

Everyone kept looking at her. At least it seemed as though she were receiving more attention than she usually did as the resident charming decoration of the household, but she ignored it as best she could. Even Clarence, trying to nudge her foot with his from across the table, only made her more determined to concentrate on the roast pheasant before her and excuse herself as soon as possible. Until Clarence proposed and she had to face reality, ignoring the entire thing and behaving in a slightly scandalous manner seemed the best plan.

"I heard the most extraordinary thing today," Lady Alvington said over the clinking of silverware.

At the same time Aunt Houton glanced in Evie's direction and frowned. Evie's heartbeat quickened. Now she would find out if the Huntleys had reported that she had sat with St. Aubyn all day, holding his arm as often as she could, and that once she'd even brushed a ladybug from his dark hair. And Saint the terrible, the scoundrel, the dead shot with a pistol, had laughed and blown it from her fingers.

"What did you hear, my lady?" Victor asked.

"I almost hesitate to say, except that it bears directly on someone at this table."

"Then you must say," Genevieve Ruddick insisted.

Evie briefly wondered whether the theatricality was on her behalf, or whether they always spoke to one another in so dramatic a fashion because otherwise the dullness of the conversation would put them all to sleep. She paid so little attention to them, and even less lately, once she'd discovered how many more important things existed in life.

"Very well." Lady Alvington leaned forward conspiratorially, though she didn't bother lowering her voice. Gossip was no fun if the servants couldn't overhear and pass it on. "Apparently the Marquis of St. Aubyn was involved in a kidnapping at that orphanage he oversees. That's why he vanished for a week."

All the blood drained from Evelyn's face. Fighting pure panic, she took several breaths, trying to keep from fainting at the dining room table. *Oh, no, no, no.* Who had heard that? Saint would never tell anyone; he'd promised her.

Everyone was definitely looking at her now, no one surprised, and her aunt the only one with the least bit of sympathy showing on her face. What was she supposed to do, lie? She couldn't do that. It would only make Saint look worse to everyone, and she couldn't bear that.

"I know . . . something about that story," she stumbled. "It sounds worse than it is. Believe me." She forced a chuckle, at the same time grabbing for her glass of Madeira. "Where on earth did you hear such a thing, my lady?"

Victor slammed his fork onto his plate with enough force to crack the fine china. "From your lips, Evie."

"Wha—"

"Imagine my surprise when Lord Alvington came calling late this afternoon with his cousins Lord and Lady Huntley. They heard *you,* my dear sister, at General Barrett's idiotic idealists' picnic, saying several . . . unfortunate things to St. Aubyn—including the fact, I believe, that you were eager to *kiss* that . . . blackguard. I would use a stronger term, but ladies are present."

"May I explain?" she asked, though she had no idea what to tell him but the truth—or as much of that as he could tolerate.

"No, you may not. What did you think," her brother pursued, "that you could behave as you like? Associate with that absolute . . . scoundrel and I would do nothing? I have questioned our aunt about your absences from her teas, and she admitted that you have been wasting your time with bloody, bastard orphans—excuse my language, ladies—at the Heart of Hope Orphanage, the very one under the authority of St. Aubyn!"

Evie looked at her aunt. "You told?" she asked, her voice so calm it surprised her.

"I'm sorry, Evie," the countess murmured. "He'd already guessed. I had no choice."

"Thank God the Huntleys went to Lord Alvington and not to the gossip sheets," Victor went on. "And thank God we have the means to make this fiasco right before any irreparable harm is done."

For a moment Evie closed her eyes, wishing they would all go away. Saint. She wanted to talk to Saint. He would have an answer for them. "And how do you intend to do that?" she asked.

Clarence gave a nervous cough. "After some discussion, and a very generous settlement on you by your brother, I have agreed to take you as my wife."

Her heart stopped. She knew it was coming, but to hear it— "You 'agreed' to marry me?" she repeated, lifting her head to gaze at him.

"And I agreed," Victor put in. "Only we few know of this nonsense, and a marriage announcement should stop any further speculation regarding the weakness of your character."

"But I don't agree." Evelyn took a deep, steadying breath. Enough was enough—and if Victor required six other people present when he attacked her, then she was more than a match for him alone. At least she could tell herself that, for the moment. "I will shout and argue every step of the way, and when people look at you, Victor, they won't be admiring your political acumen. They'll be whispering about what a tyrant you are and how horribly you've used your sister."

Her mother gasped. "Evie!"

"More likely people will be admiring my fortitude and patience in putting up with you. Obviously I've been too lenient in tolerating your selfishness and flightiness. Go to your room, and do not emerge until you agree to behave yourself. No more orphans, no more shopping with your frivolous friends, and no more conversation with St. Aubyn. Ever."

Evelyn put her napkin onto the table and slowly stood. "Whatever you think, and whatever you've been told, remember that you never heard my side of the story. And you might have thought to ask me, Victor, before you attempted to humiliate me in front of our family and friends. You will make a fine politician, but you would have been a better brother if you'd asked, and if you'd listened. Good evening."

With as much decorum as she could muster, Evie climbed the stairs, strode down the hall, entered her bedchamber, and closed the door behind her. Leaning back against it, for a long moment she simply concentrated on breathing. Then she realized she wasn't so much upset as she was angry. Turning around, she locked the door. That would be better than hearing them lock it from the outside. At least this way she could pretend that she had some control over the situation—over her own life.

She did have some control, she told herself. She could still say no. Not even Victor could force her to marry completely against her will. Of course, in return he could send her back to their estate in West Sussex and refuse to give his permission for her to wed anyone else—and he could also cut off her funds on the grounds that she'd failed to fulfill her duty to her family, so that she wouldn't be able to afford to go anywhere or do anything.

Even worse than all of that, though, was the thought of the children. Saint surely wouldn't go back on his promise to move them to their new home, but even so, she'd broken her word to them. They would think she'd abandoned them, just as everyone else in their lives had.

"No, no, no," she chanted, pacing from the door to the window and back again. Six months ago, if Victor had ordered her to marry Clarence Alvington, she would have wept, protested, and ultimately complied.

This, however, was not six months ago. She'd changed since then. She'd befriended orphans and realized she could improve their lives. She'd visited other institutions and seen how much yet remained to be done. She'd discovered how it felt to be in a man's embrace, and how significant one man's attentions could make her feel.

Evelyn shoved the window open and looked down. The dark garden lay below, with nothing between herself and the ground but wall. *"Damnation."* In romantic stories one always had a drainpipe or a rose trellis on hand for an escape—or a midnight rendezvous. She didn't even have a certain someone waiting in the shadows to bring her a ladder.

She paused, sitting in the reading chair by the window. Of course, she knew what she *wanted* to do; she wanted to go find Saint and convince him to elope with her, or to run away with her, or at least to hide her until she could figure out what to do. Saint, however, though he delighted in twists and turns, detested entanglements. If she landed on his doorstep, she would be bringing with her a knot the size of Windsor Castle.

What if he only wanted her when no one else knew, when it wasn't complicated? Slowly she leaned forward and closed the window again. If her life was going to become a nightmare, this way she at least would be able to hold on to the fantasy of loving the man Michael Halboro was on the verge of becoming. She couldn't bear being the witness to and cause of his ultimate failure. "Oh, Michael," she whispered. "What am I going to do?"

* * *

Saint glared at his solicitor. "No, I am not going to consider this further," he snapped. "Give me those papers to sign, or I will be forced to remove them from your person."

Wiggins swallowed. "I see you have considered already," he said, eye twitching as he dove into his satchel for the final set of papers. "Just initial the first three pages and sign the fourth. Both sets, please."

Saint turned the papers to face him, then with a deep breath dipped his pen and signed. "That's it then, yes? The property is mine?"

"Yes, my lord. Signing over the funds is the last step."

"Good. Go file and transfer and stamp or whatever it is you do. I want the deed by noon."

"By— Yes, my lord."

The solicitor fled the office, and Saint folded his hands behind his head, tilting his chair back against the bookcase. The orphans had their home. Buying St. Eve House, as he'd decided to call it, was probably the most frivolous thing he'd ever done. It would turn him no profit—just the opposite, in fact. It gained him no leverage over anyone. It did, however, keep him in the good graces of the one female, the one person, he valued above all others.

And with the papers signed, he could concentrate on finding a way to make her his forever. "Jansen!"

The butler skidded into the doorway. "My lord?"

"Have Cassius saddled. And get me a dozen red roses."

"Yes, my lord." He vanished again.

"Jansen!"

The butler's head reappeared. "Yes, my lord?"

"Make it two dozen red roses."

"Very good, my lord."

Saint finished his remaining paperwork, then pulled on his riding gloves. It was past nine in the morning, thanks to his solicitor's reluctance to hand over the last bit of paperwork. Yesterday Evelyn had said she planned to spend the morning at the new house, making notes on what needed to be purchased to make everything ready for the children.

He would find her there, then. And after yesterday, he didn't think he'd have much difficulty convincing her to join him in one of the private rooms for a short time. If he didn't take her again soon, he was going to explode.

Then it would be off to convince Wellington of some Cabinet post or other the two of them could propose that Prinny create for Victor Ruddick. He hummed a waltz as he made his way down to the foyer. Behaving was easier than he'd expected—particularly when he had a prize to claim at the end of the game.

"I'll return by noon for some papers Wiggins is to leave for me."

Jansen pulled open the front door. "Very good, my lord. And here are your flowers."

"Thank you."

"You are most welcome, my lord. And good luck, if I may be so bold."

Saint grinned as he swung onto Cassius' back. "You may, but don't make a habit of it."

The street running past St. Eve House was empty but for a few carriages of the older gentry who occupied the other dwellings. Saint went in anyway, using an un-latched window when he found the front door locked.

"Evelyn?" he called, his voice echoing through the empty rooms. "Miss Ruddick?"

Obviously she wasn't there. Saint returned to Cassius.

Her second most likely location would be the old orphanage, so he rode through Marylebone to Great
Titchfield Road.

The housekeeper met him on the landing. "My lord,"
she said, offering him a deep, ungainly curtsy.

"Mrs. Natham. I'm looking for Miss Ruddick. Is she
here this morning?"

The woman seemed baffled that she remained em-
ployed, but Saint had no intention of easing her confusion. Evelyn liked her, so she would stay. That was the
limit of his caring where the Iron Mop was concerned.

"No, my lord. The children have been inquiring, but
we haven't seen her for three days now."

"Hm. Very good. Thank you, Mrs. Natham." He
turned on his heel.

"My lord?"

Saint stopped. "Yes?"

"Young Randall has been telling the other children
the most amazing story—about a new home for all of
them. They are so excited, but I wondered whether . . .
Randall likes to tease, you know."

"Randall is correct." He hesitated. "I believe Miss
Ruddick wanted to inform them herself, as soon as the
papers were signed. I would appreciate if you would suggest to the infants that they act surprised when she gives
them the news."

The housekeeper smiled, the expression softening the
hard features of her face. "With pleasure, my lord. And
thank you—for the children's sake, that is."

"You are all welcome. Good day, Mrs. Natham."

It was so odd, he reflected, riding back toward the
center of Mayfair, that seeing people happy would make
him feel so . . . pleased. He'd demand an explanation of
the phenomenon from Evelyn once he tracked her down.

He caught up to Miss Barrett and Lady Dare just as they were exiting Barrett House. "Good morning, ladies," he said, doffing his hat.

"My lord," they echoed, sending a glance at one another.

"I'm looking for Miss Ruddick. I'd hoped to find her with you this morning."

Lucinda frowned, then quickly wiped the expression away. "She said yesterday that she had a . . . place to visit this morning."

Saint swung down from Cassius. "She's not there. Nor is she at the other place."

"We were to go to the museum this afternoon," Lady Dare said thoughtfully, "but she sent me a note, begging off."

Trying to maintain his relaxed stance, Saint took the note as the viscountess pulled it from the pocket of her pelisse. "It doesn't say why she canceled," he muttered to himself. In fact, he'd never known her to be so brusque with her friends.

"I'm sure her brother's merely sent her off on another of his missions." Despite the reassuring words, Lady Dare didn't look all that confident.

Both of her friends would know about Victor Ruddick's plans for Evelyn and Clarence Alvington, and he could see the speculation in their eyes without having to ask the question aloud. The Alvingtons were to have been at dinner with the Ruddicks last night. Saint's heart began hammering, filling him with an unaccustomed, unpleasant sensation—worry.

"Perhaps we should call on her, Georgie," Lucinda suggested. "Just to make certain she's feeling well."

Saint barely heard them. He was already up on Cassius again. "No need. I'll see to it."

Something was wrong. Little evidence though he had, his keenly developed sense of self-preservation told him that the morning was not as it should be. He wanted to gallop, but propriety still counted, so he settled for a fast trot to Ruddick House.

The Ruddick butler opened the door at his knock. "Lord St. Aubyn. Good morning."

"I would like to speak with Miss Ruddick, if she's in," Saint said, unable to keep the clipped impatience from his voice.

"If you'll wait in the morning room, my lord, I shall inquire."

Saint let out the breath he hadn't realized he'd been holding. She was there, anyway. She hadn't been dragged off somewhere and married to Clarence Alvington before he had a chance to do anything about it.

He paced the morning room, the need to see her creeping along his veins like a fever. She would be all right. She would come downstairs and tell him that she'd had too much wine at her brother's dull dinner and that she'd simply overslept.

"St. Aubyn."

He turned. "Ruddick." The hairs on the back of his neck pricked. Whatever was going on, it was worse than he'd anticipated. *Be polite*, he reminded himself. Evelyn wouldn't go completely against her brother's wishes in anything, and so he had to woo Victor as much as he needed to convince her of his sincerity. "Good morning."

"Good morning. My sister's not feeling well this morning, I'm afraid."

Saint's jaw clenched. *He wasn't going to see her.* "Nothing serious, I hope?" he made himself say.

"No. Just a headache. But she's not seeing anyone."

"Well. I won't keep you, then." Saint brushed by

Ruddick, returning to the hallway and handing the roses to the butler. "For Miss Ruddick."

"And St. Aubyn?" Evelyn's brother continued, following him toward the foyer.

Only Victor's presence kept Saint from storming up the stairs and breaking down doors until he found Evelyn and assured himself that she was all right. "What is it?"

"My sister is not as sensible as I could wish. She is betrothed to Clarence Alvington, and I would appreciate, gentleman to gentleman, if you would keep your distance from her."

Saint froze. *No.* When she'd mentioned it to him before, it had only been a possibility, something he had already decided he could prevent. The woman he'd fallen in love with did not become betrothed to someone else. Not when he hadn't even had a chance to win her. "She agreed to marry Alvington?"

"Of course she did. She has this family's best interests at heart. Good day, St. Aubyn. I trust you won't be calling here again."

Saint paused in the doorway as the butler pulled open the door. "You know, Ruddick, I used to think I was the worst scoundrel in London. It's somewhat reassuring to know that I was wrong. Congratulations. You now hold the title."

"If you had a sister, St. Aubyn, you might understand. Now leave, and don't come back."

Leaving Ruddick House was the hardest thing he'd ever done. He knew Evelyn was in there, and that she had to be desperately unhappy. He needed to see her. He needed to help her. He needed to do something.

Chapter 24

Can tyrants but by tyrants conquered be,
And Freedom find no champion?

—Lord Byron, *Childe Harold's*
Pilgrimage, Canto IV

Saint had grabbed Cassius' bridle away from Ruddick's groom when the butler emerged onto the front steps. "You, rag and bone man!" the servant shouted. "Don't accost our guests. You know the servants' entrance is around the back!"

Saint glanced over his shoulder in the direction the servant was yelling. No rag and bone man was anywhere in sight. With a fleeting glance in his direction, the butler disappeared back inside the house and slammed the door.

Forcing his mind back from the grim desire to beat Ruddick within an inch of his life, Saint rode Cassius down the street. Once around the corner from Chesterfield Hill, he found a young man, gave him a shilling, and handed the bay over to his care. Thank God for butlers.

Slipping along the carriage drive, he made his way to the rear of the house. The kitchen door opened as he reached it. The butler motioned him inside.

The kitchen staff seemed furiously busy with cleaning for this time of morning, but if it gave them an excuse not to see him, he had no objection. "Thank you," he muttered, following the butler toward the narrow back stairs.

"If Mr. Ruddick sees you, I'm afraid I will have to deny providing you with entry," the man returned. "But Miss Ruddick seems quite fond of you, as we are of her. She does not deserve this foul treatment. Go up to the second floor. Her bedchamber is the fourth one to your left."

Saint nodded, already halfway up the stairs. At least the butler's actions confirmed his own suspicions. Evelyn was not in this situation by choice. The hallway was empty as he emerged, and he made his way to the door the butler had indicated. Rapping softly, he leaned his ear against the hard wood. "Evelyn?"

"Go away, Victor! I will not speak to you!"

"Evelyn Marie," he called in the same low voice. "It's me. It's Saint."

He heard a rustle of material approach the door. "Saint? What are you doing here?"

"There's no key in the lock," he whispered back. "Do you know where it is?"

"I've locked it from the inside. Go away, Saint. Now. You'll only make things worse."

Saint rattled the handle. "Open the door, Evelyn. I need to talk to you."

"N . . . no."

"I'll break it down, and then everyone will know I'm here. Open it before someone sees me standing here."

For a moment he thought she wouldn't comply, but then the lock turned and she pulled open the door. He slipped inside her bedchamber, closing the door quietly behind him again.

Evelyn watched him straighten, turning to face her. She'd dreamed all the long, sleepless night of seeing him again. Now that he was here, she had no idea what he could possibly do to help her. "You shouldn't be here," she said, willing her voice to be steady. "If Victor knew, he'd pack me off to West Sussex in an instant."

The marquis looked at her for the space of a heart-beat, then closed the distance between them. Taking the sides of her face in his hands, he leaned down and kissed her, so softly, so gently, it made her want to weep.

"Your dear brother threw me out of the house a few moments ago," he murmured, kissing her again, as though he hadn't seen her in years, rather than just a day ago, "so I doubt he expects to find me anywhere in the vicinity."

"Then how did you—"

"Victor could never be as underhanded as I am, even if he tried. Tell me what happened."

She had to agree with that assessment. No one accomplished subterfuge like St. Aubyn. She wanted to throw herself into his arms, tell him all her troubles, and let him make everything right. This, though, couldn't be made right. "Victor found out about my activities at the orphanage and something about you and I, and he decided he'd had enough. Clarence Alvington agreed to marry me, apparently for a very generous dowry, and Lord Alvington agreed to give his district's votes to Victor."

Saint paced away and back again, his face hard and set. "So it's done. Signed and sealed, and you've been delivered. Did they ask you, Evelyn? Did anyone ask what you wanted?"

"Obviously not. But I stepped beyond the bounds of propriety. I knew what might happen."

"So you accept this?"

Evelyn took a ragged breath. "I wish you hadn't come here, Michael. Of course I don't want to marry that idiot. But what else can I do?"

"Leave here. With me. Right now."

Oh, God, she'd wanted to hear that so badly. "And what about my family?"

"They've sold you. Don't you dare worry about them."

"But Saint, they're my family. I've tried so hard to make a positive difference. If I ruin Victor's career, what does that say about me?"

His eyes narrowed. "That you got even."

"But I don't live by that philosophy." She ran her fingers along his lapel, unable to resist touching him.

He captured her hand, pressing her palm flat against his chest. "I won't let you marry Clarence Alvington," he said in a low, black voice she'd never heard him use before. "That is my philosophy." His heart under her fingers beat hard and fast.

"Believe me, if there's a way to escape this mess, I will do it. But I won't ruin my family name. My father was very proud of who he was, and so am I. And much as I want to hate him, Victor is a good man—if misguided about some things."

"And what about your infants, then?" he retorted, yanking her still closer. "Would you leave them to me?"

"You'll do right by them, Saint." A tear ran down her cheek, the first she'd wept since everything had fallen to pieces. "I've seen your good heart."

He released her so abruptly she staggered. "I don't

have a heart, Evelyn. That is why I . . . need . . . you. Leave with me right now. I'll buy you anything you want, take you anywhere you want to go. We'll open orphanages all over Europe, if you like. Just be with me."

She heard the desperation in his voice, and the hurt. "Michael, I can't," she whispered. "Please understand."

Saint faced the window for a long moment, the muscles across his back so taut she could see him shaking. "I understand," he finally said. "Victor gets his seat in Parliament, you make certain the children are cared for, and you live a miserable, hopeless life."

"That's not—"

He whipped around to face her. "I'll see to the first two, but I will never, *never* agree to the last." Striding forward, he kissed her again, roughly. "I'll see you tonight."

"Michael, I'm not—"

"Tonight."

He reached for the door. Frantic that he might try something even more drastic than this, she pushed against it. She might as easily have stopped a charging bear, but he halted his retreat.

"Michael, look at me."

With a shuddering breath, he faced her again.

"Promise me that you'll continue on this path you've chosen. That you'll be good."

The Marquis of St. Aubyn shook his head. "No. You don't get to feel as though you've made a sacrifice for the greater good where I'm concerned, Evelyn. I intend to get exactly what *I* want, even if you've given up."

With that, he slipped out the door and softly closed it behind him. Evelyn leaned against the door, listening for a long time, but he didn't return. Slowly she turned the key and the lock clicked shut. Even if he came back to-night, she wouldn't let him in. If she did, she would never have the strength to let him go.

Saint rode past Lord and Lady Gladstone's grand house on the way home. He didn't even realize it, how-ever, until he was two streets past there. If he needed an answer about how much he'd changed, that provided it. He didn't want Fatima Hynes or any other nameless fe-male with vacant eyes and an ample bosom. He didn't want anyone else, ever. He wanted Evelyn Marie Ruddick—and he'd be damned if he was going to let Neckcloth Alvington have her without a fight.

And if there was one thing he knew how to do better than anyone else in London, it was how to fight dirty.

"I need a message delivered to Wellington immedi-ately," he said as he entered his home.

"I'll fetch Thomason," Jansen returned, hurrying down the side corridor as Saint made his way to his of-fice. Several invitations lay stacked on the side table, and he flipped through them. Nearly a dozen, more than he used to receive. Whether anyone had begun to notice his more polite behavior or not, they had realized he was at-tending more of the Season's events.

At the bottom of the pile he found the one he'd been looking for. Thankfully he'd already accepted the invita-tion to the Dorchester ball that evening. It wouldn't give him much time, but he had little enough of that anyway.

He grabbed a paper and scrawled out a note to Wellington, offering the duke his last case of sherry if His Grace would join him at the Dorchester soiree and do him the very great favor of sending on a note inform-ing Ruddick that the duke would like Victor and his family to be in attendance as well. When Thomason appeared, Saint dispatched him immediately, instructing the footman to wait for an answer.

For a moment he considered sending a similar note to Prinny, but he needed more than a notable appearance; he needed a Cabinet posting. A seat would take too long to ensure, and Alvington had that card in his hand already. And any appointment suggested by the Regent would bog down in committee for a year. If he couldn't arrange faster results for Ruddick than Alvington could, he needn't bother.

Thomason returned in less than thirty minutes. "That was fast," Saint said, pausing in the pacing that was wearing a track in his office floor. "What was his answer?"

The footman actually backed away a step. "The . . . His Grace was not at home, my lord."

"Damnation. Did his butler say where I might find him?"

"Yes, my lord."

Saint gazed at his footman as all remaining patience fled. Being polite and considerate could go hang itself. "Then where is he?" he hissed.

"Calais."

Saint stopped. "Calais," he repeated. "The Calais in France."

"Yes, my lord. On his way to Paris. I'm very sorry. I could go after him, if you'd—"

"No. Go away. I need to think."

"Yes, my lord."

No Wellington. Prinny looked to be his only choice, though with the time and care the Regent spent in selecting his wardrobe, convincing him to attend a party on such short notice would be nearly impossible. And Prinny didn't have a reason to invite Ruddick. Victor would see through the ruse in a heartbeat. He resumed pacing again, then stopped. "Thomason!"

Everyone seemed to be lurking close by today, because both the footman and Jansen galloped into the office. "Yes, my lord? Am I to go to Calais, then, after all?"

"No. When did Wellington leave?"

"Just this morning. He wanted to make the evening tide at Dover."

Saint nodded. "Good. Nothing in the newspaper about his departure until tomorrow, then. Wait right there." He returned to his desk and grabbed another sheet of paper.

"Is there anything I can do, my lord?" Jansen asked.

"No. Yes. I will need eight coaches or other conveyances this evening." He glanced up, then went back to scrawling. "Make it ten. And I want them here by seven this evening."

"I'll see to it, my lord."

It took two attempts to get the wording right, and then he sanded and folded the letter. The seal would be a problem; after a moment's consideration he used his own, twisting the ring in the soft wax so the crest was unrecognizable.

Blowing on it, he stood, then realized Thomason was wearing the distinct black and red St. Aubyn livery. "Damn. Do you have another jacket?"

"My lord?"

"Never mind. See Pemberly before you go. Wellington's servants are in plain black, are they not?"

"Yes."

"I have something that should suffice in my wardrobe, I'm sure. You are now in Wellington's service, and you are taking this note to Ruddick House. Don't wait for an answer. Wellington's man wouldn't."

"Yes, my lord."

"You have to understand, Thomason. You must convince them that you are in Wellington's employ, that he's in town, and that you're actually too important to be delivering this note. If not, none of this will work."

The footman nodded. "I understand, my lord."

Saint took a deep breath. "Go see my valet, then."

Once the footman was gone, he changed his coat to go out again: The day was passing quickly, and he had another errand to run. Three of them, actually.

For a moment when someone began pounding on her door, Evelyn thought Saint had returned to kidnap her. She wouldn't have resisted. She shouldn't have turned him down when he offered to take her away before. He was correct; it wasn't fair that everyone got what they wanted but her.

"Evie, open this door!" Victor bellowed.

Hope fell to the floor again. "Never!"

"If I have to come in there—"

"Then you'll break my door, and you'll have to lock me in the cellar."

She heard his muffled cursing behind the door. He probably had no idea what to do when she didn't give in to him.

"Wellington has requested our presence at the Dorchester ball this evening," he said after a moment.

"I'm not going."

"He thinks you're charming, and he wishes to dance with you, Evie. You *are* going. And you'll dance with Clarence, as well, and we'll begin spreading the rumor of your engagement."

Jumping out the window was beginning to seem a sound alternative. Just as she started to yell her defiance once more, though, she remembered what Saint had said. *He would see her tonight.* Had he arranged this? He knew Wellington, certainly.

It was a chance. Not much of one, but at least if she went out, she could see her friends, and perhaps think of something to get herself out of this. And she could ask Lucinda to get a message to the children, so they would know that she hadn't forgotten them.

"I'll go," she called. "If you'll let me see my friends."

"As long as I'm there beside you, you may see anyone you wish—except for St. Aubyn."

She didn't answer that; he wouldn't believe anything she said, anyway.

As her own personal act of defiance, Evie wore the diamond heart pendant Saint had given her. No one would know its significance but the two of them, and if he was in attendance it would probably send him the wrong message—that she still hoped for his rescue—but somehow she felt stronger inside with it on.

"Evie!" Lucinda called, sweeping out of the crowd to give her a tight hug as soon as they arrived at the soiree. "We were worried about you. Are you well?"

Evelyn smiled as Georgiana and Dare arrived on Luce's heels. "I—"

"I'm afraid my sister is not feeling quite the thing," Victor interrupted. He'd strayed no more than an elbow's length from her since she'd opened her bedchamber door. "Too much excitement, I suppose," he continued.

"Excitement?" Georgie repeated, taking Evie's hand. "From what?"

"Well, we will announce it in the *Times* in the next day or so, but Clarence Alvington has proposed to Evie, and she has accepted."

For a moment her friends just stared at her.

"I . . . congratulations, Evie," Lucinda faltered first. "What a surprise."

"Indeed," Georgie echoed, her gaze searching Evie's face. "You know, you . . . you should tell my aunt about this!" She favored Victor with a friendly smile that didn't touch her eyes. "The Dowager Duchess of Wycliffe simply adores Evie."

"Yes, yes!" Lucinda seconded, grabbing Evie's other arm and pulling her forward. "Come, Evie, let's tell her!"

As the ladies dragged her willingly forward, Dare stepped between them and her brother with his usual splendid timing, putting an arm around Victor's shoulders. "Ruddick, my boy. Did I ever tell you—"

Victor shrugged free, intercepting Evie's arm from Lucinda. "As I said, Evie isn't feeling well. We only came by at Wellington's request, and then we must get her right to bed."

Georgiana's eyebrows drew into a frown. "But—"

"I'm afraid I must insist."

Evie could see her friends were growing upset, and she offered a quick smile before they began a shouting match with her brother that would hurt all of them. "It's all right. As Victor says, I'm not feeling well."

"Then . . . we must call on you tomorrow."

Her brother shook his head. "She will be feeling better on Thursday. You may call on her then."

Of course. The announcement would have run in the *London Times* by then, and news of her betrothal would be all over London. No one would be able to do anything for her after that. Not that they should have to. This was still her problem.

"Ah, there's Clarence now," Victor said, looking past

her friends. "You promised him this dance, didn't you, Evie?"

She gave him a sideways glance. Did he expect her to knit the rope for her own hanging, as well? "I don't know. Did I?"

"Yes, you did, if you're feeling up to it." He bowed to her friends. "If you'll excuse us?"

As she reluctantly allowed him to guide her away, she finally followed his gaze to the far side of the ballroom. "That isn't Clarence Alvington."

"He'll be along for the waltz. I wasn't about to let you regale your friends with your tale of woe."

Evie sighed bitterly. "You've already won, Victor. Do you have to see me miserable at *every* moment?"

"You've given me no reason to trust you."

She could pay him the same compliment. "Please just find Wellington so you can put me on display with him and we can leave."

"I don't want to appear too eager."

"Humph. If this is so important to you, *you* should dance with him."

"Sarcasm doesn't become you." He gazed at her for another moment, then placed her hand over his arm. "I don't suppose I can rely on you to behave for much longer. We'll find Wellington."

After fifteen minutes of searching and discreet inquiry, it became obvious that the duke wasn't in attendance. And Evelyn could be equally certain that Saint was absent, as well. Her heart sank even further. She hadn't expected a rescue, but seeing him would have meant . . . something.

"Damnation," Victor muttered under his breath as they returned to the crowded ballroom.

"Yes, it seems you've been jilted," she offered. "I can only wish the same fate for myself."

"That's enough. We'll stay through the waltz, and then we're going home, and you're going back to your bedchamber until Thursday."

She stopped, forcing him to a halt beside her. "And you're welcome."

He scowled. "What?"

"Hasn't it even occurred to you that I might say no, or that I might throw a tantrum in the middle of the ballroom here, or announce to all and sundry that . . . that St. Aubyn and I are lovers? What do you think that would do to your career?"

"It would ruin you," he hissed, his gaze hardening.

"Yes, it would. And believe it or not, I would actually prefer that to marriage with Clarence. However, despite what you've done to me, I truly believe that you will make a fine member of Parliament and do some good for the people of England. That," and she jabbed a finger into his chest, "is why I've kept my silence. And you are welcome."

"You may be as gracious as you want, now that you've been caught. I'm not the one who was carousing with St. Aubyn or going unchaperoned to visit filthy orphanages in Covent Garden."

Evie started to snap a reply, but as she looked at her brother's calm implacable face, she realized she would never win. He would never see that he'd done anything wrong toward her, much less admit it. But she couldn't leave one thing unsaid. "The Marquis of St. Aubyn," she returned quietly, "is more of a gentleman than Clarence Alvington could ever hope to be. You've made a poor choice all the way around."

Her brother smiled grimly. "Now you're going to attempt to convince me that you've gone mad, aren't you? Look, there's Clarence. Waltz with him, smile, and we'll leave."

Evelyn lifted her chin. "It so happens that right now I'd rather spend time with Neckcloth Alvington than you, anyway."

She met Clarence halfway, watching with a kind of detached hopelessness as he took her hand and practically licked it. Thank goodness for gloves. "My lovely, lovely Evie," he cooed, squeezing her fingers.

"Mister Alvington. I believe we are to waltz."

"You must call me Clarence."

"I'd really prefer not to," she returned, almost amused as he looked at her uncertainly. He was probably the most unlucky of the lot of conspirators. The others reaped the benefit of her sale to the Alvington family, but he would have to live with her.

The waltz began, and he slipped a hand about her waist. The sensation made her want to gag; it reminded her of what he would expect of her after they were married. The idea of lying with him as she had with Saint . . . She closed her eyes, shuddering. *Where was Michael? Didn't he know how much she wanted to see him? To at least be near him?*

The ballroom doors burst open. As Evelyn watched in openmouthed amazement, children poured into the ballroom. Ten, twenty, then more ragged children. Orphans. *Her* orphans.

The guests nearest the entrance began shrieking, moving back and to the sides of the room as if faced with a stampede of wild cattle. The orchestra squeaked to a halt, leaving the dancers stranded arm in arm in the middle of the ballroom.

"For God's sake," Clarence gasped, his face going white. "It's a revolt!"

He wasn't the only one to think the lower classes were staging a revolution. Lady Halengrove fainted, and most everyone else was stampeding over footmen for the far exits into the garden.

Evelyn, though, was looking at the tall, dark figure in the center of the chaos. Saint. He held young Rose in his arms, his expression as calm as if he were shopping for gloves on Bond Street.

As the orphans fanned out, she noticed him giving them signals. Immediately things began to make sense. Lord Alvington became boxed up against the refreshment table, while her brother suddenly became acquainted with Randall, Matthew, and two of the other older boys.

What are you doing? she mouthed at Saint, not certain whether to be embarrassed or amused.

He ignored her, instead strolling over to her brother. "Good evening, Ruddick," he said in a carrying voice.

The remainder of the crowd quieted, obviously beginning to realize that they were not in immediate danger. Evelyn edged closer, having to drag Clarence with her when he refused to relinquish his grip on her hand.

"What the devil is the meaning of this, St. Aubyn?" her brother growled over Randall's head. "You have been warned to—"

Saint dug something out of his pocket. "Here. You are now the assistant chancellor of the Exchecquer." He slapped a parchment against Victor's chest. "Congratulations."

"I—"

The marquis turned his back, strolling now straight for Evie. Her heart began to pound. He'd done it. He'd beaten Alvington in the race to get Victor into the government.

"Here," Saint said, handing Rose into Clarence's arms.

"Are you my papa?" the girl said, with such precision that Saint must have coached her on her delivery.

"I—oh, good heavens, I—"

Saint stopped before Evie. "Hello," he said quietly.

She couldn't breathe. "Hello."

"May I?" Reaching out, he took both of her hands in his. "I've brought your infants."

"I see that."

"They need you."

In the back of her mind Evie realized that the room had gone dead silent. Everyone could hear every word they said to one another, but she didn't care. Saint had come, and he was holding her hands.

"I need you, as well," he continued.

"Saint—"

"Michael," he breathed.

"Michael, how did you do this?"

He smiled, that crooked, wicked smile that made her legs weak. "You provided me with inspiration, and a source. Your literary Lady Bethson. I would do anything, you know, to give you a free choice."

A tear she hadn't felt forming ran down one cheek. "Thank you. Thank you so much."

Saint—Michael—took a shallow breath, and then, to her surprise, went down on one knee. "I lied to you earlier," he said in the same low voice.

"What?" She was going to faint. If he said he was finished with her, she was going to wither and die right there in the middle of the ballroom.

"I told you that I didn't have a heart," he continued

as he gazed up at her, his voice shaking just a little. "I do have one. I just didn't know it until I met you. You are my light. My soul craves you, and I love you with every ounce of the heart you've awakened in me. I . . . I could live without you, but I wouldn't want to. Will you marry me, Evelyn Marie?"

Her legs gave way. Evelyn sank into his arms, reaching around his shoulders to grip him so he couldn't vanish. "I love you," she whispered against his cheek. "I love you so much. You've given me everything."

"Only because you showed me how." He took her arms, holding her away a little so he could see her face. "Marry me."

"Yes. I will marry you, Michael."

Saint smiled again, reaching back into his pocket. He pulled out a small velvet box and opened it to her. Inside lay a ring with a diamond center, surrounded by a silver heart, winking at her. Saint pulled it free and slipped it onto her finger, then leaned in and kissed her. Dimly she heard children cheering, and she chuckled against his mouth.

"I tried very hard to reform you," she said, allowing him to help her to her feet. "But I have to admit that lately I've developed a new appreciation for scoundrels."

Standing himself, he kept hold of her hand, as though he couldn't make himself let go of her. "Good. Because I'm not certain how proper I can be where you're concerned, my dear."

Across the floor she saw Georgiana, Dare, and Lucinda cheering, and she laughed, leaning against Saint's strong shoulder. *You're next,* she mouthed at Lucinda.

"Orchestra!" Saint bellowed. "Play us a waltz!"

Lady Dorchester, white-faced and with several children hanging on to her arms and trying to head her off, stormed onto the dance floor. "What is the meaning of this?" she screeched. "A marriage proposal is well and good, but these filthy children cannot be here!"

"Why not?" Saint asked, swinging Evelyn into the dance and holding her much too close for propriety. "They know how to waltz."

> *A thousand hearts beat happily; and when*
> *Music arose with its voluptuous swell,*
> *Soft eyes look'd love to eyes which spake again,*
> *And all went merry as a marriage bell.*

> —Lord Byron, *Childe Harold's*
> *Pilgrimage, Canto III*

THE END